flour garden

Pamela Dangelmaier

FLOUR GARDEN
Copyright © 2016 by Pamela Dangelmaier.

This book is a work of fiction. Names, characters, businesses, organizations, places, events and incidents either are the product of the author's imagination or are used fictitiously. Any resemblance to actual persons, living or dead, events, or locales is entirely coincidental.

For information contact:
pameladangelmaier@gmail.com
www.pameladangelmaier.com

Cover Design & Illustration - Michael Dangelmaier, Red Pine Design
Interior Design - Pamela Dangelmaier
Copy Editing - Heather Conn
Author photo credit - Stefanie Fournier

ISBN: 978-0-9953322-0-1

First Edition: March 2017

10 9 8 7 6 5 4 3

Praise for Flour Garden

"Pamela writes in vivid technicolor. Each moment is artfully captured in this delightful read. Moments of tension peppered with humour and joy; this is the book you want to be trapped with under a quilt on a rainy afternoon. I spent the entire time making comparisons of the characters to the people in my own life. Flour Garden feels more like a memoir than a piece of fiction. Tuck in and enjoy the journey!" -

Carson Arthur - gardening expert, HGTV Home to Win

"How I love the vividly colourful, warm and amusing world Pamela Dangelmaier has created in this outstanding first novel, Flour Garden. Her oh-so human characters, both flawed and beautiful, opened the door to a charming community in which I wished to stay. Her compassionate, playful writing style is an absolute pleasure."

Carolyn Soper - film producer 'Sherlock Gnomes', Rocket Pictures

"Pamela Dangelmaier's Flour Garden captures the dynamics of hortsocieties with humour and affection illuminated by funny and lovable characters. This is underscored by her main concern about the nature of friendship between women, between men and women, and the drama of these relationships holds this lovely first novel together with style."

Marjorie Harris - plant consultant & garden columnist, The Globe & Mail

For

m h s

Prologue

October 2015

It was a perfect night for baking.

The sweet smell of wood smoke puffing from chimneys along the chestnut-lined streets mingled with the cool night mist to create a pleasant potpourri of autumn fragrance. As she walked home from work, Kate breathed in the crisp night air, then kicked up a pile of leaves strewn across the sidewalk. She laughed as they fell to earth and crunched underfoot. Perhaps it was the peaceful slumber of the autumnal evening. Or maybe it was the coolness of the foggy night air that nipped at Kate's cheeks, turning them the colour of the pink tam she had plopped onto her head. Whatever it was, Kate was in the mood to bake.

Some would think that after a long day at work, the last thing she would want to do would be to turn on the oven and get her hands covered with sweet dough. As the owner of one of Vancouver's most successful bakeries, Kate's Bakes on West 41st, Kate Freitag spent a good portion of her day rolling dough, tending to the ovens, and generally mucking about in the kitchen. But if you knew Kate, you knew that before she ever introduced an item to the bakery's menu, it was tweaked, tested, and tasted in the comfort and privacy of her Kerrisdale home. Ever since she had inherited the Craftsman-style house from her grandparents a number of years back, she'd pretty much made it her own, but she had left the kitchen just as it was. She felt a special, almost magical, feeling when she baked in that small kitchen. It mostly had to do with her fond childhood memories of doing the exact same thing in the exact same kitchen while learning the craft of baking from her Oma (Grandma) Margaret.

Once she'd gotten home, Kate ate a light meal, cleared the dishes, then pulled out the baking ingredients onto the kitchen counter where she and Oma had often stood side by side. Kate smiled, remembering how, as a child, she would watch her grandmother carefully mix the ingredients, then drop gooey dollops of sugary dough onto a butter-greased sheet. Kate was allowed to open the oven door, then Oma would slip the precious cargo inside. Kate would pull up a chair and sit directly in front of the oven window, legs dangling. She watched carefully as the small lumps would slowly melt and form perfect rounds of cookie goodness. This was better than TV and it came with its own sweet reward.

Tonight, Kate began to mix up what promised to be a delicious new creation. This yet-to-be-named cookie had been simmering in her head for some time and tonight, she was determined to work out the kinks. Tying her curly auburn hair into a loose bun atop her head, she rolled up her sleeves and got to work.

Kate had just added a few drops of Mexican vanilla when the phone rang. Silently cursing that she'd once again been caught with cookie dough on her hands, Kate hastily wiped them on the front of her apron and reached around the corner of the kitchen to the hallway where the phone sat in its cradle.

"Hello?"

"Kate?"

"Yes. Who's this?"

A long silence ensued. Kate wrinkled her brow, straining to hear, and waited for a reply.

"Hello?"

"You don't recognize my voice?"

In an instant, Kate knew the answer. She stood frozen, caught halfway between the warmly lit kitchen and the cool darkness of the hallway. The only hint that she recognized the caller's voice was the slight trembling of her right hand, which hung limply by her side.

"Kate, it's Sophia."

"I know."

"Kate, I'd really like to talk to you. You know, face to face. Would that be possible?"

"And how exactly is that supposed to happen, Sophia?"

Sophia cleared her throat.

"I live in Vancouver now."

Kate's free hand flew up to cover her mouth. Her eyes widened. She could feel the pounding of her heart in her throat as she tried to swallow.

"We could meet whenever or wherever you want. I want to make things right, Kate. Not just about the recipe but about everything, you know. I really need to see you—"

Dropping her hand, Kate spoke in a clenched whisper. "To be honest, Sophia, I don't need to see you. That's how we differ, you see. What you need is not what I need." Taking a deep breath, she spoke louder and with determination. "I don't know how you got this number but please don't call back."

Reaching up, almost mechanically, Kate pressed the small red button on the portable handset. The phone line went dead. Then, as though released from a stifling grasp, she slowly slid down the wall until she slumped onto the floor. Her head was throbbing. Sweat began to form small beads on her brow and her heart continued to race wildly. Kate closed her eyes and took a laboured breath, trying to keep calm.

Enclosed within the walls of her home and lost in cascading thoughts, she didn't hear the low purr of a car engine starting in the street across from her house. Nor could Kate see, as she clutched her knees close to her chest, a sleek black sports car as it hastily pulled away from the curb.

Sophia winced as her car screeched towards the traffic circle at the end of the block. In her panic to get away, she had tossed her cell phone onto the passenger seat, then tightly gripped the steering wheel as the back wheels of her BMW jumped up and over the cement curve of the roundabout. This hadn't gone at all as she had planned. Now she was running away like a criminal from the scene of a crime. Her dark eyes glanced furtively into her rear-view mirror just in time to see the shadowy row of chestnut trees in front of Kate's house fade to grey. The evening fog enveloped them in a cloak of silent mist.

Chapter One

Oma's Baking Tip

Sugar is all fine and good but if you add spices to your baked goods, you'll elevate them above the ordinary and have people coming back for more.

April 2016

Despite the inclement weather and a forecast of further rain showers into the night, some twenty members had managed to trundle into the Tuesday evening meeting of the Kerrisdale Garden Club.

"A paltry sum," mumbled Ursula St. Germain as she peered over her bifocals and took a quick head count of the attendees who had bothered to show up. *How would they be able to entice new members to join,* she thought, *if what they were greeted with was a dwindling bunch of uninspired octogenarians?*

Most were huddled together in a tight little group, surrounded by a sea of empty metal chairs. They whispered amongst themselves in hushed tones, fidgeting with their drippy umbrellas and soggy coats. Some were lingering by the kitchen, placing their homemade baked goods on the table in front of the kitchen window while chatting it up with Ethel McCormick. Her mousy little shape could be seen scurrying behind the kitchen counter as she struggled with that rather archaic contraption they called a coffee percolator, a definite holdover from the community centre's earlier days. Unfortunately, Ethel, a certified tea aficionado, had absolutely no idea what to do with the thing.

Some members were cheerfully chatting near the door with the evening's invited guest speaker, welcoming her to the club and helping her carry in some of her colourful poster boards. Others, mostly those who were slightly hard of hearing, had dutifully seated themselves near the front, trying to get comfortable on the outrageously uncomfortable metal chairs supplied by the community centre. Francine O'Dwyer, for one, had come prepared. Having given a cursory nod to Ursula, she placed her pink, crocheted seat cushion on one of the metal chairs and settled herself in, front and centre. Next to her sat Margaret Wikowski. Margaret was in the habit of taking up two metal chairs since her bulky frame could not possibly fit onto one. Unlike Francine, Margaret was in no need of chair cushions as her expansive backside was padding enough.

As Ursula continued with her manual head count, she ruminated over the fact that they'd only managed to recruit one new member in the last twelve months. Admittedly, she was an extremely enthusiastic one who had brought with her a breath of fresh air.

But come to think of it, Ursula suddenly thought, *where exactly is Kate?*

Ursula quickly scanned the room but couldn't make out Kate's tell-tale knitted tam among the rag-tag collection of Tilley rain hats and plastic hair bonnets.

The Garden Club's president let out a sigh as she glanced down at her watch. Seeing that it was exactly two minutes to seven, she carefully brushed out the wrinkles from her tweed skirt, ran a smoothing hand over her grey bob, adjusted the bifocals on the tip of her nose, and began the slow walk to the podium. It was strategically placed to the left of the small stage, or rather stage right, to be correct. Ursula loved using the theatrical terms she remembered from her community theatre days. In fact, she was prone to using them regularly in daily life, often referring to her first marriage as "the dress rehearsal" and her last as "the epilogue."

Loud laughter suddenly erupted from the back of the room. Mimi Owens was holding court in her usual fashion. She was easy enough to spot. Her tightly permed, platinum-blonde locks bobbed up and down while she animatedly shared the latest neighbourhood gossip with a small group of eager listeners. Ursula clapped her hands twice in an effort to gain the attention of the talkative crowd that had gathered around Mimi. As they slowly dispersed about the room and found their seats, Ursula tapped on the microphone and tossed a steely glance towards Lloyd Stobbs, the club's self-appointed technical guru. He flashed Ursula a toothy smile. The members of his assisted living housing co-op had recently voted him "most eligible bachelor."

Ursula's look was a silent warning that she most certainly didn't want a repeat of last month's microphone feedback fiasco. It had left her no choice but to shut off the outdated contraption Lloyd had borrowed from his co-op's Monday night bingo club and shout the remainder of her dissertation on the importance of disinfecting your garden tools. Lloyd had taken heed. Tonight, he had arrived with a brand new Panasonic RP-VK35 microphone that he'd borrowed from the co-op's Friday night karaoke club. If this one didn't work, he would have no choice but to approach the co-op's Sunday morning spiritual club. They were a sanctimonious bunch and he'd rather avoid them, if possible.

Ursula St. Germain stood ramrod straight behind the wooden podium and silently surveyed the crowd. It was easy to see that she was a doer and natural leader, someone with enough time on her hands to devote countless unpaid hours of work to the job at hand, having retired five years ago as principal at the Point Grey Preparatory School for Girls.

Ursula was just what the club needed to get things under control. Most members were more than happy, despite her tendency to be condescending, to leave the day-to-day running and organization of club matters to someone else. As long as they didn't have to do too much, most members were content to pay their dues, come to the monthly meetings, enjoy the company of fellow gardeners, hear a lecture or two, munch on a cookie, and go home to their own private worlds.

"This is your problem," Ursula had mentioned at several previous meetings. "Apathy will be your downfall. One must be involved and active or else, like the weeds that will surely encroach on an unkempt garden, we, too, will be overrun and smothered out as we take our last and final horticultural gasp before plunging into obscurity."

Ursula's valiant and dramatic pleas for help had seemingly fallen on deaf ears. In truth, some members were hard of hearing but that was beside the point.

With a clearing of her throat, Ursula began her well rehearsed monthly address.

"A warm welcome to you all. Thank you for coming this evening. I'm pleased to see that our turnout tonight is good despite the weather." The sound of her clipped, British accent cut through the air and silenced any lingering conversations.

"However, I would strongly encourage all of you to do your part to swell our ranks and make use of our new Agri-Buddy program. I need not remind you of the importance of signing up new members. Our club's very existence depends on it so I'm relying on all of you to spread the word and bring along fresh recruits. Of course, a very special thank-you goes out to our own Francine O'Dwyer for creating those attractive little member-drive posters you may have seen about town." Francine, who was known to blush at the drop of a hat, squirmed uncomfortably atop her crocheted cushion.

"I especially liked the accompanying poem she wrote. For those of you who may not have seen a copy of the poster on the centre's bulletin board as you came in this evening, I'm happy to share it with you."

Plant a seed and watch it grow
water it well and you will know
the pleasure that comes from joining our group
we'll even give tips on using worm poop.

A few stifled twitters of laughter rippled through the small crowd.

"Well, I thought it was rather catchy and something that might appeal to the younger set. So, thank you again, Francine, as I'm sure we'll reap the fruits of your labour."

Sporadic clapping broke the silence. Francine turned yet a darker shade of pink, which, strangely enough, matched the shade of her crocheted seat cushion.

"Keep in mind that our new Agri-Buddy program has its rewards," Ursula continued. "For every new member you sign up, you will receive a coupon for five dollars off your next purchase at Sam's House of Tools plus a free autographed copy of my booklet *The Taming of the Shrub*."

"Now, before we hear tonight's speaker, I would like to address a very important issue. As you all know," said Ursula, "the 46th annual Shaughnessy Garden Show will soon be upon us. Before we start with the usual club business and our evening's lecture, I would appreciate seeing a show of hands to let me know who amongst you is planning on volunteering for the event."

An awkward silence fell over the crowd, broken only by the sound of Ethel dropping the aluminum coffee filter unit in the kitchen. All eyes turned in her direction. Ethel's head popped up from behind the serving counter like a puppet that had missed its cue. With a sheepish look on her face, she mumbled something about being new to the coffee detail. Ursula stood at the podium, looking exasperated.

When Ursula's gaze fell back over the crowd, she counted four willing participants who had raised their hands. The usual eager group included the garden club's entire executive committee: Mimi Owens, club secretary and resident gossip, Margaret Wikowski, club treasurer and someone whose opulent figure was equally matched by her robust wit, and Francine O'Dwyer, the club's librarian and Ursula's former colleague at Point Grey Prep.

Not surprising, in the least, was Chester Smith's enthusiastic hand-waving, higher than all the rest. Chester usually put up his hand at every opportunity, regardless of the topic discussed. He was known to forget his hearing aid at home and regularly slept through most of the meetings.

Ursula's confidence in the success of the upcoming show was seriously waning. The audience tension was palpable yet no one else raised their hand, moved a muscle, blinked an eye or dared look at one another for fear that they would be singled out to explain. Most of the Kerrisdale Garden Club members were suffering from a serious case of indifference. Despite having been told about the seriousness of the club's lack of funds, they were far from motivated to do something about it. "Someone else will fix it, they always do," seemed the battle cry of this silent majority.

Just as Ursula opened her mouth to unleash her disappointment at this apparent garden club mutiny, the door to the community centre swung open. Kate Freitag rushed in. Her curly auburn hair was haphazardly tucked into a rain-soaked tam. She carefully balanced one of her bakery's purple-with-white-polka-dots boxes in one hand and her bright pink umbrella in the other.

Finally, thought a relieved Ursula. *Perhaps we haven't gone to hell in a hand-basket quite yet.*

"I'm so sorry I'm late," Kate said in a hushed whisper as she hastened over to the kitchen door at the side of the hall. As she glanced backwards over her shoulder, Kate couldn't help but notice the anxious look on Ursula's face.

As Kate stood dripping onto the linoleum floor, Ethel gently grasped the box of baked goods and placed them on the table next to the other goodies. Kate nodded appreciatively, then leaned her wet umbrella against the wall. Touching Ethel's arm, she whispered into her ear, "Did I interrupt something important?"

"Thank goodness," Ursula boomed loudly into the microphone. "I'm glad you've finally arrived, Kate. We were just having a show of hands to see which of our members would be willing to give of their free time to support our beloved club by volunteering for the Shaughnessy Garden Show. Unfortunately—"

Before Ursula had a chance to finish, Kate turned back to the group wearing a huge smile.

"I'm sorry to interrupt, Ursula, but I have to share some exciting news on that very topic."

Kate knew that her announcement would probably create a bit of a hubbub. She wanted everyone in the group, including dear deaf Chester, who sat in the front row, to hear what she had to say. She quickly strode towards the front of the room.

Kate climbed the steps to the stage and walked over to Ursula. Sensing that something good might be coming her way, the club president stood aside with a grin of slight trepidation on her lips, letting Kate speak into the microphone.

"Hello everyone!" Kate gave a little wave to the crowd. A uniformly cheerful "Hello" echoed back from the rows of metal chairs. Without a doubt, Kate Freitag was the most beloved member of the Kerrisdale club. Having joined their ranks around the same time that Ursula had been voted in for her second term, Kate was both the newest and youngest member of the ageing group. Because she had inherited an interest in gardening from her Oma, she had immediately felt at home with this delightful collection of senior citizens.

As much as she had previously wanted to join a gardening club like this, Kate had dedicated so much free time to her fledgling bakery that she dared not make the commitment. But now that Deb, her long-time employee and newly appointed manager, had been taking on a lot of the day-to-day responsibilities of the bakery, Kate had decided to test the waters of her newfound, albeit, limited free time. Joining the Kerrisdale Garden Club last January was one of the first things she had decided to do.

Since joining, Kate had missed only a few meetings when things at the bakery had really gone nuts. This past Valentine's Day, the line-up for her popular Honey Hearts and Sweetheart Tarts had stretched down the block. For the most part, however, she felt good about her garden club attendance record and had no regrets.

Tonight, of course, would have to be an unfortunate exception. The catering job for The Grand tomorrow morning simply had to get finished tonight. With some of her staff on vacation and others sick with the flu, Kate had no choice but to pitch in to get the job done. At least she had some good news to announce.

"Unfortunately, I can't stay for this evening's meeting." Kate turned to Ursula and shrugged apologetically. Ursula suppressed a groan.

"But I wanted to share with you a bit of good news." Taking a quick breath, she continued. "I've been asked to do a favour for my dear friend George Stanwell."

Crinkling her nose at the sound of George's name, Ursula instinctively reached for the tissue hidden beneath the cuff of her blouse. She pursed her lips.

"Some of you may know that George is the 'man in charge' at the Shaughnessy Botanical Garden and," pausing for effect, "he has asked me to take on the position of volunteer coordinator for this year's show!"

In the kitchen, Ethel let out a stifled squeal. Ursula just about dropped her cue cards.

"Even though it'll be taxing on my time, I've decided to accept the position. So, I really hope that you'll all consider volunteering for the show because Lord knows, I'll need the help." Kate smiled widely, her bright green eyes dancing with excitement.

A quiet hum of voices buzzed about the room. Kate turned to Ursula and whispered, "I'll be sure to give you a call in the next few days so that we can get started on this whole thing."

Turning back to the club members, Kate finished by saying, "I'm so sorry that I can't stay but I'm sure you'll have a lot to talk about. Please enjoy a few of my BLT Brownies at the break."

Kate hopped down off the stage and with a few furtive waves to a couple of members near the back of the hall, she left as quickly as she had arrived. No sooner had the door closed behind her than the club members exploded into excited chatter. Ursula brought their unwilling attention back to the front where she stood by, rapping on the podium with her ever-present pencil. She deftly picked up on the upbeat mood and charged forth with her appeal. (Sometimes Ursula regretted that she may have missed her true calling in life as a politician. That's why she loved being club president so much: it afforded her a modest taste of political power.)

"People, people, I know you'll agree with me in admitting how exciting it is to hear that our own sweet Kate has taken on this important and influential position at the Shaughnessy show. We don't want to disappoint her now, do we? I feel it's the opportune time to finally settle this issue about our members' participation. Are we, or are we not, going to attend and, if so, who can I call upon amongst you to volunteer?"

Almost every hand shot up, including Ethel's from the kitchen, sugar tongs and all.

Just as Ursula was beginning to jot down all of the newly acquired names, the hall door slowly opened, followed by a gush of cool night air. Thinking Kate had perhaps decided to stay after all, heads quickly turned towards the rear. A strangely familiar face peeked around the half-opened door.

"Isn't that the woman who hosts that show on TV?" whispered Mimi to Margaret out of the side of her mouth as she peered steely-eyed through her trifocals.

"I'm not sure," Margaret replied as she attempted to turn around. The flimsy metal chairs let out a painful squeak under the bulk of her buttocks. Squinting her eyes, Margaret replied, "You may be right. It sure looks an awful lot like her."

Sophia Simpson stood in the open doorway. Although her dark straight hair was pulled back in a casual ponytail, her clothes were all business. She was dressed in a dark wool overcoat, sporting a pair of high-heeled boots that matched the colour of her leather cream-coloured gloves. She looked as though she had just walked off the pages of *Town & Country* magazine. Sophia had stopped by on her way home from work at Urban TV. As she picked up on the excitement lingering in the room, her intuitive journalistic senses kicked into full gear.

Eager eyes stared at Sophia. Before anyone said a word, she spoke in a clear voice, "I'm sorry. Maybe I'm mistaken but I saw a poster at a coffee shop that said something about worm poop and I was intrigued. Am I in the right spot?"

Sophia closed the door behind her and stepped into the hall. She quickly glanced around the room, looking for a friendly face. Her eyes met Ethel's as Ethel gave her an encouraging wave from the kitchen. But Sophia was staring down at the small table set up in front of the kitchen window. A chill ran up and down her spine. Her dark eyes widened with surprise. Sophia stood, her frozen gaze fixated on an all-too-familiar item: the small, purple-with-white-polka-dots box.

Chapter Two

Oma's Baking Tip

If dough has been prepared properly, it will have its own dough memory, stretching with elasticity and bouncing back to its original shape.

By the time Kate slammed the door of her VW Bug, she was completely soaked. In her hurry to leave, she'd forgotten her pink umbrella in the hall but didn't have time to retrieve it. Why she even bothered to schlep the darn thing around with her was an ongoing riddle. She'd lost it numerous times but it always seemed to find its way back to her. As she put the car in reverse, Kate was sure that Ethel would see it on her way out of the kitchen. Maybe Ethel would drop it by the bakery on one of her daily shopping trips through the Village.

Kate felt a trickle of cold rainwater dribble down the back of her neck. Luckily, the bakery was just a couple of blocks away; she could dry her tam and raincoat in her back office. Kate slipped the wet hat off her head, tossing it onto the passenger seat. She knew her hand-knitted head coverings, gifts from Oma, were completely impractical in the rain but she couldn't bring herself to get rid of them. Oma had knit at least twenty in a rainbow of different-coloured yarns, mostly mohair, soft and fuzzy.

"You never know what colour you might need to go with your outfit," Oma had once told Kate, who had come across her tam stash in the front hall closet. Kate had inherited every one, along with the front hall closet that still contained the basket of tams.

Tonight's choice was a soft green variation that was looking a little worn. *I really should take Francine up on that offer of knitting lessons,* thought Kate. *Then I could make a few of my own and perhaps repair a few.* She said aloud: "What am I thinking? It's not like I don't have enough to do already." She brushed a stray strand of wet hair off her face and manoeuvred her bright purple car onto 41st Avenue, heading west along the rain-slicked street.

How Kate had managed to let George talk her into taking over the role of volunteer coordinator was still a blur. After their weekly Friday night dinner at Sakura Sushi on south Granville, he and Richard had invited her back to their place for "a glass of wine and a chat." She should have suspected something was up earlier when George had called and so kindly offered to pick her up from work and drive her home after dinner. Kate loved George; he was her "best friend who happened to be a boy," one of her few long-time friends who managed to stick around.

In typical dramatic fashion, George had relayed his story that evening about how his volunteer coordinator, Cynthia Critchley, had suddenly decided to "find herself." She had headed off to some famous ashram on the Gulf Islands where they grew organic vegetables and tended a flock of alpacas and mohair goats. "Actually sounds kinda nice," mumbled Kate over the rim of her wine glass, much to George's consternation.

"Honey, if you want to find yourself, get a GPS."

George was a sweetheart but not much of a spiritual seeker. His heaven could be found in the Alessi tableware and Natuzzi furniture that filled Richard and George's west-end condo. That and their annual trips to the tropical shores of St. Barts each February was all the heaven he needed.

Cynthia's departure had left George high and dry, without anyone to organize and motivate the close to two hundred volunteers they had each year at the garden show. Kate had wanted to help but was held back by thoughts of biting off more than she could chew. George, however, had been so utterly convincing. He had told her that she'd be perfect for the job and that he had secretly hoped Cynthia would quit so that he could ask Kate. Kate instinctively knew that this was a white lie but when George resorted to batting his long eyelashes and staring unabashedly at her with his pretty blue eyes, she had fallen prey to his plans.

A pleading glance towards Richard in search of moral support had brought only the cheerful reply, "Oh, he does that to all the pretty girls." Flashing an engaging smile, Richard had added, "He usually gets his way. I wish I could use that technique in court but I'd probably be charged with contempt."

Maybe it was the wine, maybe it was all the ego-pumping and blatant flattery. Or maybe it was just that Kate had read through George's pleadings and seen a man who was truly desperate for help. Regardless, she had finally agreed and had made the first public announcement of her new position at the garden club.

They seemed quite pleased, thought Kate as she glanced at her watch, figuring it would take her just five more minutes to reach her reserved parking spot at the back of the bakery. By then, the Mint Maggie Melties would just be coming out of the oven and the night crew would be putting the finishing touches on the Mom's Yums.

Kate's Bakes sat in the middle of the five-block trendy strip of West 41st Avenue in Kerrisdale, often referred to as 'the Village'. A number of newspaper articles and upscale culinary magazines had featured the bakery as "the place for unique treats" in Vancouver. As one famous food critic visiting from New York had written, "Kate's Bakes will entice the kid in you with its whimsical interior and brightly coloured shelves filled with mouth-watering goodies. The adult in you will then take one crumbly bite from any of Kate's daily, fresh-baked creations, and you'll know instantly that the word addiction can also apply to a brownie."

Part of the charm of Kate's Bakes was the unique name used for each of her tasty creations. They usually referred to someone or something special to Kate in some way. Mint Maggie Melties were named for her Oma, Margaret, Kate's culinary idol, who had taught her to bake at a very young age. Although Oma had once showed Kate how to make traditional chocolate mint melties, Kate had replaced the standard artificial mint flavouring with a generous squirt of crème de menthe, topped with an organic mint leaf. Mint Maggie Melties were born. Mom's Yums were a special soft cookie tribute to her mom, who loved apricot jam. Experimenting one day, Kate had squeezed a layer of fresh apricot preserves between two browned-butter cookies. Mom's Yums were one of her top sellers, particularly around Mother's Day.

Most popular of all, and the items that put Kate on the bakery-scene map were her BLT Brownies: bittersweet, chocolaty morsels that "blew the lid off the comfort-food scale," according to *Dine Vancouver*, an upscale culinary guide that had done a feature article on Kate's Bakes. It had not published the recipe, however; like all of Kate's special creations, that was a tightly held secret. Employees even had to sign a waiver, which Kate had gotten Richard to draw up, essentially binding them to secrecy. She had learned her lesson a couple of years ago and didn't want a repeat of that painful event.

As the traffic slowed, Kate drove quietly past the front of the store. Looking to her right through the rain-soaked window, she could see the lights emanating from the back of the shop. What luck she had had six years ago when this space had come up for lease. Situated between Happy Ho's Fruit Market and Fodo's Book Emporium, Kate's Bakes had filled the spot where Mr. Dorflinger's toy shop had once been.

The renovation from toy store to bakery had taken up all of Kate's savings. Since toy stores don't come with professional kitchen equipment and high-end convection ovens, a further bank loan, secured by putting up her inherited home as collateral, had sealed the deal. Thankfully, Kate had paid back that loan in full early last year. Kate's Bakes had been operating in the black ever since. She intended to keep it that way. Kate had even named a cookie to commemorate the event: Blackie Bites, a gooey, rich chocolate cookie with a raspberry centre. The colour symbolism had not been lost on the bank manager, who received a baker's dozen the day the loan was paid off, along with a thank-you note signed by all the bakery staff.

Pulling into the back of the bakery, Kate parked her Bug, grabbed her soaking tam, and used her master key to get into the shop. As soon as she entered, that warm, comforting fragrance enveloped her and immediately set her mind at ease. The aroma from her bakery always seemed to calm her nerves, even on the most hectic days or nights, like this evening. Kate knew they had a deadline to meet and a long list of treats to create before she could call it a night. But the warmth and coziness that seeped into every nook and cranny of the store usually allowed her to focus on the job at hand. Time often seemed to fly by.

Kate took off her rained-soaked overcoat, hung it on the hook in her office, and placed the tam on the radiator under the window. "I'm back!" she shouted towards the kitchen as she slipped on her striped apron and headed to the hand sink to wash up. The magnitude of the sheer silence echoing from inside the bakery kitchen was more than disconcerting. "Hello-ho?" she said over the sound of the water pouring from the faucet. Still no answer.

What the heck? thought Kate. She hastily rubbed her hands on the front of her apron, nearly knocking over a stack of empty delivery boxes piled near the entrance to the kitchen. She rounded the corner to see if her entire night staff had gone up in smoke.

Chapter Three

Oma's Baking Tip

Position the racks in your oven before you turn it on because no one likes to move a hot rack.

"How about that weather guy, Howie? Is he as cute in person as he appears on TV?"

"I've got a neighbour friend who owns thirteen cats. Now, that's a story worth telling!"

"Are you going to feature our club on your show? I'd definitely have to have my hair done before then but I'm sure you'd give us a bit of warning, wouldn't you, dear?"

Sophia could hardly get a word in edgewise as the cluster of star-struck gardening club members peppered her with questions during their short fifteen-minute coffee break. They had managed to barricade her into the corner next to the hallway leading to the washrooms. Any patient attempt to free herself had been met with yet another barrage of questions.

Sophia had gotten used to this sort of thing over the years: strangers coming up to her in restaurants, speaking to her as though they were the best of friends, people telling her their life stories as she waited in line for a movie or at the bank. Being asked to pose for pictures with grandmothers and children during a stroll on the beach. All this had become commonplace and nothing really surprised her much anymore. Being a face that people recognized from TV was the simple reality of her life.

Stories from the Street was now a nationally syndicated, half-hour news segment that appeared on most regional channels across the country. What had started out as a two- to three-minute time filler at a small Toronto news station had grown into a Canada-wide, highly acclaimed human-interest show. There were rumours in the industry that Sophia was likely to get a production deal soon for her own daytime talk show.

Sophia's "recognition factor," as she liked to call it, had jumped significantly since her move to Vancouver from Toronto. Since the syndication deal had come through, she was no longer a one-city gal. Her face, her demeanour, her easy style of interviewing, and her lovable girl-next-door personality had made her an instant hit across the country. The move to Vancouver was something she had welcomed; she had long envisioned coming home to her beloved city. Her success in Toronto had afforded her the bargaining clout she had needed to push the transfer through.

Nevertheless, Sophia had to fight the prevailing attitude of eastern Canada's broadcast executives that Vancouver was still a backwater. But things had changed significantly since the 2010 Winter Olympic Games. Vancouver was no longer viewed as "that granola-crunching city out west." Besides, the format of Sophia's new show gave her the opportunity to travel across the country, bringing viewers interesting, heartfelt stories so often lacking in today's television offerings. Her ratings had proved that there was a real hunger for uplifting and positive human-interest stories and that Sophia had a knack for delivering the goods. Her recent transfer to Vancouver had been viewed as a win-win situation for all involved.

Now that she had been in the city for couple of months and had settled into her newly purchased home, Sophia was determined to bring a bit of local flavour to her broadcasts. Seeing Francine's neatly handwritten poem hanging on the corkboard at her local coffee shop had piqued her interest. She had decided to drop into the garden club to see if it had any merit for a future story.

But then her confidence had been rocked when she had seen that purple-with-white-polka-dots box, the one now emptied of its contents. This obviously sweet-toothed group of gardening fanatics had devoured the entire thing.

"I'm sure I'll get around to answering all of your questions but in the meantime, perhaps one of you could answer one of mine?" Sophia smiled brightly at the uplifted faces.

Hands shot up like the first day of school when all are eager to impress the teacher.

"Why certainly, Miss Simpson. I'm sure we'd love to do that for you," chimed Margaret, who had elbowed her way into the foray of adoring fans.

"Well," Sophia said as casually as possible, "I was wondering who brought that box of goodies from Kate's Bakes?"

"Why, Kate did, dear," said Ethel from the back of the group. "She always brings a little something from her bakery whenever she comes to one of the club's meetings. It's such a treat. She really does spoil us."

"But she's not here right now, is she?" Sophia glanced nervously over the sea of grey hair, thinking she might have somehow missed Kate's auburn locks.

"Oh no, dear," said Ethel. "Kate just popped in at the beginning of the meeting. It's too bad but you just missed her. She couldn't stay but I'm sure you'll get a chance to meet her soon." Sophia's eyebrows shot upwards and she sighed in relief.

"Don't worry, Miss Simpson. Kate usually comes to every meeting and I just know that you two would hit it off. Why, you could feature her on your show. She'd love that. She's been such a success in our neighbourhood. We're all so very proud of her."

"Yes, Kate was the newest addition to our club. But now perhaps we can retire her claim to fame and pass that torch on to you." Ursula's authoritative tone cut through the hubbub as she extended her hand to Sophia and pushed herself forward through the clinging group of admirers.

"My name is Ursula St. Germain, club president, and I would like to personally welcome you to the Kerrisdale Garden Club."

"Thank you, Ursula. I'm Sophia Simpson."

A few muffled giggles of admiration bubbled up from the crowd. They still couldn't believe they had a real live celebrity in their midst. Sophia took Ursula's hand and smiled. "I'm pleased to meet you." Swallowing any further fear of the commitment and concealing that she knew absolutely nothing about gardening, she continued, "And yes, I would very much like to become your newest member. Where do I sign up?"

"Right this way, my dear, right this way." Ursula stepped in closer and scooped Sophia under her arm. "There's just the small matter of a membership form and then," she chimed in, sweeping her away to the front of the room, "we'll have you signed up and ready to go faster than you can say *Filipendula purpurea Elegans.*"

Chapter Four

Oma's Baking Tip

A warm kitchen helps your yeast rise.

"Surprise!"

Kate's mind raced through every possible celebratory configuration that could somehow explain the scene she now faced. Standing in front of her, complete in their baking regalia, stood most of her staff, grinning from ear to ear with a few flour-smeared foreheads and spatters of batter.

Kate was at an utter loss.

"Surprise for what?" She looked from smiling face to smiling face but was rewarded with only cheerful giggles. Finally, the group parted to reveal a spotlessly clean kitchen and towards the back of the room near the loading door, a collection of transport roll trolleys. These were filled from top to bottom with trays of purple-with-white-polka-dots boxes, all neatly stacked and labelled "The Grand."

"We're finished. Done. Finito!" Deb spread her arms wide with a flourish. Standing about a foot taller than anyone else in the room, Deb commanded attention. Her straight brown hair was neatly braided and coiled into a tight bun at the back of her head. She was a no- nonsense kind of gal and had been working at Kate's Bakes since it opened. Deb worked hard, was fiercely loyal to Kate, and she expected the other employees to follow her lead. Most of them had seen her recent promotion to bakery manager as a good thing because, despite her imposing presence, Deb was fair and honest and the kind of person who inspired the same in others.

"The whole order?" Kate looked at every grinning face. She was taken aback to see them all there, especially considering that most of them had already worked a full day and were due in again for tomorrow's morning shift.

"Down to the last Lilie's Lemon Tart!" Joseph stepped forward and put his hands on Kate's shoulders. His dark eyes twinkled as he smiled down at her. "We knew this catering job was a bit of a thorn in your side, boss, so we just wanted to get it done. You know, show you that we could handle it."

"Thanks for the words of wisdom, Joe, but I'm sure she doesn't appreciate the manhandling." Nudging him aside, Deb stepped in front of Kate. Bending slightly forward to look her directly in the eye, Deb wrinkled her brow, then lowered her voice.

"Look, Kate," Deb said, "fact is, you work too hard."

"I'll be the judge of that—"

"You have no time for yourself. George dropped by today, going on and on about how grateful he was that you had taken over that volunteer coordinator job for his beloved little garden show, which by the way, you're crazy to do in my opinion but we'll talk about that later—"

"Yes, we will." Kate smiled. She knew Deb well enough to know that she was just picking up speed.

"Anyways, he got me seriously thinking and a little bit worried. Actually, I was a bit pissed off that he had finagled his way into your newly acquired free time but then I figured it was up to you."

"Yes, that true. It's up to me to decide how I 'finagle' my time," said

Kate, grinning.

"What we needed to do was pull up our socks. So," said Deb, standing up straight and gesturing to the rest of the gang, "I called in the remaining staff on the promise of some free Chinese food later and we knocked this baby outta the park."

The seven-person baking crew broke into spontaneous applause.

"Well, first of all, thank you," Kate said. "Really, thank you so much, everyone, for all the hard work. I know I've said it before but I really can't say it enough: you are all very much appreciated. I totally could not run this business without you, so thanks again."

"And you, missy," said Kate, pointing playfully at Deb, "you and I will most definitely have a chat about my volunteer work at George's little garden show. Quite frankly, this," Kate wiped her hand across a freshly cleaned kneading board, "will be your sole domain for the next couple of weeks, so get used to it."

"Oh God," Joseph groaned. "Does that mean we all have to put up with Deb's antics more than usual?"

"That's right, mister." Deb turned and poked a finger into his chest." And I run a pretty tight ship so don't expect me to fix your messes like the one you made with those cookies tonight."

"Hey, that's not fair." Joseph cocked an eyebrow and nudged a thumb at Kate. "Don't let the boss in on all my shameful secrets."

"All right, all right," said Kate. "I'm sure your secrets will remain hidden, Joe. No worries there. Thanks again, everyone, for all your help but it's getting late so let's get out of here. Chinese food sounds good to me, Deb. I guess since it was your idea you'll be paying?"

Kate slipped her arm around Joseph's elbow and skipped past Deb with a conspiratorial grin on her face.

"Nice, real nice," nodded Deb as she followed the rest of the gang out of the kitchen. The hallway lights flickered slightly.

"Damn lights," she mumbled, then raised her voice. "How 'bout I split you for the Chinese and you finally pay to have these stupid flickering lights fixed?"

Turning off the bank of switches, Deb quickly followed the group out the back door. Kate's Bakes was silent again as it fell back into its sugary slumber.

Chapter Five

Oma's Baking Tip

Be careful when frying donuts in hot oil. Lower them slowly and gently because the closer your hand gets to the oil, the less likely it is to splash and burn.

Wednesday morning dawned grey and drizzly. It was the kind of day that locals brushed off, knowing that the glorious sun was hiding behind that layer of soppy clouds and could very well make a late-afternoon appearance. Non-Vancouverites, on the other hand, would cite this type of weather as the reason why they would never want to live here: too much rain.

Sophia rolled over and stared blankly at her alarm clock. She never used the alarm function because she was one of those enviable people whose internal clock let her know what time she needed to get up. Besides, Wendell never let her sleep in. His usual morning routine included getting up about fifteen minutes before Sophia even stirred, stretching his long limbs. He'd climb slowly and carefully onto the duvet and nestle himself on her stomach before he began his unrelenting purring and kneading. Sophia enjoyed these few minutes of snuggling probably as much as her tuxedo cat. The weight and warmth of his black-and-white, fur-covered body on her solar plexus, accompanied by the soft sound of his purring, was very comforting, especially on those mornings when she woke feeling anxious about the day ahead.

Those types of mornings had become increasingly rare since Sophia had progressed through her career and banished most of her old demons. However, this morning, they were back to haunt her in full force. Sophia felt nauseous with anxiety at the prospect of having to fulfill the promise that she had made the previous night.

~~

"Oh look," sighed Ethel as she came out from the community centre's kitchen to clear the leftover treats from the table. "Kate's gone and left her umbrella here again."

Sophia, who was graciously helping to clean up after the meeting, suddenly noticed the bright pink umbrella leaning up against the wall in a pool of fresh rainwater.

"Now, wouldn't that be the perfect opportunity, dear, for you two to meet?" asked Ethel. "If it's not too much of an inconvenience for you, of course. Wouldn't it be nice if you could bring Kate her umbrella tomorrow? I'm sure she'd very much appreciate it. You could use the chance to introduce yourself as our newest member, although she probably already knows who you are. There'll be no need for introductions on your part, I'm sure."

Ethel blushed a little, thinking how Kate would thank her for sending a famous person like Sophia Simpson into her bakery.

Oh, she knows me alright, thought Sophia. *The question is whether she'd let me in the door or not.*

Mistaking Sophia's furrowed brow for discontent at her bold suggestion, Ethel quickly retracted her idea.

"Of course, I'm sure you're much too busy. Come to think of it, I've got a few errands to run in the Village tomorrow so it's no problem for me to drop it off at the bakery."

Sophia smiled and found herself blurting out, "No, that's alright,

Ethel. I'm sure I could find the time."

"Now, don't you worry about it, my dear, I understand. You're a very busy lady and I wasn't thinking straight. I'll take it to her tomorrow and tell her myself about our newest member. Maybe I'll even have some fun with her and make her guess who you might be!"

Ethel chuckled at her own genius and beamed brightly. Sophia knew that Ethel's little game might bring on a worse result than expected so she swallowed hard and quickly explained.

"It's no bother at all, Ethel. In fact, I just remembered that tomorrow I have the morning off because we're doing an evening shoot on the North Shore. So, it would be my pleasure to bring it to Kate." Biting her lower lip to conceal her next little white lie, she blinked slowly and said, "Now, remind me again, where exactly is her shop?"

~ ~

Sophia, of course, knew exactly where Kate's Bakes was, having driven past it twice a day on her daily commute. She had scouted out the bakery even before she began looking in earnest last fall for a home to purchase in Kerrisdale. Since moving into the same neighbourhood as Kate, Sophia had always been careful to avoid Kate's house and to walk on the opposite side of the street from Kate's Bakes if shopping on foot. But one time she had dared to venture onto Kate's side of the street by popping into Happy Ho's, the vegetable store next to Kate's Bakes, on the premise of checking out the mangoes. In fact, she'd been peeking into Kate's front window display.

Feeling safely hidden under the cover of a wide-brimmed hat, Sophia had stared directly into the bakery's window. The sudden sound of Kate's voice from inside the store had sent her scampering into Happy Ho's, where she remained guiltily lurking amongst the bok choy and bean sprouts. She had ended up purchasing a few shitake mushrooms and an oversized cantaloupe, then had made a quick dash for the exit.

This morning, however, Sophia was really in for it. There was no going back now. Although she had hastily promised Ethel she would return Kate's umbrella, it was truly the last thing she wanted to do today. Her previous night's bravado had morphed into a crippling cowardice all too familiar to her.

Sophia took a deep breath. As she tried to focus on calming her nerves, the reality of last night's visit to the Kerrisdale Garden Club hit her full force. Sophia's eyes widened in disbelief as she lay staring at the ceiling. Without warning, she sat up straight, inadvertently launching Wendell off the duvet onto the hardwood floor. He landed on all fours but turned and meowed his displeasure in Sophia's general direction.

"Oh, my God, Wendell. I signed up to be a garden club member. What the hell was I thinking?"

In a strange way, Sophia fully expected an answer from him, her feline companion and closest confidant since Phil had dumped her two years back. Wendell's recent expulsion from the warm duvet had done nothing to improve his mood. He stared up at her with unwavering green eyes, blinked slowly, then contorted his pretty black face into a toothy yawn.

"Thanks, buddy, I can see you're not going to be much help this morning."

Sophia groaned, rolled out of bed, then slunk with resigned defeat into the *en suite* bathroom. Wendell took this opportunity to jump back onto the bed, nestle himself atop the still-warm covers, and close his eyes. If he truly could talk, he would have told her the logical solution: the appointment would have to be cancelled because it was simply too wet and grey outside to seriously consider even getting out of bed before noon.

Chapter Six

Oma's Baking Tip

If you're looking for a quick treat, you can always go the no-bake route like fudge. But any baker worth his or her salt is willing to put in the time required, which means you have to turn the oven on.

One last look in the hallway mirror, a deep breath, and Sophia felt she was as ready as ever to face her self-imposed obligation. Holding tight onto Kate's umbrella and hoping she wouldn't get too wet, she dashed across the street to her parked car. Once she got the door open, she tossed the umbrella and her briefcase onto the passenger's seat, hopped in, and quickly closed the door before the rain got the seat too wet. The drive to Kate's Bakes was short and she really could have just walked, but the decision to take the car was more a plan for a quick escape should things go terribly wrong.

While getting dressed, Sophia had run through the upcoming scenario. She couldn't seem to get this image out of her head: she is running down the street with Kate in hot pursuit, umbrella in hand, wielding it like some crazy samurai sword. It was silly, of course, but all the same, Sophia didn't want to tempt fate should the meeting not go well. Driving away quickly looked a million times better than sloppily running down the street, dodging early-morning shoppers and bus stops crowded with daily commuters. She'd like to keep her potential embarrassment to the confines of the bakery — patron free, of course.

Once she got onto West 41st, Sophia had to drive around the block twice before she was rewarded with a suitably close spot to Kate's Bakes about half a block down the street. As a large white delivery van pulled away from the curb, she manoeuvred her black BMW into the space with ease. Sophia always prided herself on her ability to parallel park. The words of her high-school driving instructor inevitably came to mind.

"The real trick, Sophia, is to pull up far enough alongside the car beside you. If you don't, you won't have enough room to angle in. If you do, it'll be like sliding a hotdog into a bun."

A then-sixteen-year-old Sophia had blushed slightly at the analogy, especially considering it came from Miss Shirkley, the stoic and matronly drivers' ed instructor at her old alma mater, St. Augustus High.

The rain was easing up. As she stared through the slowly fogging windshield, Sophia could see the storefront just a few meters ahead. It was now almost nine o'clock and the early-morning rush looked to be over. She sat for a few minutes, trying her best to judge the volume of customers going in and out. After about ten minutes of keenly watching the entrance to Kate's Bakes and noticing a slowing up of people coming out of the store with their tell-tale polka-dotted bags, she made the decision to go in.

Slipping a couple of coins into the meter and grabbing Kate's umbrella, Sophia whispered to herself, "It's now or never." She turned towards Kate's Bakes and walked steadily down the street. A warm waft of sweet, dough-smelling air greeted her about a metre from the bakery as one last patron exited the shop. Sophia took a deep breath, held her head high, and walked into the bakery. Eyes wary, she searched for that familiar face.

What greeted her was everything she had expected Kate's Bakes to be and more. If comfort could be personified in a retail space, Kate's

Bakes was just that. The second you stepped through the door, you were enveloped by the warm, soothing aromas of freshly baked pastries and breads. It was common, often comical, to see customers walk in off the street and take a deep inhalation while closing their eyes ever so slightly as a satisfied grin crossed their mouths. Sophia didn't know it, but Kate liked to refer to this as the first moment of contact: that all-important time in a baker's repertoire that could remain with someone for a lifetime.

Kate knew that a person's sense of smell was the most potent and lasting in terms of memory recognition. She wanted everyone who walked through that door to remember that they'd stepped into Kate's Bakes. The second moment of contact was when they opened their eyes and were treated to a visual delight of soft colours, rounded shapes, and a cornucopia of baked goodies that would make most people go weak at the knees. Everything in the shop was curved like the nudes in a Rubens painting: no harsh, sharp angles. It was as if the store itself had been secretly nibbling on the baking and had gone soft around the edges. Countertops, stay tables, light fixtures, and display cases were rounded and smooth, which only added to the overall sense of fluidity and softness.

The walls were painted an inviting shade of lavender, accented with large white spots reminiscent of dollops of butter cream frosting or rounds of freshly kneaded dough. The brightly lit display cases at the back of the shop were clear and meticulously clean, filled with doily-covered trays, glass pedestals, and linen-lined baskets overflowing with the most mouth-watering treats. The only holdover from Mr. Dorflinger's toy shop was the wooden floor, now marked with age but lovingly restored and lacquered to a shine with a honey-coloured finish. It grounded the space and gave it an old-time feel, which added another notch on the comfort scale.

The third and most crucial moment of contact was the first bite. This was the clincher; this was what made all of Kate's hard work worthwhile.

This was what she wanted to share with everyone who walked through that door and into her shop. So important was this moment for Kate that she sometimes secretly watched customers from behind the counter as they took their first bite of a soft cookie or a crumbly croissant. She thrilled at seeing their eyes roll slightly upwards, the smiles of tasty bliss spreading across their contented faces, and hearing the "Oh, my God, that's so good!" exclamations. It was these moments that she lived for, not because they fed her ego but simply because she had made someone happy, just for a moment or two. This was what she strived for and, because her baking was addictively delicious, this is why Kate's Bakes was such a resounding success.

"There's an umbrella stand right beside you if you want to use it," piped a smooth-sounding voice from behind the counter.

Sophia blinked back to reality and stared ahead to see a young man, clean-shaven with short-cropped, dark hair, wearing a dark purple apron and a winning smile.

"Oh, thanks," she said. Stumbling a bit over the next few words, she found the courage deep within her to say, "I'm actually returning this to Kate. Is she here?"

"You know, she really should rename that thing the magic pink boomerang." Stepping around the counter at the side of the display case, Joseph chuckled lightly. "I can't tell you how many times someone has come in to return it."

All Sophia could do was stand there, waiting for the inevitable shouting of Kate's name towards the kitchen in the back of the bakery. Or perhaps there would be a quick "Just a sec, I'll get her" or a nod over the shoulder then, "Oh, here she comes now." Somehow, though, she still managed to take in that Joseph was an extremely attractive man whose lower half, originally hidden by the bakery countertop, filled in the complete picture in a very pleasing way. Surprisingly, he didn't seem to recognize her and that made him all the more attractive. Sophia, however, really wasn't prepared for what he said next.

"She's not here right now."

Relief suddenly flooded through Sophia's every pore. She felt pent-up tension dissolve from her shoulders. Maybe she wasn't as ready to do this as she had thought. But at least she could now speak freely, knowing Kate was nowhere in sight. Standing within centimetres of an extremely attractive man, who smelled appealingly of freshly baked lemon scones, made her words flood out in a babbling dribble of monologue.

"Oh, that's okay. I just wanted to return it to her on my way to work. She'll probably be missing it today, the weather's so bad, but at least she can use it later. I really didn't expect to see her so no worries. If you could just give this to her that would be great." Thrusting the pink umbrella into Joseph's hand, she turned to make a hasty retreat.

The bell above the store's door jangled loudly. Sophia almost bumped into a stout little woman whose clear plastic rain bonnet was snugly tied under her chin. The older woman looked up and squinted her eyes as she stared open-mouthed at Sophia. Sophia had seen that kind of look before. Feeling that her cover might soon be blown, she rushed on with her explanation.

"Oh, and sorry I'm not buying anything today. On a diet, you know." She made a beeline for the escape route. Grabbing the door handle, she barely heard the jingling of the bell attached to the hinge at the top of the door as it mixed with the sound of Joseph's voice behind her.

"Who should I say returned it?"

"Just tell her it was a friend from the garden club," she replied sheep-ishly. Without looking back, Sophia quickly scampered out the door and disappeared into the crowd of people slowly climbing onto the number 39 bus.

As he watched her hurried retreat out the door with the dingle -dangle of the bell chiming in her wake, Joseph had an odd sense that he knew her from somewhere. But he shrugged it off, realizing that he thought that about many women, especially the attractive ones. With a shake of his head, he turned and smiled at the older woman who was eyeing the banana bran muffins in the display case.

"I'll be with you in a moment, ma'am." Joseph continued on through to Kate's office in the back. As he hung Kate's pink umbrella on the coat rack next to her office couch, he was still trying to figure out where he'd seen Sophia's face.

Definitely attractive but skittish, that one, thought Joseph as he headed back to the plastic-bonneted customer up front. *But then again, those gardening club people are always a bit weird.*

Chapter Seven

Oma's Baking Tip

A well written recipe will list all ingredients in the order they will be added in the preparation instructions.

Kettle boiling, egg poaching, and a slice of whole grain bread in the toaster: all was right this morning in Ursula's world. As she finished her usual morning ablutions and padded about the kitchen in her terry robe, with hair rolled up in a matching apricot-coloured towel, she couldn't help but hum a little ditty as she set the breakfast nook for one.

At long last, she mused, *our garden club will be saved.*

Even in her most vivid imaginings, never would Ursula have concocted the perfect storm of circumstances that had occurred the night before. Teetering on the brink of disaster with an uninspired motley crew of initial volunteers, there was no way that she could have saved them from themselves. The Kerrisdale Garden Club was headed for imminent disaster, an inevitable and embarrassing degeneration — had it not been for those two, dare she say, inspired young women who had come to their rescue.

Reaching up into the cupboard to grab her Brown Betty tea pot, Ursula removed the stout little lid and filled the pot with a bit of boiling water from the kettle. Swirling it around and around, careful not to let the hot water shoot out of the spout, she poured the liquid into the sink. A small tin of PG Tips loose-leaf tea stood at the ready. She scooped a couple of teaspoons full into the pot, followed by a good dose of boiling water. The aroma of the strong, black tea rose out of the pot and was quickly captured, like a genie in a bottle. Ursula replaced the lid and covered the pot with one of her crocheted cozies.

The teapot sat decorously on the table next to the bone-china sugar bowl and the jar of homemade raspberry preserves. The poached egg and toast sat squarely on one of Ursula's Royal Doulton Provence Rouge plates. A copy of the morning's paper lay ready, already turned and folded to the crossword section along with a pen, a well-worn copy of *Chambers Concise Crossword Dictionary*, extra reading glasses, and the portable phone. Ursula was now prepared to begin her breakfast.

And so began each day, as it had like clockwork for many years, or at least since Rupert had passed. Before his death, Ursula had gone through the same motions every morning. Now she had reduced the breakfast portion by half. She, of course, left the small creamer of milk in the fridge as she preferred her tea with just sugar. She also kept the obituary section tucked quietly away in the back portion of the newspaper.

Ursula's late husband Rupert had fostered a morbid fascination for obituaries and had insisted on vigilantly reading through them each morning. This did not concern Ursula except when Rupert had found the name of someone they knew, no matter how vaguely, and had insisted on reading aloud their last literary tribute while Ursula feigned interest and quietly sipped her tea. These constant early morning reminders of her own mortality were probably why Ursula had never issued an obituary after Rupert died. She hadn't been able to bring herself to write one, knowing that perhaps somewhere, someone else was enduring the same onslaught of deathly declarations read aloud to them over the morning's toast and eggs. *One less obituary was probably a good thing*, she thought.

Settling in, Ursula poured herself a large cup of tea, prepped with just the right amount of sugar, and began to dip into her poached egg and toast. Breakfast in her nook was one of her favourite times of the day. Unlike mornings in the past, when things had seemed rushed while she had cleared away the dishes, sent Rupert on his way, and gotten herself finished and out the door. The realities of her retirement suited her just fine. She now lounged her way through the early-morning hours without a twinge of guilt as she casually worked on the day's crossword while nibbling on a piece of toast and jam.

This particular morning had brought with it a grey gauze of dampness that blanketed her back garden in a dewy, wet sheen. The breakfast nook jutted out slightly from the first-floor level and looked out onto the back yard through three panes of bay windows. Decorated at the top with single sheets of leaded glass, their green-and-purple art deco motifs cast a colourful glow across the kitchen floor. Ursula adored her backyard. Having the opportunity to admire it every morning was one of the reasons she now lingered so long over breakfast.

Years of loving care and attention to detail had rewarded her with a pleasing vista that was the envy of the neighbourhood. Ursula had fussed over her garden like a new mother over her first-born. Most first-borns eventually moved out but her "baby" settled in, matured, and was in constant need of attention. It was the kind of attention she was willing to give and the rewards were her own to savour. A deep sense of satisfaction coursed through her veins, especially now in early April as the garden came to life again. Tulips, daffodils, snowdrops, and crocuses, all of which had been carefully tucked into the soil the previous fall, now filled the yard, both front and back, with a riot of colour and fragrance.

Dunking a slice of toast into the creamy centre of her poached egg, Ursula returned her thoughts to last night's meeting. It couldn't have gone any better had she orchestrated the entire thing herself. How fortuitous it was, she thought, that Kate had announced her role as the volunteer coordinator followed closely by the induction of their newest, and dare she say, sole celebrity member of the club, Sophia Simpson.

Admittedly, Ursula, whose taste in television viewing was exclusively reserved for Friday-night mysteries on the Knowledge Network or the occasional British literature series on PBS, had never seen any of Sophia's television clips. Yet, Sophia was not entirely unknown to Ursula. Certainly the star-struck reaction of the other garden club members upon her arrival last evening was a strong indication of her celebrity status. Ursula had immediately begun calculating the extreme advantage of having such a media-integrated individual within their ranks.

Surely Sophia would be interested in doing a feature on the club, perhaps even tying it into our involvement in the Shaughnessy Garden Show, thought Ursula as she took a long sip of her sweet, strong tea.

Reaching across the table to the manila membership folder, which she had placed there last night, Ursula flipped open the cover and retrieved Sophia's hand-written application form.

Lovely script, thought Ursula, who couldn't help herself when it came to the fine details of such things: a throwback to her days at Point Grey Prep.

Wiping her hands on a cloth napkin, she mumbled, "Ah, yes, here it is."

Grabbing the portable phone and dialling the number, Ursula took one last quick sip of tea to warm her throat and waited for the connection to go through. The line rang once then went immediately into a pre-recorded message.

"Hmmmph," groaned Ursula as she rolled her eyes. She disliked leaving phone messages because she resented having to edit herself on the spot without due preparation. These thoughts, however, were banished as she heard the impending beep. With a hasty clearing of her throat, she did her best to convey her thoughts as quickly as possible without sounding rushed.

"Hello, Sophia, it's Ursula St. Germain from the Kerrisdale Garden Club. It was lovely to meet you last night and I wanted to again thank you for signing up as a new member. I know I should keep this short so I'll get to the point." Picking up the pace, she rushed on, "I have an excellent idea for your television show that I believe would be mutually beneficial for you and for our little garden club. As well, there is another member of our club whom you did not have the opportunity to meet last night but whom I strongly believe would be a great asset to such a venture. She just happens to be this year's volunteer coordinator for the upcoming Shaughnessy Garden Show and could therefore afford you behind-the-scene access and information that would make your story more interesting and exciting."

Ursula gasped and sucked in a quick breath. "Please call me back at your earliest convenience and let me know what you think. As I said before, it could be a wonderful thing for you and Kate—"

Beep.

"Drat!" With an exasperated sigh, Ursula held the phone at arm's length and stared at it, as if waiting for an apology.

She quickly dismissed the idea of calling back. Nothing was worse than leaving a two-part, disjointed message in which you spend half the time in the second recording apologizing for being cut off in the first. Ursula was sure that Sophia, who presented an utmost professional persona, would understand the gist of what she had just said and would return her call forthwith, after checking her call display, of course, for Ursula's phone number.

Hoping for better luck with her second call, Ursula dialled the number from her roster and awaited the familiar voice on the other end. Her face drooped slightly, eyes narrowing and lips pursed, as she impatiently listened to the second disappointment of the morning.

"Hi, Kate here. I'm probably out doing some bakery-related something or other so leave me a quick message and I promise, honest, to get back to you soon. Thanks!"

Beep.

With no hesitation this time but having some difficulty masking the slight annoyance in her voice, Ursula proceeded quickly and efficiently lest she be cut off once again.

"Hello, Kate, Ursula here. We're very excited about your announcement and the garden club is looking forward to working with you on the upcoming garden show. You did, however, miss a rather important update at the club: we have a brand new member! I'm going to take the liberty of saying that I believe this new member will be most interested in meeting you. You see, her name is Sophia Simpson, a name I'm sure you're very familiar with, and I'm working on her potential involvement in featuring the garden club on her television show. I realize this is short notice but I would really appreciate your cooperation and was hoping that the three of us could get together some time soon to discuss the project. So, please call me back, dear, as soon as you can. Until then, take care and," she breathed a sigh of relief, knowing that she'd managed to fit it all in without being cut off, "happy baking."

The last bit did sound a tad contrived but Ursula so wanted this idea of hers to work. She was willing, at least for now, to "sugar it up a bit," as Ursula's mother used to say when giving her advice on how to deal with belligerent men and small children — not that Kate fell into either category but it couldn't hurt.

Having completed her morning tasks, Ursula sensed it was time to get dressed. She cleared the breakfast dishes from the table and turned to go upstairs. But a knock at the front door made her start. She tiptoed to the entrance hall, not wanting to let the visitor know that she was at home. Normally, she would have peered suspiciously through the eyehole and then opened the door without hesitation. However, Ursula never presented herself to the world in an unkempt way. Fully dressed, hair done, and makeup on was the only way others would ever see her. Never in a bathrobe and certainly not with her wet hair bundled up atop her head in a hand towel.

Peering through the peephole, Ursula watched as the postal delivery woman walked down the front steps. Only until she was safely ensconced behind the wheel of her red-and-white delivery truck and had pulled away from the curb did Ursula dare to open the front door. Allowing just enough room for her to peek out, she glanced down to see the familiar packaging of her favourite mail-order plant company.

"Ah, my summer bulbs!" With childlike glee, she quietly closed the front door, leaving the package on her front step for later retrieval once she was dressed.

"The morning has turned out not so badly at all," she murmured to herself as she climbed the stairs to her bedroom. "Not badly at all, indeed."

Chapter Eight

Oma's Baking Tip

You, too, will learn from every loaf. Persevere through the bad and you'll get to the good, I promise.

Getting out of bed this Wednesday morning as soon as the alarm clock had chimed seven, Kate trotted into the bathroom and took a long, hot shower. Her weekly Wednesday visits to see her mom were one of the few times that she allowed herself an extra hour of sleep in the morning. She had a newly crafted arrangement with Deb, her bakery manager, that Wednesday mornings were Deb's day to open the shop and oversee its running until Kate's arrival, some time in the late afternoon. This arrangement had worked out well since Kate had first suggested it last year after her mom's fall and subsequent move to the assisted living facility in West Vancouver.

The last year for both Kate and Deb had been an adjustment as Kate had allowed herself the rare freedom of being "bakery free" for a few hours. Deb had secretly relished the opportunity to play boss once a week.

The long drive through downtown, over the Lions Gate Bridge and into West Van was best reserved for after 9 a.m. so that the hurried rush of standstill, morning commuter traffic could die down. At first, Kate wasn't sure what to do during the first few hours of freedom before she left to see her mom. She was used to rising at 5 a.m. and being out the door and into the shop by 5:45: a daily routine she had practised for years. For the first couple of months of the new arrangement she felt strangely guilty, as though she was somehow playing mid-week hooky and should be working instead. Kate simply didn't know what to do. At first, she had convinced herself that she could spend the first few hours helping out in the bakery before leaving. But Deb had put the kibosh to that idea last August: "No."

"What do you mean, 'No'? If I want to come in and help out, that's my decision."

Blocking Kate from coming any farther than the back entranceway that first Wednesday of the arrangement, Deb had stood her ground firmly.

"I don't want to sound pushy, Kate, but I think I'm the only one here who will tell you the truth to your face and the truth is: you need to take this time for yourself."

"Yes, I know that's what we agreed but it's only for the first few hours until traffic—"

"I don't care what you do but please don't come to the shop. You've trained us all well enough that we can practically do everything blind-folded and we're happy to do it." Nudging Kate closer towards the back door, Deb had continued her lecture.

"I'm serious now, Kate, you need to just take some time for your-self. Read a book, do some gardening like you said you would or, I don't know, learn how to knit or something."

Kate had smiled. "Actually I'd thought about asking one of the ladies from the garden club to teach me how to knit."

"There you go." Deb had grinned widely, placing her hands on her hips. "Or, you could just sit and do like. . . nothing. Now, that's a novel idea, isn't it?"

"I think you know me well enough, Deb, to know that I'm not the type to just sit and do nothing."

"Well, there's always room for improvement, isn't there?"

Moving forward, Deb had placed a lanky arm over Kate's shoulder, turned her around, and led her slowly to the back door of the shop.

"Now, get in your cute little car and drive home. Make yourself a cup of tea or something and say 'hi' to your mom from all of us. We'll see you later this afternoon."

With a final nudge, Kate had found herself standing like a reprimanded child in the back parking lot. She had turned to see Deb giving her a quick wave as she had closed the door of the bakery. Staring at the hand-painted words "Employees Only" scrolled neatly across the heavy metal door, Kate could not have helped but smile. She was grateful to have Deb in her life.

Now, some nine months later, they had all settled into a comfortable routine. Sometimes she still instinctively woke at five but she'd force herself to lie quietly in bed, often spending the time semi-dreaming about new recipes. Vegan and gluten-free concoctions had been occupying her mind of late because she'd noticed an increased demand for them. Her customers' pleasure was always paramount in her mind, no matter what their dietary predilections were.

This morning, Kate had managed to sleep in until 7 a.m. After a shower, she trundled downstairs and, like every morning, pushed through the waiter door from the hallway and stepped into her small kitchen. The door, which swung freely in two directions, had been there since she could remember. In fact, her Oma and Opa had installed two: one that led from the hallway into the kitchen and one at the other end of the kitchen that led into the dining room. As a child, the doors had always fascinated Kate and she remembered asking her Oma once why they had them. Oma had said that they were ideal when you had guests over for a dinner party because if your arms were laden with appetizers or dinner drinks, you didn't need to use any hands to open the door.

Instead, you just pushed it with a free elbow or walked out backwards. "You only have to be careful," Oma said, "that no one's trying to push on the door from the opposite side at the same time you're trying to push it out!" Kate lived alone so there wasn't much chance of that happening.

Kate's heritage home was located two blocks south of West 41st on a cozy, tree-lined street aptly named Maple Drive. The neighbourhood, with its neatly trimmed houses and meticulously manicured lawns, was more than just a childhood memory for Kate. Having spent many a summer vacation comfortably ensconced in the second-storey bedroom of her grandparents' home with its white chenille bedspread, doll-like writing desk, and a porthole-shaped window in the walk-in closet that overlooked the front yard, Kate was connected to this place in an intimate, family way that ran deep into her heart.

Having grown up with no siblings, Kate had relished the opportunity to spend her entire summer vacations with her Oma and Opa and the many neighbourhood children who had lived within a chestnut's toss of their front door. Her parents, Norbert and Sylvia Freitag, had both been university anthropology professors who, to quote a precocious eight-year-old Kate, "went on tediously boring overseas research trips" during the summer months. Those special summers with her grandparents had been so enjoyable for Kate that she had been careful to reassure her parents each June that they weren't abandoning her but rather giving her grandparents time to "get to know me better." Privately, they had chuckled at that remark, especially considering her Oma and Opa saw her throughout the year; they just lived across the city from where Kate had grown up.

Even from a young age, Kate had always had a knack for saying the right thing to the right person at the right time to make them feel that whatever decision they were making at that moment was a good one. It's what had made her parents feel their summer departures were tolerable. It's also why she never seemed, as a boss, to have a problem holding onto staff. This innate ability to see through and satisfy others' needs while often fulfilling her own goals was one of the main reasons she had been so successful with both her bakery and her personal life, for the most part. In an uncanny and simple way, Kate often gave people a sense of hope: hope for themselves, hope for a better future, hope that all was well in the world.

A postcard tacked to the bulletin board beside her desk at the bakery summed this all up. It hung next to a faded, curled newspaper article about the bakery's opening day and a makeshift frame made out of plastic tape and wooden stir sticks, which held the first dollar they had earned that day. On the front side of the now-slightly-faded postcard were five simple words in white type on a black background, "You gotta give 'em hope." On the back was a slightly faded stamp reading "In memoriam of Harvey Milk, Mayor of Castro Street."(Milk, California's first openly gay politician, was assassinated in 1978 by a former colleague while serving as city supervisor in San Francisco.)

Carefully written in the neatest of handwriting, the card said, "Milk & cookies anyone? Somehow we thought Harvey Milk's words of hope summed it up best. Not only does your kind of hope come from the heart but it's also wrapped up inside the most delicious, melt-in-your-mouth chocolate croissants. Honey, that's the kind of hope we live for! We wish you all the success in the world and we both know that you'll 'rise' to the occasion. Love, George & Richard P.S. Do we get a family discount?"

George and Richard were two of Kate's closest friends and confidants. She had met George at a charity tea she was catering; she had been running a dessert-catering business from a small rented space on Commercial Drive. George was then the store manager for one of the city's most prestigious floral designers. Their fateful meeting occurred in the bustling loading dock of the hotel where the charity event was being held. George had insisted that his delivery truck be allowed to unload first since his floral wares were "perishable, delicate, and not something that could be slung about like a tray of brownies."

Kate had stopped dead in her tracks and, turning to face him, had looked him up and down as though assessing her opponent. Unmoved, George had stared back as he ran a furtive hand through his salt-and-pepper hair. His neatly trimmed moustache had barely hid the sardonic smirk that had played across his lips. As he had taken a deep breath to aid in his mini-tirade, his light blue cashmere sweater had stretched even more tightly over his broad chest.

But he didn't have a chance to speak. Kate's eyes had flared as she let him know that not only was she not about to "sling her brownies about" but rather she would treat them and the other fine baked goods waiting in the back of the idling truck with the respect that they deserved, considering they were to be enjoyed by the parents and relatives of the terminally ill children for whom this benefit was being held.

George's eyes had narrowed. An uncomfortable silence had ensued. Looking like a chastised altar boy, George had rubbed his chin and conceded, "I apologize. You're absolutely right. Please go ahead and unload first. My arrangements can wait."

Then he had smiled at her. That all-consuming sincere and glittering sweet smile had gotten him into so much trouble in the past but now was reserved solely for those whom he truly liked. The effect had been immediate. Kate couldn't help but smile in return. As she unloaded the first of many trays, she had offered him a Mint Maggie Meltie in an attempt to smooth things over. It had worked. After that day, they became friends for life.

Soon after that fateful meeting, George had gone on a singles cruise in the Bahamas and promptly fell in love with Richard, a Vancouver-based lawyer whose quiet charm matched his uncanny good looks. George couldn't wait to introduce his new beau to Kate over crêpes at a West End café. Kate had laughed while George and Richard had shared stories of their misadventures aboard the Imperial Caribbean's *Pearl of the Sea*. She had known immediately that she had had the rare good luck of making two lifelong friends in less than six months.

The sound of the waiter door swinging shut brought Kate out of her short reverie and she reached up to the cupboard for one of her mugs. Setting her Gaggia coffeemaker to "double coffee," she quickly warmed some cream while the heady aroma of freshly ground coffee filled the air. Closing her eyes and breathing deeply, Kate silently thanked George and Richard for this precious Christmas gift. Her "Italian Stallion" was well used and she often wondered how she had lived without it. Clutching her mug, she walked back upstairs and began the thirty-minute ritual of drying her hair. Once satisfied that her unruly locks were somewhat in control, Kate pulled on a pair of jeans and a light sage-green pullover. A quick glance in the mirror, a dab of mascara, and a hint of blush and Kate was ready to start the day. She eagerly swallowed the delicious coffee.

Grabbing her now-empty mug, Kate headed back downstairs for breakfast and another cup of coffee. Once the dishes were cleared away, she pulled out her card box and pencil crayons and sat down at the dining room table to begin work on her mom's card.

Ever since her mother's fall, Kate had reinstated the old tradition of card-writing that had so delighted her mother when Kate was a young girl. She knew that her mother adored these simple expressions of affection; she had decorated her small but neat apartment with examples of Kate's work. Some of them were even raised to the status of "art," having been framed and hung on the wall. Even though Kate thought her drawing abilities had peaked at around age ten, she had taken Deb's advice and deftly found something to occupy the few hours she had to spare before driving across town to visit her mom.

Initially, guilt had plagued Kate when she and her mom had picked out her room at the Ambleside Arms. "But I feel terrible, mom. Can't you come live with me?" she had said. "There's plenty of room and we could make do somehow."

"Oh, darling, you know that wouldn't work. Oma Freitag's house wasn't built to accommodate a wheelchair. And besides, you heard the doctor. I need round-the-clock attention from 'a qualified staff of individuals.'"

"Well, maybe he was just saying that because he owns shares in this place."

"Don't be silly, Kate. You know as well as I do that I absolutely do need the help. I would never in a million years expect you to give up all that you have worked so hard to accomplish just so you could nurse me." Luckily, Kate's mom had left off the phrase "in my final days," which Kate had feared she might say.

"Oh, mom, I hate this."

"I do, too, dear, but you really aren't that far away. If you plan to come and visit me every Wednesday like you said, it'll be just like the old days when you'd come by on Friday nights with Benjamin."

Kate had swallowed hard. Realizing that she had touched on a sore point, Sylvia had reached up and patted Kate's hand.

"I'm sorry, Kate, I didn't mean—"

"That's okay, mom, really. I miss him too but," Kate took a deep breath and squeezed her mother's hand, "you're right. This probably is the best place for you. Deb has agreed to take care of the shop on Wednesday mornings so I'll be by to visit every week."

"That'll be nice, honey. Don't you worry too much about me. I may be in a wheelchair but I'm still as feisty as ever."

Of that Kate had no doubt. What her mother didn't know, however, was that Kate had had a subsequent meeting with Ambleside Arms' director and head nurse. After listening to all their well intentioned platitudes, she had explained that she would be visiting regularly and if she ever got wind of anything untoward regarding her mother's care and well-being, she would pursue legal action to the fullest extent of the law. It's not that Kate didn't trust the staff to do a good job; she had done her research on the place and had gotten many positive reviews from the people she had spoken to briefly. She was just fiercely protective of her mother, especially in the last few years. They had both experienced significant loss: three months after Kate's father, Norbert, had died from a stroke, her fiancé, Benjamin, had been killed in a car accident near Whistler. Their tiny family had gotten very tiny indeed and Kate was holding on as tightly as possible to what was left.

This Wednesday morning had dawned grey and drizzly, much like the day her father had passed away. Sensing that her mom might be thinking of that too, Kate decided to create something really cheerful for her. Maybe a quick sketch of the delicate little daffodils that lined the front walkway. Then, to go along with the card, she'd pick a few and make a little posey for mom to put on her small kitchen table.

Kate finished the card within an hour, signing it simply:

For Mom, delicate daffodils dripping with dew,
I've picked a few to give to you.
With nodding heads, they smell so sweet
and whisper softly, "I love you."

Kate smiled and gave the card a little kiss. Tucking it into its envelope, she set it on the front table by the door where she kept her keys and other "droppables." Grabbing a pair of scissors from the junk drawer in the kitchen, she passed through the swinging door into the front hallway, slipped on a pair of rubber boots and an old raincoat, and stepped outside. Pausing at the top of the bright red steps that led up to her front door, Kate took a deep, languid breath. She loved the smell of Vancouver on a rainy day, especially in this neighbourhood. It was an indescribably sweet mixture of dewy grass, moss, and cedar, tinged with the lightest fragrance of salty ocean air. Pulling the hood of her rain jacket over her hair, she carefully made her way down the front porch steps and onto the paved pathway that led to the sidewalk.

Kate headed directly to a large clump of mini daffodils that were bending over under the weight of the rain. She planned to cut a nice hand-sized bunch of the delicate little flowers since nothing much else was blooming in her garden this early in the season. She knew these simple, graceful stems spoke volumes and she didn't think she needed to add anything more. Once back up the steps and inside, she toed off the rubber boots and walked towards the kitchen to place the flowers beside the sink. Intending to bind them up with a bit of green ribbon, she quickly removed her drippy raincoat. That's when she noticed the red light blinking on her phone.

"I only just went out for a second," she muttered to herself as she reached into the closet for a hanger. The bakery wasn't open yet but the early crew had arrived a few hours ago. Realizing that it might be an urgent message, she quickly hung up the coat and grabbed the phone from its cradle.

Although Kate was relieved to hear that it was just Ursula calling about last evening's garden club meeting, this vanished as soon as she heard Ursula mention the newest member. Sophia's name dropped like a lead ball. The rest of the message was a muffled blur of stuffy British accent. Startled back to reality by the insistent beeping of the phone clenched in her hand, Kate set it back down and stood stupefied in the hallway.

That fateful evening last October came roaring back with a vengeance. She had stood in the exact same spot. The trembling in her stomach had felt just as nauseating. Despite her sincere efforts to forget that conversation, Kate had found herself in the months since playing it over and over in her head. Each time, she had concocted more sophisticated, witty retorts to Sophia's pleadings for reconciliation. The disturbing reruns of "the Sophia call" had significantly subsided as of late. Kate couldn't remember the last time she had been swept away with thoughts of that night. But now it all came back in a terrifying instant — and this time, it wasn't even Sophia who had called.

Chapter Nine

Oma's Baking Tip

Don't worry about spilt milk. There's usually more in the jug and besides, the cat gets an unexpected treat.

"Yes, that is exactly how you make an idiot of yourself!"

Windows shut and wipers pulsing, Sophia grumbled out loud as she pulled away from the curb and glided her car into the morning's traffic. Heading east on 41st Avenue, she eventually turned left on Cambie and made her way north to the Urban TV studios on West 4th. Feeling disgusted with her performance back at the bakery, Sophia felt like crying. Presented with a perfectly good opportunity to come face to face with Kate, she had bolted like a bat out of hell when it became obvious that Kate wasn't even there.

As she cruised along in stop-and-go traffic, Sophia continued mumbling under her breath. Soon the mumblings became a full-blown one-way conversation. The funny thing was that with the introduction of Bluetooth technology, she knew that she could get away with it. Talking to yourself in your car or even while standing in line at the grocery store was no longer cause for concern from innocent bystanders. The automatic assumption was that you were talking to someone on your cell phone. The clear line that used to mark the difference between a "crazy person" and a "sane individual" had been permanently blurred beyond recognition. Sophia often took advantage of this assumption and carried on conversations with herself in the confines of her car, especially when she was trying to work out a particularly sticky problem.

Glancing quickly to her left, Sophia briefly caught the eye of a fellow commuter. She smiled curtly then, turning her eyes forward, she unabashedly continued her solitary tirade.

"You could have left a note. You could have told that guy who you were. He obviously didn't recognize you so you could have at least left your name. A business card. Something. No, you just ran like a baby out of the store and down the street with not so much as a courteous thank you and goodbye. That guy probably thinks, and he's right, that you are a complete moron. That's right, a complete moron who slunk in with Kate's little pink umbrella and then just as quickly dashed out of the store. What is he going to say to her?"

Stepping on the gas, Sophia quickly changed lanes, then lowered her voice an octave, doing her best to imitate Joseph's smooth tones. "Oh, hi, Kate. Some nutty woman came in today and returned your umbrella. Don't ask me who she is because she didn't say. She just shoved it at me and ran out of the bakery. Oh yeah, she did mention one thing: she's from that garden club of yours." Resuming her normal voice, Sophia continued, undeterred.

"Great! Not only will judgement be passed on me, a complete stranger to that guy, but now all those sweet old ladies from the garden club will be tarred with the same brush."

Sophia could go on like this for hours. It was one of the things that she was prone to: externalized monologue conversations, usually self-deprecating and negative. She had been working on changing this, and many other things, but hadn't always been successful. When Phil had left her, she'd finally come to the stark realization that her personal life was in shambles and she had no one to blame but herself. Every once in a while, she had slipped back into the same rut but now she usually recognized the signs before they got out of hand; she mentally changed the conversation going on inside, or like today, outside her head.

As Sophia sat waiting for another light to change, she closed her eyes and tried to focus on her breath. The sharp sound of a car horn from behind brought her back to reality. The light had changed and she jumped forward into the flowing traffic. Thankfully, she wasn't too far from the studio. Sophia drove more calmly down the last stretch of city streets and eventually parked her BMW in its reserved spot in the alleyway behind Urban TV's five-storey brick building on West 4th Avenue.

Rain was still coming down pretty hard and the wind had picked up. Large droplets of rain lashed Sophia from all directions. Holding her briefcase above her head, she dashed as fast as she could along the alleyway. Rounding the corner, she splashed through the small parking lot behind the old brick building, doing her best to avoid the larger puddles that had accumulated like miniature lakes in the pavement cracks. By the time she reached the studio door, however, she was soaked.

Cursing under her breath, Sophia paused for a moment in the brightly lit entranceway and wiped her boots on the already soaked rug. A small pool of water was beginning to accumulate at her feet as rain dripped off her coat and onto the floor. She reached up to brush back her hair and immediately realized that it was a lost cause. Her dark locks now clung limply to her head like a wet mop. Sophia mentally thanked her production assistant, Genevieve, for cancelling their shoot on the North Shore today. The thought of going back out into this downpour was definitely not her idea of a good time. Instead, she'd take her time going up to her office and pop in to see Marcie in H&M first.

Careful not to slip on the polished concrete floor, Sophia stepped up to the reception desk and gave the elderly gentleman behind the counter a quick wink.

"Hi, Carl. How was your night?"

While Sophia signed the day's docket, Carl set his coffee mug down, brushed a few donut crumbs off the front of his dark blue uniform, and fumbled around in his desk drawer.

"Oh fine," he said, handing her the security lanyard with a wide grin. Every employee who wanted access past reception had to wear one of these plastic pouches around their neck. It contained a picture ID card, stating their name and department as well as an electronic fob that allowed them access to certain secure areas of the building.

Raising an eyebrow, he continued, "You look a bit soaked there, Miss Simpson. Ever thought of getting yourself an umbrella?" Carl chuckled as he initialled the docket next to Sophia's name.

"No, actually, but that probably would be a good idea." Sophia slipped the lanyard around her neck and picked up her drippy briefcase, giving it a shake.

"Yeah, my wife keeps buying them for me but I just keep losing them. I guess I'm always hoping someone will return them to me but they never do."

Nodding in agreement, Sophia headed in the direction of Marcie and her drying equipment. Just before she reached the studio door at the end of the corridor, she stopped and turned to face Carl, who had gone back to munching his donut.

"You never know, Carl," she said in a loud voice, "maybe some day, someone will return that umbrella of yours. Stranger things have been known to happen."

"Ain't that the truth, Miss Simpson."

Giving him a quick wave, Sophia bent down to pass the fob over the black keypad near the double swing doors. The little red light in the centre of the console turned green and with a push of one hand, she entered the studio. Taking a sharp left, she quickly walked down the long, fluorescent-lit hallway, nodding briefly to one of the cameramen as he passed. Within a few seconds, she arrived at her destination. Lit more warmly than the other rooms in production, Hair and Makeup was also one of the most cheerful workspaces in the entire building.

This was mostly due to the presence of Marcie Mitchell, head stylist and resident mom figure to pretty much everyone who worked at the station. Marcie had been employed at the Vancouver studio of Urban TV since the late eighties, longer than most anyone else. No one, not even the self-absorbed evening news co-anchor, David Burwell, had a bad word to say about Marcie. She was always ready with a charming smile and ever respectful: what was said in Marcie's domain remained in Marcie's domain. And she was a wizard at making anyone look like a million bucks. She knew everyone's secrets, of course, but her lips were sealed. For those little "cosmetic" secrets that couldn't disappear by Marcie keeping her mouth shut, she deftly covered up with a dab of foundation and a quick spray of temporary hair colour.

Sophia popped her head around the corner. To her relief, Marcie was alone, her back turned to the door. She was sitting in one of the makeup chairs, sipping a cup of coffee, her mascara lashes blinking slowly as her bright green eyes absorbed the contents of a colourful, picture-laden magazine. Not wanting to startle her, Sophia whispered, "Hey there, Marcie."

Twirling around in her chair, Marcie beamed and set her magazine on the makeup counter. Marcie's heart-warming smile could melt almost anyone. Even though she was well into her sixties, she certainly didn't look the part. Her bleached-blonde, curly hair, youthful makeup, and chunky costume jewellery gave her the appearance of a woman much younger. Despite being close to retirement, Marcie could win over the confidence of even the most stoic clients with her bubbly personality and cheerful disposition.

"Hi, hon. Oh my, you look drenched. Don't you own an umbrella?"

"Don't get me started."

Plunking herself down in one of the black leather swivel chairs, Sophia spun around to look at herself more clearly in the bank of mirrors on the opposite wall. Frowning, she lifted a lock of wet black hair off her forehead and tossed it backwards.

"Would you mind drying me up a bit?"

"Course not. Evelyn won't be in for her makeup for another half hour so it's just you and me, girl."

Marcie set down her coffee cup and quickly grabbed a curling brush and her hair blower from the rolling cart in the corner of the room. Walking back to Sophia, she looked into the bank of mirrors to assess the situation.

"Yup. We've got some work to do. But nothing I can't handle, right?" Marcie giggled. "Oh, and help yourself to some coffee if you like and," she leaned in close to Sophia's ear and whispered, "you have got to try one of those!"

Pointing a free elbow in the direction of the far corner of the room, Marcie smiled like a Cheshire cat. Sophia swivelled a bit in her chair and, following Marcie's gaze, found herself staring at a small purple-with-white-polka-dots box. Misinterpreting Sophia's silence as mutual admiration, Marcie chattered on, "I know. I know. You've tried them, right? I couldn't believe them when I first took a bite. Her stuff is off-the-charts, melt-in-your-mouth, get-me-outta- here-before-I-get-too-fat good!"

In a flash, Marcie had set down the hair dryer and brush, grabbed the box, and deftly flipped open the lid. Standing in front of Sophia, box in hand, she looked exactly like one of those perky hosts on the Home Buying Network.

"Ta da! These are so delicious, so yummy, I bet you won't be able to have just one. Believe you me, if this is the last thing you eat before you die, Miss Sophia Simpson, then you will have lived a fulfilled and satisfied life!"

"Oh, come on." Sophia waved her away. "They're just brownies. How good can they be?"

"That's what I thought but then my neighbour, Pattie, she told me about this awesome bakery on West 41st and said I absolutely had to go there. She said that she's been going there for years, and sure, it does kinda show on her hips, but that's beside the point. Pattie kept bugging me so this morning on my way to work, I did a little detour and picked up a box of these brownies."

Sophia squirmed in her chair, thinking of the bizarre consequences she would have faced if she had run into Marcie on the way in or out of the bakery this morning. That would have made an awkward situation even more excruciatingly embarrassing.

Marcie was on a roll. "It's called Kate's Bakes and they've got lots and lots of yummy things. When I was peering through the display case this morning, this really cute guy in an adorable purple apron asked if he could help and I asked him which one was their most popular item. He told me that these here brownies were their bestseller. They're called, now get this, this is so sweet: BLT Brownies. Apparently, they have something to do with the owner's old flame. I think he said his name was Benjamin or something. Sounds like a story I'd like to hear, eh?"

Turning to set the box back down on the small counter behind her, Marcie didn't see the stunned look on Sophia's face. Sophia swallowed hard and did her best to fight back the tears she felt burning in the corners of her eyes.

Marcie had gone to retrieve a plate and a paper napkin from her coffee counter. She returned with a single brownie nestled onto the centre of the plate. Handing it to Sophia, she said, "Apparently, the owner, Kate, makes up endearing names for pretty much every bakery treat they sell. I saw stuff like Mom's Yums and Maggie's Mint Melties. Really, hon, you must try one. Even just a wee little bite? God, listen to me! I sound like a drug dealer."

Laughing joyfully, Marcie smiled down at Sophia who, now holding the plate in her hand, still hadn't gathered herself together.

"Oh, I'm sorry, hon. I hope I haven't upset you. Are you on one of those cabbage diets or something?" Reaching out to take the plate back, Marcie shook her head. "I really should have asked before shoving that thing at you. Sorry."

Sophia looked up at her and held tightly onto the little white plate.

"No, it's okay, Marcie. I'm just being silly. It's just that this brownie reminded me of something." Struggling for words, she continued, "I had a friend once who used to make the most delicious pastries and stuff. We shared an apartment way back when while we were both going to college and . . ." She glanced down at the enticingly dark brown morsel on the plate. "I just miss her, that's all."

Placing a sympathetic hand on her shoulder, Marcie lowered her voice. "I know what that's like. I mean, it's not exactly the same but I had a Polish boyfriend once who used to make homemade perogies. After we broke up, whenever I saw a perogie, I'd turn into a blubbering fool. You should have seen me at my cousin Kelly's wedding. She married a guy from Vegreville, big Ukrainian wedding. I spent most of the evening at the hall crying. Everybody thought it was because of the bride. Luckily, they didn't know it was because of the cheese and potato perogie platter."

Sophia smiled. Marcie was an angel.

"Hey, I just had an idea." Putting her hands on her hips, Marcie continued, "Why don't you consider doing a story on that Kate's Bakes? It's the cutest little place, all decked out in polka dots and stuff. I bet you anything, judging from how delicious those brownies are, that the owner Kate is probably as sweet as pie — excuse the pun. Besides, it might just be the best way for you to get over missing your friend. You know, just like me at that wedding. You see, back then, I decided I'd had enough moping around because of that stupid Johann so I loaded my plate full of those damn cheese and potato perogies and ate my fill. Well, you never saw so many plump, prairie women smile at one time. I was the hit of the party!"

Picking up the brush from the counter, Marcie ran a hand over Sophia's head, then slowly began to brush her dark curls.

"Well, enough babbling, right? Let's get to drying you out so that you don't spend the rest of your day looking like a drowned rat."

Marcie gave Sophia's shoulder another squeeze and with practised skill, began styling her hair.

Looking down at the singular brownie staring up at her from the small white plate, Sophia took a deep breath, picked it up, and took a bite. She closed her eyes as the taste of rich chocolate coated her mouth like a soft cloud of sweetness. As she savoured the delicious flavour, a rush of memories filled her mind. For a flicker of a second, she saw herself and Kate sitting on the floor of their shared studio apartment, nibbling on Kate's Friday-night baking and gossiping about the guys in their Applied Business Practice class, one of whom was Benjamin.

When she opened her eyes, she saw Marcie smiling conspiratorially at her in the mirror.

"Amazing, aren't they?"

"Mmmhmmm," hummed Sophia as she closed her eyes again, lost in bittersweet memories. Marcie's hair dryer droned on, warming her head and shoulders and blowing bits of brownie crumbs onto the floor.

~~

Later that morning, completely dry and feeling refreshed after her visit with Marcie, Sophia sat comfortably behind her desk in her corner unit office on the fifth floor of the Urban TV building. She'd had to fight to get this prime spot on the top floor but now, staring out at the North Shore mountains, she knew it had been worth haggling over with her new bosses. Tucking her hands behind her head, she leaned back in her leather chair and sighed. It had been quite a morning.

Who says you need an umbrella? she thought.

A wide swathe of sunshine penetrated through the grey, soppy clouds, lighting the buildings and roadways in its path so that everything glistened and sparkled. A light breeze was blowing, causing ripples to appear on the surface of puddles. The early tulips, which had begun to bloom in the rooftop garden across the street, nodded back and forth in time with the gusts. Sophia watched a lone seagull float downward, a straggler that had perhaps been buffeted this way from

False Creek. It lingered easily in the air, floating without effort on the unseen support and then, nudged downward by the changing wind, it landed gracefully on a nearby street lamp.

Sophia's mood had decidedly lifted. Talking with Marcie, even though Sophia had not revealed to her the truth about her previous friendship with Kate, had softened the blow of this morning's awkward trip to the bakery. She smiled to herself as she remembered Marcie's ill-advised suggestion that she do a piece on Kate's Bakes.

Wouldn't that just be about the worst thing you could do right now? she asked herself. *I can just imagine Genevieve cold-calling the bakery to see if Kate would be interested. Genevieve may be able to charm influential spiritual leaders and celebrities but I wonder how she'd fair with Kate?*

Sophia looked through the glass partition to see Genevieve, her hard-working reliable assistant, sitting at her desk, typing notes into her laptop while cradling the phone against her shoulder. Her small stature, demure appearance, and soft-spoken voice hid the fierce determination of a twenty-four-year-old journalism graduate who hardly ever took no for an answer. She had the uncanny skill of scrounging up the most interesting and exciting leads for Sophia. It was Genevieve who had gotten Sophia a personal audience with the Dalai Lama last summer when he visited Vancouver to attend a peace conference — a coveted slot that most reporters would have given their eye teeth for. How she had done it was a complete mystery but Sophia suspected it had something to do with the fact that Genevieve's mother taught religious history in the Asian Studies department at UBC and was on the advisory board for the conference. Genevieve was not above using "familiar" connections if they proved useful.

Catching Sophia's eye, Genevieve made a "yak, yak" gesture with her free hand as she listened to an obviously long-winded caller. Besides being her personal assistant, Genevieve was also Sophia's official gate-keeper. By the bored expression on Genevieve's face, Sophia figured she was probably listening to someone drone on with a segment suggestion, and not a particularly good one. Sophia glanced out the panel of windows and watched as the last droplets of rainwater dribbled down the glass. They picked up speed, as they conjoined with other little rivulets, to create a miniature landscape of water lines flowing downwards to the ledge. From there, they disappeared out of sight, presumably carried off by gravity to the pavement below.

Her thoughts returned to Marcie's suggestion about doing a piece on Kate's Bakes. *Nope. Out of the question*, she thought. *I've rocked the boat enough as it is and I don't want Genevieve getting caught up in my personal business.*

Sophia thought it best to handle these things on her own. She certainly didn't want a repeat of last fall's ill-fated phone call. Even though she had felt like a fool after leaving the bakery this morning, no one was the wiser. In truth, Sophia had never planned to be in this situation to begin with. Yes, she had desperately wanted to talk to Kate but was still weighing her options when she saw that poster at the coffee bar. Who would have thought that that little sign would lead her right to Kate? Sophia's intentions for showing up at the Kerrisdale Community Centre were solely professional but one thing had led to another. Before she knew it, she had joined the club and the next morning, was in Kate's Bakes under the premise of returning her umbrella. Was it fate?

Sophia sighed. The whole garden club meeting thing was really serendipitous. Thinking back now, she probably should never have signed up as a new member. This was getting messy already. Sophia started to get that sickening feeling again. Rubbing her temples, she closed her eyes.

"All I need is a few moments alone with her to explain, that's all," she mumbled. Opening her eyes, she stared back out the windows and caught sight of the seagull still sitting atop his perch on the lamppost across the street. As though on cue, he arched his neck backwards and let out a cry. Even though Sophia couldn't hear him through the office's double-paned windows, she knew the call all too well. Having grown up in Vancouver, the sound of seagulls screeching in the wind was etched into her memory forever. It was a piercing squawk: lonely and strangely mournful. She watched as the bird suddenly took flight again, its white chest thrust forward into the wind. Catching an upward gust of air, it banked to the right and disappeared over the top of a building further down the street.

Turning back to her desk, Sophia tossed Marcie's idea of doing a segment on Kate's Bakes into her mental wastepaper basket. There had to be another way, just not that way. Adjusting herself in her chair, Sophia decided it was time to stop daydreaming and get back to work. She now noticed the blinking red light on her telephone console. Grabbing a pen, Sophia pressed the loudspeaker button and began listening to her messages. The first couple were relatively unimportant, just Harry from editing reminding her of their meeting later on that afternoon to go over the animal rescue piece and another from the dry cleaners. The third one stopped her cold.

As soon as she recognized the accent, she quickly picked up the receiver so that no one else could eavesdrop. Sophia replayed the message. With resigned determination, she dialled the number on her display pad and waited. After exactly two rings, a woman's voice with a clipped British accent answered.

"Hello? Ursula St. Germain speaking."

Chapter Ten

Oma's Baking Tip

Nobody likes a soggy-bottomed pie so be sure to make holes in the top of your pastry crust to allow the steam to escape.

"Hi, George, it's me." Kate's voice cracked.

"Hi, you. So tell me, how did the garden club take your news last night? I'm sure the old Germain Shepherd was tickled pink." George's disdain for the Kerrisdale Garden Club's president was palpable. They had both met years ago when they had co-chaired the floral arrangement judging at one of the Shaughnessy Garden Shows. Their sense of the artistic was on opposite ends of the scale, matched only by their intense dislike for one another. Agreeing on whom to give the best-in-show blue ribbon that year had been an epic battle of wits. George had vowed never again to co-anything with that woman.

The sound of George's voice seemed to uncork the last bit of bottled-up emotion Kate had managed to suppress while hurriedly getting ready to visit her mom. By distracting herself with last-minute chores, she had successfully kept the tears at bay. The delicate little posey had been tied and set, card attached, by the front door in a small glass vase.

When she had reached into the closet for a fresh, dry tam, she'd paused and held the soft pink Merino wool hat in her trembling hands. Perhaps it was the fond memory of her Oma who had lovingly knit it so many years ago. Or maybe Kate had simply reached her emotional limit. But she had found herself running to the bathroom in search of a tissue. Staring at her red-rimmed eyes in the antique bathroom mirror above the sink, she had decided it was finally time to talk to somebody. George was her somebody.

"Now, don't tell me you're having second thoughts already." Pressing his cell phone tightly against his ear, George leaned forward and tore a scrap off his desk's notepad and balled it up in his fist. "I just got off the phone with our marketing manager, Pauline, and told her that you've accepted the position. They're planning on printing the—"

"I'm not calling about that." Kate's voice sounded flat.

Relief flooded across George's face as he joyfully tossed the paper ball in the general direction of his wastepaper basket. He missed. George was never good at throwing things except tantrums.

"Well, thank God because you just sent my high blood pressure through the roof!"

"Listen, George, I need to talk to you about something. Can we meet for coffee later today? Just you and me. Would that be okay?" Kate's voice was barely above a whisper.

George lowered his voice. "Are you alright? You sound upset." There was no immediate reply. "Did you want me to come over? I can do that, you know." George was standing now.

Kate bit her bottom lip and squeezed her eyes shut to hold back the flood of tears she knew was about to pour out of her.

George didn't need any more prompting. "I'm coming over." Reaching for his coat on the back of his chair, George slammed his laptop closed and headed for his office door.

"You can't." Wiping a wayward tear that had strayed from the corner of her eye, Kate took a deep breath and continued, "I'm on my way out the door to see mom."

"Well, how about I meet you there and take you both out for lunch? Afterwards, you and I can slip away for a private chat. Besides, I need a good excuse to get out of here. My new intern Stacey is driving me nuts. I'm afraid if I don't leave soon, I might just do something I regret later."

"I can't be away from the bakery for that long." Kate's voice trembled slightly and she let out another sigh.

"My God, you sound like a leaking tire. This is serious. And you most certainly can be away from the bakery for however long it takes me to patch you up! Even if I have to call Deb and tell her myself."

"She'd love that." Kate managed a weak smile.

"Oh, I know she would. That's why I'm half-hoping you'll say yes so that I can really make her day."

A small laugh trickled out of Kate.

"Now, that's better." George fumbled with his coat. Having managed to slip it on, he took a glancing assessment of himself in the mirror next to the door.

"I love you, George."

He stopped short. "I love you too, hon. Now, are you going to make that call or are you going to allow one of your best employees to be tortured by the likes of me?"

"Don't worry. I'll call and I guess I'll see you at mom's. She'll be thrilled."

"So will I." Tucking his cell phone into his jacket pocket, George turned the door handle and stepped into the reception room. "Stacey! Hold all my calls, if you even know what that means."

Chapter Eleven

Oma's Baking Tip

When in doubt, add chocolate.

George's lunch idea was exactly what Kate needed. She bundled the last of her things for the day into her VW Bug and headed for the North Shore. Before she'd left the house, Kate had called ahead to let her mom know that George had decided to take them both out. Sylvia could barely contain her excitement, not only because it gave her an opportunity to get dressed up, but also because, like Kate, she simply adored George's company. Kate knew that it was because George was educated, witty, and observant, ever the gentleman — traits her father had had in abundance. Traits that Benjamin had shared as well.

Pulling onto West 41st Avenue, Kate drove slowly past the bakery but managed to stare straight ahead. She knew that if she caught a glimpse of it, she might have to pull over to compose herself. After the phone message from Ursula and the mention of Sophia's name, her head had been swirling with memories. As so often happened, when they settled, they settled on thoughts of Benjamin.

It had only been three years since the accident but to Kate, it seemed at times like this, when her emotions were laid bare, that it was only yesterday when she'd opened her front door to find a grim-faced police officer standing on her front step. As she turned left onto Granville Street, Kate began to think of all that had happened since that evening when her world was shaken to its core. She swallowed hard and tightly gripped the steering wheel as a wave of emotion swept upwards from her stomach and sat like a clenched fist in her throat. She shook her head and marvelled at how, after so much time had passed, she could so easily conjure up those feelings of loss and sadness.

The bakery had saved her. Pouring hours of time into her work with singular focus and determination, she had managed to knead through the lumps of pain. But like with this morning, lingering wisps of sadness would occasionally waft through her mind like the faint scent of smoke from a distant fire.

As Kate crossed over the Burrard Street Bridge and into the clogged traffic of the downtown core, she took a deep breath and allowed herself to think of a night, just over a year ago, when a shift had finally come. It was the second anniversary of Benjamin's death and Kate had decided it was time to break the silence.

On the first anniversary she had invited both Richard and George, her mom, and Deb over for dinner. Done mostly out of a sincere fear of being alone on that day, Kate had busied herself with preparing a four-course meal and spending time in the company of her dearest friends and family. Conversation that evening had only hinted at the reason for their gathering. Everyone had taken their cue from Kate, not wanting to upset her more than was already visible.

The second anniversary, however, had been different. Upon arrival, everyone had not been greeted with the somewhat ghostly and self-absorbed version of Kate that they had grown accustomed to in the months following Benjamin's accident. Instead, they had encountered an exuberant cheerful version, reminiscent of the "old" Kate who used to be engaged to a wonderful guy named Benjamin. Having taken all their coats and gotten her guests settled in the front room with a drink, Kate had taken a seat by the roaring fire and stared quietly at her lap. The room had been silent for an awkward moment, all eyes on Kate. She had looked up and simply said, "I've made a decision." She had announced, "I've decided that I'm not going to grieve for Benjamin anymore."

"Oh, Kate." Her mom had lifted a hand to her chest, as though trying to hold back the rush of sadness that welled inside her. She had often felt helpless in the wake of her daughter's loss because she herself had been still trying to cope with her own.

"It's okay, mom. I'm not going to forget him. How could I?" Kate had glanced around the room. "He is a constant reminder in my life. I see him in all of you." Placing her glass down on the coffee table, she had continued. "But it suddenly hit me last week as I was going through the motions of getting ready for tonight's dinner. I was planning the menu and I got stuck on the dessert. I couldn't think of a thing. Imagine me, of all people, who couldn't figure out what to serve for dessert!" A loud sigh had accentuated her frustration as she stared upwards, reliving those exasperating moments in the kitchen where she had literally begged for some kind of divine intervention to alleviate her suffering.

The room had gone silent.

"Actually, it was a good thing that none of you were here to witness the disaster. I literally tore through that kitchen like a madwoman and it took me three hours to clean up the mess."

"Oh, God," Deb had moaned.

"Yeah, I was off the hook," Kate had confessed.

"Why didn't you call?" George had set down his glass and moved to sit next to Kate. Taking her hand in his, he had gently said, "You know we would have been over here in a heartbeat."

"Oh, I know you would have," Kate had said with a smile, "and I appreciate it." She had taken a deep breath and continued, "but I kinda had to go through that. I've been keeping it down for too long. To tell you the truth, I think Benjamin would have gotten a kick out of it."

"What, of you having a mini mental breakdown in your kitchen?"

This time, Deb had spoken up.

"Well, yes, that too, but I was thinking more about the revelation that came from it."

All eyes had been on Kate.

"I finally figured out that he's really not coming back. Benjamin was killed in a head-on collision with that freight truck on the Sea to Sky highway just outside of Whistler on September 5, 2013. Those are the facts."

Sylvia had reached for her purse to retrieve a handkerchief. Despite having seen her mother beginning to crumble under the weight of her words, Kate had continued. "We're not going to get married and we're not going to be raising a family together."

An earnest look of concern had passed between Richard and George. Sylvia had stared at her daughter with a tinge of fear in her eyes as she had dabbed at them with her tissue. Deb had simply sat still, obviously uncomfortable at not knowing how to deal with the raw emotion spilled forth in front of her.

Glancing towards her mom, who was now openly crying, Kate had said softly, "Don't worry, mom, I'm not crazy. I know it's hard to hear but it's just the truth and I need to move on." Kate had stood and walked over to Sylvia.

"In that moment, while I sat on the kitchen floor among piles of spilt flour and cracked eggs, I realized that Benjamin would always be with me. But I had to let him go because if I didn't, I'd die too, only really slowly, over time, bit by bit. . . It had already started." She had looked down.

Sylvia had stood up and run a trembling hand through Kate's hair. "I'm so proud of you, honey. You've been through so much, what with your father's death and then Benjamin's. And yet, you always seem to somehow land on your feet. I just hate to hear you talk like that. It sounds so matter-of-fact."

As a tear had run down Sylvia's cheek, Kate had gently brushed it away with her hand.

"It's okay, mom, it really is." Smiling, she had said, "I'm alright, really. I want you to know that. All of you." Turning, she had looked at George, still sitting by the window, Richard alone on the couch and then to Deb, who had sat forlornly in the corner.

"I loved Benjamin. I mean, I still do. And so, sitting in that messy kitchen, strewn with the ingredients that make up my life, I literally picked up the pieces and baked something that will always remind me of him. Something that will always make me smile. Hopefully, it will bring a smile to others as well." Standing up and moving towards the kitchen, Kate had added, "I know it's a little early for dessert but. . ."

She had disappeared around the corner and within seconds, had returned with a tray stacked high with milky chocolate brownies.

"Introducing my 'kitchen revelation' and the newest member of Kate's Bakes signature collection: BLT Brownies."

George had stood up and joined Richard by the couch. Deb had walked over to have a closer inspection, the baker in her having come alive. She had been hugely relieved for an opportunity to help swing the mood of the room in a different direction.

"These look delicious, Kate." Deb had beamed.

"Oh, and they are! And a total stroke of genius, if I don't say so myself."

"And why, pray tell, did you name them BLT Brownies?" Richard had not been able to wait to hear the story about this one.

"Yes, dear. Why BLT? That's a sandwich, isn't it?" Sylvia had now gathered herself together and was genuinely intrigued by her daughter's handling of her grief.

"Well, mom. . ." Kate had paused slightly. "It's really quite simple. As I sat there in the kitchen, I remembered that Benjamin adored these brownies. He was always asking me to make them. Because they were so special to him, I didn't make them at the bakery. Well, as of tomorrow, everyone's going to get a chance to enjoy these as much as he did. And every smile I see on my customers' faces, after they've taken that first bite, will be my gift to Benjamin for all the smiles he gave me. So, you see, calling them BLT's was the obvious choice because," Kate had looked down at the tray full of brownies and smiled, "they're Benjamin Loves These — BLT's."

The fact that Kate had used the present tense as opposed to the past was not lost on anyone in the room that night. As they had each taken a bite, savouring the rich chocolaty flavour and the surprisingly soft, creamy centre, it was Sylvia who, having wiped a wayward crumb from her lap, had announced, "Why, yes. Benjamin Loves These Brownies really is the perfect name, isn't it?"

There hadn't been a dry eye in the room.

The sound of a discordant horn startled Kate as memories of that evening flashed away in the blink of an eye. Somehow, without even knowing how she had done it, she had driven most of the way to her mom's apartment and was now approaching the Marine Drive off-ramp from the Lions Gate Bridge. Glancing at the clock on her dashboard, she gripped the steering wheel and with renewed vigour, stepped on the gas pedal. If she had daydreamed the drive away and George had somehow managed to get to her mom's faster than she did, Kate knew she'd have some explaining to do. There was already way too much explaining to do. Kate held her breath as she zoomed through a yellow light and careened her Bug around the final corner. The fluffy pink blossoms of the cherry trees outside her mom's nursing home winked at her from a distance.

Chapter Twelve

Oma's Baking Tip

Adding salt to your baked goods not only enhances the flavour but it gives croissants, breads, and muffins a nice, golden colour. Forgot your salt? Your sweet treats and breads will come out pale.

Lunch with Sylvia that blustery Wednesday afternoon ended similarly to that second anniversary evening last September, with laughter and reminiscing: a huge relief for Kate, who was having a difficult time holding it together. She was thankful for George's calming presence. Sylvia certainly more than enjoyed the company and the delicious lunch. As was his style, George phoned ahead to a nice little Italian bistro he knew on Marine Drive and made reservations for noon. This allowed enough time for him to organize things swiftly at the office, give Richard a quick call, and drive through downtown and over the bridge to Sylvia's apartment.

D'angelo himself greeted them warmly at the door and led them to a small table near the window with a clear view of the harbour. They dined on George's pre-ordered menu of arugula salad, gorgonzola and porcini mushroom risotto, and zabaglione with plums. There were no complaints from his two guests, who savoured each bite and thanked him for his choices. The conversation remained light. George entertained Sylvia with the latest plans for the garden show, including the appointment of Kate as the new volunteer coordinator. Smiling through the inevitable questions about time constraints and potential bakery conflicts, Sylvia chided. "Mother's Day is just around the corner, Kate, and you know how crazy your shop is then." But Kate was able to breeze through this portion of the meal and assure her mother that all was well without revealing her underlying thoughts about the unsettling phone message she had received earlier that morning.

After driving Sylvia back to her apartment, and assuring her that they would talk again soon, Kate gave her mom a hug.

"Thank you, again, for the card." Sylvia gestured to the table next to the couch, "And I love the flowers, dear."

Kate smiled and quickly turned to leave. George saw the emotion coming forth from her. Sensing that Kate really needed to talk, he walked over to Sylvia and gave her a kiss on the cheek.

"You have a wonderful daughter, Sylvia. But who could expect less from such a wonderful woman?"

"Oh, George. You're such a charmer." Blushing slightly, Sylvia squeezed his hand. "Now get along, you two. I'm sure you both have things to do, places to go, and people to see."

As they headed for the elevator, Kate and George briefly discussed where they would meet up. They quickly decided that because the weather was still holding, they'd chance a quick walk down by the beach. After taking their separate vehicles, they arrived within minutes at the mostly deserted parking lot adjacent to the beach-access walkway at Ambleside Park. The rain had been sporadic that morning. Thinking it might be a good idea to bring along a little insurance, Kate reached behind her seat for her umbrella. She came up empty-handed.

Rolling her eyes, she thought of the many times she had mislaid her favourite pink umbrella. As she buttoned her raincoat up to her chin, she remembered that she had taken the umbrella with her to the garden club meeting last night. It had been the box of brownies' sole protector against wayward drops of rain as she had madly dashed across the parking lot to the hall.

I wonder who'll be bringing it by this time? Kate thought as she grabbed her tam and shoved it into her purse. She had left her umbrella at club meetings on several occasions and it was faithfully returned to her every time. Usually, Ethel or Mimi stopped by the bakery the next day to return it. One time, it had been Lloyd and she had had a heck of a time shooing him out the door. A free box of Duncan's Donuts, named in honour of the sympathetic policeman who was so kind to Kate after Benjamin's death, had done the trick. It had been a small price to pay so that she could finally get on with her day. She secretly hoped it wouldn't be Lloyd today.

George had parked his car a few stalls down. He now stood outside her door, tapping lightly on the window. "All set?" His muffled voice chimed behind the closed window.

Opening the door, Kate replied, "As set as I'll ever be, I guess."

Climbing out of her car, she linked arms with George. They headed towards the rain-soaked path that clung to the beach and afforded an excellent view of Stanley Park and the waters beyond. There weren't too many people out, only the occasional dog walker and a jogger or two. The sky was still overcast but thankfully, the rain had let up. The salty breeze coming off of the water was refreshing and cool.

George and Kate walked in silence as they turned right along the path dotted with a matrix of interlocking puddles. They quietly picked their way along, managing to avoid getting their shoes soaked above the sole-line. Kate let out a soft sigh. Sensing that she was now perhaps ready to spill the beans, George asked, "So, what's up?"

"She called."

Kate's voice was barely above a whisper.

George tensed because he instinctively knew who "she" was. He was one of the few people in Kate's life who was privy to the intimate details of how her friendship with Sophia had gone sour. Not even her mother had been told the whole story. George suspected that this was because Kate didn't want to upset Sylvia. Kate had attributed the distance between the once-inseparable girlfriends to busy lives and blossoming careers.

"When?"

"Seven months ago."

George now glanced sideways at Kate. "And it's taken you this long to tell me?"

Kate realized the absurdity of her answer and smiled weakly up at George.

"I didn't tell you about it because I didn't think it was so important at the time."

"Well, obviously it wasn't, until now."

"You're right." She paused. "It wasn't really important. That's why I didn't mention it. But now it's happened again."

"She called again?"

"Well, not her, but Ursula St. Germain."

George stood still and turned to Kate. "What? St. Germain? What does she have to do with Sophia?"

"That's what I thought, too, when I heard her message this morning."

"Okay, wait a second, hon. You're not making any sense. Why don't you start from Sophia's first phone call. When was it?"

"Early last October."

A gust of wind tossed Kate's hair about in a wild flurry. Reaching into her handbag, she pulled out the pink knit tam she had shoved in there earlier and skillfully pulled it onto the top of her head. She managed to tuck a few wayward wisps of curly auburn hair in under the edges.

"You always remind me of Audrey Hepburn when you wear those tams." George smiled.

"Thanks. Oma was very 'Breakfast at Tiffany's,' I guess."

Kate paused again, not sure where or how to begin.

"So, tell me about the call already. I'm dying here."

"All right." Kate swallowed hard and reached down to hold his hand for extra comfort and a little bit of warmth from the cool spring breeze. She began.

George, of course, knew that Sophia was back in town. He and Richard had stumbled across one of her shows on a rare stay-at-home-and-watch-TV night. Having only heard about Sophia and having seen the occasional snapshot in Kate's old photo albums, he had admitted that Sophia was stunningly beautiful but that was as far as George's appreciation for her extended. In defence of Kate and the disappointments she had experienced with Sophia, George, in particular, was not beyond sardonic remarks. They were, of course, delivered in a playful, offhand way but everything from Sophia's interviewing style to her clothing had come under his meticulous scrutiny.

At first, George had wanted to pick up the phone and call Kate, informing her of Sophia's return but Richard had advised against it.

"Why stir things up? It'll only make her feel bad. Besides, she probably already knows and has rightly chosen to simply ignore her. I think we should too." Richard was always the voice of reason. He couldn't help it. That's what four years of law school and twelve at the bar will do to you.

George had heeded Richard's advice then, but now, listening to Kate as they slowly walked along the winding path, he doubted whether his judgement call had been correct. He cringed inwardly as Kate recalled the evening back in October, complete with her hallway slide to the floor.

"I thought it was done then. I mean, I was pretty clear to her when she called. I never heard back from her after that, so why bother worrying you about it? It was over, as far as I was concerned."

Kate knew this sounded weak. Maybe George was hurt that she decided not to share the news with him about the late-night call but at the time, it seemed the right thing to do.

"But then, as I was getting ready to come see mom this morning, I got a phone message. I was out front picking some flowers and I missed the call. I thought it might be the bakery but it was a message from Ursula."

A bit of rain started to pepper down so George opened up his umbrella, tucked Kate in a bit closer, and held it over their heads as best he could. An elderly woman whizzed past on a bright red electric scooter. Her poncho-covered poodle, perched in the front basket, yapped a parting "hello" as they headed off down the path with her Canadian flag whipping in the wind at the end of its flexible pole.

"She told me that Sophia had showed up at the garden club meeting last night."

"What? You mean she just showed up out of the blue? Did you see her?" George was getting really excited now.

"No, I didn't see her or else you definitely would have heard from me earlier." Kate sighed. "No, I just stopped by quickly last night to let everyone know about my decision to head up the volunteers for the show."

George smiled. He was still thrilled that Kate had agreed to take the position.

"I left early and went back to the shop because we had a big job to finish for The Grand. I had no idea what went on afterwards but apparently, Sophia showed up at some point and joined the club."

"Pardon me? She joined the club? Let me get this straight: she just walked into your garden club and joined it? Like that's a perfectly normal thing to do?" This all came out in one fell swoop, George's gushing emotion pouring out like the wet drops all around them.

"I guess so. I have no idea why she was even there. But the worst part is that somehow, Ursula's now got this fabulous idea that the three of us are going to happily do a kind of mini-documentary with Sophia at the helm, all about the gardening show and the club and, and, and . . ." Kate's worry raged to the surface now.

George stopped walking and turned to Kate. His mind was racing.

National exposure on Sophia's television show would be a godsend for the Shaughnessy Garden Show. Attendance totals had been in a steady decline over the last couple of years and the show was in a real risk of cancellation. Being featured on Sophia's show would definitely boost its exposure, potentially ensuring its continued success. He, of course, stifled these thoughts for Kate's sake.

"But how does she know you two know each other?"

"I'm assuming she doesn't because she said there was someone new whom she thought I'd like to meet and—"

"Just say no," interrupted George. "You don't have to do anything you don't want to. Even if St. Germain thinks it's a good idea — trust me, I know from experience — it doesn't mean that it is."

"I know, but how am I supposed to turn her down? You know our club is suffering and the exposure would be fantastic." She looked up at him. "And you have to admit, it would be great advertising for the garden show too." George was shocked by the truth of her last statement, mostly because it matched his inner thoughts. He would hate to admit to Kate that since she had mentioned Sophia's intentions to do a segment on the garden show, he had even entertained the idea of having Sophia on-site.

"Look, Kate, the garden show will do just fine with or without Sophia Simpson," he lied, "and your garden club will carry on as it always has. St. Germain is, if anything, a resourceful woman. She'll think of something else."

"Oh, no she won't. You know her well enough. She's like a dog with a bone. Once she gets an idea into her head, she doesn't let it go." Looking past George to the open ocean, Kate added, "and that's what worries me the most. This is going to get personal and ugly. I can just see it now."

"Not if you stand up to her and simply say no." George put his hand under Kate's chin and turned her face towards his. His tone was gentle and reassuring. "Look, if it makes you feel more comfortable, let St. Germain do the segment on the garden club and the show. Who cares? Just don't involve yourself. Plead 'too-busy syndrome' or something like that."

He looked Kate intently in the eyes, sensing that she was almost on the verge of tears again. A jogger approached. Even though she had a pair of pink ear buds dangling from under her skullcap, George leaned in closer and spoke in hushed tones.

"You don't owe her anything, Kate, and you certainly don't owe Sophia anything. If she wants to worm her way into your garden club, then let her. I bet she won't last a meeting or two. Once she figures out that you're onto her game, she'll move on. Once a coward, always a coward, I say."

The jogger splashed past them, giving a smile and mouthing a 'hello' as she glided on her way down the winding path. George raised his voice slightly, "She'll bore quickly, I'm sure. Perhaps she'll get a story out of it but that'll be it. She'll move on to other things and life will go on."

"You know the funny thing, though?" Kate looked at George. "Why is she being so persistent? I mean, I think I made it pretty clear that I didn't want to continue our friendship, not after how she virtually ignored me after Benjamin's death. And the cookie thing was downright underhanded."

"I know, I know." George was lost in his own thoughts. They had gone over this many times, trying to figure out the motives behind Sophia's actions but always came up with the same conclusion: she cared more about her career than her friendship to Kate. Unfortunately, there was no way to sugar-coat that reality.

"Maybe she's finally figured it out." Kate was thinking aloud.

"Figured what out?"

"That her career isn't everything. That friendship actually means something and has value. That hurting your very best friend by giving no support whatsoever when they really needed it and then stealing a traditional family recipe from me and taking recognition for it is not the way to elicit trust and understanding."

"Wow. You sure give her a lot of credit for self-discovery and internal development." George couldn't help the sarcasm. "Perhaps that interview she did with the Dalai Lama last summer had some kind of lingering effect."

"I'm serious, George. I'm wondering if she really has got it." Kate stopped walking and turned to him. "I mean, what if she has? Isn't it my responsibility to respond?"

"You have absolutely no responsibility whatsoever! Have you forgotten how she treated you after Ben died?" Of course, George knew the question was rhetorical but he couldn't believe Kate was even considering giving Sophia another chance. "And what about the gingerbread recipe?"

"I know. Stupid, huh? I guess I'm just a sucker for punishment."

"Oh no, you're not and don't you even think about going down that route." George's mother-hen instincts were in full swing now. "Face it, Kate. She dumped you. Left you high and not-so-dry after Ben's death. She stayed in Toronto, didn't bother to show up for the funeral, and barely got in touch with you for two years. To make matters worse, she steals one of your Oma's cookie recipes and promotes it as her own on a nationally syndicated holiday cooking special and gets rave reviews and cook book deals. Honey, if that's not enough to tell you that she's not worth pursuing as a friend then I don't know what is."

"Everybody can make mistakes, right?"

"Oh God, now you're sounding like Oprah. Listen, I don't want to play the baddy here but I don't think she's worth it. She wasn't kind to you then and I don't see how and why she would suddenly be having a change of heart."

"I heard Philip left her."

"Well, surprise, surprise. Come on, Kate. Don't you see it? She's way too involved in her career to care about anybody else but herself. Even her boyfriend leaves her."

Turning to Kate, George asked, "How, by the way, did you know that?"

"Oh," Kate mumbled, slightly embarrassed, "I've Googled her a couple of times and we both belong to the same online alumni group from college. People talk."

"You've been lurking online?"

"Well, not exactly lurking but I have been curious. There's nothing wrong with that."

Realizing that he'd done the same thing many times with ex-boyfriends and former classmates from his old high school in Toronto, George dropped the subject and came to the point.

"So, listen. You've got to make a decision. Do you want to risk it or not? 'Cause you know, you may just be headed for another huge disappointment. Do you think you could handle it? More importantly, is she really worth the effort?"

"I've been thinking about it a lot. Ever since that call last October and despite everything she's done, despite the fact that she really hurt me. God, she stole one of Oma's recipes. I don't know, I guess sometimes I just miss her." Kate seemed both resolved and exasperated.

"Get a cat. They're way more loyal than she'll ever be."

"No, seriously, George. Sophia and I really connected way back when. She was my first real grownup girlfriend. Someone I shared my hopes and dreams with. We used to laugh so much and we totally got each other. But now I'm not sure how to get it back, or even if it's possible."

Stopping to look at George, Kate continued, "I guess what I'm really saying is: Do I want to start over again?"

"That, my dear, is the million-dollar question. If you're looking for my advice, I'd say keep the door shut for a while, for a long, long while. If you're really determined to make a go of it again, let her make the moves. Let her show you that she's sincere but guard yourself because I don't trust her. She certainly hasn't given you any reason up to now to trust her."

"No, she hasn't. I know you're right. But maybe she's changed."

"I hope, for your sake, that she has but I don't know," George said, shaking his head. "If you're determined to forge ahead with this crazy plan of yours, you know I'll be there for you. I just wish that you would have called me back in October. I feel like a bit of a jerk."

"And why would you feel like a jerk?"

George shrugged. "I feel like I need to protect you sometimes. I know that sounds corny but I can't help myself. Richard says it's the mother hen in me."

"Well, whatever it is, I don't mind at all." Kate gave George an unexpected hug.

He looked down at her and placed a hand on the side of her face.

"Maybe working with Ursula on that project would be a neutral start. She'd be professionally obligated to act a certain way and St. Germain could be the buffer between the two of you."

"Get a room!" yelled a cyclist with a laugh as he pedalled by.

"I would if my husband was here!" shouted George to the cyclist's mud-splattered back. The bike rider wobbled a bit but carried on his way.

Laughing, Kate and George turned back towards the parking lot.

"I guess we should get going." Seeing that the rain had once again let up, George pulled the umbrella down, gave it a shake, and wrapped the Velcro strap in place.

"Yeah, they're probably wondering where the heck I got to, back at the bakery."

"Oh, no need to worry about that. I called Deb after I talked to you and told her that I was stealing you away for the afternoon and didn't know when I would be getting you back."

"She was probably thrilled to hear that news."

"Actually, she was. I think that girl's got an eye on your job."

Kate laughed. "Well, she's not going to get it. Remember: the name of the place is Kate's Bakes not Deb's Desserts."

"True, my dear, so very true."

Chapter Thirteen

Oma's Baking Tip

Always break your eggs into a separate bowl just in case you get a rotten one. Then you won't ruin the batter.

Mimi slapped the sixth and final card down in front of Francine. The four ladies seated around Mimi's large oak dining room table were now ready to begin the game. Mimi was casually staring into her freshly fanned set of cards and adjusting her feet so that her mini-dachshund Willawiener could comfortably settle across the top of her ostrich-feather slippers. Finally, she voiced what had been on her mind since the last garden meeting.

"So, ladies, do you really think this Sophia person is interested in gardening or do you think she just wants to spy on us so that she can do a story on what seniors get up to at night?"

Mimi always liked to get their weekly crib game started with a bit of controversial conjecture. She also liked to listen to talk radio and was a regular subscriber to *Celebrity* magazine, a publication notorious for "inside stories from reliable yet anonymous sources."

"Well, I sure know what I'd like to be getting up to at night but it doesn't have anything to do with gardening!" Margaret, who sat opposite Mimi, pulled her cards close to her face to stifle an exploding laugh. Francine went decidedly pink while fumbling to re-count the cards in her hand and Ethel gave Margaret a little kick under the table.

"Honestly, Margaret," Ethel said. "You have the worst sense of humour."

"Oh, I wasn't joking. Didn't you see how Lloyd was looking at me last meeting? I mean, really, if I had wanted that fellow I would have made my move at the last member competition when he was judging my roses."

"Now, seriously, Margaret." Mimi looked up over her trifocals and stared across the table at her card partner. "You don't honestly think Lloyd is really interested in you? Doesn't he have a girlfriend in his complex?"

"Oh, I should think he does," said Francine, who had finally worked up enough courage to enter the fray. "In fact, he was telling me all about her during the coffee break. He's taking her to the Kenny Rogers concert at the casino later this month. Something about paying her back for the microphone, whatever that means."

Ethel reached over and cut the deck about three quarters of the way through. As she turned over the top card, Mimi let out a little squeak. "Well, look who's turned up? Looks like I'm the lucky one to get a man today."

Placing the jack of hearts on the top of the stack, Mimi picked her peg and placed it two holes from the start. Having made the first move, she forged ahead. "Well, I should think she wouldn't be his only lady friend. In fact, my friend Susan, who lives over on West 45th next to that old dilapidated house, you know the one that went into foreclosure last year because that couple divorced and he refused to pay her out, and then their son from Montreal got involved and it became a real mess. . ."

Taking a quick breath, she continued, "Well anyways, my friend Susan has a friend whose name is Doris and Doris lives just down the street from Lloyd' housing co-op. Apparently, Doris is one of those nosy types of people who watches over the whole neighbourhood like a hawk and knows everything that's going on." Mimi paused long enough to suck in another much-needed breath.

The other ladies exchanged a knowing look.

". . . Well, Doris says she often sees him with different women. You know, coming and going. And according to her, it happens at any time of day or night!"

"You don't say? Well, that doesn't surprise me in the least." Laying a three of clubs on the table, Ethel continued with a nod towards Margaret. "Remember last month how he behaved towards our guest speaker, you know that lovely Dutch woman who was speaking about creating natural curvature in the garden? While I was pouring her a tea at the break, Lloyd pushed his way to the front of the line just so he could stand beside her. He was going on and on about how he would like to get some advice on putting some curvature into his garden. I felt sorry for the poor thing so I engaged her in a conversation about my trip to Keuekenhof last year. He eventually got the hint and sulked all the way back to his microphone board. At this rate, we'll be lucky to get another female guest speaker for anything. Someone should really talk to him."

Margaret smiled slyly and laid a three of diamonds on the table. "That's six for two, my dears. Looks like we're off to a running start, Mimi." She leapfrogged Mimi's peg and placed hers two holes farther along the board.

"At least he left Sophia Simpson alone last night." Francine gently laid down a three of hearts. "I do believe that's nine for six." Smiling across the table to Ethel, she moved her peg from the starter position and placed it two ahead of Margaret's.

"Well, well. These ladies mean business, Margaret. We'd best be on our toes today." Mimi took a sip of her diet cola and reshuffled the cards.

"They haven't got a hope in hell," replied Margaret with a smirk, "certainly not if I can help it." Fanning her cards evenly in her hand, she looked over to Ethel, who was sitting to her right. "Lloyd probably left that TV woman alone because he was all nervous, thinking he didn't want to ruin his chances of getting on her show." Margaret looked to Mimi for agreement.

"You're absolutely right, Margaret, and that brings me back to my original question: Do you or do you not think that her visiting us was just a ruse to get some inside information?"

Mimi quickly glanced around the table at her card-mates, hoping that someone would engage. They all simply stared back at her, not sure how to respond. Sensing her urgency was falling on deaf ears, she continued, voice raised for emphasis in the hopes that it would elicit some kind of response.

"Don't you understand? She could be one of those mole types, you know, trying to infiltrate our ranks only to deceive us in her false friendliness. Then she'll throw us all in front of the proverbial bus by portraying us to the public at large as a boring, bumbling group of old biddies." Mimi was getting fired up. She hastily smacked a five of spades on the table and looked anxiously around, her steely blue eyes flashing above the rims of her glasses.

Ethel glanced quickly at Francine, then nervously shuffled the cards in her hand. "I think perhaps you're being a bit too dramatic, Mimi. I mean, have you ever watched Sophia's Stories from the Street? They're very well intentioned and she's always putting a positive spin on things."

Mimi was ready with her reply. "Ah yes, that may be true but what do we know about her ratings? Perhaps they're slipping? Who knows, they often change the format of these reality-type shows so they can grab new viewers. I don't know." Pursing her lips, Mimi lowered her voice and whispered, "There's something about her that just doesn't ring true for me. She seems like she's hiding something."

"Oh, for goodness sake, Mimi! How, pray tell, did you manage to deduce all of that in the short time you had to observe her at the meeting?" Ethel slapped a five of clubs on the table and announced, "That's ten for two!" Grabbing her peg, she gleefully stuck it two holes ahead on the board, surpassing Mimi and Margaret once again.

Not to be distracted, Mimi quickly countered, "It's just a gift of mine. I've always been able to sense the false ones. That's why I'm sitting here now with all of you."

A communal gasp filled the room. All eyes were now frozen on Mimi. Realizing they had misunderstood her intention, Mimi held up her card-free hand. "Oh, not you, you sillies. . . You're not false. I know that each and every one of you is true, dear, and sweet." She winked at Francine, whom she knew to be particularly sensitive. "But you will notice that I have never, and will never, invite Ursula St. Germain to join our little group. Besides, being a fifth wheel, she's also a perfect example of what I'm talking about. Why, I wouldn't trust that woman farther than I could spit. Even though I grew up in East Van, don't think for a minute that I can spit very far."

A short silence ensued, broken only by the sound of Margaret sipping a large gulp from her now-cold tea.

"We'll just have to wait and see," said Francine meekly. "I personally think Sophia Simpson is lovely. And she did like my poem about the worms so maybe she is as nice as she appears to be on TV."

Not yet having had her fill, Mimi carried on. "Ah yes, but how often have we heard about celebrity types being completely different than their on-air persona? She could be a wolf in sheep's clothing for all we know."

The image of Sophia in a hairy wolf's suit engaged Francine's thoughts long enough for Ethel to pipe in, "Well, I'm sure Ursula will be the first to find out the truth. Even though you may not like her, you must admit that she's very good at judging personalities. I can't imagine that she'd let anyone just use us without getting something in return."

At the mention of Ursula, Francine unconsciously straightened her back and brushed a hand over her hair. "Oh, you are most right there, Ethel. Ursula does not suffer fools easily. But I'm sure this is all just silliness because I'm convinced that Sophia is a lovely person, just like Kate."

Seeing she wasn't getting anywhere with her chosen theme of disgruntlement, Mimi let it drop for the moment and pretended to concentrate on her hand. It was Margaret's turn.

"It's really too bad that those two didn't get an opportunity to meet." Staring at the fan of cards in her hand, Margaret let out a disappointed sigh. "Go." Grasping a handful of salted nuts from the bowl at her elbow, she deftly popped them into her mouth and mumbled, "Given their age and the fact they're both such successful businesswomen, I'm sure they would have gotten along like two peas in a pod."

"Oh, but they will have met by now," said Ethel. "You see, Kate forgot her umbrella again and at the end of the night, while we were cleaning up, Sophia kindly agreed to bring it to her the next day. Apparently, she lives nearby and said she could drop it by the bakery the next morning."

"Well then, at least that's one new relationship we won't have to meddle in, yet." Mimi was sounding a bit put off. "You all seem convinced that Sophia is a darling person so perhaps I am wrong and those two will have hit it off in an instant. But I'll tell you this, the next time I stop by the bakery, I'm going to be sure to have a little chat with Kate and ask her how it went. Maybe now having talked to her herself she has a much better idea about Sophia's intentions than we do."

"Oh yes, I'm sure she will," said Francine. "You know, those young people, they connect up right away. Why, I wouldn't be surprised if they're already friends on that Bookface thing in the interweb."

With an impish grin, she gently laid a queen of hearts on the pile and chirped, "That's two for thirty-one. Well, well, Ethel, I do believe we're on a winning streak. Perhaps we should buy some lottery tickets, you and I." Francine giggled with delight as Ethel moved their peg two spaces farther on the board. Margaret stared in disbelief across the table at her now-silent crib partner.

Mimi rolled her eyes and took a disgruntled bite out of her devilled egg sandwich. She tossed the remainder to Willaweiner, who sat perched in anticipation at her feet. If there was one thing she couldn't stand, it was not being right. That and losing at crib.

Chapter Fourteen

Oma's Baking Tip

Milk gone sour? Don't throw it out! Use it to make the most delicious cakes, pancakes or waffles.

At Ursula's suggestion, they decided to meet at the Piccadilly Tea Room, a fashionable café she knew well and one where she hoped they could speak privately. Having enjoyed high tea there on many occasions, she was confident that the servers would be polite and discreet. The last thing she wanted was to have some star-struck waitress start gushing over Sophia like the garden club members had done earlier that week. When making the reservation, Ursula had purposely name-dropped, knowing that mentioning Sophia Simpson would perhaps garner the kind of tactful attention that Ursula was looking for. It had worked. The staff member who took the reservation assured Ursula that they would be seated at their most discreet table and their server would be informed beforehand of the mitigating circumstances.

This prearranged date was very important to Ursula and she envisioned it being a quiet and proper meeting of like minds. From the tone of Sophia's voice when she had returned Ursula's call on Wednesday morning, she could tell that her segment suggestion had struck gold. Sophia certainly appeared enthusiastic, although she did detect a change in tone once she had brought up the topic of involving Kate. Perhaps Ursula was interpreting too much but she had a sense that Sophia was nervous about meeting Kate.

Odd reaction, she had thought at the time, *for someone who makes her living probing into the lives of strangers.*

But Sophia's reply had been downright normal compared to Kate's. *I'm concerned that poor girl has too much on her plate,* thought Ursula as she laid down the receiver. The conversation had been awkwardly stilted and augmented with pregnant pauses. Reluctantly, Kate had agreed to meet with Ursula and Sophia today but given her strange behaviour on the phone, Ursula was hoping against all odds that she did intend to show up.

Ursula had made the reservation for 3:45 but told both Sophia and Kate that the time was 4 p.m. She wanted to make absolutely sure that she was the first to arrive so that she could conveniently greet them at the table. She arrived punctually. Having checked her coat, she gave her name to the hostess, who stood behind a neatly placed podium, not unlike the one Ursula used during the garden club meetings.

"St. Germain?" The hostess scanned the reservation book with the tip of her index finger. Having found the discreet little star next to the name, she looked up with a pleasant smile and said, "Yes, I see we have you seated in the sun room. Please follow me, ma'am."

As they walked through the restaurant, Ursula smiled politely at the occasional pair of raised eyes that met her as she strolled past. She straightened her back and walked with gliding purpose. The tinkling sound of china teacups being set in their saucers mingled with the hushed tones of polite conversation. Soft notes of classical music filtered in from unseen speakers hidden in the Victorian-style décor. Everywhere were fresh flowers, which added their fragrance to the comforting smells of steeping tea and freshly baked pastries.

To her utter relief, Ursula was delighted to see that children were in the minority. Those present appeared to be well behaved and suitably dressed, although she did spot one boy with running shoes— clean ones, but running shoes all the same. There were also no strategically placed flat-screen TVs blasting the latest sports event and no overly friendly staff introducing themselves by their first name and stating the obvious such as, "Hi guys, I'm Jake and I'll be your waiter this afternoon." Ursula cringed at the thought. She had a severe aversion to being lumped into that generic group called "guys" as it only proved her hypothesis that the younger generation was quickly slipping into the abyss of poor etiquette.

Ursula let out a sigh of satisfaction. She felt perfectly at home here and patted herself on the back for choosing such an ideal locale for her "meeting of minds."

They rounded a corner and entered the more private and secluded sun room.

"Your table, ma'am."

The hostess gestured to a quaint spot near the rear of the room with a view of the back deck and garden. The table was set for three with a small bouquet of daffodils and fragrant little grape hyacinths tastefully placed in a lead-crystal vase at the centre. The sterling silver cutlery gleamed in the afternoon sun and the white linen serviettes were neatly laid beside the Royal Doulton china plates. *This is the perfect spot*, thought Ursula. *It's somewhat distant from other tables and cheerfully lit with natural light to allow pleasant conversation to flow.*

So much was riding on this meeting and Ursula was desperate to make things work. The setting, as always, was of extreme importance and this one did not disappoint. Ursula seated herself with her back to the large panel windows so that she could see when Sophia and Kate approached.

"Would you care for anything while you wait for your guests to arrive?" asked the hostess.

"No, thank you. You've been most kind. I would like to request, however, that the bill be presented to me once the other two ladies have left. They are my personal guests and I don't wish them to be bothered with the mechanics of payment."

"Absolutely, ma'am. I'll be sure to pass your wishes on to your server."

"Thank you." Ursula was pleased and wriggled herself into her seat.

"You're most welcome and enjoy your tea." With that, the hostess slipped away and left Ursula alone. Glancing over her shoulder, Ursula peered out into the brightly lit garden. She admired the collection of colourful spring blooms that swayed in the light breeze. *Someone has put a bit of thought into this garden,* she mused. *Someone not unlike myself.* She grinned.

Turning back to look into the restaurant, Ursula straightened her linen napkin and slowly rotated the little vase to admire each of the delicate flowers.

She heard Sophia before she saw her. Laughter erupted from around the corner as her voice rose above the cultured ambience. "Well, be sure to give me a call. It's been a long time and I'd love to catch up." There was a somewhat muffled reply followed by more girlish laughter.

Ursula froze in her seat.

Had someone recognized Sophia already?

This is exactly the type of intrusion that she was trying desperately to avoid. To her chagrin, the conversation continued.

"I'll give you a call next week, Jan. Maybe we can do sushi or something? That would be great."

There was a slight pause, then Sophia appeared around the corner, led by the same hostess who had seated Ursula. The hostess gestured in the direction of Ursula, said a parting word to Sophia, and quietly took her leave. Dressed in a tailored dark-grey suit and a light blue blouse, Sophia looked the epitome of business style. Feminine and confident. Ursula was duly impressed. Pushing her chair back, she came forward to greet her with an open hand.

"Sophia. I'm so glad you could make it."

Taking her hand, Sophia smiled. "I am too." Glancing over Ursula's shoulder at the empty table behind, she asked, "I take it our other guest hasn't arrived yet?"

"No, but I do expect her at any moment." Looking down at her watch, she added, "She isn't late yet so let's just hope that she could tear herself away from that bakery of hers."

Sensing some relief in Sophia's posture, Ursula smiled graciously and turned to the table. "Please, please have a seat."

Sophia took the chair to Ursula's right. Fumbling about in her bag, she eventually pulled out a small notebook and pen. Looking up, she met Ursula's curious eyes. "Oh, I hope you don't mind me taking a few notes. It'll help me once I get back to the studio to begin formulating scene ideas and such."

"Not at all, dear. You go right ahead. I'm sure you know best what to do."

During an awkward pause, Ursula noticed that Sophia was shifting nervously in her chair, looking towards the entrance of the sun room.

"No need to worry. Kate is usually very punctual. I'm sure she'll be here any minute."

"Oh, it's not that," she lied. "I'm just excited to see her. I've heard so much about her from some of the garden club ladies."

Ursula sensed that Sophia was hiding something but before she could needle a bit further into her thoughts, she was blindsided by Sophia's sudden confession.

"To be honest, Ursula," she lowered her voice, "Kate and I know each other quite well."

Ursula blinked and turned to stare at Sophia. She had no idea that these two had met before, let alone knew each other well.

Why hasn't either one said anything? Pushing her glasses farther up on her nose, she looked inquiringly at Sophia and said in a soft whisper, "I'm sorry, did you say you knew each other?"

Before Sophia could answer, the hostess interrupted them, "Here you are, ma'am."

They both looked up to see Kate standing silently in front of them. Her hair was pulled back in a loose braid and she wore a colourful pink-and-yellow, floral-patterned spring dress. Her demeanor was calm yet Ursula noticed that Kate was clutching her purse tightly to her chest.

Breaking the spell of unspoken words, Kate turned to the hostess. "Thank you, Melanie. Please say hello to Gerard and tell him I'm sure his pastries will be delightful."

"I will, Ms. Freitag. Thank you. Enjoy your tea."

Ursula's head was swimming. The anonymity of her meeting had completely dissolved into a web of unexpected interconnectedness. Sophia had blown her cover by chatting loudly with an acquaintance in the restaurant, leaving the door essentially wide open for further intrusions and looky-loos. Kate was apparently on a first-name basis with the Piccadilly's hostess and pastry chef. To top it off, these two knew each other well but had somehow failed to inform Ursula. She teetered a bit as she stood up but recovered quickly by holding fast to the edge of the linen-covered table.

"So glad you could come, Kate," Ursula said shakily. "I'm to understand that you know our other guest, Sophia?" Ursula gestured to Sophia, who was sitting next to her, eyes slightly downcast, quiet as a mouse.

Kate raised an eyebrow in Sophia's direction. Recovering quickly, Kate replied, "Yes, we've met before." She paused and then, looking directly at Sophia, said without a hint of expression, "Hello, Sophia." The words seemed to catch in her throat but she maintained her poise and looked directly into Sophia's eyes.

Relieved that Kate had acknowledged her, Sophia smiled and replied, "Hello, Kate." She got up out of her chair but Kate had now taken the initiative to move towards her seat on the other side of Ursula, leaving Sophia standing alone, looking embarrassed and out of place. Having settled into her chair, Kate avoided Sophia's eyes and focused entirely on Ursula.

"I had some difficulty getting away today and I may just have to leave early," said Kate, her predetermined early-exit excuse coming off without a glitch, "but I'm sure we can cover all we need to in a short amount of time." She smiled demurely at Ursula and then busied herself with straightening the napkin on her lap. Sophia, in the meantime, had picked up the tea menu, intently perusing the choices of blends available.

"Yes, I'm sure," was all that Ursula could manage. She was still feeling out of sorts and hoped that the waitress would soon arrive to take their order. A good sip of hot, strong tea would do her just fine about now.

An uncomfortable silence ensued, filled in only by the lyrical tones of Vivaldi's Four Seasons playing softly in the background. Ursula didn't know what to do. She looked at Kate, who was gazing at the bright yellow daffodils that filled the outdoor terrace, and then to Sophia, who was still fixated on the menu. They both seemed preoccupied with their own thoughts, almost oblivious to Ursula's presence.

Odd, she thought. *If these two know each other so well, why weren't they engaging in conversation?* Ursula was stumped but she certainly wasn't about to let the situation get out of control. This meeting was far too important. She was going to get her garden club segment produced regardless of any obstacles, seen or unseen, that might cross her path.

"So!" Ursula broke the uncomfortable silence and folded her hands together on her lap. Both Kate and Sophia turned to stare at Ursula while still avoiding locking eyes or saying a word to one another. Ever the politician looking to do a good spin on events, Ursula boldly continued with her plan. "I must say that I'm surprised that you two know each other." Smiling broadly, she paused in anticipation of the explanation that never came. Clearing her throat, she pushed on. "But I'm wonderfully relieved to discover this bit of exciting news as I'm sure it will make our job so much easier."

Ursula waited for the affirmative responses but after a few protracted seconds of silence, they did not come.

Sophia sat silently.

Kate quietly cleared her throat.

The seconds ticked by. Ursula bided her time by glancing from Sophia to Kate and back. It was more than obvious that these two so-called acquaintances had nothing to say to one another. The situation presented a bit of a conundrum for Ursula but nothing outside of her spectrum of expertise. Bit by bit, she would get to the bottom of the situation but what was important now was getting through this meeting with a contingency plan for the future.

Experience had taught Ursula that there was no sense in beating around the bush. Straightforward talk, poignant and to the point, always helped clear situations despite how uncomfortable it might be for those involved. Similar to waiting in silence for the confession to come from some under-aged teenage girls who had lit a cigarette in the washroom, ex-school-principal Ursula St. Germain sat in determined silence. The cat would soon be out of the bag. It was just a matter of time.

As the stillness bore down like a heavy weight, it was Kate who finally broke the icy silence. "I'm sorry, Ursula." She looked at Ursula in earnest. "I should have mentioned that we knew each other but I guess I didn't think it was too important."

The confession now having been given freely, Ursula smiled benevolently at Kate. One of the silent partners had finally spoken. She placed her hand on Kate's, patting it gently. "Important? Why, Kate dear, it's of the utmost importance."

Ursula glanced towards the still-silent Sophia and then back to Kate. "If you two actually know each other, we'll be able to accomplish so much more. That is. . ." Ursula was now unflinchingly speaking of the elephant obviously sitting in the room with them, "as long as you two are actually speaking to one another, because if not. . ." Her words trailed off into a soft whisper.

The elephant blasted its trunk.

They had been on speaking terms once. Less than five years ago, three-hour phone conversations had sometimes been the norm. Kate and Sophia had been the best of friends, sharing all the intimate details about their loves and lives, but that was before everything fell apart and they had ended up like this. Sophia placed the burden of responsibility for their failed friendship squarely on her own shoulders, knowing that it was entirely her fault. Benjamin had tragically died and she didn't show for the funeral. Then she succumbed to Phil's suggestions and stolen that cookie recipe. Her television career had really taken off then and the more successful she became, the guiltier she had felt. As time passed her guilt morphed into a debilitating monster that rendered her unable to connect with her one-time friend.

She felt paralysed, a traitor who had abandoned her best friend in her time of need. Her cloak of guilt had only gotten heavier with time.

"Tea, Sophia? Which kind of tea?" Ursula's voice broke through Sophia's thoughts like a cannon shot. Startled, Sophia looked up from the menu that she had been clutching tightly in her hands and realized that she had completely zoned out. Embarrassed by being caught off-guard while the flood of memories still lingered in her mind like a thick fog, she swallowed hard and said, "I hear the house tea is delicious."

"Then house tea it shall be." Ursula said this directly to the petite waitress standing demurely beside Kate, hands folded neatly behind her back. Sophia's embarrassment now cut a notch deeper. She realized that Ursula, Kate, and the waitress had all been staring at her, awaiting an answer while she had stared blankly into her memory bank.

As the waitress exited the room, Sophia looked at Ursula and explained. "My apologies, Ursula. I was lost in my thoughts." Glancing quickly at Kate, who was now looking directly at her, she continued. "You wanted to know if Kate and I were speaking to one another and I think an explanation is in order."

Kate winced but Sophia continued.

"Kate and I have been friends for many years," she began, faltering a bit as she continued, "but we lost touch. I moved to Toronto a number of years ago and my career left very little time for relationships."

Kate moved uneasily in her chair and looked the other way but Ursula was hanging on every word.

"I'm afraid our lack of communication over the last while has been my fault and since my return to Vancouver I . . ." Sophia paused long enough to see Kate throw her a glance that said in no uncertain terms: "Don't you dare."

"I uh, I just haven't had the time to get in touch. This is actually the first time I've seen Kate in about five years."

Kate's jaw tightened and she refolded the white linen napkin that lay in her lap.

"Well, then it's time to celebrate!" chimed Ursula. Touching both of their arms, she bubbled with delight. "Old friends reunited. What could be more special than that? And to think it was me who brought you together after so many years."

Kate and Sophia both smiled weakly at Ursula. They knew that there was no going back now. Their future, at least for the duration of this project, was now set in stone, especially if Ursula had anything to do with it.

"Ah, the tea has arrived. Shall I pour?"

Ursula smiled at the waitress as she placed the steaming pot on the table along with a small tray of freshly cut lemon slices, crystallized sugar, and milk. As Ursula deftly filled each of their china cups with the warm, steaming brew, the corner of her mouth crooked slightly upwards with self-satisfaction. Not only were her plans of promoting the club through a highly visible television show now within reach, it appeared she was also personally responsible for bringing two long-lost friends back together after a lengthy and obviously difficult separation. She marvelled at her uncanny ability to coax harmony out of disorder, just like in her garden. Surely, the credit for all her hard work would come to her in good time.

They'll all thank me one day, Ursula mused as she filled the tea cups. *The entire garden club and these two ladies will be forever grateful for my selfless deeds of dedication and compassion. I just know that I will be rewarded for my efforts, at the very least with a singular line credit at the end of the television segment.*

Ursula paused and envisioned herself watching the shows credits as they slowly rolled upwards on her television screen.

Our thanks to Ursula St. Germain, president of the Kerrisdale Garden Club, faithful garden warrior, friend to all: plant and man.

Ursula smiled broadly. "Sugar, anyone?"

Chapter Fifteen

Oma's Baking Tip

Get yourself a couple of silicon mats for baking. Cookies will simply slide off them, they're easy to clean in soapy water, and they'll last for years.

The water lapped gently at the sandy shore with a liquid tempo punctuated by the occasional cry of a sea bird. Early morning sunshine streamed down, warm and promising, and a soft wind blew in from the west. George reached down and clasped Richard's hand as they strolled barefoot along the deserted shoreline. He sighed contentedly, taking a deep breath of salty air, then turned to smile at Richard.

The tropical peacefulness was suddenly broken by the repetitive sound of distant beeping. Like a bothersome mosquito, it now became insistent. George blinked, willing it to go away but it was unrelenting and only seemed to get louder.

As he stared into Richard's face, it began to blur in and out of focus like heat waves on black tarmac. George watched as the entire scene vanished into a starry void, filled only with the sound of that unrelenting beeping. Instinctively reaching out with an arm that felt like lead, he batted frantically in the general direction of that grating noise in an attempt to get it to stop.

The sound of shattering glass filled the air, followed by a profound, knowing silence that something expensive had just been significantly reduced in value.

"George? What the hell was that?" Richard's voice was filled with muffled annoyance.

George's eyes popped open and he stared blankly at the ceiling. In an instant, he came to the realization of exactly where he was. In bed. Next to Richard. Even though he couldn't see him clearly without his glasses, George could tell by the sound of Richard's groggy voice that he had been startled awake. George felt him lean over top of him and strain to look over the side of the bed. The crystal lamp lay in a shattered mess on the floor. Next to it, in a tangle of electrical cord, was the now-silent and blinking digital alarm clock.

"Oh, for God's sake, George, you just broke the lamp." Flopping back over onto his side of the bed, Richard let out an exasperated sigh. "And you just scared the hell out of me."

Leaning over the side of the bed to get a better look himself, George mumbled, "Sorry, I was having a dream and that beeping was really annoying me. Dammit, that lamp cost a fortune and it's probably irreplaceable."

"To hell with the lamp. What about me? You scared the bejesus out of me. I hope at least it was a good dream."

Trying not to think that he now had to go on the hunt for a replacement lamp, George rolled over and laid his arm across Richard's chest. Snuggling in, he said, "Actually, it was. You were in it."

"And?"

"Well, we were walking down a beach all alone. It was morning time, the sun was shining and—"

Beep! Beep! Beep!

"Oh, for the love of God!" cried George. He ripped off the covers and swung his feet over the side of the bed. At the same time, Richard bolted upright, grabbing George's elbow in an attempt to pull him back.

"Watch out for the shards," he cried.

Too late. George's right foot landed on top of the alarm clock, magically silencing it, but his left foot came down directly onto a pile of broken crystal.

"Shit!" shrieked George. Reaching down, he pulled his left foot over his right knee and squeezed it tightly. A piece of broken crystal had lodged itself in the sole of his foot. He instinctively pulled it out but in doing so, he had opened the floodgates and the wound began to bleed. "Uh oh," he murmured as the colour drained from his face. He slumped backwards onto the bed.

George was never very good with blood. It was one reason he had chosen a career in horticulture and not, as his parents had wished, in medicine. Chances of drawing blood while doing gardening were slim to none unless you managed to snip yourself with a sharp pair of pruning shears or prick your finger with a thorny rose stem. He had carefully managed to avoid both in all the years he'd been gardening.

Richard was up and out of bed, assessing the situation. "Just lie there, George, and try to breathe. I'll be back in a flash."

"Uh huh." The room began to spin as George tried his best not to succumb to the dizzying feeling inside his head.

Grabbing a towel from the rack, Richard dashed out of the *en suite* and carefully picked his way over to where George lay half-slumped across the bed. A few droplets of blood glistened on the floor underneath George's left foot, which now dangled limply over the edge of the mattress. Trying not to think about the possibility of having to take the world's-worst-patient to the doctor for stitches, Richard bent down and tightly wrapped the towel around George's bleeding foot.

"I hope you didn't use one of the new bamboo ones I just bought," George said weakly. "They weren't cheap and the colour perfectly matches the striation in the travertine tiles in the bathroom."

"No," Richard lied. *At least George was getting back to his old self already*, thought Richard. *Only he would think of colour- matching towels and tiles at a time like this.*

Now that George's foot was safely enclosed in a soft, and apparently expensive bamboo towel, Richard went back to the bathroom to get something to wipe the floor. Rummaging around under the sink, he found a small white washcloth. Holding it under running water, he wrung it out and turned to go back into the bedroom.

"I hope you're not using a white cloth to clean floor." George's voice still sounded weak but firm.

Oh, for God's sake, Richard mumbled to himself. Speaking louder, he said, "So which one should I use then?"

"Downstairs in the laundry room is a green bucket that Marguerite uses with some cleaning supplies in it. She probably has a couple of old rags in there somewhere that you can use. Grab them and some paper towels too." George's voice trailed off.

Definitely on the mend, thought Richard as he bounded downstairs two steps at a time to fetch the supplies.

By the time he returned, George was sitting up with both feet still dangling over the side of the bed. Some of the colour had returned to his face but his lips were distinctly pale. He was staring straight ahead in the direction of the bay window, purposely avoiding eye contact with bloody stain beneath his feet.

"I told you not to use the new bamboo towel," he grumped.

"Well, I guess I didn't hear you. Besides, we have to go shopping for a new lamp so why not get a couple of new towels while we're at it?"

Richard's attempt at lightening the mood fell flat. George was now definitely in a sulk. Richard knew the best thing to do was to keep things simple and straightforward and get the hell out of the house as soon as possible. While George pouted, Richard cleaned up the floor. He swept the remaining bits and pieces of the ruined lamp into a dustpan and placed the clock back onto George's nightstand.

"So," said Richard, who sat beside George, wiping his hands with one of the clean rags, "can I have a good look at your foot now?"

"Well, I guess I can't stop you." In typical George fashion, he continued, "But I'm telling you right now, I am not going to the doctor. No stitches. Got it? Besides, I have an important meeting this morning that I simply can't miss."

"Be reasonable, George. If your foot needs stitches, then your foot needs stitches. The meeting may just have to wait because I'm certainly not going to sew your foot back together and I'm sure you don't want to ruin any more towels with," he paused, "you know. B-L-O-O-D."

"Spelling it out doesn't make me feel any less queasy." George swayed a bit and leaned his head onto Richard's shoulder. "I'm an idiot, sorry," George said, pouting.

Taking his hand and giving it a squeeze, Richard said, "It's okay. You're out of sorts. I mean, that's one helluva way to wake up in the morning."

"I know, I'm sorry. I don't know why I got so frantic," said George, nodding in the direction of the nightstand, "but that damn alarm clock was so annoying and I was dreaming that we were walking on the beach so peacefully and calmly and it ruined it all." He let out a big sigh. "And now we're down one lamp and a bathroom towel and I probably have to have orthopedic surgery."

Although George was definitely a drama queen, years of being together had taught Richard exactly how to handle these types of incidents.

"Look, hon. First things first. Let me have a good look at your foot and if the bleeding has. . ."

George hiccupped and swallowed hard.

"Sorry, forgot." Starting again, Richard said, "Let me look at it and we'll decide if a trip to the doctor is in order. If not, I'll get you bandaged up and we'll have some breakfast."

"Bleh." George held a hand to his mouth.

"Okay, no breakfast, just coffee, and you'll head off to your important meeting. I, in the meantime, will go to work, litigate a few ne'er-dowells, and meet you at Bloom around 5:30 just in time to go shopping for a new lamp. How's that sound?"

"Fine. Except they have a better selection of lamps at EQ. And Waterworks is just down the street from there so we could look for some new towels at the same time."

He's mending, thought Richard. "Now, let's have a look at your foot."

Kneeling onto the floor in front of George, Richard carefully unbound the towel. To his relief, the bleeding had slowed significantly and the size of the wound was little more than one centimetre long.

"Good news, my dear." Smiling up at George, who had gone back to staring out the window, Richard told him, "Just a surface wound. Nothing a little ointment and a bandage can't fix. You may have some trouble walking on it, though, but let's hope for the best."

Richard headed into the bathroom to get the first aid kit and dispose of the bloodied towel.

"There's nothing more pathetic than a limpy old queen," George shouted from the bed.

Coming out of the bathroom with supplies in hand, Richard replied, "Actually, I find limpy old queens quite attractive." Richard smiled. "They're so helpless and they can't run fast from robust fellas like me."

George smiled for the first time that morning. "You're too good to me."

"You're right, I am. Now, lift your foot."

Once the wound had been properly cleaned, ointment applied, and a large bandage attached, Richard started to gather up the remnants of his doctoring and headed back again to the bathroom. Over his shoulder, he said, "So, who's the important meeting with?"

"Sophia."

Richard stopped and whipped his head around the corner. "Sophia? *The* Sophia?"

"Yes, *the* Sophia. Her assistant called the other day to request a meeting. Apparently, she wants to talk to me about setting up some kind of supposed filming schedule for the garden show."

Richard was intrigued. "Well, isn't that interesting. Does Kate know about this meeting?"

Pausing slightly, George replied, "Apparently not or I would have heard from her."

"And you haven't told her about this meeting?" Richard stepped back into the bedroom, arms crossed, now fully intrigued.

"No. I haven't. I made a conscious choice not to because I want to speak to Ms. Simpson on my own and, well, perhaps give her a piece of my mind, if you must know the truth." George harrumphed.

"You can't do that, George."

"Why not? She deserves it after all she's put Kate through. Or do you think that what she did was okay?"

"It's not a matter of whether or not it was okay. The crux of the issue is that you don't know what Kate is thinking. Didn't she say to you last week that the three of them were going to have some kind of meeting? Her, Sophia, and that woman from the garden club?"

"Ursula St. Germain."

"Yes, that's right. Didn't they have some kind of get-together?"

"As far as I know, yes."

"Well, maybe it went well. Maybe they're best buds again."

"I highly doubt that." George rolled his eyes at Richard.

Acquiescing, Richard continued. "Well, okay, that may be a bit of an exaggeration, but maybe if you dump on Sophia, you'll ruin something that Kate may be working on, namely rebuilding her relationship with her."

"Since when did you become the great psychologist?" George said snippily.

"Since my job is to do exactly that: mediate between warring parties. And if you don't know that by now, George, then I don't really know what to say." He turned and walked into the bathroom. George knew he had ticked him off but he couldn't seem to help himself. Kate was his best friend, he was angry with Sophia, and he needed to vent that anger somehow.

"I still think she owes Kate an apology." George raised his voice.

Nothing but silence emanated from the bathroom.

George looked down at his carefully bandaged foot. No sign of blood, the entire mess cleaned up, sanitized and set right. He sighed. "Okay, okay, so I'll call Kate and tell her. Is that what you wanted to hear?"

Beep. Beep. Beep.

"Goddamn it!" blurted George as he reached over and slammed his hand on top of the alarm clock.

Richard poked his head out of the bathroom. With a sly smile, he said, "That sounds a lot like your conscience, Mr. Stanwell, coming back to remind you that if you keep pushing the proverbial snooze button in your life, it will only be silent for a while."

George turned his face away from Richard's. "Oh, shut up and have a shower already."

He hated it when Richard was right, which when it came to the more sensitive issues in life, he usually was.

Chapter Sixteen

Oma's Baking Tip

If you want to add coffee flavour to your baked goods, use dry instant instead of fresh. It won't add any extra liquid and the coffee flavour is much more concentrated.

Thankfully, Richard left quietly with a short peck on the cheek and a promise to call later that day to see how things went. He spared George any further lectures on the right thing to do and simply let him ruminate about what he referred to as "the next steps in his progression to enlightenment."

George wasn't due into work until 9:30 and his meeting with Sophia was set for 10 a.m. It was Wednesday so he knew he could reach Kate at home, or at least he hoped so because his curiosity was killing him. Why hadn't she called to tell him about her luncheon date with Sophia and Ursula? Did it actually happen or had it been cancelled? Did she know about Sophia's plan to call him and set up an appointment? It just didn't make sense that Kate hadn't gotten in touch. As much as he hated to admit it, Richard was right: he should have checked with her first to see what was going on before he had agreed to meet with Sophia.

As he hobbled over to the kitchen chair, his foot still smarting from his early-morning injury, George was careful not to spill the double espresso he was balancing with one hand. Once he'd settled comfortably in the chair, he reached for the hands-free and dialled Kate's number.

"Hello?"

"Hi, sweetie."

"Oh hi, George. Just give me a second, I've got my hands covered in dough." George heard the plunk of the phone ungraciously falling onto the hall table. "Sorry!" shouted Kate from the kitchen. He heard a tap running. In a few moments, she was back, albeit slightly out of breath.

"So, what's up?"

"Well, that's why I called, to ask you."

"Oh, right. I guess you got my message then." Kate walked with the phone to the living room and settled herself onto the couch. The cookie dough she had started could wait.

"What message?" George cocked an eyebrow. He was meticulous about returning phone calls. If someone had left him a message, especially Kate, he returned it immediately, even if it was to say that he had no time at the moment and would call again later.

"I left a message with your new assistant. What's her name again?"

"Stacey." George rolled his eyes. He knew in an instant where this was going.

"Right, Stacey. I called you yesterday afternoon but you were out so I left a message."

George sighed dramatically.

"I'm assuming from the tone of your voice that you didn't get it."

"You are assuming right." George scrunched his eyes tight. This morning was going from bad to worse to soap-opera dramatic in one fell swoop. His tone was now decidedly dark.

"No. No I didn't get it," he said with a sigh, "and to tell you the truth, I've just about had it with that Stacey."

"Look, George, perhaps it just slipped her mind and she forgot to write it down. I mean, I didn't make it sound so ultra-important either so—"

He cut her off. "Any time anyone phones and leaves a message for me, it's important. That certainly is not her judgement call to make," he huffed, "and I'm tired of her antics. Last week, she 'accidentally' deleted an entire database containing the new plant introductions for next spring. Thank God I had a backup. And," he paused to give credence to the importance of his next point, "she's a two-finger typer! I never could stand two-finger typers. They drive me nuts. No," he said decidedly, "she's done. I've had it. I'm going to fire her today."

Kate cringed. Abruptly changing the subject, she asked, "So, how's your morning going otherwise?"

"Oh God, don't even get me started." Leaning his elbows on the table, George continued, "I was wrenched out of bed this morning from a most wonderful dream by our damn alarm clock. My feeble attempt at trying to get it to stop resulted in one of our best crystal lamps crashing to the floor, after which, I had the fortitude to slam my left foot into a pile of shards, causing myself due injury." He was just getting rolling.

"Then, my dear husband, in all his wisdom, decides to create a tourniquet out of one of our best bath towels. To top it all off, he followed that with a lecture on proper friend etiquette and the importance of not making assumptions, blah, blah, blah." George's voice ground down to a rumble.

Kate let the silence sink in for a bit then asked, "How's your foot?"

Now that some of the steam had been aired, George replied flatly, "Fine. Richard bandaged it and I only have a bit of a limp. But having a shower this morning was simply impossible. Of course, I still have to deal with a trashed lamp and the towel that now looks like it went through World War III." Visualizing the bloodstain sent a wave of nausea through his system and he downed his double espresso in one gulp.

Aware of George's sensitivity to anything gory, Kate chose her words carefully. "Well, I'm glad you didn't have to go to the doctor. Does it hurt?"

"Only if I stand on it. Right now, I have my pretty little ass settled into a kitchen chair and it's only a short hobble from here to the car."

Kate smiled. Sometimes George could be a real pouter.

"Well, why don't you just call into work and tell them that you'll be a bit late? Better still, take the day off and rest up. Lord knows, you work hard enough as it is."

"That's just it." The conversation was now coming full circle again. "I have to go into work because I have a meeting this morning with a dear friend of yours." His slightly sarcastic tone did not escape Kate.

Confused by his comment, she said, "And who would that be?"

"Sophia."

"Oh."

"Yes, oh. Did you know she would call me and ask for a meeting?"

"Well, yes. Sort of, I mean," Kate hesitated, a bit flustered, "that's why I left you a message. But I didn't think she'd get in touch with you that quick."

"Well, she did and she has and now I've got a meeting with her in," he glanced at his watch, "exactly one-and-half hours. I'm going to kill Stacey."

"Look, don't be angry with Stacey. People make mistakes. When you think about it, it's actually my fault because I should have known when you didn't call back right away that something was up. I should have called you back again." Continuing on, she said, "We had a meeting: me, Ursula, and Sophia."

"So, you went through with it, you little devil, and you actually saw her? Like face to face?"

"Yes. It wasn't easy, George, I can tell you that."

"Oh, you poor thing. Was it awful? Did you fight? What did St. Germain do? Oh God, I can't stand it! Tell me all the juicy details." Wiggling in his chair, he wished the coffee machine wasn't so far away.

"Only if you promise not to fire Stacey."

"Oh, don't worry about Stacey. I'll give her a piece of my mind and send her to a typing class. All will be well. Enough chit chat. Now, tell me already."

"Well, it started when I got back to the bakery last Wednesday. Apparently, Sophia had been by earlier that morning,"

"You don't say!" exclaimed George. He was hanging on her every word.

"When I got back after our walk along the beach, Joseph said that someone from the garden club had dropped off my umbrella. As usual I'd left it at the garden meeting on Tuesday night."

"The plot thickens. Go on, go on."

"I assumed it was Mimi or Ethel but he said that whoever it was was a bit of a looker."

George laughed out loud. "Kettle pot black."

"May I remind you George that you're married?"

"Okay, okay. So what happened next?"

"Well, he said whoever had dropped it off didn't look like one of my usual gardening club pals. How did he put it? She was "young, pretty, and didn't wear glasses on a chain." Apparently, she was really nervous too and practically ran out of the store. He said it was kind of weird. I guess she asked for me but when she found out that I wasn't there, she shoved the umbrella at him and just ran out the door."

"Like the scared little rabbit she is." George was really looking forward to his meeting with Sophia.

"But you know what it made me realize, George? It must have taken a lot of courage to walk into my bakery."

"Either that or a brazen disregard for your feelings." He paused, then added with sarcasm, "My, my, now doesn't that sound like a recurring theme?"

"No, I don't think so. Not this time. In fact, I now know so. I think she was making an honest attempt to reconnect with me. After I thought about it for a while, I decided to take Ursula up on her offer for the three of us to meet. Don't get me wrong. I still don't trust her one hundred percent but I couldn't just ignore her now, could I?"

"Yes, actually you could have. But we've been down this road before, Kate, and you know how I feel. It'll take a lot of convincing to change my mind."

"I know, George, but hear me out. I called Ursula back that afternoon and eventually we set up a time to meet at the Piccadilly—" George cut her off mid-sentence.

"I love that place! They have the best croissants." Catching his faux pas, he quickly added, "After yours, of course."

Kate laughed. George's mood was decidedly improving.

"That's okay, George. They do have the best croissants. But anyways, back to our meeting. We got together this past Monday afternoon and despite a rocky start, it actually went quite well."

"That's it? A rocky start? And then it went quite well?" George let out an exasperated sigh. "It's like pulling teeth with you! Details. Details, dear. You can't leave out the details," he paused, "but hurry, I've got to get going in five minutes."

Kate told him about the awkward start to their meeting, how they sat in silence for so long, and then how she finally broke the ice by admitting to Ursula that she and Sophia already knew each other.

"That must have blown her away. St. Germain is such a control freak I'm sure you rocked her boat a bit." George grinned.

"I guess she was a bit off-kilter but, honestly, I was so wound up in my own thoughts at the time I really didn't even notice. My heart was beating a million times a minute. God, I could barely talk."

"And what did Sophia say?" George's eyes narrowed.

"She was even worse. She hardly said anything at all. She sat there most of the time smiling meekly at Ursula and rarely ever made eye contact with me. She was definitely nervous as hell."

"And how did that make you feel?" George surprised even himself with that question. Perhaps Richard's sensitivity was rubbing off on him.

"As weird as it sounds, and as angry as I am with her still. . ." Kate paused, "I felt kind of sorry for her."

"Sorry for her? Come on, Kate, she brought this all on herself. She's the one who dumped your friendship in the toilet and left you high and dry when you really could have used a friend. And don't even get me started on that stolen recipe."

Realizing the truth of his words, Kate stared out the window and into the street. The sun was just breaking through the boughs of the large chestnut tree in her front yard. Skies were clear and it was going to be a beautiful day.

"Kate?"

"Sorry, I was just thinking about what you said."

"So, you feel sorry for her. But what about her? Does she feel sorry for you?"

"I'm not sure but she certainly had an air of guilt around her. I don't know," said Kate, shaking her head, "it was hard to tell. She was being very professional, once she started talking, and she spoke more with Ursula than with me."

"That doesn't surprise me at all. And now what?" George said. "She's going to be walking through my office door this morning. What the hell am I supposed to say to her now?"

"I don't know, George. I guess it's really your call. I'm sure all she wants to do is obtain permission from you to do some filming on the premises during the garden show. Nothing more than that."

"I realize that and, to be honest, I'm not going to put any stones in her way when it comes to the production. That would be foolhardy. However, I'm talking more on a personal level. Remember, she doesn't really know me at all. You and I weren't friends before she left for Toronto and I've never met her in person."

"You know, you're right. I've never had the opportunity to tell her about you and Richard."

"Exactly!" He sat up straight in his chair and declared, "So, I have essentially two choices here: one, I can treat her as a stranger, someone I know absolutely nothing about other than she is a professional television personality with a nation-wide following of adoring fans or, two: I can let her in on the fact that I actually know her very well, vicariously that is, and that I don't particularly trust her nor do I particularly care for her considering how she has treated my BFF over the last couple of years."

"George, if I could make a suggestion. . ." Kate pleaded.

Barrelling on, he continued, "Actually no, you may not. As I said earlier, I will not put any stones in her way when it comes to the production but I'm not at all convinced that she deserves my respect. That, my dear, is something she most definitely will have to earn. So," he glanced at his watch before he finished, "I will, therefore, dutifully listen to what she has to say and . . ." Kate clutched the phone close to her ear.

"Yes, yes what will you do?"

"Play the rest by ear. Improvisation, my dear, has been the saving grace of my life."

"Oh, George, don't go and do something stupid. I don't want to make her feel any worse than she probably does right now."

"Not to worry, Kate. I'll let my conscience be my guide. To quote my insightful husband, "If you keep pushing the snooze button, it will only be silent for a while.""

"Huh?"

"No time to explain, dear. This old queen has to totter along now. I'll call you after the meeting to let you know how it went. Kisses."

With that, he hung up and Kate was left wondering exactly what his conscience was going to guide him to do. She hoped for Sophia's sake that it wasn't going to be a trip down memory lane.

Chapter Seventeen

Oma's Baking Tip

It's easy to be seduced by the beautiful pictures in baking books but you need only ask one question to know if the recipe is right for you: Does it call for butter or margarine?

"It wasn't intentional, Mr. Stanwell. I'm sorry." Stacey stood meekly in front of George's desk, trying her best to hide behind the slender arching branch of orchid flowers that hung gracefully across the top of his computer screen.

"Intentional or not, Stacey, you managed to cause me a fair amount of personal embarrassment. Given the fact that I now walk like a one-legged buccaneer from the chorus line of the *Pirates of Penzance,* I am in no need of further affronts to my character."

Stacey wasn't sure what the *Pirates of Penzance* was but it didn't matter. Now into her second month of working as George's personal assistant, she was getting used to his flair for the fanciful. Anything was better than her last job at the insurance agency where her previous boss, Mr. Sneedstone, would spend long hours explaining the ins and outs of personal injury deductibles, pro-rated cancellation fees, and indemnification. She would always be grateful to her Uncle Sid, who worked as a tour guide at Shaughnessy Gardens, for rescuing her from certain death by boredom. He had mentioned the job opening he'd seen on the Garden's bulletin board and had given her a glowing recommendation.

Despite the fact that she may have exaggerated a little bit about her actual "skills" on her résumé, Stacey still managed to get the job. One of those so-called skills included "an obsessive love of gardening." In reality, Stacey owned one sorry-looking spider plant that hung droopily in a dusty macramé hanger in the corner of her kitchen. Nor did her skill set include a lightning-fast typing speed of sixty words per minute. She was pretty sure that George had already noticed her clumsy two-fingered attempts at using the computer keyboard but she secretly hoped that it didn't really matter.

"I know I should have written it down and, you know, I probably did but somehow I must have misplaced it. Or maybe it got shredded by accident. I'm really sorry," Stacey said with a slight tone of desperation creeping into her voice.

"Well, regardless, it simply can't happen again. From now on, I'm asking that you write every call received into your notebook. And I mean every call, whether you take a message or not. Once you've given a message to me, put a tick mark by the call. If I find that there are messages without ticks or, even worse, I find out that you have not passed a message on to me, I'm sorry, Stacey but," he paused ever so slightly, hoping to convey the seriousness of his warning, "I'm going to have to let you go."

Stacey's face reddened. George noticed the change in her demeanour. Not wanting to bring on a crying fit, he softened his tone.

"Look, Stacey. I know you're new to this and I'm willing to give you a break but I cannot afford to have more mistakes made, especially with the garden show looming in the distance. Trust me when I say things are going to get crazy around here. You are going to have to be extremely organized or things will begin to unravel very quickly."

Stacey turned her head slightly and quickly brushed a tear from her eye. She stood up straight and summoned her courage. "You can count on me, Mr. Stanwell. I'll do the very best I can and I promise I won't disappoint you again."

"Good. Now get back to work and scuttle up a notebook so you can begin your message log right away, okay?"

"Aye, aye sir!" Turning on her heels, she quickly left the room and closed the door quietly behind her.

Oh God, thought George as he rolled his eyes, *my pathetic little limp has now inspired a pirate theme around here. Lord help us.*

Having settled the issue with Stacey in the hopes that she would take his threats seriously, George now had only a few minutes to compose himself before Sophia's scheduled arrival. On the drive over, he had determined that he was going to let her do most of the talking. That way, he could feel her out and, depending on what she said and how she said it, it would be either sink or swim for the famous Ms. Simpson.

George adjusted his tie in the reflection of his monitor. Pleased with his appearance, he was jolted back to reality by an internal page on his handset. Knowing that his guest had probably now arrived, he cleared his throat and gently pressed the hands-free button.

"Yes, Stacey?" he said smoothly, knowing she, too, would have it on speaker phone.

"Ms. Simpson is here to see you. Would you like me to bring her into your office?"

Thinking it might be best to let Sophia come to him rather than wobbling his way down the hall, George readily agreed to Stacey's suggestion. He quickly got up from his chair and gingerly made his way towards the front of his desk, casually leaning himself against the edge. With one hand in his pocket and the other dangling nonchalantly by his side, he felt as prepared as ever for what was about to walk through his door.

Within a few seconds, a somewhat star-struck Stacey appeared with Sophia following close behind. As she stood framed by the doorway,

George's initial thoughts were that Sophia was much taller than he had imagined and she obviously had impeccable taste in clothes. She was wearing a tailored, dark-blue wool suit with a bright red, silk blouse. Her slender legs extended gracefully below the hem of her skirt, revealing perfectly shaped knees, something George had always found very attractive, but rare, in women. Her silky dark hair fell casually over her shoulders. She smiled brilliantly, revealing perfectly white teeth. George was instantly smitten. Gathering his composure, he stepped forward, swallowing the pain that shot up from his foot, smiled appreciatively, and extended his hand towards Sophia.

"George Stanwell. I'm pleased to make your acquaintance." Formal was always best, he thought, especially at the beginning. *You can always move in for the kill later.*

Sophia took his hand and shook it firmly, signifying that she was a woman who meant business. George found himself slightly taken aback by her confident presence. Now that she was significantly closer, he was able to smell her perfume, expensive and probably French, and to admire the exquisite diamond pendant earrings that hung gracefully from her small lobes. She quickly glanced at her watch and then looked at him directly. Her bright green eyes were mesmerizing. George could feel himself going slightly weak at the knees.

"I'm sorry I'm somewhat late. I was held back at the studio for a few moments and it took me longer than expected to get here."

"No apologies needed." George suddenly realized that he wasn't even aware that she was over twenty minutes late, having been so wound up in his own affairs to even notice. "In fact," he stumbled slightly over his words, "I've really nothing better to do at the moment."

I can't believe you just said that, blurted the voice inside George's head. *Nothing better to do? For God's sake, man, pull yourself together.*

Strangely enough, George found his heart was beating quickly. Was it because he was secretly hiding that he knew intimate details about this woman, more than she would ever guess, or was it some kind of strange personal magnetism?

Odd, he thought. George normally felt this kind of schoolboy giddiness only when some new handsome gardener was introduced to him on the grounds or whenever he bumped into his ex, Steve, at the drycleaners. Steve was a fireman "with special skills" and even though they had had only a short romance, George still got a secret little tingle whenever he saw him.

Clearing his throat and gesturing to the table and chair set in the corner of his office, he said, "Please take a seat, Ms. Simpson." Leaning his head in the general direction of his assistant but not taking his eyes off of Sophia, he said, "Stacey, would you please bring us some coffee? I assume you'd like a cup, Ms. Simpson? We have a very nice espresso machine."

"Yes, actually, I would adore one." Breaking her gaze with George, Sophia turned to Stacey, who now stood in the doorway and continued, "Thank you, Stacey. I would appreciate that very much. I take it black."

"You're welcome, Ms. Simpson," said Stacey with a blush. "I'll be right back."

George gestured for Sophia to take a seat, then settled himself as gracefully as he could into the chair opposite her, doing his best to hide his limp. Since he certainly didn't want to get into a discussion about the how's and why's of his injury, he did his best to mask the pain shooting up through his foot and into his leg.

George liked to conduct personal meetings while seated around the small coffee table in the far corner of his office. Next to a large, floor-to-ceiling window, the comfortable grouping afforded one of the best views of the expansive gardens. He preferred the intimacy this afforded rather than having his guest sit opposite him, peering over the wide expanse of his desk. Despite outward appearances, George had learned early in his career that you get the best work and creative ideas out of some people if you treat them more as an equal instead of playing the authority card. He reserved that one for some of the cutthroat Dutch plant suppliers he knew or meddling garden club presidents like Ursula St. Germain.

"So," said George as he leaned back into his chair and crossed his legs, "Your assistant mentioned that you wanted to discuss the possibility of doing some filming during our upcoming garden show."

Sophia leaned against the back of her chair and crossed her legs at the ankle, giving George a clear view of her satiny stockings and high heel shoes. There was a sudden flash of red and George practically leapt forward out of his seat.

"Oh my God! Are those Louboutins?"

"Yes, actually they are," said Sophia, a wide grin spreading across her face. Leaning forward and placing a slender hand on her right foot, she whispered conspiratorially, "and I got them on sale, if you can believe it."

"On sale? Well, aren't you lucky? They look amazing, especially with that outfit. A perfect match." George looked up from her shoes and caught her eye. He suddenly realized that all his pretences of playing the big tough guy had just flown out the window.

Sophia laughed. "You know, you're probably the only man who has ever taken an interest in my shoes, let alone recognized the designer, so I take that as a huge compliment." She looked him directly in the eyes and continued, "You know, George, I think you and I are going to get along swimmingly."

Before he could help himself, he blurted out, "I do believe you're right, Ms. Simpson."

"Oh, call me Sophia. Ms. Simpson sounds so stuffy. Since we may be working closely with one another in the coming months, I figure there's no need to be so formal. Don't you agree?"

George stared at her blankly, mesmerized for the moment by the sheer magnitude of her presence. *What the hell is going on here,* he thought. *This is the woman who stole a beloved family recipe from Kate and prostituted it throughout the media for her own personal gain just two years ago. She's supposed to be the enemy, the friendship destroyer, the cold-hearted one who left your best friend to fend for herself in her serious time of need. You should hate her right now. You should be kicking her out the door but no, instead, you sit here ogling her designer shoes and agreeing to have a jolly old time of it over the next few months. Kate will never forgive you and Richard is going to get all smug. You'll never hear the end of it.*

"Your coffees." Stacey had silently appeared with a small tray. She set it down on the table and turned to leave.

"Thanks again, Stacey." Sophia gave her a little wave and Stacey retreated appreciatively back to her desk.

"So, tell me, George. What made you decide to become the head of one of Vancouver's most celebrated horticultural gardens?"

The question took him a bit off guard. He was still reeling from his thoughts of betrayal and he certainly wasn't expecting to have to talk about himself.

"I just kind of fell into it. Literally." He gingerly picked up his coffee and took a small sip. He enjoyed telling this story although Richard had grown bored of it years ago and always excused himself whenever a new acquaintance happened to ask George about it.

"Fell, like stumbled across the opportunity, or do you mean fell, like literally, fell?" Sophia smiled.

"Well, both. It's a funny story." Placing his coffee cup back on the saucer, he continued, "The previous director was an older chap, Thomas Dawson. You may have heard of him. He was the one who had the brilliant idea of opening up the gardens to an annual flower show back in the seventies. Anyways, Thomas was getting on in years and a tumble off his back porch put him out of commission one month before the show was scheduled to start five years ago."

"Don't tell me," Sophia picked up her cup and gave it a little blow to cool the contents. "You came in and saved the day." She winked and George felt himself blushing.

"Actually, yes. I mean, it certainly wasn't chivalrous or anything like that but the show did come off without a hitch. After six months of re-habilitation, Thomas made the surprise decision to retire. I guess the powers-that-be decided that since I was already doing a satisfactory job, they may as well extend my contract and," he paused, gesturing around him, "here I am."

"And yet, despite your best efforts, I understand that the garden show has been struggling financially for a number of years and there is a real possibility that it will be cancelled," she said matter-of-factly.

"Why, yes." George stumbled a bit, wondering where she had found out this information. "That is true."

"And to help matters a bit," Sophia continued, "you and your husband Richard have made significant contributions to the garden's heritage fund for the preservation and upkeep of both the orchid greenhouse and the Japanese pagoda, both of which have fallen into disrepair over the last number of years."

George paused and looked her directly in the eye. "May I ask how you happen to know that bit of information?" His curiosity was now piqued and he leaned forward in his chair.

"Oh, I have my sources." Taking a sip of her coffee, she looked up at him with an innocent glance and said, "and it's certainly nothing to be ashamed of, now is it?"

George flinched inwardly. *Did she just say what I thought she said? Be ashamed, I think not!* His thoughts became very clear as he realized he was talking to a reporter who obviously had done her homework, both business and personal. Fact-gathering was her job. The question was, how many facts had she gathered? Was there any way she could pos-sibly know of his relationship to Kate? Straightening his tie, he figured now was the time to cut to the chase.

"I'm never ashamed of anything I do, my dear, or of the relationships I maintain."

The old George had now sprung back to life. Like snapping out of a dream, not unlike his experience earlier this morning, George Stanwell was now fully awake. As though to give him a physical reminder of how his day had begun, his foot throbbed within its soft leather loafer. He tensed his jaw and continued in a cool tone.

"Well, I see you've done your homework, and to your credit too. I appreciate that in someone. But you must also realize that I've done my homework too."

George lowered his gaze on Sophia and stared at her without blinking.

Taken aback by his sudden change in demeanour, she asked, "And what exactly does that mean, George?" A slightly cautious smile crossed her lips.

"Well, I obviously know why you're here. Let me state for the record that I will not stand in your way at all. In fact, as the official representative and spokesman for the Shaughnessy Horticultural Gardens, I welcome you and your film crew. If there is anything we can do to assist you with your production, please let me know."

Sitting up straighter in her chair, Sophia said, "Why, thank you, George. That will be most helpful and I—"

"But," he continued, cutting her off, "you must know, Ms. Simpson, that I neither wholly respect you nor do I completely trust you."

"Pardon me?"

Sophia swallowed hard and placed her coffee cup back in its saucer.

"You see, there are things in your past that I am privy to. Based on those actions, I will let you know that I intend to deal with you solely on a professional level. Once the production has come to an end, I sincerely don't believe that we will remain anything but business cards gathering dust in one another's desk drawers."

"Excuse me, George, but I don't quite understand. What exactly do you mean when you say 'things in my past'?

Sophia's eyes narrowed as her hands gripped the arms of her chair. There was a light knock at the door as Stacey appeared with another small tray. She quickly entered the office and stood in front of the pair.

"Sorry to interrupt but I thought you might like a little treat to go with your coffees. Carol in HR picked these up on the way to work today and they're just delicious," she gushed. "She even said they were one of your favourites, Mr. Stanwell."

George would normally have cut Stacey off before she even had the opportunity to enter his office during an important meeting but with one glance at her tray, he kept his mouth shut.

Stacey leaned forward and placed the small plate of Georgie-Porgie Puddin' Pies on the table. A neatly folded purple napkin with white polka dots peeked out from underneath the cream-coloured tartlets.

Sophia stared at the baked goods, then shot a look to George who was staring at her with a satisfied grin.

"Why, thank you, Stacey. That was most thoughtful." Shooing her out of the room with a casual wave of his left hand, George waited until the door was firmly shut before he leaned back in his chair.

"I believe you are quite familiar with the person responsible for these delicious creations, Ms. Simpson. They come from a very well known bakery here in town, owned by my dear friend and close confidante, Kate Freitag. Please do have one."

Cocking one eyebrow and lowering his voice to a whisper, he let her have it.

"I'm told they're from a secret, old family recipe."

Chapter Eighteen

Oma's Baking Tip

Using a cooling rack speeds up the cooling process by allowing air to pass beneath the cookies. It helps keep the cookies crisp by allowing steam to evaporate from underneath, rather than trapping it and making them soft.

Kate was in the midst of transferring a tray of freshly baked cookies into the portable rack near the convection oven when she stopped, frozen by what George had just said.

"You didn't."

Dropping the still-hot tray on the nearby counter, she turned and stared. "Oh, George, tell me you didn't."

George had unexpectedly arrived at Kate's Bakes just before closing, insistent that he immediately talk to Kate. Most of the staff were cleaning up the display cases at the front of the store so it afforded he and Kate a bit of alone time in the kitchen.

"Why should I be ashamed of it, Kate? She was asking for it, let me tell you. Coming into my office this morning all primed and ready to go. She almost had me completely seduced with her fancy French shoes and her light-hearted chit chat. But I saw through it immediately." He blinked.

"You're lying. I know it. You didn't see through anything, even if there was something to see through."

Kate moved towards George, wiping her hands on her apron. "She had you going, didn't she?"

George didn't answer. Instead, he just stood there, uncharacteristically quiet and still without any traceable expression. Kate knew this was a telltale sign that he was hiding something.

"See, I told you. She has that effect on people. But what I don't understand is: Why did you suddenly turn on her? Why couldn't you have just had a normal, professional conversation about the filming and left it at that?" Kate was letting her frustration show. George went on the defensive.

"Well, she pushed me into it." George was starting to sound a bit like a schoolboy who'd been goaded on by others to do some naughty deed. Kate wasn't buying any of it.

"Oh, baloney, George. Nobody pushes you into anything. What exactly did she say?"

Looking around to ensure that none of Kate's staff was lingering near the doorway to the kitchen, he continued in a slightly hushed tone.

"Well, we were having a perfectly normal conversation about how I'd gotten the position at the gardens when all of sudden, she pounced on me with all sorts of details about the financials. She went on and on about how the garden show was struggling and threatened by cancellation. She even mentioned my and Richard's contribution to the heritage fund and suggested," he lowered his voice even more, "that she knew about Richard and I and that our marriage was nothing to be ashamed of. The gall of that woman." George's eyes flared wide as he placed his hands defiantly on his hips.

"And so? What do you care what she thinks about you and Richard? And isn't all of that other stuff public information?"

"Well, yes," he stammered, "I guess so, even though the financials are supposed to be private."

"Not when some other reporter has already done a big spread on it in the newspaper. When was that, George? Last May, if I recall? If I remember correctly, you weren't too happy about it then either."

"All right. All right. So, it's not a corporate secret. Although I don't give a damn about what she thinks about Richard and I, I do resent the homophobic tones in which it was suggested I had something to be ashamed about. If you had been there, you would have seen what I mean. God, it was the way she oh-so-nonchalantly let these hurtful little tidbits tumble into the conversation. It was like she was trying to impress me or something with her behind-the-scenes info. I'm sorry, Kate, but I just couldn't help myself."

"No, you're not sorry. What you really want to say is that she one-upped you. You wanted to show her that you knew more about her than she did about you."

Staring him right in the eyes, she concluded, "Oh, George, you're so insecure sometimes."

Kate turned her back on him and walked towards the cookie tray she had set down earlier. She looked over her shoulder and said, "You may have just ruined everything, you know."

George's hurt ego now sparked into action. "Quite frankly, I thought everything was already ruined. So, how could I have made matters worse?"

Kate sighed. Her back was still turned to him and she stared down at her flour-covered shoes. She was a tornado of emotions and was having a hard time understanding what she was feeling. To some degree, George was right: things were already ruined between her and Sophia. But, on the other hand, they might have been salvageable. The real question, once again, was whether or not Kate was willing to try to rebuild the friendship.

She felt George's warm hands on her shoulders. His closeness filled her eyes with tears of frustration and regret.

"Look, I'm sorry, hon," he said quietly. "I should have kept my big fat mouth shut and just let her do her job. It's just that I'm still so angry with her and what she did to you. I couldn't help myself. If I'm honest, it felt good when I did it. But seeing you now," he turned her around and looked down into her eyes, "well, it just breaks my heart and I—"

"It's okay, George." She smiled weakly. "I guess I should never have thought this could have worked itself out anyways. Too many bad memories clouding the view."

"Hey Kate!" Deb shouted from the kitchen doorway that led to the back offices. "Phone's for you. Someone called Sophia?"

George grabbed both her shoulders tightly. Looking like the proverbial deer caught in the headlights, he stammered, "You don't have to talk to her right now. You can get Deb to take a message."

"You can't hide forever, George. You should know that better than anyone else."

Her meaning did not escape him. He looked away, contemplating the depth of what she had just said. After a moment, he relented, "Go. She's waiting." Standing aside, he let Kate pass and watched as she walked towards the doorway.

Before she reached the hallway, Kate turned and said, "I didn't really want to be on TV anyways. They say the camera adds ten pounds and there's nothing worse than a chubby baker." The words trailed off softly and then she was gone.

Absent-mindedly grabbing one of the warm cookies off the tray, George took a huge bite. But his own internal bitterness masked the sweet flavour of the chocolate as it slowly melted in his mouth. He swallowed hard and leaned against the stainless-steel counter. His foot was throbbing again, so he closed his eyes, hoping the pain would pass.

"Are you still hanging around?" Deb suddenly appeared within a few metres of George, trying to look mildly annoyed by his presence.

In no mood to indulge in the sarcastic repartee that they usually enjoyed, he replied, "Yes, that is, if you don't mind."

"Well, you know I do but that's another matter." She smiled and looked at the cookie tray on the counter behind his back. "Hey! Those are for paying customers, you know."

"I know, so sue me."

George walked past her, heading for the back door. "Hey, tell Kate," he looked back at her, his brow furrowed, "Aw, just tell her I said good-bye."

Deb frowned and watched as he headed, shoulders slumped, down the hallway, an obvious limp hampering his usual graceful gait.

Chapter Nineteen

Oma's Baking Tip

Did a recipe not work for you? Attempt it once again but then move on. Life is short, ingredients cost money, and there are lots of other recipes in the world to try.

"Hello?"

"Hi, Kate, it's Sophia."

Kate said nothing. Her heart pounded in her throat, burning like a hot coal. She shut her eyes and sighed.

"Look, Kate, I know this is awkward and you've probably already spoken with George but I wanted to have a chance to explain."

"Explain what?" Kate's tone was flat. She'd gotten into the habit of keeping her guard up when talking with Sophia and this time wasn't any different.

"Well, explain why I left his office so abruptly. I'm sure he's told you everything already."

Feeling like she couldn't lie at this point, Kate simply replied, "He's told me some."

"You know, he said some things that really hurt."

I know how that feels, thought Kate.

"But for the most part, what he said was right." Feeling the moment had finally come to wipe the slate clean, Sophia confessed, "I treated you like crap, Kate, and God, I'm really, really sorry."

Kate quickly opened her eyes and looked up at the framed picture of Benjamin on her desk. A silent tear ran down her cheek.

After a few moments of silence, Kate spoke. "I don't know, Sophia," Kate's voice was unsteady. "I'm really torn and . . ."

Desperation crept into Sophia's voice. "If it's about the gingerbread recipe, I can explain that."

Kate sighed. Her thoughts were swirling together in a blur. Without thinking, she blurted out, *"Gestolen ist gestolen"* (literally, "Stolen is stolen," meaning "What's done is done").

"What?"

"Just a phrase my Oma used to use."

"What does it mean?"

Debating whether she should say or bluntly tell her to go look it up, Kate thought about her options while drawing figure eights on her monitor with her computer mouse.

"Look, it doesn't matter."

Sophia interjected, "What does matter is that you give me a chance."

"It's not that easy, Sophia. I can't just forget everything that's happened. I know that we've been thrown together with this gardening club thing but I think I'm just going to do what needs to be done. Don't expect more—"

"I'm planning on mentioning the bakery, you know, as a sort of side plug. Maybe we could feature your BLT Brownies." Sophia swallowed fast, trying to get the words out quickly before Kate stopped her. "I'm sure it'll do your business a world of good."

"Stop right there." Kate's voice was cold and tempered. The wound that she thought had at least healed enough to simply be a jagged scar on her heart felt like it had been ripped apart. The emotion it encased came gushing forth. "You have no idea what you're talking about." Her voice trembling, she continued, "And you have no right, Sophia, no right at all to even mention his name."

Sophia cringed on the other side of the phone line. "Oh, Kate, I'm so sorry. I shouldn't have," she stuttered.

"Damn right you shouldn't have. Don't you dare pull Benjamin into this!"

Exasperated, Kate felt trapped. If she could, she would quit this thing right now, tell George to find someone else to head up the volunteer program, and tell Ursula to go it alone with Sophia. But she knew in her heart's heart that she couldn't. She didn't want to appear to be just like Sophia: someone who easily abandoned her friends in times of need. No, that she wouldn't do.

"Look, Kate, I'm sorry. I'm so sorry. I just thought it would be a good thing."

"Well, you thought wrong and your apology is a couple of years too late."

There was silence on the other end of the phone.

"You know what, Sophia, I've gotta go. The bakery's closing up and I—"

Sophia cut her off. "Don't hang up, Kate. I really need to finish this with you."

"It is finished, Sophia."

She hung up, not waiting for an answer. George was right. She should have listened to him. How did she manage to get sucked in again? Kicking herself for playing the fool, she sunk her head into her hands and sobbed. It had been so long since Kate had really cried; even she was surprised by the intensity of her tears. What with the success of the bakery and the relative stability of her personal life, even without a love interest, she had managed to pull things together. But this conversation with Sophia had torn a hole in her carefully created façade.

Kate was sick with anger and disappointment. The bitter tears that dripped through her fingers were saturated with the sadness of five years' worth of unsettled grief. She, of course, had thought about Benjamin every day since his death and had somehow managed to control her feelings of loss. But Sophia's words had changed all that. Kate realized in a split second that she really hadn't finished grieving for him. Despite her best efforts and her proclamations that "All was well," she had a long, long way to go.

Glancing up, Kate gazed at the framed picture on her desk. The wind-tussled hair, the easy grin, the little scar above his left eye that Benjamin had gotten playing baseball as a kid. . . Her heart ached to touch his face again and tell him that she loved him.

There was a knock at the door.

Grabbing a tissue from her desk drawer, Kate quickly wiped her face and nose. Looking intently at the computer screen, she feigned interest in the spreadsheet that glared back at her, then said quietly, "George?"

Deb turned the knob and poked her head in the door. "No, it's just me. Mr. Grumpy Pants left a few minutes ago. The next time you see him, tell him he owes you for a cookie."

"More like I owe him," Kate whispered softly. Swivelling around in her chair, she looked red-eyed at Deb. "Time to cash out?"

Deb's intuition told her that Kate had been crying. Not wanting to embarrass her, she quickly said, "Yeah, but don't worry about it. I'll do it." She paused, "You just finish up here and I'll do the rest."

"Thanks, Deb." Kate managed a smile.

"No problem." Closing the door quietly behind her, Deb's boss-in-charge mode kicked into full gear. Kate could hear her barking out orders to the remaining staff through the closed office door and was thankful that she had sensed her vulnerability.

Deb's kindness was the sort of friend-to-friend behaviour she had always expected from Sophia but now realized she would never get. After all that had happened, Sophia still didn't understand. Kate was tired of trying to hold onto something that would never be. In that moment of recognition, she mentally broke off her connection to Sophia. Even though Kate knew that she had to have contact with her in the near future, she also knew that that contact would be emotionless and un-binding.

This is what she knew she could handle. This was the way it was going to be.

She smiled slightly at Benjamin's picture and said, "It's time. Right, honey?"

Chapter Twenty

Oma's Baking Tip

Pure vanilla extract is as simple as that: pure, not artificial.

The cell phone line went dead. Sophia stared unbelievingly through the windshield and out into the empty parking lot. The day had gone terribly wrong, starting with her miserable meeting with George Stanwell, followed by this heart-wrenching call to Kate from the confines of her car.

Sophia had managed to struggle through the day but by late afternoon, her conscience was telling her to get a hold of Kate and try to explain. Try to apologize yet once again. It was like she couldn't let go of it, even though Kate had told her in no uncertain terms that she didn't want to have Sophia as a friend anymore. But there had been too many wrongs done. She had quietly said goodnight to Genevieve and slipped out the back way. Calling Kate from her car had provided her with the privacy she knew she had needed. In the end, it didn't matter because the conversation had lasted less than a minute.

A tear peaked at the corner of Sophia's eye and slipped down her cheek. She inhaled haltingly and with her exhale came an uncontrolled flood of tears. Placing her hands on the steering wheel, she hung her head and let the salty tears drop onto her lap. They were the only silent witnesses to her pain. There was no holding them back.

Sophia was startled by a soft knocking at her window. Raising her head, she saw Marcie peering in through the driver's-side window. A look of concern shadowed her face.

"You okay, hon?" Her voice was muffled but clear and wracked with concern.

Wiping the tears from under her eyes, Sophia turned the car keys a notch and pressed the driver's window button.

"I'm fine." She ran a hand through her hair. "I just have a bit of a head-ache and was resting."

Marcie wasn't born yesterday, as they say, and immediately clued into Sophia's attempt at a cover-up. Marcie liked Sophia. She was one of the few celebrities she'd worked with who was kind and not completely self-obsessed. They had made easy friends although this had been kept within the confines of the TV station.

Marcie had just finished up for the day and was walking across the lot to her car when she had seen Sophia, hands gripping the steering wheel and her shoulders shuddering with sobs. Marcie simply couldn't just walk by. She had to stop and find out what was happening.

"Oh, sweetie, it looks to me like more than just a headache. Do you need someone to talk to?" She reached through the window and placed a consoling hand on Sophia's shoulder.

Sophia paused for a moment. Without hesitation, she turned to Marcie and whispered, "That would be nice, thanks."

"Listen, why don't I run over and get my car and then you hop in. We can go get a bite to eat or, if you'd prefer, you can come to my place. I don't live that far from here and I make a pretty mean spaghetti." She smiled and gave Sophia's shoulder a squeeze.

Realizing the privacy of Marcie's kitchen would be significantly bet-ter than spilling her guts in a public place, Sophia forced a smile.

"Dinner at your place sounds good." She grabbed a tissue from her purse and blew her nose. "But you don't have to drive. I can follow you."

"Are you sure you're okay to drive? I hate to say it but you look pretty upset."

"I'm okay. Honest. Besides, it'll save you having to drive back here after dinner."

"Well, all right but just in case I lose you in traffic. . ." Marcie reached into her oversized handbag and grabbed a scrap of paper and a pen. She quickly scribbled something and handed it back to Sophia. "That's my cell number and address. Call me if you get lost and I'll give you directions. I basically live at Main and 12th near Heritage Hall. Do you know it?"

Taking the piece of paper and placing it next to her on the passenger seat, Sophia turned and nodded. "Are you really sure, Marcie? What about your boyfriend? Sorry, I forgot his name."

"Who, Ted? Oh, don't worry about him. It's Wednesday night. He's got his ham radio club meeting and they don't finish up until late. So, let's hit the road, missy, get you some vittles, and see if we can't cheer you up a notch or two." She gave Sophia a little wave then hurried off to her car parked near the end of the lot.

Thank God for Marcie, thought Sophia. At this point, it seemed like she was Sophia's only friend.

The drive to Marcie's was mostly uneventful. Sophia followed her closely. Although she almost lost her at Broadway, she managed to squeak through the light. Marcie had given her a big thumbs up in her rear-view mirror. Once they turned onto 12th Avenue, Marcie rolled down her window and pointed at a pink stucco house in the middle of the block. She headed around the corner and into the alleyway behind. Sophia followed but then realized that there was parking for only one vehicle. After circling the block two times, she managed to find a vacant spot just up the street from Marcie's fifties-style home.

Sophia walked the short distance to Marcie's house. Opening the ironwork gate at the front, she let herself into the garden. Tiny but neat,

Marcie's front garden was a little oasis of spring. Daffodils and crocuses popped up everywhere in a random but endearing pattern. Here and there, colourful teapots poked through the soil, appearing to have been abandoned there after some whimsical mad-hatter tea party. The stone walkway was short to the front steps and before she reached the top step, the front door swung open. Marcie appeared with a warm smile.

"Welcome to my humble abode." She spread her arms wide. "I'm sure it's nothing like the new place you just bought but I think it's homey."

"It's wonderful, Marcie." Turning to the garden, Sophia continued, "Your front garden is adorable. So many pretty flowers. And I love the teapots."

"Oh, you noticed those? I used to collect them until one day, it suddenly dawned on me that I had way too many. But I didn't have the heart to throw them all away." Pointing out towards the garden, she added, "So, I recycled them, so to speak."

"Well, they look adorable," Sophia smiled.

"Come in. Come in. There's no need to stand around outside."

Taking Sophia's coat and hanging it on a hook in the tiny enclosed porch, Marcie gestured to the open door behind her.

"The kitchen's right through there. I'll fix us something to drink and then I'll get started on dinner."

Following Marcie's lead, Sophia ventured into the house and was immediately struck by the quaintness of the decor. It was like she had stepped back into the 1950s. The living room was furnished with a vintage, brown, tweed-coloured couch, an elliptical coffee table, and a small cocktail cabinet, set off in the corner, filled with pineapple-themed accessories. The kitchen was no less enchanting with its black-and-white-checkered linoleum floor. In the far corner, beneath a starburst clock, stood a Formica kitchen table surrounded by diner-style chairs with bright red vinyl upholstered seats.

The style totally suited Marcie. Sophia often thought that Marcie reminded her of the kind of waitresses that used to work at the Varsity Grill on the corner of Broadway and Granville. That was back in the day when she and Kate would go in and get the $5.99 Tuesday night special, complete with meatloaf, mashed potatoes, gravy, and a chocolate fudge sundae for dessert. The waitresses matched the diner décor, down to their pink, ruffled uniforms, bouffant hairdos, and name tags centred on lace ruffles, declaring their names in big black letters. Edith, Sally, and Midge were a few of the names she remembered. Marcie would have fit right in.

"Grab a seat. Can I get you something to drink? An iced tea or—?" Marcie had already opened the fridge door and was bent over, rummaging about while reaching into the back of the refrigerator. "Darn, looks like Ted drank the last of the pink grapefruit cocktail. Sorry, I can't offer you that."

"Iced tea would be just fine, thanks." Sophia pulled out a kitchen chair and sat down. While Marcie busied herself with the glasses and tea, Sophia asked, "So how long have you lived here?"

"Oh, forever, it seems. Actually, I grew up in this house."

"You did? Wow. I've never known anyone who's lived in one house their entire life."

"Well, actually, I did move out for a while but then my dad passed away. When my mom got older, I moved back in to help." Turning to face Sophia with two tall glasses in her hands, Marcie moved towards the kitchen table and set them down. "Then when she died, I inherited the place and I just couldn't bring myself to sell it. So, here I am!"

"I'm sorry to hear about your parents, Marcie. It sounds like they passed away pretty close together."

"They did. My dad died in 1998 and my mom only lasted three years after that." She paused, "I think she died of a broken heart. The doctors say it was angina but I know better." Turning away and busying herself with some pots and pans, Marcie continued, "And that is why we need to find out what's going on with you, missy, because if there's one thing I can recognize, it's a broken heart." She turned with one hand on her hip and smiled encouragingly at Sophia. "So, what's his name?"

Sophia started to laugh nervously.

"Did I say something funny?"

"In kind of a way you did." Taking a sip of the cold iced tea, Sophia swallowed and continued. "Her name is Kate."

Turning on her heels and flushed with embarrassment, Marcie almost dropped the pot she was about to fill with water for the pasta. "Oh, my God, Sophia. I'm sorry. I didn't realize. I should have just kept my mouth shut. Stupid me." Turning back to the sink, she turned the faucet on full blast. Out of embarrassment, she continued to fill the empty air by talking at a much louder pitch so that she could be heard over the running water.

"I really should have known better. I did the same thing last year at the Christmas party with Grace, who works one of the cameras on the news floor. There I was going on and on about how beautiful her engagement ring was and that she must have hooked herself a real hottie because the ring wasn't a cheap one and he must have a good job and blah, blah, blah. All the time I was blubbering on I hadn't realized that her fiancée Cindy," she shut off the faucet and lowered her tone, "was standing right next to her. I felt like such an idiot when Grace introduced her. Afterwards, I ended up drinking far too many rum and eggnogs and Carl had to give me a lift home. I'm still a little embarrassed every time I see Grace in the cafeteria. She's totally cool about it but I still feel like a nimrod."

Grabbing the heavy pot out of the sink, Marcie placed it on the gas stove and turned it onto high heat.

"So," turning back to face Sophia, she smiled timidly and asked, "your girlfriend's name is Kate?"

"She's not my girlfriend." Sophia said slowly. "Well, she used to be my girlfriend but not in that way."

"Oh." Marcie was totally confused. "So you aren't gay?" She followed that quickly with, "Not that there would be anything wrong with that if you were, you know what I mean?"

"Yes, I know what you mean. No, I'm not gay but I think your 'heart' instincts were right." Sophia looked down at her iced tea then continued. "I think I may just have a broken heart. But it's all my own fault and I don't know how to fix it." Her tears welled up again. Marcie rushed over from the stove, grabbing the pink, crocheted-covered box of tissues off the counter. Placing them in front of Sophia, she sat down opposite her and took one of her hands. "Oh, sweetie, don't cry. I'm sure we'll be able to figure it out."

"I'm not so sure we can." Sophia's voice cracked. "You see, I'm not really the person I appear to be. I've done some really bad things and I've treated Kate terribly. I don't blame her for hating me but I can't help but want to fix it and let her know how sorry I am for all the bad stuff I did." Engulfed in her grief and oblivious that she barely knew Marcie, Sophia felt compelled to tell her the whole story. She figured the best place to start was that fateful night in Toronto. *Yes,* she thought, *that awful night and Phil.* With a heavy sigh, she began.

~ ~

Sophia lay quietly, staring off into the darkness of her bedroom. A sliver of light came from the crack beneath the *en suite* bathroom door. Phil had forgotten to shut the light off again. It was one of those little things that annoyed her but not enough to mention it for the umpteenth time. She hated to sound like a nag and he probably wouldn't listen anyway.

"You've been quiet tonight," he said as he adjusted the pillow behind his head. Unlike other lovers she'd had in the past, Phil wasn't the kind of guy who got all dopey and sleepy after making love. He usually liked to chat or watch a bit of TV. Tonight was no different except for the fact that Sophia wasn't much interested in conversation.

"Oh, it's nothing," she said. Sophia propped herself up on her elbows. All evening she'd managed to avoid this conversation but she'd suddenly gotten tired of changing the subject so she let slip, "I've just been getting a bit of flack at work and I'm not sure what to do about it." She regretted it instantly.

"What kind of flack?" She could feel Phil's eyes staring at her in the darkness.

"Well, I had a production meeting with Bill this morning and he hinted that perhaps my ratings were slumping a bit. I mean, he didn't say it in those exact words but I got his meaning."

"That's funny." Phil leaned over and turned on the bedside light. "He didn't say anything to me when we played golf last week."

"You talk about me with Bill?" Stunned that Phil would discuss her work with her boss over golf, Sophia sat up straight.

"Well, yeah."

"Oh, great!" Sophia shook her head and got up, heading for the bathroom. "That's fantastic, Phil! Do you also discuss how often we sleep together?"

"Well, no not exactly but—"

Sophia swung around and stared at Phil. "Oh, my God, Phil. You're kidding, right?"

"Of course I am," he said in a conciliatory tone. Seeing how upset she had gotten, there was no way he was going to tell the truth. "I'm just kidding." In a gesture of surrender, he threw his arms up in the air. "So, shoot me for trying to make a joke."

Sophia turned and pushed open the bathroom door. Closing it hard behind her, she stood in front of the sink and stared at herself in the mirror. A slight shudder went through her body. She felt that sickening feeling well up inside her once again. She could hear the TV turn on in the bedroom as Phil searched for something distracting to watch.

This morning's meeting had gone worse than she had let on. It wasn't a production meeting at all. She had been called into Bill's office and blindsided by his factual tirade about the station's sinking ratings. She soon learned that she had been singled out to bear the responsibility for the downslide because she was the station's newest feature host and therefore, the most expendable. She had been told in no uncertain terms that she needed to up her profile significantly, and the station's ratings by the end of the quarter, or she would not be welcomed back after Christmas. Sophia had left the meeting assuring Bill that all would be well. She had promptly gone to the private women's bathroom on the second floor and vomited.

All her hard work over the last eight months had not seemed to impress anyone at work. Even if it had, as she suspected, she was obviously being used as a scapegoat for factors out of her control. Sophia had left work early that day and aimlessly driven around the city until a call from Phil had steered her in the direction of their favourite restaurant. She had managed to pull herself together during dinner and figured she'd done a pretty good job hiding her true feelings while they were in bed. But Phil's so-called joke had cleaved her façade and broken her wide open.

Sophia turned on the tap and splashed some cold water on her face. Her hands trembled as she ran her fingers through her dark hair. She felt hot tears, then pain well up in her chest. An unexpected gasp ripped from her throat.

"Babe? You okay in there?" Phil shouted over the sound of the TV.

Quickly wiping her face with a damp cloth, Sophia replied, "Yeah, I'll be out in a sec."

Feeling a chill run through her body, she pulled on her terry robe and cinched it tight at the waist. Looking back at the mirror, she blinked slowly and tried to smile. She didn't want Phil to know how she was truly feeling. If he knew how often she struggled with anxiety and lack of confidence, he would leave her for sure. Even though he wasn't the perfect partner, he was better than being alone. But that was a copout and she knew it.

"That's better," he said, smiling from the bed and patting the pillow next to him. "I saved you a spot."

Sophia settled herself on top of the duvet and leaned back against his outstretched arm.

"Look, babe, I'm sorry. I didn't want to upset you but maybe it isn't a bad thing that I talk to Bill. I get inside info sometimes, which isn't so terrible, right?"

Sophia remained closemouthed next to him.

"I mean, don't forget who got you the job in the first place, right?"

Sophia turned and looked him in the face. "Got me the job?" she said with incredulity. "Got me the job? I got me the job, Phil. You told me about the opening but I was the one who sat through those exhausting interviews and made nice during that awful dinner with Bill. You got me nothing except an introduction."

Pulling his arm out from behind her and grabbing the channel changer, he said, "I wouldn't be so sure about that."

"What do you mean?"

"Well . . ." Phil wasn't looking at her but staring at the TV with feigned interest as he slowly surfed through the channels. "Think about it, Sophia. Why would Urban TV hire a, excuse the term, 'nobody,' whose only real experience was as the weather girl at some small-town cable station?" He glanced back at her with a raised eyebrow.

"I'd like to think it was because they saw my potential."

Phil guffawed. "Oh, come on, Sophia. You're not that naïve, are you? Didn't you ever stop to think that maybe, just maybe, it had something to do with someone pulling a few strings for you?"

"And that someone was you, I take it?" she said with a slight tone of annoyance.

"Bingo. See, you're not as naïve as I thought you were." He smiled and patted her leg, still staring at the TV.

"You're a bastard, Phil."

"Yes, that's true. I am a bastard, at least that's what a lot of people tell me," he said, raising a finger, "but I'm a bastard with a fairly healthy bank account. I also happen to know a lot of important and influential people and," he paused for emphasis, "I ain't bad in bed either, right?"

Sophia could feel herself go cold. Why did she put up with this? I really should kick him out. Instead, she just lay there frozen, the hard reality of his words ringing in her ears.

"Look, babe, I don't want to upset you. You're obviously under a lot of stress at work. But maybe there's something I can do, you know, to help." He flavoured his patronizing tone with just enough niceness to have it mistaken for genuine concern.

Sophia didn't say anything. Today, had been a roller coaster ride and she felt like she still had not yet hit the final straight stretch.

Phil sighed and looked back to the TV. Without waiting for a reply, he said, "What you need is something high profile. Something that exposes you to a national audience with the possibility of syndication."

Finally coming out of her daze, Sophia said, her voice now bitter, "Since when did you become such a media expert?"

"Since most of our clients are in the media biz. I've been in the legal profession long enough to know that it pays to know your client's business, inside and out." Giving her thigh a quick squeeze, he continued, "Look, Sophia, it's no skin off my teeth but if you want to impress Bill and the gang, you need to do something pretty special."

"What?" Her voice was getting louder. "Like sleep with him?" Sophia almost choked on the words.

Phil threw his head back and laughed. Shaking his head, he turned to Sophia and smiled. "Listen, Sophia, I don't give a shit who you sleep with but frankly, I think it's below you to go that route."

Sophia turned away and clutched her housecoat close to her chest.

"I mean it, Sophia. You can listen to me or not but whatever you do is your choice."

"Damn right."

Phil sighed. Aimlessly flipping through the channels, he suddenly stopped. A sly smile spread over his face. He quickly glanced at Sophia, who was still lying propped up against her pillow with arms crossed angrily over her chest.

"Look, Sophia. Let me spell it out to you, as I see it."

"Go right ahead. It's not like I can stop you or anything."

"All right then. One: You're about to lose your job. Two: You're talented as hell and three: I have the perfect solution for you."

Phil turned up the volume of the TV. "Look. That," he said, gesturing towards the now-blaring TV, "is the answer to your prayers, hon."

Staring at the TV, Sophia didn't get it. It was a repeat episode of the popular Maurice and Nate show. They were interviewing a designer about her new fall collection of handbags.

"See? Those guys are big. Their show is seen by millions. I happen to know," he paused for dramatic effect, "that they're planning a Christmas special this year."

Still not understanding how this all tied into her current problem, Sophia snapped, "And this is important because—?"

"Because according to one of my clients, who happens to provide their on-set clothing, they're looking for celebrities to contribute content to their special: namely, celebrities offering family Christmas recipes. You know, that cozy shit that people go bonkers for at that time of year."

"Oh, come on, Phil," Sophia scoffed. "When was the last time you saw me in the kitchen?" This was just plain stupid, she thought.

"I know you can't cook or bake, Sophia, but they," he said, pointing at the screen, "don't know that. And my lips are sealed." He smiled contentedly.

"That's all fine and good, Phil, however, there's one important ingredient missing in your fancy-pants equation."

"Gee, and I thought I'd had it all figured out," he said slyly.

"What the hell am I supposed to offer up as a cherished family recipe? My mother was a lousy cook. Baking was something we picked up at the local grocery store."

"Ah, yes," Phil said, "that may be true but what about that old friend of yours out west. What's her name — Kate? Isn't she supposed to be some kind of baking genius?"

Sophia turned slowly and looked at Phil. "I don't think that's such a great idea. The last time I talked to Kate was a couple of years ago." Her voice trailed off as she stared down at her clenched hands.

"Oh, right. I remember now: you didn't go to her fiancé's funeral, right? Yeah, that's a bit of a bitch. Not sure how you're going to fan the flames of friendship after that snub."

Completely oblivious to Sophia's cold stare, Phil plunged onwards with his plan. "But who said you had to talk to her? You could probably get around that by just remembering one of her recipes, couldn't you? I mean, you guys lived together, right? Don't tell me your journalistic powers of observation were vacant in those days." Phil chuckled and turned the volume down on the TV.

"You mean, totally cheat?"

"Yeah, why not?"

"Because that's not what I do. Besides, if I did manage to remember one of her recipes, I'd have to ask Kate for permission and she would probably say no. Those recipes are like her babies."

"Okay then. Don't ask."

"You mean steal a recipe? You're really joking now, right?"

"No, I'm totally serious. I have no idea how you're going to get a recipe of hers but trust me, babe," said Phil, who was now standing and heading towards the bathroom, "that," he tapped the TV screen as he walked past, "is the answer to your prayers."

"And here I thought you were," Sophia said dully.

"Yeah, right. I may be the best thing you've slept with in years but I'm smart enough to know that I'm certainly not the answer to all your prayers." Phil closed the bathroom door abruptly.

Sophia shot Phil her middle finger, sighed, and stared up at the television. It flickered bright and dark and the images slowly began to blur. She closed her eyes and sunk her head into the pillow. The voices of

Maurice and Nate swirled around her. Her thoughts went unexpectedly to the shoebox full of mementoes that she kept under the stairs in her storage room. Amidst the old concert ticket stubs and fading Polaroid shots from her high-school days, she knew there was a stained and dog-eared, postcard-sized recipe card, one of her secret souvenirs from her college days. Maybe Kate wouldn't really mind. It was just a recipe. It could mean the difference between a career and no career. She'd understand, wouldn't she?

~ ~

"Oh, my God, you mean that wasn't your own gingerbread recipe?" Marcie blurted out as she and Sophia sat drinking coffee in the living room after dinner. "You know, when that Christmas special aired, it was the first time I ever saw you!"

Marcie set her coffee cup down on the table. "I remember it like yesterday. Ted and I were sitting right here on this couch. I forced him to watch it because I was planning on having a Christmas party that year. I thought I could get some good ideas on decorating and cooking."

"Yeah, well now you know. I'm a total and utter fraud. And a terrible friend. I should have called her more after Ben died. I should have shown up for the funeral. Done something." Sophia had cried herself out hours ago but she still hung her head down in self-defeat.

"Oh, come on, Sophia. People make mistakes." Marcie wrinkled her brow. "Trust me, after my parents passed away, I heard nothing from a number of people. I now understand that some people simply can't handle death. They love you to pieces but just don't know what to do or say when someone passes away. The fact that you were living in Toronto and wound up in your career doesn't totally excuse you from expressing your sympathy or flying out for the funeral. But it's reasonable to understand why you weren't available to her."

"We did talk for a bit when she called to give me the bad news and I did send a card and flowers to the funeral. . ."

"I'm glad you did. See? You weren't totally unsympathetic." Reaching down, Marcie placed her hand on Sophia's and gave it a quick squeeze.

"Let's hope that when you become good friends again, you can clear the air on that particular topic. Although you 'borrowed' the recipe, it did boost your career, didn't it?" She smiled at Sophia. "Maybe Kate was secretly happy for you. Who knows?"

"Oh, I seriously doubt that. Did you know that her cookie recipe went viral after that?"

"No, what do you mean?"

"Almost every food blogger on the planet re-posted that episode clip on their blog along with the recipe. Of course, they gave me the entire credit for it. I was interviewed by no fewer than six different lifestyle magazines. I even got a cook book offer from one of the major publishing houses in New York."

"Oh, my God! All because of that recipe?"

"Yup. And Kate must have known. Foodies know foodies and I'm sure word spread quickly. Worst of all, I did absolutely nothing to give her the credit she deserved or explain to her why I did it in the first place. At least, not at that moment. I was so caught up in the flurry of attention that I almost started to believe that the gingerbread recipe was indeed an old family secret that I, in all my wisdom, had decided to share with the world. God, Marcie, if you knew my two grandmothers, you would know that baking cookies was either impossible, improbable or impractical for either one of them."

"But have you tried since then to apologize and explain everything to Kate?" Marcie looked sympathetically at Sophia.

"Yes. Many times, but I keep screwing up. It's like I start to explain myself and then I say something stupid like I did today on the phone to her."

"What did you say?"

"Well, we're planning this extended shoot about the Shaughnessy Garden Show—"

"Oh, I love that Garden Show! I go every year, rain or shine. They have the best displays." Realizing she'd cut Sophia off, Marcie bit her lip and said, "Sorry. Go ahead. What's up with the shoot?"

"Kate and I crossed paths because of the show. I was looking for a new topic and stumbled across a little poster hanging at the coffee shop down the street from my place. It was advertising a garden club meeting. Anyways, I show up, and not that Kate was there, but I found out that she was a regular member. Long story short: I plunge ahead with the idea of doing an episode on the Garden Show, with a focus on this particular garden club's participation, maybe even a mention or two about her bakery. In the back of my mind, I figured it would be a great way to reconnect with Kate but it has gone from bad to worse in less than a week."

Shaking her head, Sophia glanced at her watch. "Look, I've been keeping you far too long and Ted is probably due home any minute. I should really go."

"You don't have to go. Ted can always set up shop in the basement. Besides, he likes it down there in his man cave." Marcie smiled. She didn't think she should let Sophia go just yet. They hadn't really gotten to solving the problem.

"You just stay where you are. We need to figure out a plan of attack. Sorry, bad choice of words." Getting up from the couch, Marcie continued, "There has got to be a solution to this and I am not letting you go until we figure one out. Solutions require ice cream so I'll be right back, okay, sweetie?" Marcie walked past her and into the kitchen. Sophia acquiesced easily. She needed somebody to figure this one out because she had run out of ideas.

"Besides," shouted Marcie from the kitchen, "I wouldn't mind a free ticket to the Shaughnessy Garden Show. So, if I can figure something out, maybe you can swing it?"

"Sure," shouted Sophia. She thought to herself, *If you can figure this one out, Marcie, I'll buy you a lifetime pass to the gardens. I'm sure George*

Stanwell could use the money.

Chapter Twenty-one

Oma's Baking Tip

If a recipe states "Mix until just combined," believe it. Overmixing can make your dough tough, chewy, and dry.

It was Friday evening and Kate was famished. She always looked forward to her Friday- night sushi dinners with George and Richard. Even though it was pouring rain outside, she had managed to arrive on time. Her two friends, however, were now fashionably late. By the time George and Richard had entered the restaurant, Kate was sitting, shoeless and comfortable, in their usual booth. She heard them before she saw them; this evening's discussion centred on Richard's new camel-hair coat.

"I told you it wasn't practical," George said in a scolding tone. "It'll be ruined before the spring is up."

"And I told you before, I don't care if it's practical. I bought it because I like it and it's warm. Even though I'm smart enough to know that it doesn't rain in the desert, I have the fullest confidence that this camel hair will weather the deluge just fine."

Peeking his head through the panelled curtain, Richard whispered to avoid surprising her, "Hi, Kate."

George flung back the curtain dramatically. "I'm sure there's no need to whisper. She probably heard your dissertation on the wicking abilities of camel hair all the way back here from the front of the restaurant. Right, Kate?" George winked.

"Right." She smiled and looked at her watch. "You two are late. What's up?"

Having removed his shoes and coat, Richard slid in on the opposite side.

"Old man Stanwell is still smarting from his lamp incident and the going is a bit slower than usual."

"I certainly am not!" piped George from the edge of the booth, where he was untying his shoes. "I can walk perfectly fine. It's just that Mr. Rush-along here has no time to dally because his precious new coat was getting wet in the rain."

"Oh, come on, you two. Give it a rest. At this rate, you'll be divorced before you even get a chance to celebrate your third anniversary. I didn't spend countless hours making your wedding cake for nothing, you know."

Any mention of their wedding was always a good smoother-over because both Richard and George got sentimental when it came to memories of that day. George now shuffled over to Richard's side and gave his hand a squeeze.

"You're right. Enough bickering." George leaned over and gave Kate a peck on the cheek. "And you, my darling, how are you?" George was mostly asking this question for Richard's benefit; he already knew how Kate was doing since they'd spent over an hour on the phone Wednesday evening after Sophia's phone call to the shop.

"Yes, how are you doing?" repeated Richard. "George wouldn't tell me much. He just said that you had a call from Sophia after their meeting, which by the way," he looked sternly at George, "I still don't think was handled well."

"Don't start up again." George looked disapprovingly at Richard. "We've already discussed this ad nauseam and what's done is done. She deserved to hear the truth and as far as I'm concerned, I was doing her a favour by letting her know."

Richard shook his head in disbelief. Sometimes there was no getting through to George.

Kate broke into the conversation. "So, did you want to know what she said or not?" She smiled coyly at George. "Because as much as I hate to admit it, George was actually right."

Turning slowly, George smiled smugly at Richard. "See, I told you."

The waitress Hanako appeared, kneeled on the edge of the booth, and bowed.

"Good evening. Would you like menus or same as usual?" Hanako smiled sweetly at the small group. They had been coming regularly to Sakura Sushi for some time and often ordered the same dishes. Once in a while, they liked to try something new so Hanako had gotten into the habit of always asking beforehand.

Bowing his head slightly, George smiled back. "Thank you, Hanako." Glancing quickly at Kate and getting a nod of approval, he continued. "I think we'll go with the usual tonight except could you please bring a small bottle of saké? We have a little something to celebrate."

Bowing again, Hanako left as quietly as she came, closing the cloth panels behind her.

Richard was now intrigued and goaded Kate to continue with her story.

"So, what's the big mystery?"

"Well, not so much a mystery but more a revelation. George already told you that while we were talking in the bakery, Sophia called all of a sudden." Kate looked off above their heads, slightly distracted. "I certainly wasn't expecting it."

"Well, who would?" asked George. "Especially considering how she had behaved in my office and then storming out, pretending to be so upset and all."

Richard stared at George. "You didn't tell me that part."

"Yes, I did. I told you that she got up and left all of a sudden. She didn't even finish the coffee that Stacey had brought her. And she didn't take one bite out of those delicious tarts either."

"Okay, wait just a second." Richard's exasperation was cracking through the surface. "You didn't say anything about tarts. What tarts? No offense," he said, glancing quickly at Kate, "but hopefully not some of Kate's?"

George and Kate looked at each other and George began to giggle. Shrugging his shoulders, he said, "It wasn't me who brought them in."

"This is just going from bad to worse. Will somebody please tell me exactly what happened?" Richard looked eagerly at both of them.

"Alright, alright." George started to use one of his chopsticks as a kind of conductor's wand, tapping the table to punctuate each successive point. "Let's see. Stacey brought Sophia into my office, asked if she wanted coffee, and left. Sophia and I had a little discussion and then she stealthily put me off-kilter by showing me her fancy shoes."

"That'll do it every time," Richard with a smirk.

"No, really, you should have seen those shoes. Anyways, after we got all chummy, she started to pummel me with questions about how I got my job and about the financial state of affairs at the garden. Then she switched gears and flat out insulted me with a rather homophobic observation about you and I."

"Homophobic? What did she say exactly?" Richard was now curious. He didn't know Sophia at all but "homophobe" was not a label he would readily attach to her.

Defensively, George continued, "Well, she mentioned you as my husband and that 'it was nothing to be ashamed of.'"

"Really? She said that?" Richard's eyebrows knitted together and he looked quizzically at Kate. "Does she have a problem with us? I would never have thought that."

"I don't know. I wouldn't have thought that either. But once you hear the whole story, you might begin to question your ideas about her too."

"May I finish?" George asked calmly.

"Yes, yes. Okay." Richard sighed and ran a hand through his thick black hair.

"So, that kind of did it for me and then I let her have it. The truth, that is."

"And the truth was what exactly?" asked Richard.

"The truth," George continued in a measured tone, "was that although I didn't respect her and suspected her to be a total fraud, I was willing to overlook these things and work together with her on this little project of hers."

"Really. How pleasant of you." Richard wasn't sounding impressed.

"Yes, really." Sitting up straighter, George smiled proudly. "And that's when Stacey, bless her heart, appeared with the tarts."

"Kate's tarts?" Richard looked to Kate.

"Yes. I guess someone from George's office stopped by in the morning and bought some Georgie-Porgie pies." Kate looked down and straightened the chop sticks that lay in front of her. "They ended up in front of Sophia."

"I thought it was a brilliant stroke of luck. You see, it gave me the perfect opportunity to let haughty Ms. Simpson in on the fact that I knew everything about her and that Kate and I were the best of friends." With a feeling of self-satisfaction, George played out a drum roll on the table with the tips of his chopsticks. "That's when she abruptly excused herself and left. Strangely enough, I haven't heard from her since."

"And you're proud of that?" Richard was sometimes taken aback by George's lack of sensitivity and simple glee at the cost of others' feelings. He didn't do it often but enough to make Richard inwardly cringe with embarrassment.

"Well, not exactly proud but certainly, my load has been lightened." George leaned back and gestured towards Kate. "And before you go prosecuting me for bad behaviour, I ask you, dear barrister, to hear the testimony of our dear Kate, who I am sure will now convince you that

Ms. Sophia Simpson is indeed all that we suspected and therefore, undeserving of our trust and friendship."

"Oh, my God. You really missed your calling." Richard looked to Kate for some relief.

Kate shrugged her shoulders. "As dramatic as George is—"

"Hey! That's not fair." George leaned forward.

"Sorry." Looking towards Richard, she continued, "He's right, Richard. Sophia hasn't changed a bit. She called me later that day and tried to explain what had happened in George's office."

"Did she have a decent explanation?" Richard hoped Kate's news was a little more sensible.

"Not exactly. It sounded more like excuses. But the worst part was . . ." Kate stopped for a moment and looked down. George reached over and touched her hand. He knew what was coming and wanted her to go on.

"She made a really bad attempt at apologizing for everything and then," Kate swallowed hard, "she said that she was planning on doing a side story about the bakery and she wanted to feature. . ." Kate stopped suddenly. Her emotions were still close to the surface. George squeezed her hand.

"Go on, Kate. Tell him," George urged softly.

Taking a second to gather her thoughts, she continued. "She wanted to feature my BLT Brownies. Talk about Ben. She said it would help business."

With indignation, George looked to Richard. "Okay, if that's not enough to convince you that this woman is bad news, then I don't know what is."

"Your saké." Hanako appeared out of nowhere, tray in hand, with a warm carafe of saké and three small ceramic cups.

George turned and smiled. "Perfect timing."

Hanako carefully poured each cup, then handed them, one by one, to each guest. With a quick bow, she was gone.

"And so, I propose a toast." George lifted his cup in the air, "Here's to letting go of the old. And here's to friendship." Smiling at Kate, he continued, "True friendship."

Kate smiled back. They all downed their drinks. No sooner had they swallowed than Richard started up again.

"Okay, so, I still don't get it."

"Oh, my God, Richard." George turned in his seat. "What don't you get? I would think it's pretty clear: Sophia has not changed her ways and once again, she's disappointed our poor Kate and strung her along. I'd have thought you were smart enough to figure that one out."

Keeping his tone even and focussing on Kate, Richard continued, "If Sophia is such a manipulative person and so 'out to get you,' why does she continue to try and have contact with you?"

Shrugging her shoulders, Kate replied, "Well, I can only assume that she's getting some kind of thrill out of it. Either that or she sees me, the garden club, the bakery, I don't know, as some kind of stepping stone to her career."

"That doesn't make sense." Richard set his cup down and looked at George. "Now, before you go all off on me again, consider the facts: one, Sophia Simpson is, whether you both want to admit it or not, a rather large celebrity who certainly doesn't need to step on any one of us to advance her career."

"Yes, but—" interjected George with a finger raised in the air.

"Let me finish." Richard continued, "and two: it seems highly unlikely that someone who has wronged you in the past, and I will admit that her previous behaviour was less than stellar, would suddenly come out of the woodwork to begin doing it again. Sophia is not a sociopath and I highly doubt, despite her shortcomings, that she gets some kind of pleasure out of your misery."

Kate looked down at her empty cup. Pushing it over to George, she said, "Can I have some more?"

"Sure, honey. See?" Turning to Richard, "Your lousy explanation is driving her to drink."

Richard smiled. "I highly doubt that. So, to conclude, I put forth an alternative reasoning. I believe that Sophia is trying her best to reconnect with you but, and there is a big 'but' here, she doesn't know how."

"Oh, come on, Richard," snapped George. "Doesn't know how? This is a woman who makes her living communicating with people. Why the hell wouldn't she know how to communicate with Kate? And let's not forget her homophobic remark!"

"I'll get to that in a second. Listen, Sophia is an onscreen personality. Yes, she makes her living interviewing people from all walks of life but what is her personal life like?" Turning to George, Richard asked, "Didn't you tell me that her boyfriend had left her?"

"Yes, I did. Isn't that right, Kate?"

"As far as I know, Phil left her for another woman," Kate said softly.

"And does she have anyone else?" asked Richard.

"I have no idea," replied Kate distractedly. "Probably not."

"And why not?" asked Richard.

"Because her career is too important to her to develop any relationships." The truth spilled out of Kate so quickly, she surprised herself.

"Exactly!" Richard looked at both of them expectantly. "Don't you see?"

"See what?" said George, taking a sip of his second cup of saké.

"Her career has been too important for her to develop any meaningful relationships." He said it slowly, hoping the logic would settle in. Kate picked up on it right away.

"You mean to say that now that her career has taken off, she wants to improve her personal life?"

"Yes, I do." Richard smiled. "And you are the first name on her list."

Even George was quiet now. There was some sense to what Richard was saying, but neither he nor Kate was ready to admit it.

"And what about the remark she made in my office about you and me?" George was still smarting about that one.

174

"Are you absolutely sure she was referring to you and me? Didn't you say she also mentioned something about our contribution to the restoration fund? Could that have been what she was referring too instead?"

With eyes lifted to the ceiling, George was mentally recalling the conversation.

"Well, if that was what she was referring to, then she meant it in a," he stumbled across the words, "nice way."

"Maybe she did."

George looked at Kate, who was staring at her empty saké cup. Not wanting to lose his conspiracy-theory accomplice, he quickly said, "No. I simply don't believe it. She's got other motives and I can't believe that her intentions have been good. Right, Kate?"

Kate looked up and smiled briefly at George, then looked at Richard. Shaking her head, she said, "You know, guys, I don't know what to think anymore. All I know is that I'm tired of all this back and forth. So, even if her intentions are good," she laid her palms flat on the table, "I'm not willing at this point to give her much more thought."

"Excuse me." Hanako's voice wafted in like a welcome soft breeze. "Your dinner is ready." Carrying a large tray, she set it down on the table and began to unload the plates of sushi and tempura onto the table. After she had carefully placed each dish in front of them, she bowed and left.

"I'm sorry if I upset you." Richard reached over and touched Kate's arm. "I just thought you might not have really considered all the angles."

"You're right. I haven't but I don't really want to talk about it anymore." Kate was getting that exhausted feeling again. Whenever she thought she had Sophia figured out, everything went topsy-turvy and she had to rethink her position. It was getting tiring. This evening was meant to be an enjoyable wind-down to the week with friends.

"Why don't you tell me about something else? What's going on at work these days?" Kate picked up a shrimp tempura and took a small bite, hoping that Richard would acquiesce and change the subject.

Taking his cue to leave the topic of Sophia alone, Richard scrambled for something to change the mood at the table. "Well," he said, "I'm really not supposed to talk about things but it's not that secret so," he leaned in closer, "one of our new clients," he nodded towards Kate, "is an acquaintance of yours."

"Really?" George always perked up when a bit of inside information was being leaked.

"Yes, I mean it's not that exciting, but we're handling the sale of the Varsity Grill. Seems Mr. Leung is thinking of retiring and there are no heirs, so he's considering liquidating the whole thing."

"No!" Kate almost dropped her tempura in the soy sauce. "The Varsity is such an old-time favourite hangout, it's like a city institution. If he closes, I won't have any place to go for Chinese."

"Seriously?" George laughed. "You live in Vancouver or did you forget?"

"I know that." Kate smiled, "But the Varsity. I love that place. I just went there the other night with the all of the bakery staff." Softening her tone, she continued, "Gosh, we used to practically live in that place when I was in college." Kate's next mouthful lingered at the end of her chopsticks.

"You did? With whom?" Richard picked up a spiced scallop roll and popped it in his mouth.

Kate was silent for a moment, then said, "With Sophia."

Richard felt George kick him under the table. Swallowing his mouthful quickly, he smiled weakly at Kate.

George leaned away from the table and pulled one of the curtain panels to the side, his voice cutting through the air.

"Hanako, honey? I think we're gonna need more saké!"

Chapter Twenty-two

Oma's Baking Tip

Use spotty bananas in your baking: they're sweeter and more flavourful.

They hardly had time to sit down before Mimi began to explain. All that the ladies knew was that Mimi had called each one of them the day before to let them know that she had some exciting news to share with them. She had said that they'd best show up for their regular crib game or they'd be missing out on something really big. Mimi loved to create suspenseful drama. She'd learned from the best, having been a loyal devotee of almost every syndicated soap opera since cable television had been introduced.

Barely able to control her excitement, Mimi almost spilled the jug of lemonade she had prepared but a quick grab by Ethel saved the day. Once they had all taken their normal seats around her dining room table, she began.

"I'd just like to remind you all before we begin that I was right." Mimi could barely suppress her glee. Margaret raised an eyebrow. Francine shrugged as she turned to Ethel to see if she knew what Mimi was talking about. Setting the lemonade atop a crocheted doily, Mimi continued, "I'm always right when it comes to things like this. I hope that in the future you will all at least acknowledge this fact without me having to constantly defend myself."

"What exactly are you talking about?" asked Margaret, holding out her glass to be filled. She'd been obsessing all day yesterday and this morning about Mimi's mysterious phone call and could hardly wait to get here today to hear the exciting news. She had practically run up the street from her house at the end of the block. Given her corpulent size, it had been more of a waddle than a sprint. She had still managed to arrive at precisely 1 p.m., their usual meeting time on Thursday afternoons. Margaret was parched and a sip of cool lemonade would hit the spot.

Mimi poured Margaret an almost overflowing glass, then continued around the table, dispensing the jug's contents into each remaining empty glass. Barely taking a moment to catch her breath, she spoke in a hushed tone. "I'm talking about Sophia Simpson! Did I not say the last time we met that her one-and-only purpose in showing up to our garden meeting a couple of weeks ago was to spy on us so that she could use that information to create some kind of defamatory show?"

"Well, yes, you did insinuate that." Francine sensed that Mimi was far from finished. She kept her comment short and quickly took a sip of her drink in hopes that the focus would be shifted away from her.

"Well, I'm here to tell you ladies that I was right!" As she slammed the empty jug on the table, the other three gave a start. Margaret began to choke on a half-swallowed mouthful. Willaweiner let out a sharp yelp and scurried, tail between her legs, to the sanctity of her plush-pillowed dog bed near the front door.

"Oh, Margaret, do get a hold of yourself." Mimi frowned, her painted eyebrows crinkling like crushed tissue paper. "It's exactly that kind of tottering old behaviour we are going to have to eradicate in order to appear young, fresh, and vibrant for Ms. Simpson."

"I'm sorry, Mimi," said Ethel, shaking her head as she finally spoke up, "but you aren't making any sense at all. Quite frankly, the suspense is killing us, so out with it already."

Mimi had them where she wanted them; she was delighted to know that they were all hanging on her every word. She slowly descended onto the seat of her chair at the head of the table and pointedly looked each one directly in the eye. Carefully and with as much punctuated emphasis as possible, she continued.

"I got a call from Ursula yesterday."

"Ursula? She actually called you?" Margaret was stunned. Ursula would normally never call Mimi. Their mutual dislike and distrust was blatantly obvious to anyone who had ever witnessed their garden club encounters.

"Yes, she did and we chatted rather nicely for quite some time."

"Really?" Francine raised an eyebrow. As Ursula's closest associate, Francine felt that surely she should have been the one to receive Ursula's phone call. Even though she had absolutely no idea what was discussed, she was visibly miffed. Feigning disinterest in the conversation, she started shuffling the deck of cards that lay in the middle of the table.

"Oh, the card game can wait." Mimi shot a firm look to Francine. "What I've got to tell you will surely sour any desire to play cards at this moment in time."

Francine gathered the cards together and meekly placed them back in the middle of the table. A moment of suspended silence hung in the air, then Mimi finally came out with it.

"Ursula wanted to warn us that Sophia Simpson is planning on having a film crew come to the volunteer meeting at the Shaughnessy Gardens next week and," she took a long, slow inhalation, "according to Ursula, we are to show up in our very best attire and be on our very best behaviour so that our garden club makes a good impression."

"Oh, my!" Ethel squeaked with excitement.

"But I don't have a hair appointment until the twenty-third. What am I supposed to do?" Margaret began rummaging through her purse, looking for her date book.

"Why didn't she call me with this news?" Francine was still smarting from the slight of not being the chosen one and hadn't yet fully realized the impact of Mimi's statement.

The three ladies began chattering amongst themselves, each excitedly talking over the other, while Mimi sat back in her chair and slowly sipped her lemonade. *They'll thank me soon enough,* she thought.

A few minutes passed. Finally, Margaret looked over to Mimi, who was contentedly nibbling on one of the devilled-egg sandwiches she had prepared with crusts removed on white bread. It was her favourite card-playing snack. Before Margaret could say something, Mimi wiped her lips with a paper napkin and said, "Yes, dear?" followed by a knowing smile.

"So, let me get this right." Ethel and Francine immediately stopped talking about the colour of skirts they were going to wear to listen to Margaret's question.

"Sophia Simpson will be showing up with an actual film crew to film us at the volunteer meeting?" Heart racing and barely catching her breath, Margaret quickly continued, "And we," she pointed around the table, "are going to be on TV? Real TV?" The last question came out so high-pitched with excitement that Willaweiner began to bark. She was only silenced after Mimi grabbed a handful of salted peanuts and tossed them into the hallway. The decidedly overweight miniature dachshund dashed after them.

"Yes, that's right. However, you are all forgetting the real motive behind this whole fiasco! I told you last time that I don't trust that Sophia Simpson and I still believe she has ulterior motives. As far as I'm concerned, she has no real intent of doing a nice little story about our garden club. Oh no, she's looking to dig a little deeper than that. In fact, I still strongly suspect that her real, true motive is to make one of those 'mockumentaries' and show us up as a bunch of doddering old fools."

"What's a mockumentary?" Francine whispered.

"Anything with the word 'mock' in it can't be good," Margaret huffed.

"I had mock chicken once and it wasn't very good at all. In fact, it was downright nasty."

"But why would you think that, Mimi? Sophia seemed like such a nice person." Ethel remembered her conversation with Sophia at the end of the garden club meeting last week and her willingness to return the umbrella to Kate the next day. "Don't you remember the umbrella?"

"Yes, interesting that you should mention that umbrella, Ethel," Mimi replied. "You see, I was talking with my friend Gloria the other day. You remember Gloria? She was the one I told you about whose husband left her for their Filipino maid, poor thing. Anyways, Gloria and I were having a chat while standing in line at the bank the other morning and she told me a very interesting story."

Taking a sip from her lemonade and sitting back in her chair, she continued, "Apparently, Sophia did turn up at Kate's Bakes the very next day with that pink umbrella in hand."

"See, I told you. She is a nice person!" Ethel crossed her arms and nodded contentedly.

"Ah yes, but according to Gloria, she wasn't so nice about how she actually returned it. You see, Gloria went into the bakery that morning to buy some low-fat muffins for her Weight Watchers group. She said that Sophia practically ran her over in an effort to get out of the shop quickly. According to Gloria, Sophia pretty much threw the umbrella at that handsome young man who works there, Joseph's his name, you know the one: good looking, not too short, nice teeth, and," Mimi added, taking a deep breath, "she stormed out of the store without leaving her name. Now, that is not what I call 'nice' behaviour."

Ethel remained silent while she pondered the reality of the situation as Mimi had presented it. The she spoke up. "Well, perhaps Gloria was mistaken or even overexaggerated the situation... You know what dieting can do, light-headiness and all."

"Most certainly not," replied a defiant Mimi, "because Gloria said that Joseph even commented to her, as he put her muffins in a box, that some people can be a bit bad-mannered in the morning but he always took it with a grain of salt. Now, why would he say that if she hadn't acted in a rude way?"

Stumped, Ethel said no more.

Margaret now spoke up. "So, let me get this straight. You believe that Sophia Simpson is setting us up? That she thinks she can get some kind of footage of us garden club members looking and acting old and feeble so that she can use this footage in a kind of mocking report on the state of the," she cleared her throat, "aged?"

"You have hit the nail on the head, my dear Margaret. Cupcake?" Mimi smiled broadly. Her theory had found resonance and now, at last, the real fun could begin.

"But it's simply not true!" sighed Francine. "We're not feeble old biddies. I like to think of us as active contributing members of society. Isn't that why we go to the garden club, to connect with others and beautify our own little patches of earth so that our whole community benefits? I still walk without a cane and do my own cleaning and laundry. I'm not some sorry old widow sitting in a wheelchair dribbling lukewarm soup down the front of my blouse!" Francine was getting really riled up. Mimi feared things might get out of hand.

"That is correct, Francine. You, me. . . why, all of us here are healthy, smart, active women who deserve much more respect than the likes of someone like Sophia Simpson is obviously willing to extend to us. " She paused for effect. "So, I have come up with a plan."

Ethel, who had remained silent while pondering this strange new image of Sophia, finally succumbed to the prevailing mood. "And what do you propose we do?" she asked.

Mimi grinned. She had managed to convince them all.

"Ladies, I say we go shopping!" Laying her hands on the table, she stood up and pushed her chair backwards. Willawiener, who had fallen asleep at her feet after her salty snack, was startled awake and let out a sharp bark.

"What? Right now?" Francine gestured at the table laid out for cards.

"Oh, the card game can wait. We need to do some serious shopping. I simply refuse to let any of you show up in something you've rummaged from the back of your closets. We need to show this Simpson woman that we are hip and trendy women so that her whole plan to show us up as withering old cronies is blown to Timbuktu. Besides, you all know how long it takes Ethel to find shoes, so let's get a move on."

Chapter Twenty-three

Oma's Baking Tip

Store your nuts in air-tight containers if possible — better yet, keep their shells on.

"It's just this way."

Stacey pointed down a long corridor to a set of double doors at the end. She didn't mind staying late this evening as it afforded her an opportunity to hobnob with Sophia Simpson, something she couldn't wait to brag about to her roommate, Vickie. She was a huge Sophia fan and couldn't believe it when Stacey came home two weeks ago bursting with pride that she'd actually met Sophia, even served her coffee and pastries. Tonight's escapades would surely keep Vickie entertained later for hours; she had even promised to do the cleaning for a month if Stacey was able to get her an autograph.

George had given Stacey the job of assisting Sophia and her crew with their set-up this evening. He would be showing up later, he said, because he didn't want to be bothered with the "technicalities" of orienting Sophia. After the recent revelations from Richard during their sushi dinner a while back, he was slightly hesitant to see Sophia again.

If he could avoid having to deal with her in a one-on-one situation, he would.

"Just be sure to be on your best behaviour and whatever you do, don't let her out of your sight," he had told Stacey. "I don't want her wandering off and getting lost." These had been his terse instructions before leaving for a quick dinner with a promise to return shortly before 7 p.m.

Stacey had interpreted his instructions as an honest concern for Sophia's welfare. She had neglected to note the slight tone of sarcasm in his voice. Pulling on the handle of the door, Stacey swung it open and kicked down the doorstop so that it stayed ajar. Reaching to her right, she flicked on a bank of switches. The small auditorium was illuminated in soft lighting.

"Oh, this is perfect," said Sophia as she turned to her cameraman Brian. "Maybe we can start here in the hallway, you know, getting a few comments from the volunteers as they trundle in. Then it'd be best for you two to set up in the corner down there." She gestured to a little alcove at the bottom of the stage. "That way, you can get some audience reaction and have a good shot of the speaker's positions. What do you think?"

"Sounds good." Brian set down one of the heavy reinforced cases he and Hank had carried with them from the parking lot. He pushed a hand through his thinning brown hair and hiked his jeans a little higher. "We'll have to go back and get the other boxes."

"I can get you a cart, if you like," piped Stacey. "It might make the trek a little easier."

"Oh, that's okay. We've got our own." Hank, the soundman from the crew, took the heavy loop of cable hanging over his shoulder and flung it onto the floor. Despite the tell-tale signs of middle age (short-cropped grey hair and a slight beer belly), Hank still had the strength of a much younger man.

Brian took the opportunity to wink at Stacey. "But you can come along anyways, sweetheart. Probably never seen the inside of a mobile sound truck, have you?"

Sophia chuckled to herself. She'd been working with Brian and Hank, one of Urban TV's best mobile crews, since last September. In that short time, Brian had never missed an opportunity to hit on any seemingly single young women he encountered. Sophia knew that he was harmless, like an annoying mosquito that kept buzzing around.

Feeling sure that Stacey could handle herself, Sophia walked into the auditorium and headed down the steps.

"You guys go on ahead. I'll just hang out here." She reached the bottom of the auditorium and stood staring at the darkened stage.

"Are you sure you'll be okay?" Stacey stood at the top of the steps. "Mr. Stanwell wanted to make sure that you had everything you needed." Remembering her promise to George, she looked back to see Brian and Hank heading down the hallway. Slightly deflated, she mumbled, "I should probably stay here with you, I guess?"

"Oh, I'll be fine." Turning and giving her a little wave, Sophia continued, "You go on with the guys. I'm sure they'll enjoy your company."

"Are you sure?" Not waiting for an answer, Stacey quickly turned and ran off to catch up with Brian and Hank. Her girlish laughter bounced off the walls of the empty hallway, then slowly faded as the three of them disappeared from sight.

Sophia turned and headed for the steps that led up to the stage. The auditorium, Stacey had told her, had been added to the gardens in the eighties and, aside from the gardens, was probably the most used part of the facility. This is where they held their master gardener classes as well as a regularly scheduled program of speakers throughout the year, which offered everything from talks on shade gardening to invasive plants.

As she climbed the steps to the stage, Sophia could feel a slight unsteadiness in her knees. Taking a deep breath, she stood in the darkness of centre stage and looked out to the empty hall. She instinctively pressed her right hand against her stomach, trying to quell the butterflies fluttering there. As she stood in the darkness, she reminded herself that this large space would soon be filled with quirky characters. People obsessed with plants. The kind of interesting people she loved to interview. So, perhaps tonight wouldn't be a bad experience after all.

Still, thoughts of what had transpired last week with George and her last conversation with Kate came rushing back in her head. The subsequent plans, hashed out with Marcie over the remaining scoops of ice cream, had made her feel even more uneasy. Tonight was the night those plans would go into effect. Hopefully, if all went well and neither one of them screwed up, she and Marcie would be able to rebuild her crumbled relationship with Kate.

Sophia still wasn't a hundred percent convinced that it would work. She'd even had second thoughts the next morning and had approached her production manager about putting the whole garden show project on the back burner. Vince had simply said no. When Sophia had first approached him with the idea a couple of weeks back, he thought the show had real merit. Because he was convinced it would be a winning episode, he told her to continue as planned.

So, Sophia had followed his directive as well as succumbing to Marcie's "plan of attack." It would be a great piece, she knew, but now, following the plan that she and Marcie had agreed on, Sophia would approach the entire project from a purely businesslike point of view. No more trying to convince Kate of the merits of rebuilding their friendship. That job would be left to Marcie. All in good time.

Sophia heard voices in the hallway. Not wanting to appear like an actor giving a soliloquy at centre stage, she moved off to the right with the intention of heading down the steps to the first row of seats.

"Oh, I see they've already arrived." George's voice was clear and clipped. "Hopefully, they haven't left her wandering around here somewhere. All I need now is for that woman to pop out unexpectedly."

Acting on instinct, Sophia quickly ducked behind the curtains at stage right. It looked like she might have already managed to fail at step one of the plan. According to Marcie, Sophia had to take the initiative of apologizing to George, even though there was really nothing to apologize for. Marcie recognized that George Stanwell was an important figure in winning over Kate's trust. He was like a surly gatekeeper who needed to be treated with respect, flattered wherever possible, and convinced of Sophia's sincere intentions above all costs. Marcie said she knew George's type well, having worked in the theatre business for many years before "retiring" to the regular hours, benefits, and salaried pay offered by the television studio.

"He's just a pussy cat, I bet," Marcie had said as she carefully instructed Sophia last week between mouthfuls of chocolate swirl ice cream. "He'll be very distrustful at first but if you treat him nice, drop a flattering remark or two and give him what he wants, which is probably a piece of the spotlight, you'll have him won over in no time. Trust me. I knew a guy just like him when I worked at the Maple Leaf Theatre. Stanley could be the moodiest guy around but if you were nice to him, complimented his looks, you know, fed his ego a little bit, he was like a kitty on catnip."

"Well, it doesn't look like there's anybody else in here so they probably all went together on a tour." Richard walked past George and into the auditorium. He threw his coat over the back of a seat. "So, what time is Kate supposed to show up?"

"She said around 7 p.m. The meeting is supposed to start at eight but she wanted to get here early so that we could go over our notes and deal with this film crew."

Tapping his toe on one of the boxes that Brian had set down, George continued, "I'm shocked that they would just dump their equipment here without anybody looking out for it. If this is what I think it is, this stuff is expensive."

Taking a deep breath and knowing that she had to overcome her fear, Sophia stepped out from behind the curtain. "That's what I'm here for."

Jumping back and clutching his chest, George let out a little shriek.

"Oh, for the love of God, woman, you just about gave me a coronary!"

"Don't be so silly, George." Richard started to walk down the steps towards the stage. Arm extended, he reached up to shake Sophia's hand. "Hello. You must be Sophia Simpson. I'm Richard O'Connor."

Disarmed by his calm self-introduction, Sophia suddenly felt much more at ease.

"Pleased to meet you." Kneeling slightly, she took his hand. Sensing the awkwardness of her position, she stood up. Straightening her navy-blue pencil skirt, she smiled down at him. "I guess I should come down there."

Turning away from Richard, Sophia quickly walked over to the short staircase at the side of the stage. In the meantime, George had made his way down the auditorium steps and now stood beside Richard, arms crossed and looking slightly perturbed.

Still smarting from the sudden shock, George had hoped his first encounter with Sophia would have been a bit more controlled. He hated looking the fool.

"I see you two have now met?"

"Yes, and I must say, George," said Richard, turning and smiling brightly at Sophia, "you were absolutely right. Sophia is even more gorgeous in person than she is on TV."

Sophia's eyes widened. Somehow, she couldn't imagine George having confided something like that. But at this moment, she was willing to accept any comment that made this awkward situation bearable. She sensed that perhaps Richard was trying his best to do the same. In an instant, camaraderie had developed between the two of them.

Preferring to take the neutral approach, George smiled tersely, then swept past Sophia and up onto the stage.

"You don't happen to know where Stacey is, do you?" His question lingered in the air as he disappeared behind the thick curtain. Suddenly, the stage was flooded with light.

"She's gone back to the sound truck with a couple of my guys to help them carry in the rest of the equipment. They should be back any moment now." Sophia looked at Richard, then shrugged her shoulders. In a hushed tone, she said, "I'm guessing she was probably supposed to stay with me?"

"I guess," said Richard with a grin. "But not to worry. I'll get George busy doing other stuff. You just do your thing and don't worry about him."

Sophia appreciated Richard's "inside help." After quietly thanking him, she started up the steps of the auditorium and out the door in search of Stacey and her crew.

Coming out onto the stage, George stared at Richard and sputtered, "So, where the hell did she go now?"

"She's gone to find her crew. Look, George. We talked about this before we came. You have got to stop being so disagreeable. Let her do her job. Stay out of her way and above all, try to be civil. It won't hurt, you know. Remember, she's doing the gardens a huge favour by shooting this. It will bring in a lot of needed attention and if you play your cards right, it could be the saving grace you need to keep the show afloat."

"I know. I know. It's just that I told Stacey not to leave her alone and we come in here to find her traipsing about all by herself. Or didn't you happen to notice that she was obviously spying on us from behind that curtain?"

"She wasn't spying. She probably went up on the stage to check out the lighting or something and we surprised her."

"Whatever." George waved a hand of dismissal. "I see it's taken mere seconds for you to succumb to her womanly ways."

Moving off the stage, George headed past Richard and back up the steps to the auditorium doors. "I have to find out where Boris is. He's supposed to set up the podium and the mikes. Can you wait here for Kate and let her know that I'll be right back?"

"Yes, dear."

George huffed and disappeared out the door. Richard planned to take a seat near the auditorium entrance so that he could see Kate as soon as she walked down the hallway. As he propped the second door open to get a better view, he heard a voice calling down the hallway to him.

"Hello? Young man?"

Richard turned to see a slightly portly woman teetering down the hallway on shoes that were either too tight or too high or both. Waving frantically with one arm, the other cradling a large tote bag, Ursula cried out again, "Would you be so kind as to give me some assistance?"

Richard rushed forward. Before he knew it, the oversized bag containing what he thought was this woman's personal rock collection was thrust upon him as she linked her arm in his for stability.

"I appreciate your assistance." Puffing loudly, she managed to take a deep breath and compose herself before they continued towards the auditorium.

Richard was immediately engulfed in a cloud of floral perfume. It reminded him of his third-grade teacher Miss Vivian, who had had a penchant for strongly scented floral perfume and bright pink lipstick. She had also liked to kiss the boys in his class, Richard included, on the cheek. Richard hoped inwardly that his small gesture of kindness today would not be rewarded in the same way.

"Are you volunteering for the garden show?"

They were moving at a more manageable pace and had almost reached the open auditorium doors.

"Actually, no," Richard said, "I'm just here to help a friend."

"Oh, and who might she be?"

She's a nosy one, thought Richard. Realizing that no harm could come from keeping an elderly lady entertained, he continued, "Actually it's a he. George Stanwell."

Richard felt the woman stiffen as she tore her arm away from his. Her demeanour changed instantly as she looked up at him with an unabashed look of disdain.

"Oh, I see. Well, thank you for your help, young man." Ursula ungraciously grabbed the bag from his other arm and slung it onto one of the auditorium seats. "I'll just wait here then for someone else to turn up."

Feeling like he'd just been given the royal snub, Richard did his best to be kind. "I'm sure someone will be along soon enough." Smiling, he turned and ventured out of the auditorium in search of better company.

Adjusting the glasses on her nose, Ursula glanced backwards as the sound of Richard's footsteps faded down the corridor. *You'd best get yourself under control*, she thought. *There will most likely be other George Stanwell peons hanging about this evening and you do wish to make a good impression, don't you?*

Taking a seat in the back row and turning slightly so that she could see out the open auditorium doors, Ursula felt grateful for the call she had received last week from Sophia's assistant, Genevieve. She had let her know that a film crew would be on hand for tonight's meeting. That had allowed Ursula just enough time to have her hair done and go shopping for a new tweed outfit as well as a pair of raised loafers that were, unfortunately, causing her some discomfort this evening. Yet, she was determined not to let the searing pain in her right foot hinder her ability to perform for the camera in a professional and stately manner.

A few minutes after the call, Ursula had immediately gotten in touch with Mimi and passed on the news about the camera crew's pending appearance. Choosing Mimi was strategic and slightly brilliant, she mused. It saved her having to make countless calls to various board members and garden club members at large. Being the gossip that she was, Mimi would spread the word faster than Ursula could ever hope to do. Ursula had conveniently neglected to reveal to Mimi the planned extent of Sophia's episode on the garden club as she did not wish to overwhelm Mimi with the facts. Mimi had her uses and keeping the lid on any insider information was certainly not in her repertoire. *No*, Ursula thought, *best to slowly feed her tidbits of information than toss all the cards on the table at once.*

Ursula had been sure, however, to press upon Mimi the importance of letting all the garden club members know that their outward appearance for the volunteer meeting was critical. Showing up in gumboots or mud-stained rain slickers would be frowned upon. Ursula hoped only that their collective imaginings of appearing in an episode of Stories from the Street would spur them on, not only to show up for tonight's important meeting but to come dressed appropriately. She fully imagined that they would act in accordance with her expectations of seasoned representatives of the Kerrisdale Garden Club.

Ursula was startled back to reality when she heard the quick pace of footsteps coming from the hallway leading up to the auditorium. A few seconds passed before she recognized who was making their way towards the open doors of the hall. Her tell-tale tam, tonight a cheerful raspberry pink, and curly auburn hair, which bounced about her shoulders like it had a life of its own, were a dead giveaway.

"Kate! Dear, how nice to see you." Ursula got up from her seat. Grabbing her clipboard out of her bag and ignoring the pinching pain in her right baby toe, she walked steadily towards the doorway to greet Kate as she entered the auditorium.

"Hi." Kate stood on her tiptoes, doing her best to peek over Ursula's shoulders. "Are you the only one here?"

"Yes, I guess the important people show up well ahead of schedule." Looking down at the notes she had prepared for the evening, Ursula continued, "Were you expecting someone else at this time? I thought you and I could go over the notes I made and perhaps do a bit of rehearsing at the podium before the crowds show up."

So many things were wrong with what Ursula had just said, Kate didn't know where to begin. She certainly didn't have any intention of sharing the podium with Ursula. There would be many other garden club members from across the city attending and although the Kerrisdale club was dear to her heart, she had to be careful not to play favourites.

Over sushi last week, George had filled Kate in on this important point, having experienced what he called the worst case of "volunteer revolt" a previous year when favouritism had reared its ugly head. The lesson he had learned was simple: When it came to volunteer politics, it was always best to remain neutral.

"Pretend you're the human manifestation of Switzerland and all will be well on the western front," he had said, "because you don't want to end up like Diane Morgenstern. She was forced to quit the volunteer co-ordinator position before the show even started. She made the deadly mistake of pitting two rival garden club presidents against one another."

"And how exactly did she do that?" Kate had wondered if she was really cut out for this role.

"During the first orientation evening, she decided to hold what she called a spur-of-the-moment vote. She asked for two volunteers to step forward, informing the crowd that she was looking to fill the position of vice-chair. Two ladies eagerly went up to the stage. One just happened to be Diane's own club president, Lucy Vanderhoofner, and the other, Penelope Fairfax, a rival president from across town. After allowing them each a brief self-introduction, she then asked for a show of hands to determine which of the two would be her new duly elected vice-chair."

"Well, that sounds reasonable, doesn't it?" Kate asked innocently.

"It does indeed, if the vote had been fair. But Diane and Lucy had conspired to put the word out to their own garden club members and had subsequently filled the audience with every registered, breathing member from their own club, past and present. The hall was filled to capacity. Apparently, there had been a promise of free donuts and a bus trip to the Bradner Daffodil Show out in the Valley later that month as payment in kind for a vote. Unfortunately for Diane and Lucy, their club members took the voting a bit too seriously. They came armed with homemade banners, originally hidden from view, which were then suddenly hoisted high, accompanied by a chorus of various noisemakers, which they tooted at the top of their lungs right at the time of the vote. One old guy even had a bullhorn and was chanting, "Lu-cy! Lu-cy!

"Penelope Fairfax and her supporters were not impressed. Needless to say, trouble ensued and a few volunteers had to be physically removed from the auditorium. I'll tell you, pushing a wheelchair down the length of that hallway with an angry octogenarian threatening to whack you with her cardboard glitter sign is not fun. Ask Richard. He tried to break up a fight between two little old ladies and got canewhacked on his shins for his efforts. So, remember this one special word, my dear Kate, and all will be well: Switzerland."

Kate's thoughts returned to the present and she smiled kindly at Ursula. In her most congenial voice, she said, "I'm under strict orders to follow a certain protocol this evening and unfortunately, that means that you will not be able to come up to the podium to speak."

Ursula's stunned silence spoke volumes. After a brief few moments of awkward stillness, Ursula replied, "Well, we don't want to break with protocol now, do we? I suppose this has something to do with George Stanwell. He never did care for me and I have to admit, the feeling is mutual. But be that as it may, I'll just sit here quietly and do as I am told." Taking her seat again, she stared forward, giving the distinct impression that their short-lived conversation had come to an end.

Kate didn't know what to say. Ursula was obviously disappointed. Kate wanted to be careful not to create any additional friction between her and George, so she improvised. "Actually, Ursula, it was my idea."

Ursula turned and stared at her in disbelief.

Not letting on that this was a sudden decision, Kate continued, "I'd prefer that you don't join me on stage because I'm very concerned that the presence of this film crew will be distracting for the volunteers and I really need you to take charge of Sophia and her crew."

Lowering her voice to a whisper, she leaned in and continued, "You know, direct them, keep them focused and above all, keep the volunteers in check. I have a feeling that once they see Sophia and her crew here, there could potentially be a lot of star-struck ladies and the occasional gent looking for their five minutes of fame. If you get my meaning?" Kate didn't blink, praying Ursula would take the bait.

Glancing over her shoulder to see if anyone was within hearing range, Ursula looked back at Kate with a suppressed smile.

"I know exactly what you mean, my dear. Leave it to me. I didn't win director of the year five times running at the West Point Grey Ladies Auxiliary Theatre Ensemble for nothing, you know."

Kate surprised herself by the sudden genius of her plan. Even though she had not intended it, she realized that putting Ursula in charge of Sophia and her crew would allow Kate to focus on the task at hand and perhaps even save her having to deal with Sophia at all.

A rumble of voices behind them quickly ended their private conversation.

"Like I said, Boris, we're going to need one podium set up stage right, fully miked, and the auxiliary stage lighting turned on. Then we're going to need some of the folding tables set up near the door so that the ladies can sign in the volunteers."

George was leading Richard and Boris along the hallway. Directly behind them were Sophia, Stacey, Hank, and Brian. Hank was pushing a large dolly stacked with a number of black, reinforced packing cases. All four were laughing with abandon at something that Brian had just said.

"Here come the troops," said Ursula, clutching her clipboard close to her chest. "To your station, my dear, and break a leg." Winking at Kate, Ursula turned and marched unceremoniously past George and his group and aimed straight for Sophia. "Oh, Sophia dear, I'm glad you're here at last. We have a number of things to discuss, you and I."

George was instantly relieved that the "Germain Shepherd" had ignored him, having swept past him in a cloud of sweet perfume on her way to accost Sophia. Perfect. *Those two will keep each other well entertained, I'm sure,* he mused. Eyeing Kate, he opened his arms wide and gave her a big hug.

"Kate, I'm so glad you decided to finally show." He pulled her in close, then whispered in her ear, "Sophia's already up to her old tricks but don't tell Richard. He's fallen head over heels in love with her." Releasing his embrace, he held Kate at arm's length. "So, where would you like the podium to be? Boris here is at your beck and call, right, Boris?"

Boris Mackenzie had been the head custodian at the gardens since the dawn of time. He had been hired by Thomas Dawson way back when the gardens were a new venture in 1978, and he had clocked many, many hours since then. George had gone to retrieve him from his private sanctuary: a modified storage closet near the back of the building. Complete with a hot plate, bar fridge, and the obligatory girlie calendars, Boris had set up shop there years ago. The décor had not changed much since then.

Boris was an avowed bachelor, which could probably account for his penchant for cheap plaid shirts that smelled of stale sweat and an overall appearance best described as scruffy. But Boris was invaluable. Whereas the resident horticulturalists knew the gardens like the backs of their gardening gloves, Boris knew every nook and cranny of the interior spaces, including the auditorium, library, display racks, and offices. He was familiar with every light switch, furnace vent, bathroom towel dispenser, and dead-bolt lock. There was literally nothing that Boris couldn't fix with a screwdriver and strip of duct tape.

Along with his untidy appearance came a prickly attitude. He certainly did not enjoy being told what to do since he most assuredly already knew what to do and probably had done it a thousand times. Hence, his hasty response to George's directive.

"Yeah. Yeah. It's not like I haven't set up the podium before. Whaddya think I am, some high-school punk or something, eh?"

Boris pushed past George, grumbling something unintelligible, and ambled up the steps to the stage, where he disappeared behind the curtain.

"He seems," Richard said, smiling stiffly at George, "efficient."

"Oh, Boris? He's harmless. You just have to ignore his attitude because deep down, he's a pretty good guy and really knows what he's doing."

"Funny," said Richard, looking into George's bright blue eyes, "I know someone like that too."

George rolled his eyes and pushed Richard to the side. "I bet you say that to all the girls." Catching Kate's eye, George raised his voice above the din of chatter now filling the auditorium.

"Kate, if you wouldn't mind doing a sound check with Boris as soon as he's set up, that would be great."

Kate gave George's hand a squeeze. "I'll go up there now, then you and I can chat quickly about the itinerary for tonight." Kate walked silently past Sophia, who was glancing distractedly at Ursula's clipboard, and began to ascend the steps of the stage.

Seeing an opportunity to break away from Ursula, Sophia quickly excused herself and positioned herself directly in front of George. "I'm sorry if I startled you earlier." She smiled.

Taken aback by her proximity, George forced a grin to disguise his surprise. Remembering what Richard had said earlier, he did his best to sound congenial. "No need to apologize. I'm sure you didn't mean it."

"Do you think perhaps I might get a short interview with you before the hubbub begins? I think it would lend a great deal to the telling of the story if you could give us a bit of background on the garden show as well as fill in the viewers on what typically goes on during the volunteer meeting. Besides, you'd look great on camera and the viewers always love a handsome face."

Hoping she didn't sound insincere, Sophia stared directly into George's eyes. Marcie's rule of flattery was one Sophia knew well, having employed it on many occasions. But with George, it was a different matter, considering what had happened in his office just a few short days before. She held his gaze.

George blushed slightly. "Well, if you think it would help, I'm sure I could pull myself away for a minute or two."

The corners of Sophia's mouth curled upwards. *Hook. Line. And sinker.*

"Perhaps we could find a quiet corner somewhere. I'll grab Hank and Brian and we can get started." She stepped back to get the camera crew but suddenly turned to George and said in a hushed whisper, "Oh, and we'll do a quick run-through before we tape. That way, you can perhaps let me know if any of my questions make you feel uncomfortable. I realize I overstepped my boundaries the other day so I want to be sure that that doesn't happen again." Sophia flashed him a winning smile. George found himself nodding silently in agreement. She turned and walked towards Hank and Brian, who were beginning to unpack the boxes near the back of the theatre.

When George realized that he was gawking at her, he gave his head a little shake and looked back over his shoulder to see Richard smiling at him while giving him two thumbs up from across the room.

Whatever, he mouthed silently. He was not about to admit that Richard might be right about Sophia. A growing sense of giddiness began to well up inside him at the mere thought of being interviewed by *the* Sophia Simpson. He had always fancied himself as someone who would look good on TV.

Suddenly, George realized that he wasn't wearing a tie. He always wore ties to work. His collection of silks rivalled only his collection of shoes but this evening, he had flippantly decided to dress casually. Now a cold sweat broke out across his back.

"Pssssst!" Gesturing wildly with his hands, George tried to get Richard's attention but he had his back turned, staring at something in the hallway leading to the auditorium.

Deciding it would be more discreet to walk up and talk to him directly, George bounded up the few steps and grabbed Richard's shoulder.

"We have got to get me a shirt and tie and I mean now!"

Richard turned and smiled at George, "Of course, whatever you say. But first, you've got to have a look at that." Richard pointed his thumb in the direction of the auditorium entrance. It took all of George's inner strength to suppress the wave of laughter that immediately shook his body. "Oh. My. God." His grip tightened on Richard's shoulder.

Teetering on shoes much too high for their slightly swollen ankles, dressed in clothing that better suited a group of twenty-somethings, and sporting hairdos that looked like they could stand on their own, Mimi, Ethel, Francine, and Margaret clattered their way down the hallway towards the auditorium. They had linked arms for support, which made them look more like a wayward band of can-can girls than a group of elderly garden club members.

"Yoo-hoo, Ursula! We're here!" shouted Mimi, who was linked in on the end of the line. She waved her one free arm. "Is there some place you'd like us to set up the volunteer table?" Mimi slipped slightly but Ethel clutched her tightly; thankfully, they avoided an ungraceful tumble.

Ursula, who had been nattering on at the TV crew about the importance of enunciation when speaking to a large crowd, turned and, much to Hank and Brian's relief, ascended the steps of the auditorium. At about the point where George and Richard were standing, she got her first glimpse of the motley crew of garden club members. Her face blanched. She felt faint. George was forced to prop her up before she hit the ground as he and Richard guided her to the closest seat. Richard fanned her with the clipboard he'd wrenched from her grasp. George screamed at Stacey to get a glass of water. Ursula pinched her eyes shut as she gulped for air. All she could think was that her carefully laid plans had just gone down in flames.

Chapter Twenty-four

Oma's Baking Tip

The best way to tell if the dough has risen enough is by look and feel. It will look soft and puffy. If you lightly press your thumb into the dough, it will leave an indentation.

"What were you thinking?" hissed Ursula as she sequestered Mimi and her gang in the ladies' washroom. "Do you have any idea how ridiculous you all look?" Francine, Margaret, and Ethel cowered in the corner next to the hand dryers.

"I don't think we look ridiculous," said Mimi with a pout. "In fact, the salesgirls were quite adamant that we all looked at least ten years younger."

"Well, that may be so but a ten-year-younger-looking clown is still a clown!" Ursula threw her arms up in the air, then grasped the edge of the counter. She gripped it so tightly that her knuckles turned white. Staring into the mirror, she glared at Mimi's reflection and silently shook her head. Mimi stared back at her, her normally platinum-blonde hair now tinged a grapey purple and permed as tight as a poodle. She was wearing an off-the-shoulder halter dress made from satiny white material covered in large gold lamé circles. A cocktail purse, consisting of interlocking gold sequins, hung from her shoulder. Her high-heeled shoes had little pompoms of caramel-coloured feathers on the toes, which fluttered each time she took a step.

"I think we look fantastic," blurted Mimi in retort. "Besides, you said that we should make sure to dress appropriately because Sophia Simpson would be here with her camera crew and you didn't want us looking like a bunch of old, dowdy women." She shifted her weight to the other foot, nearly sending her for another tumble.

"You see? You see?" raged Ursula. "You can't even stand up straight." Turning back to face the group, she railed, "And instead of dressing appropriately as I have obviously done, you four have instead decided to embarrass us all with your outrageous get-ups and quirky hairdos."

Francine now regretted allowing the hairdresser to dye her hair a light shade of pink while Ethel was having serious doubts about the cornrows that patterned part of her head. Margaret tugged incessantly at the lime green mini-skirt she was wearing but was unsuccessful in getting it to lengthen.

Ever-defiant, Mimi continued, "Well, we think we look terrific, don't we, girls?"

A few mumbled, "Why yes" and "I do believe so." Their responses evaporating like wisps of steam in the fluorescent-lit bathroom.

"That may be true but trust me, you look ridiculous. Quite frankly, you are an embarrassment not only to the Kerrisdale Garden Club but to gardeners in general."

Taking a deep breath, Ursula held her hands tightly behind her back and scrutinized the group of women who stood before her. "I'm sorry, ladies, but as president of the Kerrisdale Garden Club, you have left me with no other choice than to insist that you go home immediately and either change your outfits and remove that garish makeup — unfortunately, nothing can be done about your hair— and return here immediately or," she paused, breathing deeply, "do not come back at all. I will find someone to take your places at the volunteer table."

Mimi's jaw fell open. Instinctively, she clutched her shimmering purse to her chest.

"But you can't do that." Francine stepped forward, her bedazzled jean jacket glittering in the mirrors above the row of sinks. "We spent a lot of time and money on these outfits. I don't think it's right that you send us home like a bunch of reprimanded school girls."

"You shock me the most of all, Francine." Turning on her old friend, Ursula continued in an authoritative tone, "I certainly expected more from you than this. I see now that you have obviously been keeping bad company. I thought you would have known better, having seen things like this during our time at Point Grey." Ursula stared coldly at Francine, who now retreated to the line of ladies, her pride wounded. Tears welled up in Francine's eyes.

Margaret glared at Ursula. Defiantly folding her arms across her chest, she blared, "Now, just hold on, Ursula. You have absolutely no right to talk to us like that when all we wanted to do was—"

There was a loud knock at the door. A soft voice could be heard through the crack.

"Excuse me, would it be possible for me to join your conversation?"

It was Sophia. Ursula's face immediately reddened.

"Now, you've done it," she whispered through clenched teeth to the cowering group. "I can't save you now. It's done."

Raising her voice, Ursula continued, "Please, do come in, Sophia. I'm sure the ladies would love to speak to you." The sarcasm in her voice did not go unnoticed by the foursome, who were quickly trying to straighten themselves.

"Well, this is a tight fit, isn't it?" Sophia said with a smile. "I'm sorry if I'm interrupting anything but I couldn't help but notice how nicely you four ladies were dressed. I was wondering if it would possible to get a shot of you all later. Perhaps a quick interview too?"

Mimi squeaked. Francine and Margaret smiled from ear to ear. Ethel lightly touched her cornrows, and tucked behind her ear a wayward bead attached to one of her hair extensions.

Ursula's jaw dropped. Firmly grabbing hold of Sophia's elbow, she pulled her close and whispered in her ear, "May we have a quick word outside, Sophia dear?"

Not waiting for an answer, she tugged Sophia towards the exit, flung the door open, and pulled her into the empty hallway.

Freeing her arm from Ursula's vise-like grip, Sophia stared at her, shocked by her assertive behaviour. Ursula turned away. Despite the pain in her foot, she began pacing the floor in front of the ladies' room.

"You can't. You simply can't. It will ruin everything."

"What can't I do?"

Ursula gestured towards the closed grey door. "Them! You can't, you simply cannot feature them in your story. They look ridiculous and certainly, by no means, represent our garden club in any way that I, as president, would find appropriate."

Ursula stood with hands on her hips. She knew full well that she was risking everything by making demands of Sophia but she was determined to ensure that this story was an inspiration to people and not something to be laughed at.

"But don't you see, Ursula? They're perfect. I'll admit that their outfits are over the top but that is exactly the kind of thing my viewership loves to see. They crave seeing people different than themselves, who do courageous or funny things, who live their lives unapologetically, following their own dreams and making them a reality. It's people like those ladies in there that make my show so popular."

"You can't be serious. Those women are the type of people your viewership looks up to?" Ursula's brow knitted and her pupils narrowed to sharp pin points. "Because if that is the case, then I have to question the validity of this entire project."

"Don't get me wrong, Ursula. There are plenty of viewers who will be intrigued and inspired by your story as well. In fact, there are many stories to be told here, not the least of which is Kate and her ability to rise above tragic circumstances to become a successful businesswoman in her own right."

"Tragic circumstances? What in heaven's name are you talking about?" Ursula was not going to be sidetracked that easily. She sensed Sophia was trying to butter her up to get her to agree to allow the ladies, now trapped in the washroom, to have their five minutes of fame.

Glancing from side to side to ensure no one was within hearing distance, Sophia now leaned in closer, "You don't know about Ben?"

"Ben? Who is Ben?"

"Shhhh. Not so loud. Kate may just turn up at any moment."

Ursula now found herself intrigued by what Sophia was saying. She shuffled less than a metre closer to hear further revelations.

"Kate's fiancé, who was killed in a car accident five years ago. She never told you?"

"Why would she tell me? I'm the president of the garden club she attends, not her best friend or close relative." Ursula was all common sense when it came to things like this. However, it did cross her mind that she might have once heard Ben's obituary read aloud by her late husband over breakfast.

"Well, all the more reason to admire her fortitude and strength, don't you think?" Sophia smiled warmly at Ursula. "And to be honest, Ursula, Kate is one of the main reasons I'm doing this story."

Ursula looked up sharply and stared at Sophia in disbelief. "You mean to say that you're using our garden club and the garden show as a kind of front to dig deeper into Kate's affairs? Are we simply a means to an end for you?"

"No, of course not. I fully intend on presenting an insightful story about the garden club, its members, the garden show, and everything and everyone involved in it. What I'm trying to say is that we need to give credence to those people in this story who are making a difference in their community. That, Ursula, not only includes you but those four women now cowering in the ladies' washroom," said Sophia, looking over her shoulder once again, "and Kate too. But I can't do it on my own. I need your full cooperation and support because without it, I fear this entire project will have to be shelved. You see, you're probably the most important figure in this entire thing because you hold it all together: the garden club, the show, the various participants, why, even George Stanwell."

Ursula's face soured at the mention of his name. "What in God's name do I have to do with that narcissistic man?"

"Well, I just had a quick interview with him. He mentioned that it was only through the continued support of local garden clubs and their membership that the Shaughnessy show was even able to exist."

"I still don't see how that statement proves that I 'hold it all together' for Mr. Stanwell."

"Ah yes, but don't you see? If you were to pull your support out of this show, others would soon follow. Whether you are aware or not, you are an important figure in the garden, excuse the phrase, milieu. My assistant Genevieve has done her research. It appears that among the twenty or so garden clubs within our urban centre, yours has existed the longest and therefore, is the most respected. And if the most respected garden club were to pull out of the show, others would surely follow, and Mr. Stanwell would most likely be out of a job."

Despite the flattery, Ursula was still not convinced of Sophia's theory. "I find it highly unlikely that if the garden show were to fail, Mr. Stanwell would be looking for work elsewhere. He is too ensconced in his position to let it slip through his hands that easily."

"But you're forgetting one very important point, Ursula: money. The garden show has been struggling for the last couple of years. Since this show is one of the garden's main sources of revenue, it is up to George to ensure its success. If it fails, I highly doubt that the board of directors would be inclined to reinstate him for another term. In fact, I've already spoken with their CFO and she tells me that their annual general meeting will happen shortly after the close of this year's show. If it is determined that this year's show is again a financial failure, she said, 'Steps will have to be taken to remedy the situation.' Read into it as you wish, but experience has taught me that that means heads will roll, and George Stanwell's head is at the top.'"

As much as she hated to admit it, Ursula suddenly realized how vital George was to the scheme of all things. Although she disliked him intensely, the future of the garden show and the gardens, for that matter, hung in the balance. She would love to see him fired but that would most likely be the death knell for the show. Without this yearly gathering of horti-buffs, the future of the Kerrisdale Garden Club also looked bleak.

Clearing her throat and running a hand over her thick grey hair, Ursula looked straight at Sophia. "What do you want me to do?"

Glancing quickly over Ursula's shoulder, Sophia saw Marcie peeking around the corner of the hallway, giving her a thumbs-up. Part two of their plan had come off without a hitch: Garner the support of Ursula St. Germain and you will turn the Germain Shepherd into a lovable lapdog willing to chase after any stick you toss.

The door to the ladies' room, which had stood slightly ajar for the last few minutes, now closed quietly. Mimi turned to the huddled group cowering behind her in the tiled room.

"Well, girls, it's a good thing you took my advice because now, despite your protestations, we are going to be famous!"

The ladies' room erupted into a cacophony of excited giggles. They all jockeyed for room in front of the mirror to make last-minute adjustments before their big interview.

Chapter Twenty-five

Oma's Baking Tip

If your Bundt cake is stuck in the pan, try steaming it out. Pour a bit of boiling water over a kitchen towel, then drape it over the top of the pan. The warm pan and moisture from the towel will create steam, which helps release the cake once it's cool.

"And so, in conclusion, I would like to thank you all for coming out and showing your support for this year's garden show. I have no doubt that with your help, it will be a resounding success." Kate smiled appreciatively and gathered up her stack of notes from the podium.

Applause filled the auditorium as the three hundred or so eager volunteers beamed with enthusiasm at the end of her welcoming speech. George moved towards the podium and smiling broadly at Kate, he turned to the microphone.

"Thank you ever so much, Kate. On behalf of the Shaughnessy Gardens, I would like to sincerely thank you for your willingness to take on the role of volunteer coordinator for this year's show. By the looks of it," said George, now gesturing to the capacity-filled room, "we will have enough people to fill all of the positions. Those of you who have already completed your volunteer forms may now deposit them at the entrance to the auditorium at the volunteer table. If you still need to fill one out, more are available near the entrance. As Kate mentioned earlier, you will be contacted within a week or so. We'll let you know where we have slotted you and we look forward to seeing everyone again at the subcommittee meetings. Thank you, everyone, and good night!"

As applause once again filled the auditorium, George turned his back slightly to the crowd. Discreetly placing a hand over the microphone, he said quietly, "Now, let's get the hell out of here. I need a drink." Smiling back at the audience, which had begun to move slowly towards the back of the theatre, he gave a little wave, grabbed Kate's hand, and led her off the stage.

"You were fantastic!" Richard gave Kate a quick squeeze as they stepped onto the auditorium floor.

"Fantastic? Brilliant is more like it. I don't think I've ever seen such an enthusiastic crowd." George put his arm around Kate and pulled her close. "If the baking thing doesn't work out, honey, you could certainly give Tony Robbins a run for his money."

Kate laughed but stopped short when she saw Sophia approaching down the steps of the hall. "Here we go," she said softly. To her surprise, Sophia didn't so much as look at her. Instead, she walked right up to George. Reaching out to straighten his tie, she said, "We got some great footage, George. I'm sure we'll be able to use quite a bit of it. I particularly liked the part where you told the story of that past meeting where you almost had to call the riot police."

"Well, a little brevity always helps to break the ice." George was blushing. Kate looked to Richard for some nonverbal clarification. None was forthcoming as he simply shrugged his shoulders.

"I've got the boys packing up their gear now so we'll be out of your hair soon. Thanks again for being such a great sport. I appreciate it."

Sophia looked at Richard and extended her hand. "Nice to meet you, Richard. I hope we'll get a chance to know each other better in the next little while." Turning slightly to Kate but not meeting her eyes, Sophia said lightly, "'Bye, Kate." She turned and quickly ascended the steps towards the exit.

"Isn't she delightful?" gushed George.

Before Kate could answer, a soft voice pulled her attention to the right.

"Kate?"

A woman, sixtyish with curly blonde hair and bobbly, bubble-gum-coloured earrings, smiled brightly at her, extending her hand.

"Hi, Kate. My name is Marcie."

"Hello." Not wanting to be rude, Kate took Marcie's hand, shaking it lightly. "Can I help you with something?"

"Actually, it's me who can help you, I think. I mean, if you're willing."

Intrigued, Kate said with a smile, "With what?"

"Well, I don't want to seem too bold but I'm a hair-and-makeup artist and there's nowhere on this form where I can offer my services. I understand from the ladies at the volunteer table that Sophia Simpson will be doing an entire feature on the garden show?"

"Oh, my God! You're just what we need." George beamed. "Where were you an hour ago?" He thought back to his private interview with Sophia: all he could think about then was whether or not his hair was sitting flat and his brow wasn't too shiny. Richard had been no help at all, leaning against the wall of the hallway, smiling conspicuously while George did his best to appear calm and collected.

George thrust his hand towards Marcie, shaking hers vigorously. "George Stanwell, very pleased to meet you indeed. And where, may I ask, have you worked, Marcie? Not that I want to look a gift horse in the mouth but it would be comforting to know that you've had some kind of professional experience." Richard elbowed George in the ribs, hoping to remind him that he was, indeed, looking a gift horse in the mouth.

"Ouch. Just ignore my husband here, Marcie. Richard may be good looking and makes a dashing figure in court but he has no idea about what it takes to be presentable on TV." George threw a stern look at Richard.

Marcie giggled knowingly. "Well, suffice to say, I've had loads of professional experience. Let's see, back in the day, I studied at the Dwight School of Hair and Design after which, I landed my first job with the Maple Leaf Theatre in West Vancouver."

"Don't tell me you knew Stanley Chisholm?" George placed a hand on his hip, shaking his head in disbelief.

"Actually, yes. Stanley was a good friend of mine." Marcie couldn't believe her luck. Stanley was the "pussycat" she had described to Sophia when they began hatching their plan of attack.

"You're hired!" George enthusiastically swung around to face Kate. "Right, Kate? You think it's a good idea, don't you? I mean, if we're going to constantly be in the limelight, we certainly need to look our best, and Marcie here obviously knows what she's doing. Stanley Chisholm was the artistic director at the Maple Leaf Theatre and he did not suffer fools gladly. Trust me, if Marcie here worked with him, then she's good."

"I suppose. But do you really think it's necessary? No offence, Marcie, but I really don't plan on being in front of the camera that much." Kate smiled shyly, tucking her podium notes under her arm.

"What do you mean?" replied Marcie. "Didn't you notice that the cameraman had you in his sights practically the whole time you were on stage? He only just stopped filming you when Sophia Simpson left a minute ago."

"Really? I didn't notice." Kate peered over Marcie's shoulder to see if she could get a glimpse of the TV crew.

"Well, notice you should, my dear. I'm going to override you on this point. We absolutely would love your assistance, Marcie." Pulling out a business card from his breast pocket, George handed one to Marcie. "All my contact numbers are there, including my cell and email, so be sure to stay in touch." Marcie took the card and dropped it into her large green leather purse. "Can we count on you to be on hand whenever we may require you in the next couple of weeks?"

"Why, sure. I'm only just a phone call away. My number's right there." Thrusting her volunteer form into Kate's hand, Marcie thought how brilliant a move it had been for her to take her vacation for the next three weeks. She could be extremely flexible and on call at the drop of a hat without revealing her true place of work and her connection to Sophia.

"Thanks, and by the way," asked Kate, glancing up from the volunteer form and looking at Marcie, "which garden club do you belong to?"

"Oh, I don't actually belong to any one in particular. I just like to plant seeds and watch them grow." Giving Kate a little wink, Marcie turned and disappeared into the remaining remnants of volunteers.

"Now, things are really coming together." Clapping his hands, George put his arms tightly around Kate and Richard. "Drink anyone? I'm buying."

Chapter Twenty-six

Oma's Baking Tip

If you want to add a bit of zip to a recipe, use lemon zest. Unlike the juice of a lemon, which can result in too much liquid or acidity, zest doesn't throw off the chemistry of the recipe — and baking, like any good relationship, is all about chemistry.

Kate woke to the rhythmic chirping of chickadees. An industrious pair of doting parents had built a nest in the tree outside her bedroom window and were busy this morning gathering food for their ravenous babies. Each time they flew a fresh morsel into the nest, the young ones let out a chatter of tweets.

Turning on her side, Kate looked at the clock and was amazed that it was just past 7 a.m. Normally, on her day off, she lounged in bed until at least 8:30 but she felt rested enough this morning to consider getting up. Pulling her pillow higher behind her head, she shimmied herself into a sitting position. Looking out of the window, she had a good view of the chestnut tree that grew on the west side of the house, the one now home to a new family of chickadees. At the base of the tree lay her beloved sunken garden. Soon it would be overflowing with hostas and ferns, surrounded on all sides by a moss-covered, stone retaining wall that her Opa had built back in the fifties. Hidden among the shade plants were inconspicuous stone sculptures of frogs and gnomes, their grey-and-yellow lichen patina belying their age.

The sunken garden had been Kate's favourite playground as a child. Slightly hidden from view and protected from above by the expansive boughs of the chestnut tree, she would while away the hours, playing hide-and-seek with the neighbourhood cats or nestle herself into one of the cushioned wicker chairs with a good book. Oma would occasionally appear offering lemonade and cookies and little Kate couldn't imagine a better place to be in the whole world.

From her position in bed now, she couldn't see the shade garden but she could see through the chestnut tree and into the alleyway that curved along the west side of the house. This was another aspect of her home that she loved. In a neighbourhood known for its charming houses and well kept gardens, it was rare to find one that could be considered a quiet corner lot. Most of the forties-style bungalows were either sandwiched between other houses or had a street running down one side, open to parking and traffic at all times of day and night. Kate's alleyway around the side of the house was rarely used, except for the garbage truck on Monday mornings or the occasional neighbours driving around the back to access their yard. Nobody on her short street used the garage buildings at the back of their lots to park their cars. They were either too small, in need of serious repair or as was the case with Kate's, filled to capacity with gardening tools, recycling bins, bicycles, and an assortment of I'll-clean-that-junk-out-one-day stuff.

Kate stretched her arms above her head, then ran her fingers through her wavy hair. As a few of her fingers got caught in a tangle of curls, her thoughts ran to that nice woman who had suddenly appeared at the end of the meeting last night. Marcie seemed like the kind of person who could easily become a friend. Something about her carefree way of talking and that twinkle in her eye made Kate want to know her better. Even though she thought it was silly to have a hair-and-makeup person, George had seemed convinced that it was a good idea. *Besides,* she thought as she threw the duvet off to the side and got out of bed, *I may just get a few good tips on what to do with this shaggy mess.*

Glancing down at her cell phone on the nightstand, Kate saw, to her relief, that there were no text messages from the bakery or from George, whom she fully expected to hear from this morning. They had a lot of work to do today, sorting through the volunteer forms and assigning groups, but Kate knew that George wouldn't call until at least 9 a.m. Not because he respected her right to have a bit of extra sleep but more likely because she knew he was a lost cause until at least 8 a.m. After that, he would have his usual two espressos, choose his outfit for the day, shower, shave, and get dressed.

As Kate trundled off to the bathroom, she felt glad that they had made plans to meet at her house around 9:30 this morning. It meant that she could take her time getting ready and George would have time to check in at work before they spent a leisurely time discussing their plans for the show.

After a nice long shower, Kate pulled a light, floral-patterned dress over her head, swept her damp curls into a quick bun, and headed downstairs. Today, she was going to make George his favourite break-fast pastry, Sour Puss Scones, a super-flaky, lemon-and-cranberry treat named after her neighbour's cat, Puss Puss. Although Kate loved ani-mals, she swore that Puss Puss, an elderly calico, had a feline version of bipolar disorder because she could be sweet one minute and a furry tornado of fangs and nails the next.

Clear spring sunshine was flooding the kitchen through the break-fast-nook window, setting the mood for what Kate felt sure was going to be a productive day. She pressed the warmup button on her coffee ma-chine as she walked past the counter towards the pantry near the back door. After tying the laces of Oma's striped apron around her waist, she piled the dry ingredients into her arms and headed back to the counter to begin making the dough.

The coffee machine beeped as she grabbed her favourite mug and pressed the digital display. The machine whirred and purred as it created a perfect crema-topped cup of freshly ground brew.

Turning the oven on to 375 degrees Fahrenheit, Kate started to measure out the dry ingredients into a large metal bowl. She knew the recipe by heart, having made hundreds of small and large batches over the years. It felt good to let the soft powder of the flour sift through her hands as she mixed in a small amount of sugar and baking powder. Setting the bowl aside, she dusted off her hands and grabbed her cup of coffee. After pouring a generous amount of soy cream into the cup, Kate savoured the first sip, which was always the most satisfying of all. Holding the warm coffee mug in both hands, she stared out the window above the kitchen table and smiled.

She was thinking of last night and again, felt the same sense of relief that had occupied her mind the entire drive home. Despite her trepidations, everything had gone well. Even her encounters with Sophia had been surprisingly minimal and inconsequential. It seemed as though Sophia was more concerned about George than anyone else and that suited Kate fine. The less attention she drew from Sophia, the better as it had allowed her to perform her duties as volunteer coordinator unencumbered. The only time she had felt any real unease was when Marcie had mentioned that the cameraman had spent a lot of time focused on her. Kate hadn't really noticed, as she had been more concerned with getting her introduction speech done. By the sound of the applause at the end of her talk, she had felt confident that people had taken to heart her encouraging words.

Kate truly hoped, for George's sake, that this show was a success this year. For all of his bravado, she knew that it meant a lot to him and that's really why she had agreed to take on the role.

George had been, and still was, her rock-solid place. He had been there when the police officer had knocked on her door to give her the bad news about Ben and he had stayed by her side throughout the whole ordeal. She couldn't have asked for a more loyal friend. He certainly had picked up the pieces of her life and helped her put them back together. She would never forget that. Even though he could be unbearably self-centred at times, Kate loved him dearly and was thankful that he had stumbled into her life.

Richard, of course, was just as meaningful as George. Kate always appreciated his common sense and unflappable demeanour. She'd given some thought to what Richard had said the last time they had gone for sushi. Even though she was tiring of rehashing the whole Sophia thing, she had to admit that his explanation of her actions had made some sense. Kate was a realist, though, and she wasn't about to let her guard down that quickly. She had already made up her mind to keep a cool distance from Sophia and let the cards fall where they may.

The sound of the phone ringing snapped her back into the present. Setting her coffee on the counter, Kate pushed through the waiter door to the hallway.

"Good morning, sunshine."

"Hi, George, up so early?"

"Yes, and I have Richard to thank for that. He had to be up for some Law Society meeting or something and as usual, was a bit clunky getting out of bed. So, how did you sleep?"

"Fine, I guess. I'm glad I only had a sparkling water last night. The roads were pretty slick on the way home. How did you two fare?"

"All I can say is that I'm glad it was Richard's turn to be the designated driver. After those two scotches, I was in no position to get our asses back home."

"Two?"

"It was two, wasn't it?"

Kate laughed. "George, you kill me. You had at least four. For a moment there, Richard and I thought you were having your own little private party."

"Well, I guess I was just relieved that everything went so smoothly last night. A boy's allowed to celebrate a little, right?"

"Of course." Kate pushed through the kitchen door. Grabbing her coffee with her free hand, she sat down at the kitchen table.

"Guess what I'm doing?" Kate took a small sip of her coffee and closed her eyes, letting the morning sun warm her face.

"Now that's the sixty-four-dollar question. Are you dressed?"

"George!"

Laughing naughtily, he continued, "Well, how should I know? From what I can guess, you could be stark naked practising yoga positions on the living-room floor."

"You should know me well enough to know that one: I wouldn't walk around naked except within the confines of my bathroom; two: I'm terrible at yoga; and three: if I was good at yoga, which I'm not, I certainly wouldn't be doing it naked."

"All right. All right. You're baking."

"Oh, man, you're no fun."

"Am I right?"

Letting out a slightly defeated sigh, she said, "Yes, of course you're right."

"Well, what else would you be doing? Of course, you could be doing it naked."

"And you could get your mind out of the gutter."

"That is probably a lost cause, my dear, but I do know you all too well, Kate Freitag!"

"That you do, George. In fact, I was just thinking this morning about how well you know me. I don't know if I say this enough," Kate whispered into the phone, "but I really do love you, Mr. George Stanwell."

George blushed. "Now, you stop that. Don't go getting all mushy on me first thing in the morning. You're as bad as Richard."

Kate laughed. "I can't help it. You just bring it out in me."

"I bring a lot of things out in a lot of people but rarely do they tell me they love me because of it."

"Well, I think you're adorable and I can't wait for you to come over so I can feed you some of these. . ." Kate let her sentence drift off in an expectant whisper.

George picked up on the clue right away. "Sour Puss Scones?"

"Yup."

"I'm over in twenty," he said earnestly.

Kate laughed at his eagerness. "I thought you had to go to the office first."

"Office schmoffice. I'll just call Stacey from my car. Anyways, I really don't need to stop in there this morning. You took all the forms with you last night, right?"

"Yes, but I haven't sorted them."

"That's okay. We'll do that together as we nibble on scones and perform sun salutations while contemplating our navels. But maybe you should get dressed first." George laughed.

"You're terrible. I don't know how Richard puts up with you."

"Trust me, darling, I don't know either. See you soon." Kate heard a kiss in the phone and then he was gone.

Twenty minutes was hardly any time at all. Kate put the hands-free on the kitchen table and went back to her mixing bowl. She had best get cracking and get those scones into the oven because if George was one thing, he was punctual.

Chapter Twenty-seven

Oma's Baking Tip

If your recipe calls for softened butter and you don't have time to wait for it to get to room temperature, simply grate some frozen butter. Grated butter will soften in the same amount of time it takes to heat the oven.

Sophia drove slowly along Main Street, stop-and-start the whole way. Morning traffic seemed to be getting worse but she didn't have to be in the office until later that morning to go over the shots from the night before. She had made plans with Marcie to meet her at her house at around nine and by the looks of it, she would make it just in time.

She parked her car around back since Marcie had told her that Ted would be gone for the day and his spot out back would be free. She had barely shut the driver's-side door when Marcie came bounding out the screen door, smiling broadly, and holding her arms wide.

"It's working! It's working!" Grabbing Sophia by the hand, she led her breathlessly up the back steps and into the kitchen.

"Don't mind the mess. Ted just left for work and I haven't had a chance to clean up the dishes. Take a seat." As Marcie gestured to one of the empty kitchen chairs, Sophia sat down, wishing she had had an appetite for breakfast. But the thought of eating anything made her stomach churn.

"So, tell me all about what happened on your end." Marcie wiped a hand across her forehead and tucked a loose clump of her curly blonde locks behind her left ear.

Marcie could hardly control her excitement. She had been very discreet last night, barely making eye contact with Sophia. It wasn't until she had noticed Brian and Hank set up in the corner with their equipment that she realized their plan might hit a slight snag. The last thing they needed was for one of those guys to recognize her and let the cat out of the bag. So, Marcie had been very careful to bury herself among the crowd of volunteers and to keep a low profile as much as possible.

Marcie had sent Sophia a quick text message once she'd left the hall. It was rather cryptic but she was sure that Sophia had gotten the gist. "Foot in door. Pussy cat purred. How 'bout u?"

Sophia's short reply had made it clear that things were going well. "Dog didn't bite. Cat didn't scratch. Can we meet tomorrow morning?" Marcie had replied right away, "Coffee. My place at 9. Park out back. Can't wait!"

Marcie grabbed a used coffee mug and the remnants of a toasted bagel from the kitchen table and carried them to the sink. Over the sound of the running tap, she turned her head to Sophie. "So, what happened? I barely got a wink of sleep last night just thinking about it. Coffee?"

"Yes, please. Just cream." Sophie loved Marcie's enthusiasm but was still feeling a bit awkward about last night. It's not that she had lied or anything; she knew that she was manipulating people and it didn't sit right with her. Her quietness was not lost on Marcie, who shut off the tap and turned to face her.

"You're not having second thoughts, are you?" Marcie leaned back on the sink. "Don't worry, Sophia, everything will work out just fine. I got to speak to Kate last night and I can see why you'd want to be back in her good books. She seems really nice."

"She is and that's the problem. I'm the not-nice one. Why should I ever think that she'd want to be my friend again? After all I've done and here I am scheming and planning, manipulating circumstances for my benefit."

"Hold on. Hold on." Marcie grabbed a tea towel to dry her hands and plunked herself down in the chair opposite Sophia. "Now, don't start down that path again. I thought we'd been through all this already?"

Marcie smiled encouragingly at Sophia, who was staring down at the table, unable or unwilling to look her in the eyes.

"You are not a bad person, Sophia. I'll admit that you've made some mistakes along the way but haven't we all?"

Sophia glanced up briefly, then looked away.

"The difference is this: you're willing to make a change. You recognized that you made some mistakes with Kate and you want to make up for it, start again. The problem is, up to now, you've only made matters worse — or at least it seems so." Marcie stood up and walked over to the coffee machine. "But now you have a solid plan and with my help, which, by the way, I'm more than happy to give, you'll be best friends with Kate in no time at all."

"That's all fine and good, Marcie, but what about the manipulation? What about keeping your identity secret from Kate? If she ever finds out about our little plan, there will be no turning back. She'll hate me for sure and that will be the end of it."

Returning to the table with two filled coffee mugs, Marcie set them down and pulled her chair closer to Sophia.

"How could she find out? I can tell you right now that she didn't suspect a thing last night. Her friend George was all excited about me offering to do their hair and makeup."

"George would get excited about something like that." Sophia smiled a bit but it was fleeting. "Come on, Marcie, she could easily find out. I totally forgot that Brian and Hank both know you. If they see you, they're bound to say something and she'll put two and two together.

Oh, God, I knew this wouldn't work." Letting her head fall into her hands, Sophia let out a frustrated sigh.

"Look, Sophia, I thought about that too. I didn't like having to sneak around, making sure that Hank and Brian didn't see me. So, that's why I've come up with our next plan of attack."

"Oh God. . ."

"I'm going to tell Kate the truth! Well, not the whole truth because that will only complicate things."

Sophia looked up from her hands, her mouth half-open in surprise.

"What do you think about me telling her the truth about where I work? Or should I say, where I worked?"

"What do you mean?"

"Well, I think we have no choice but to tell her that I work at the station if we want to cover the Hank-and-Brian angle. But I don't think it's a good idea for her to know that I still work at the TV station because then she may think that we're manipulating the situation."

"Which is exactly what we're doing."

"I know, but it's for a good cause."

Sophia shook her head.

"She's going to see through this one."

"No, she won't because I'm going to tell her that I worked at the station — past tense. That will explain how I potentially know Hank and Brian should they happen to recognize me, or whatever. If she thinks I retired shortly after you started working there, she has no reason to believe that you and I have any kind of real connection. Brian and Hank would, of course, know me but only fleetingly."

"This is getting too complicated. And besides, what if one of the guys says something like 'See you at work' or something like that?"

Marcie chewed the corner of her lip, silenced for only a moment.

"Well, then I'll just have to make something up on the spot. I'll tell Kate we're having an alumni-golf-tournament fundraiser or something. Oh, I don't know. I wouldn't worry about it. At work I have nothing to do with those two guys. They only know me from seeing my face around the station. They probably don't even know what I do."

"This sounds pretty shaky. I don't know. What if she asks how you found out about the volunteer night?"

"She certainly doesn't have to know that I found out about it through you. I mean, why would she even suspect something like that? There have been ads in the paper, you know. I've seen them. And I'm certainly not about to tell her that we came up with this amazing plan to get you two back together as friends because I found you crying in the parking lot, right?"

Sophia stared blankly at her, wondering where this was going to lead.

"So, if she asks, and she won't, I'll simply tell her that I saw one of those ads in the paper asking for volunteers to show up to the meeting last night. I was intrigued by the whole garden show thing, being a bit of a gardener myself and since I'm retired, ha!"

Marcie scooped two heaping teaspoons of sugar into her coffee and stirred wildly, satisfied with her ingenious plan.

"And then, once I got there, of course, I saw a need for a hair-and-makeup person since Sophia Simpson, from my old TV station, was doing a show on the show . . . and that is why I decided to volunteer my skills. Simple as that. Bagel?"

"No, thank you. Look, Marcie, this is really important to me. I truly see this as my last chance to make things up with Kate." Sophia looked pleadingly at Marcie. "Do you really think this is going to work?"

"Yes. I. Do." Licking her coffee spoon, Marcie got up to grab another bagel from the counter.

"Simple as that. You just think it'll work without a hitch?"

"Yup." Opening the fridge door, Marcie grabbed some butter and a jar of plum jam.

"And have you also thought about the future? Let's say this does work and Kate and I become the best of friends again. Will she ever know the truth about our plan? Is she ever going to find out who you really are?"

"Sure she will." Sitting back down, Marcie began to spread some butter on half of the bagel.

"And you don't think that'll ruin it?" Sophia stared at Marcie in disbelief.

"Nope. And before you go and ask me the obvious," said Marcie, unscrewing the mason jar lid and spreading a large dollop of plum jam on top of the butter-smeared bagel, "it's because I think this whole thing will make for a story that you two will laugh over and probably tell your grandchildren about."

Biting into the bagel, Marcie chewed contentedly. "Sure you don't want one?"

"No, thanks, really." Sophia wasn't letting up. "And when exactly does the real truth come out?"

"Oh, not until you guys have truly buried the hatchet. It would be too risky to mention anything before then but you'll know when the time is right."

"You make it sound so easy. I'm terrified, Marcie. I'm so afraid that she's going to hate me even more than before that I'm seriously considering trashing the whole project."

Swallowing hard, Marcie grabbed her hand. "Don't do it, Sophia. I promise you everything will work out okay. Just let me talk to her. I've got really good people skills. That's what you get from working in my profession for thirty-some-odd years."

Sophia leaned back in her chair, staring up at the ceiling.

"Look. Let me have a chat with her. If you don't notice a thawing of the iceberg the next time you see her, then we'll stop, okay?" Marcie smiled again at Sophia.

"Really? If she doesn't warm up to me the next time I see her, we'll call it quits?"

"Yes. But I swear to God, Sophia, you're going to be pleasantly surprised."

"What are you going to say to her?" Sophia leaned forward, both elbows on the table.

"I'm not sure yet but I do know that I'm going to do something with that wild hair of hers. Believe me, all I have to do is get her in my chair, run a brush over her scalp, and she'll be putty in my hands."

"She does have pretty crazy hair." Sophia smiled for the first time since coming into the kitchen.

"That she does." Nodding her head, Marcie tried one more time. "Are you really sure you don't want a bagel? I made the jam myself."

"Oh, all right, but only half a slice."

"Good!"

Marcie got up from the table and walked the few steps to the counter. Grabbing half a bagel from the bag, she snagged a plate from the cupboard and then laughed. "And don't worry about George Stanwell. He and I are practically best friends already."

"George is an interesting character. He's very protective of Kate so watch your step with him. One wrong move and he'll bite your head off. Trust me, I know."

"Oh, he's just an old softie. Nothing a bit of discreet eye makeup and a spray tan won't fix."

Returning to the table, Marcie set the plate down and handed Sophia a butter knife.

"You've got lots of goodies in your bag of tricks, I guess?"

"More than you can imagine. If I have to, I'll use 'em all. Cheers!" Raising her coffee mug, Marcie clinked it against Sophia's. "Here's to friendship."

Sophia grinned slightly. "Here's to not getting caught."

Chapter Twenty-eight

Oma's Baking Tip

To keep a skin from forming over puddings and custards, just sprinkle a small amount of granulated sugar over the top.

Taking in the satisfactory view of six neatly stacked piles of paper, George and Kate let out a shared sigh of relief as the final form was placed on the pile next to Kate's right elbow.

"Last one!" Kate beamed as she popped the remaining morsel of scone into her mouth and chewed contentedly.

"Thank God. I don't want to sound ungrateful, but what the hell? That was a lot of forms." George leaned back, his manicured hands clasped behind his head.

"Ah yes, but remember: a lot of forms means a lot of eager volunteers. So, you don't need to worry too much about the show this year."

Kate picked up their plates and empty coffee mugs, pushed back the dining room chair, and made her way towards the kitchen.

"Oh, this is just the beginning, honey. I mean, it's fantastic that we've got all these volunteers but now I have to deal with the vendors and their never-ending lists of 'needs,' which, believe you me, is incredibly demanding and quite unbearable."

"George, you're impossible. Is there no pleasing you?" Kate turned to look at him with a questioning smile. Gathering their empty plates she headed into the kitchen.

"You're right. There is no pleasing me. That, my dear, is why most people — employees, cashiers at the grocery store, parking valets, and the like — tremble at the sight of me and do things for me to keep me happy. It's my secret weapon."

"Not so secret now that you've told me," shouted Kate from behind the kitchen door.

Raising his voice, George replied, "Ah yes, but I know for a fact that you are good at keeping secrets. Besides, who would you tell? Sophia?"

George's little joke evaporated silently into the air. Realizing his indiscretion, he quickly countered. "Of course, I know that you wouldn't actually be talking to her or at least not within the next little while or perhaps at all but. . ."

"It's okay, George."

Kate was leaning on the door jamb, arms crossed but smiling. She had a damp tea towel slung across her shoulder.

"I know we didn't talk much about her last night but for the gardens' sake, I'm glad you're getting along with her," said Kate. "You know, I'm just going to let things flow. I want this show to go as smoothly as you do and if Sophia's episode brings the gardens some positive exposure, then I'm all for that."

George could hear Richard's voice in his head. "Whatever you do, be mindful of Kate's feelings today," he had mumbled as he headed for the shower that morning. "I think it's good that you're getting along with Sophia on a professional level but keep in mind what Kate said at Sushi last week: she just wants to get this thing over with. I'm sure, by that, she means in a distant, hands-off kind of way, so please don't go Sophia-izing everything." With that, Richard had disappeared into the slate-stone enclosure of their walk-in shower and George was left to ruminate in bed.

Looking up at Kate as she stood in the door jamb, George took a deep breath and said, "You're absolutely right, my dear. I am getting along with her but believe me," he said as he sat up and straightened his green silk tie, "it's completely professional, nothing else. We're not seeing each other privately or anything like that, so no need to worry."

"Oh, George, you crack me up." Kate started to turn back to the kitchen when the phone rang.

Walking the short distance to the hallway, she blew him a kiss. George smiled appreciatively as she picked up the receiver.

"Hello?"

"Hi, Kate? This is Marcie, you know, from last night at the volunteer meeting?"

Kate was surprised that Marcie had somehow gotten her home phone number. Before she could ask, Marcie continued.

"I bet you're wondering how I got your number. Well, it's a funny story really. I was leaving the meeting last night and I literally ran into Sophia Simpson." There was silence at Kate's end. Not wanting to lose her too quickly, Marcie continued. "No, really, I ran into her. I mean, I bumped into her in the parking lot. Not with my car or anything like that but I accidentally ran into her because I wasn't looking where I was going and the next thing you know, wham! But don't worry, she's not hurt. The only thing that happened to me was I dropped my car keys. We spent the next five minutes scrambling around in the dark trying to find them. It was a funny sight, I'll tell ya."

As Marcie quickly took a breath, Kate seized the opportunity to interject.

"Hey, Marcie," Kate said as she turned and looked at George with raised eyebrows, "how did you get my number?"

"Oh right, your number. Sorry, I tend to run off at the mouth a bit but I'm glad you asked. I thought you might wonder and don't worry, it's totally legit. You see, I used to work at the same TV station that Sophia works at now. Isn't that funny?"

Kate wrinkled her brow and tossed her head at George, who scrambled to his feet and made a silent beeline for the hallway so he could hear as much of the conversation as possible. As he stood beside Kate, she gave a little shrug of her shoulders and held the receiver at an angle so that George could listen in.

"I guess so." Kate wasn't quite satisfied and this new revelation that Marcie and Sophia worked at the same TV station got her head spinning.

"I didn't get a chance last night to mention that after I finished working at the Maple Leaf Theatre, I landed a choice gig at Urban TV. But I retired last year."

George silently mouthed, OMG! He received an elbow in the ribs and a silencing glance from Kate. Marcie barged on.

"So, anyways, Sophia and I got chatting about the station and some of the people that work there and how she's getting along in Vancouver and all that kind of stuff. Then," Marcie's voice became even more animated as she added, "we started talking about this new doc she's doing on the garden show and one thing led to another. Before you know it, I had your number!"

Sensing Marcie needed to breathe, Kate took the opportunity to cut in.

"Sophia gave you my number?"

"Yeah, I thought it was sweet too. I told her that I had offered to do your hair and makeup and she thought that was a great idea. I guess I'm kind of an overeager person, sorry, but I just flat out asked her if she had your number. Well, it didn't surprise me that she did and then she just gave it to me. Right there in the parking lot."

"Okay." Kate was thinking this was all a bit odd but considering how enthusiastic Marcie obviously was, she didn't think it was necessarily bad. "So, what can I do for you?" Kate glanced at George, who was hanging on every word.

"I was wondering if you wanted to get together today. I actually called your bakery first but they told me today was your day off so I called you here. I hope you don't mind but maybe it'll work out great. That is, if you don't have anything to do this afternoon?"

Marcie's sincerity was palpable. Kate had the same feeling now as she had had last night that Marcie could become a good friend. Something about her melted Kate's guard and made her feel at ease.

"I'm not really too busy. I have to go see my mom for lunch but after that, I'm free. What were you thinking?" Kate looked questioningly to George, who replied with shrugged shoulders. He could hardly stand it and was having trouble keeping still.

"I thought maybe we could play with your hair a bit. I've got a couple of styles I think you'd like and—"

Kate cut Marcie off mid-sentence.

"Okay. Sounds like fun. Where should we meet?"

"I've got a little studio in my house, if you'd like to meet here. I live just off of Main on 12th Avenue. My hubby is at work so we'll have the place to ourselves. Would 3 p.m. be okay?"

"Sounds fine. So what's your number, just in case I get lost?"

"You can get me any time on my cell at 778-493-2020. My house is at 352 12th Ave. Did you get all that?"

George grabbed the phone and held it between their bending heads so that Kate could scribble down her information.

"Yup. I'll see you then around three."

"Sounds good, Kate. I can't wait to get my hands into your hair. See you later."

George stifled a giggle. Kate wrenched the phone away and turned her back.

"See you."

Sloppily setting the phone back in its docking station, Kate looked at George and shook her head.

"You are the most impossible person!"

"Well, sorry," George said with a shrug, "but it was just how she said she couldn't wait to get her hands into your hair. Good thing she mentioned her 'hubby' or I'd be thinking she just flirted with you."

"Oh God, George. You think everyone's flirting with everyone. All the time. Everywhere." Kate threw the tea towel at him and walked off to the kitchen.

"Well, it's true, isn't it?" George followed like a scolded puppy.

~

Marcie gingerly pushed the loudspeaker button on her phone and looked up at Sophia.

"That went well." Marcie smiled with an eager grin.

Sophia's face lay buried within her hands.

"We are so dead."

Chapter Twenty-nine

Oma's Baking Tip

"Folding" is a gentler mixing technique than "stirring" or "mixing."
Use it where tenderness is desired.

Adjusting the purple tam on her head, Kate took a deep breath and hoped for the best. She kept reminding herself on the drive over about what her mom had said as they had sat drinking their coffees after lunch.

"She sounds lovely, dear. Who knows? This Marcie may just turn out to be a good friend. I know all too well that you're never too old to make new friends. All it takes is the recognition that you have something in common, a similar experience or talent, and voilà! The chemistry begins."

Kate wondered what the chemical combination was between her and Marcie. Because she knew so little about her, she was at a loss as to what it might be. All she did know was that Marcie seemed sincere, sweet, and approachable. She had an impish twinkle in her eye and Kate liked that: it meant that she wasn't a foreigner to fun. Fun was definitely something that Kate could use more of in her life.

Had she known that the "something in common" was Sophia, Kate probably would have made her excuses earlier and then taken a right on Broadway instead of a left and headed straight for the bakery. With no idea what the attraction truly was, she now stood innocently on the front porch of Marcie's quaint little house.

"Oh, I do like a girl who's punctual." Marcie greeted Kate with a big smile, hands on hips, and a pick comb sticking out of her blonde curls.

Clutching the small purple paper bag in her hands, Kate offered it to Marcie.

"I thought you'd like to have a little something. As a kind of a thank-you for having me over."

Hastily opening the crinkly top, Marcie peeked inside and took a deep breath, savouring the lemony fragrance emitting from between the folds.

With a satisfied sigh, she said, "You're a girl after my own heart. Kind of gives me the shivers."

Kate blushed slightly, remembering George's remarks from earlier this morning.

"Oh, it's nothing. Just a few Sour Puss Scones I made this morning."

Blush fading, Kate continued, "I really do appreciate you offering to do my hair today, Marcie, although it does seem a bit premature." Kate stepped into the enclosed porch that smelled faintly of lilac and rubber boots.

Helping her with her coat, Marcie countered matter-of-factly. "I like to get a good look at my clients before any big performance. That way, there'll be no surprises down the road." Marcie grinned. "And besides, I had this strange feeling that you and I could become good friends." Marcie winked. "I mean, that's what I said to my hubby Ted this morning."

Marcie laughed. "You wanna know what he said?" Without waiting for a reply, she scooped Kate around the waist and led her into the living room.

"He said, 'Marcie, hon, you make friends with everybody and that's what I love about you the most.'" Marcie stood still in the middle of the room. "My Ted's a good guy."

"So, you're married?" Kate asked, trying not to look too distracted by the adorable way Marcie had decorated her house.

"Well, not exactly married but if twenty years of co-habitation counts for anything, I guess we're as close to being married as you can get. Tea?"

"Actually, I just finished a coffee with my mom, so no thanks. Not right now. Maybe later."

"Good idea. Then we can have a nibble on those scones you brought. That is, if I can keep my hands off of them."

Marcie walked through to the kitchen and carefully placed the purple bag on the counter. Turning back to Kate, who was now mesmerized by all the knick-knacks and tchotchkes that adorned Marcie's living room, Marcie crossed her arms and gave Kate a wide grin.

"So, my little red-headed baker extraordinaire, let's get started." Without missing a beat, she gracefully pulled the soft purple covering from Kate's head. A jumble of auburn locks tumbled down around her shoulders.

"Wow. That's a lot of curls!"

Kate smiled. If she had a dollar for every time someone said that, she'd be well on her way to opening a second bakery.

"I got them from my dad. Even though he kept his hair short, I've seen pictures from when he was a kid and he definitely had a full head of unruly curls, just like me."

Marcie chuckled. "The only thing I inherited from my dad was an insatiable sweet tooth and a fat lot of good it's done me." Gesturing to her ample bosom and derrière, Marcie let out an infectious giggle. "At least, I've always got a soft place to land, right?"

Kate laughed too. "And you're a girl after my heart because without people like you, I'd be out of business."

They both smiled. Sensing the time was right to move on, Marcie gestured towards the basement stairs.

"Time for the dungeon, my dear."

Kate looked at Marcie with a fleeting glimpse of apprehension.

"Only kidding! My studio is actually quite nice. Ted did a fantastic job converting my dad's old tool room into a fully functioning salon. There was a thought that maybe I would use it to do some freelance work, you know, hair-cutting and styling for weddings and things, but quite frankly, I don't have enough time."

She grabbed Kate's hand and led her down the stairs.

"Come on. Let's go have some fun."

The basement was surprisingly spacious and well lit, not at all like Kate's, which was in dire need of a cleaning. Since she hardly went down there, it always got relegated to the bottom of her to-do list.

The steep wooden stairs of Marcie's basement opened up into a large, sparsely furnished den. They walked past an oversized desk that stood in one corner. Kate couldn't help but slow up slightly and stare. The solid oak monstrosity supported an organized jumble of strange electrical boxes covered with knobs and buttons. A set of large headphones hung off a hook to the side and an old-fashioned microphone stood clamped in a small stand. Little lights blinked and flashed. The whole thing looked strangely like something from an East Berlin bunker in the days of the Cold War.

Before Kate could formulate the question in her head, Marcie seemed to read her mind.

"Don't mind Ted's mess. He's a ham radio buff. Actually spoke to the space station last week. At least that's what he said, but I think it was just one of his buddies having a lark."

Kate laughed. Marcie was proving to be a total delight. Kate could feel the knots of apprehension loosening and a real sense of camaraderie building between them. She spoke without thinking. "My fiancé Ben liked to tinker with radios too."

Marcie paused, then turned to smile at Kate. She inwardly braced herself for what she knew would be the response. Sophia had already told her all about Ben. She asked politely, "Does he belong to a club?"

Kate took a breath and continued without hesitation. "Actually, no. Ben died in a car accident a couple of years back."

Marcie felt like she had just snagged a tangle of hair with a sharp comb. Sympathy welled up inside her. She found it hard not to tear up but knew inherently that all of this was a necessary evil in getting to the core of what was troubling the relationship between Kate and Sophia. She could only hope that some day, Kate would forgive her. Acting on instinct, Marcie reached out and pulled Kate into a big hug.

"I'm so sorry, hon."

Kate didn't mind getting this sudden expression of consolation from Marcie. She had been right: she was a soft place to land. Not only did she wear her heart on her sleeve but her genuine concern seemed to make that okay. Years of distance from the evening of the crash had slightly dulled Kate's emotional response to the telling of Ben's story.

After a moment or two of silent consolation, Marcie gently pulled back and held Kate at arm's length. "You and I are going to have a lot to talk about, I can see that now." Giving Kate's cheek a soft touch, she turned and with a flourish, opened the door that stood closed directly behind her. Switching on the lights, she stepped aside and gestured to Kate.

"Welcome to Marcie the Maven's Makeover Haven — where magic happens and mum's the word!"

"You crack me up." Kate walked forward and poked her head inside. It was like stepping into a French boudoir complete with pink-and-black accessories, plush, velvety seats, and ornately decorated antique mirrors.

"Holy cow, this is fabulous!" Kate turned to Marcie. "You did this all yourself?"

"Well, I picked out the furnishings and, of course, the practical stuff like the pneumatic chair and adjustable sink but Ted did the rest."

"I've got to get me a Ted one of these days. That's for sure," Kate mused.

"If he had brother, I'd let you know but as it is, there's only one Ted. So, sorry, hon, he's spoken for." Gesturing to the salon chair, Marcie continued, "So, have a seat and let's see what we can come up with."

Kate scrambled up onto the chair and stared at her reflection in the antique mirror. Marcie was right, she really did need to do something with this mop of curls. Settling in, Kate sighed and looked at Marcie's reflection.

"Have your way with me. I have absolutely no idea what to do with this," said Kate, tossing a handful of curls over her shoulder. "And by the looks of it, you do. So, go ahead. I trust you."

Marcie felt another pang of guilt as she carefully ran her fingers through the back of Kate's locks. She kept reminding herself that it was all for a good cause. She imagined that some day she, Sophia, and Kate would sit around and have a good chuckle about all of this. Her fingers encountered a small tangle that pulled her thoughts back to the present. Grabbing a soft-toothed brush from her accessory stand, she began brushing Kate's hair.

"If you don't mind, I'd love to hear about Ben. I mean, if he was close to you, he had to have been a pretty good guy, I figure."

Kate didn't mind Marcie probing further. Even though she'd told the story countless times, she missed having a real heart-to-heart about what she really felt. Strangely enough, even though they had just met, Kate felt as though she could open up to Marcie and tell her everything.

And so the conversation flowed, slowly at first, but like the untangling of Kate's curls, the story unravelled at its own pace. Kate told her everything, from the awful night of Ben's accident and the ensuing minefield of emotions that she had wandered through since then.

"My mom was wonderful, of course, but we were both still recovering from the loss of my dad and," said Kate, pausing as she looked down at her hands, "my best friend at the time kind of abandoned me."

"Oh, honey, that's horrible." Turning her back, Marcie reached for a handful of hairpins that she didn't really need. Again, she knew what was coming and couldn't bear to look at Kate's reflection in the mirror as the truth came out.

"Actually, you know her."

"I do?"

With her back still slightly turned, Marcie busied herself with imaginary necessities in the top drawer of the counter behind her.

Kate swallowed, not sure how Marcie would react.

"Yes, it was Sophia."

Marcie froze and slowly turned to look at Kate in the mirror.

"Our Sophia?"

Her voice cracked slightly as she clutched the edge of the drawer.

"Yes, our Sophia."

Kate looked up, unsure of how Marcie would react to the news. As far as she understood, Marcie was fond of Sophia but had no clue about their past friendship. Kate figured Sophia would be too embarrassed to tell anyone about it.

Marcie pulled up an extra chair and sat down beside Kate. She reached for her hand and held it gently.

"Well, hon, I'm not making any excuses but maybe there's a few things you need to know about our Sophia."

Chapter Thirty

Oma's Baking Tip

Knowing when your cake is baked is crucial. Simply stick a toothpick into the centre of the cake. It should come out clean, with no streaks of batter.

Driving was difficult. Despite her brilliant new hairdo and a bit of fresh makeup to cover her tear-stained eyelids, Kate felt like a mess. Although she gripped the steering wheel firmly, she couldn't stop her hands from trembling. Her thoughts kept darting back and forth to snippets of conversation with Marcie.

After everything Marcie had just told her, Kate found her mind wandering off to places she never thought she would go. The unnerving revelations about Sophia were things she could never have imagined. Everything was slowly beginning to make sense. Kate slammed on her brakes, narrowly missing a bumper-to-bumper collision with a taxi.

Enough is enough, she thought. Kate had made it almost the whole way back to the bakery but instead of following West 41st, she veered off on Arbutus and headed down a few quiet side streets, ending up at one of her favourite childhood playgrounds: Maple Grove Park. Comfortably nestled into the residential neighbourhood and boasting some of the largest maple trees in the area, this park had been her Sherwood Forest as a child, filled with adventures, hidden pathways, and maple leaves the size of her head.

Kate often found herself drawn to this little oasis of solitude. It was always quiet here. Even though the bustling city buzzed around its edges, Maple Grove Park was peaceful and welcoming. Each season brought its own cloak of colour and scents to the park's exterior but the inner peace she found here was present throughout the year.

The early May sunshine streamed through the newly leafed-out trees, creating a soft green haze across the park's lawn. Kate found herself on a narrow, gravel path that led from the small parking lot that ran the entire length of the east side of the park. Crunching along, her shoes kicking bits of gravel ahead of her, Kate clutched her light spring coat and took a deep breath.

Why had Marcie's stories about Sophia affected her in this way? It's not like she hadn't thought of these scenarios herself. Why, even Richard had suggested that Sophia was sincere in her attempts to make up with her. She'd even said these things aloud to George when they had walked along Ambleside Beach a couple of weeks ago. So, why was she so deeply affected by this now?

Kate walked past a flowerbed blooming gloriously with red-and-yellow tulips, their stems swaying gently in the soft, mid-spring breeze. She thought about the many times she had asked herself the simple question: Why? Why had Sophia neglected her when Ben had died? Why had she then gone on to steal one of her Oma's recipes in what seemed a clear case of shameless self-promotion? Kate could never figure out the reasons for these actions. That was, until today.

Marcie had said she'd worked briefly with Sophia at the TV station and they had struck up a short-lived friendship. It wasn't that they weren't friends anymore. According to Marcie, after her retirement from the TV station, she hadn't seen much of Sophia until yesterday, when they had bumped into each other at the volunteer meeting.

Kate knew from her own experience that Marcie had a way of enlisting trust. She could imagine how Sophia would have told her things while sitting in her makeup room at the studio. As soon as Marcie had run her fingers through Kate's tangled locks, she had felt like she could tell her anything. She figured this was exactly what had happened to Sophia.

Kate's stroll took her to the north end of the park, where most of the large maple trees stood in majestic silence. The sunlight streamed through their upper branches in broken beams, creating a shadowy pattern of light and dark along the winding path. In the years since Sophia had left for Toronto and all the things that had gone on since then, Kate could never figure out what had hurt more: Sophia's poor attempts at condolence or the recipe incident. Both were forms of betrayal. Although completely different in their makeup, they had cut Kate to the core. Her best friend had abandoned her, leaving her to figure out why.

But since getting to know Marcie better, Kate was now privy to some of Sophia's history in Toronto. She had received an inside look into perhaps what had made Sophia do the things she did.

"She puts on a good front but I think she's dealing with a lot of demons. Sophia didn't go into details but I definitely got the impression that she has a lot of past regrets. I suspect she's done things she's ashamed of." Marcie leaned in as she rinsed Kate's locks with warm water. "You know, to further her career."

After applying a handful of almond-scented conditioner and working it through her wet curls, she had continued, "And that so-called boyfriend of hers. What was his name? Oh yeah, Phil. Well, Mr. Phil was no help at all. He treated her like crap and then dumped her for another woman."

As Marcie turned on the faucet and rinsed the conditioner from Kate's hair, she continued with the revelations. "I remember last fall, I was getting her ready for an interview and Sophia told me that she had done something the night before that was really stupid. She was quite upset about it and I think she needed to get it off her chest, but she never did tell me exactly what was going on. All I knew is that it involved some old friend of hers and that she tried to apologize to them. I got the sense that Sophia had hurt this person in some way, maybe even cheated them in the past. Who woulda thunk that that someone was you?"

Kate stopped near the trunk of one of the majestic Maples and suddenly came to the realization that she now felt sorry for Sophia. Those beginning years in Toronto had obviously been very difficult for her. Kate didn't know much about the TV industry but she could guess that it was pretty cut-throat. It was all starting to make sense. Sophia's obsession with getting ahead in that dog-eat-dog world would have left little time for dealing with personal tragedies. Maybe her stealing the recipe was more out of desperation than anything else.

Perhaps Richard's explanation over sushi the other night was right after all.

Kate stepped forward into a warm beam of sunshine that had broken through the maze of branches and newly formed leaves that tussled in the breeze. She stared ahead.

I can forgive her for this, she thought.

Kate's heart felt like it would burst out of her chest. She let out a hastened breath. She had cried a bit in Marcie's chair when she had told her about Sophia's guilt but now, in this singular beam of light, standing alone among the maple trees, Kate couldn't stop the tears from flowing.

She missed Sophia. Terribly. They had been such close friends and when Sophia had left for Toronto, Kate had had a foreboding sense that things would change between them. Ultimately, she was right but had no idea how right she was going to be. Grabbing a handkerchief from her coat pocket, Kate wiped away the tears cooling on her cheek. She knew she was going out on a limb and that some people in her life would probably disapprove but Kate sorely missed Sophia. Again, she thought of what her mom had said that morning, "All it takes is the recognition that you have something in common, a similar experience or talent, and voilà! The chemistry begins."

Kate realized now that she was willing to let the chemistry begin again with Sophia. Stepping around a large tree trunk, Kate headed back across the lawn to the parking lot. As she was fiddling with her car keys, a voice chimed in behind her. She turned to see a young woman standing on the path with an overloaded baby stroller.

"Hi! Sorry to bother you but aren't you Kate from Kate's Bakes?"

"Yes." Kate smiled. Strangers didn't often recognize her but every time it happened, it took her by surprise.

The young woman smiled. "I thought it was you. I've seen you in the bakery a couple of times and, of course, I'd have recognized that hair anywhere." The woman giggled. "I just have to tell you, I love your stuff. Everything is so delicious and everyone who works at your bakery is so kind."

Stepping a little closer to her admirer and hoping that her recent crying episode would be mistaken for a bit of cold, Kate said, "Aw, that's so nice of you to say that. I'll be sure to tell everybody at the bakery. They love hearing stuff like that."

"Oh, and if you want my vote for the best thing on the menu, it's got to be your BLT Brownies."

Kate nodded. She'd heard this many times before and it always made her smile.

Continuing, the young mom said, "I remember years ago you used to have gingerbread but I haven't seen them in a long time. They were the best."

Kate often regretted having removed them from her menu. Each time a customer mentioned them, she felt a little twang of guilt as if she had let them down in some way. But today was different. For the first time since Sophia had misused the recipe, she felt that maybe, just maybe, she could offer them again.

"Yeah, they were the best, weren't they? Maybe we'll bring them back again some time."

"I wish you would. They tasted like, well, like coming home."

"Thanks, I'll remember that."

The baby hidden under a lavender-coloured blanket began to stir and let out a loud cry.

Smiling broadly, the young woman made a move to continue on her way. "It was nice meeting you. If I don't keep moving, this little one is going to start putting up a fuss."

"Take care and thanks again."

Kate opened the car door and sat behind the wheel. As she watched the woman with her baby disappear into the maple trees at the far end of the path, she closed her eyes and took a deep breath. Maybe it was time to bring back Oma's gingerbread. But first, she needed to settle things with Sophia. Maybe then, they could make a grand reappearance at Kate's Bakes.

She fished her cell phone out of her purse and dialled George's number. She needed to share with him her decision to reconnect with Sophia. If there was anyone who knew anything about making a grand reappearance, it was George. His number rang once.

"Hello?"

"What do you know about making peace offerings?"

Recognizing her voice immediately, George smiled and looked away from the spreadsheet that glared at him from his monitor.

"Nothing, honey, but if you're looking to disturb the peace, I'm your man. What's up?"

Without hesitation, Kate told him. "I've decided to give Sophia another chance."

"Wait a second." Kate could hear him putting his phone down and walking across his office. "Don't let any other calls through and don't let anyone in. I'm busy," he barked. Within seconds, he was back on the receiver.

"I'm all ears. Now tell me all about it and don't you dare leave out one juicy detail."

Chapter Thirty-one

Oma's Baking Tip

Always have a frozen sweet loaf or cookies on hand for unexpected guests. No one, especially a baker, likes to get caught with their pantry down!

"Ladies. Gentlemen. I need all of you to please take your seats!"

Ursula's pleadings could barely be heard over the rumble of voices that filled the Kerrisdale Community Centre. The number of people who had turned up to this meeting, the first one since the volunteer orientation night the previous week, had overwhelmed her. To her astonishment, every last metal chair had been pulled from the stacks and there was standing room only towards the back of the room. She even had to shoo deaf old Chester from his usual seat near the front of the stage and send him packing in the direction of the kitchen with promises that Ethel would find him a suitable spot to sit.

A large and animated group had crowded around Sophia and her crew, who were doing their best to set up their equipment near the back corner of the room. Lloyd had taken it upon himself to assist in crowd control but was doing a mediocre job at keeping the excited, mostly female onlookers from holding their distance. He enjoyed being so close to so many older ladies but found it difficult to ask them to step back. Sophia, accustomed to this kind of adoration, simply smiled and did her best to answer the multitude of questions and compliments tossed at her amidst excited giggles and requests for autographs.

If anyone was to blame, it was Mimi. After overhearing Ursula's and Sophia's conversation outside the ladies' washroom at the volunteer meeting, she had taken to heart the real possibility that the garden show and, ultimately, this garden club were on the brink of disaster. Even though Ursula had been nagging the club for months, it was Sophia Simpson's pleadings to Ursula to cooperate with the television project that had convinced Mimi that the situation was, indeed, dire. Of course, Sophia's compliments about Mimi's gold lamé outfit that evening had helped immensely. Mimi now ranked herself among Sophia's biggest fans.

Mimi felt it was her civic duty to spread the word among the Kerrisdale community that a TV crew was going to film their upcoming meeting. If they wanted to get an up-close-and-personal experience with the famous Sophia Simpson, they had best show up and join the club. She was adamant, however, that no looky-loos would be allowed in, only card-carrying members. Francine and Margaret were busy at the sign-in desk, doing their best to handle all the new inductees.

It's amazing what a bit of promotion can do. After their ego-boosting interviews with Sophia last week, each of the cribbage players had gone on the rampage, excitedly calling every friend they knew and encouraging them to come to the next meeting. The success of these calls had spurred Mimi into high gear. As club secretary, she had the most updated version of the current and past membership list. With this in hand, and Willawiener in tow, she had headed off to the library to make a number of photocopies.

Calling each of the cribbage ladies on Wednesday evening, Mimi had simply said: "Be sure to show up tomorrow with your cell phone fully charged. We're not going to play crib but rather 'Go fish.'" Intrigued by her cryptic message, everyone, including Ethel, whose granddaughter had recently convinced her to carry a cell phone, came "charged" and ready to go.

Mimi had converted her living room into a makeshift call centre. Plying the ladies with copious amounts of lemonade and matrimonial cake, she had given each of them the duty of calling every member on her allotted list. Promises of on-air appearances and potential personal interviews with Sophia Simpson had enticed them with lines like: "She's just a delight in person," or "I don't see why she wouldn't want to interview you too."

It had worked. The hall now thundered with the voices of close to two hundred people. Ethel was concerned that the coffee and goodies would run out.

At Ursula's urging, Lloyd had left his post as protector to the stars and reluctantly returned to his usual position behind the soundboard. After he had cranked the volume on the microphone to the max, Ursula's voice boomed loudly over the crowd, cutting through their conversations like a sharp pair of pruning clippers snipping off an unruly branch.

"Ladies and gentlemen, I must ask you again to please take your seats!"

The jumble of voices quickly died off. All heads turned towards the stage, where Ursula stood poised behind the podium.

"Thank you. Now, as I said, if you would all please take a seat, we will begin."

Ursula could hardly contain her excitement. Never in the history of the Kerrisdale Garden Club had she experienced a turnout like this. If she was a different person, she would have been at a loss for words. Despite her inner elation at the sight of this filled-to-capacity-crowd, she kept her cool and appeared in complete control.

"I would like to welcome all of you, new and old members, to the monthly meeting of the Kerrisdale Garden Club, Vancouver's oldest and most respected garden club. I see a few familiar faces in the crowd and many whom I have not yet had the pleasure of meeting. But all in good time."

Fumbling slightly with her notes, she continued. "Tonight, we have the distinct pleasure of welcoming Miss Sophia Simpson to our little gathering."

The hall erupted into joyous applause and everyone, including Chester, who had been corralled into kitchen duty with Ethel, gawked adoringly at Sophia. The popular on-air personality gave a little wave, then turned to say something to Hank, who stood behind her with a microphone boom in hand.

Almost shouting to regain their attention, Ursula boldly continued, "Yes, it's quite exciting, I know, but more importantly, we are here, as gardeners, to fulfill our duty as stewards of this planet: to continue the legacy of those, past and present, who have dedicated themselves to beautifying our surroundings and ensuring that that which we leave behind for future generations is viable, natural, and sustainable."

The ensuing silence sucked the room of all its energy. Ursula instantly realized her blunder. Wanting to sustain the excited momentum of the evening, she instantly changed tactics and continued, "Of course, the prospect of having our little garden club featured by one of the nation's most respected and, may I say, adored, television celebrities is something worth celebrating, don't you think?"

Thunderous applause and cheers filled the room. Ursula smiled and gave a small nod towards Sophia. *If it's a celebrity they need to keep them here, then a celebrity they shall have,* she thought.

No one noticed as Kate slipped silently into the hall and disappeared into the kitchen. Once again, she'd been held up at the bakery, this time by the new electrician she'd hired to fix the troublesome lighting in the kitchen. Norm, her regular go-to guy for all things electrical, was away on vacation and the company had sent someone new named Gord instead. All Kate cared about was that Gord got it fixed. She was tired of hearing Deb sarcastically complain that the flickering lights were giving her headaches. She claimed that the ongoing dimness was causing some of the staff to mix up the butter and the butter cream.

Gord had taken more time than Kate had anticipated since he had the unfortunate gift of the gab, going on and on about mundane things like wattages and voltages and surge protection outlets and the like. When he had finally finished and the flickering had been repaired, he had cleared away his gear and Kate had hastily paid him. She had then grabbed a large box of mixed pastries from the day-olds, set aside for tomorrow, and rushed over to attend the meeting.

"Hi, Ethel," Kate whispered as she sneaked into the small kitchen. "What the heck happened? Where did all these people come from?"

"Oh, Kate, thank God you're here." Ethel's voice was filled with concern. "It looks like our telephone canvassing was a huge success. But now I'm worried that I won't be able to handle them all. Just look at that crowd!"

Kate set her purple box down and peeked out the opening above the kitchen counter. All the regulars were there but she didn't recognize most of the faces. Ursula was taking command, as usual, from her elevated position on the stage and were focused on her. Kate turned her head to the left just in time to see Sophia duck in behind a monitor set on wheels, deep in discussion with one of her crew. Quickly pulling her head back into the kitchen, Kate turned to Ethel.

"Don't worry, Ethel. We'll get it all done. I'm going to pop back to the shop and grab some extra supplies and baking. I won't be long."

"Oh, bless your heart, Kate. I was beginning to think we'd run out before we even started. It's just Chester and me back here." Gesturing in the direction of the sink, Ethel let out a slightly defeated sigh, knowing that Kate would understand the awkwardness of having someone like hearing-impaired Chester in the kitchen.

Kate tapped Chester on the shoulder as he stood at the sink rinsing out coffee cups. He turned and smiled broadly at her. Making sure he was looking her in the eyes, Kate carefully enunciated her words and raised her voice to be heard.

"Hey, Chester. Want to come for a ride? I could sure use your help."

"Sure, Kate." Chester smiled easily and wiped his hands on his pants. "And you don't have to shout. I can hear you just fine."

Kate stared, then looked at Ethel, who shrugged her shoulders.

"Oh, I just put on that deaf act to bug old St. Germain." He chuckled and grabbed his coat, which he'd thrown over a chair in the corner of the kitchen. "Gives me kind of a cheap thrill, I guess, getting her goat."

Kate smiled and shook her head.

"Well, I never!" Ethel stood with her hand over her mouth and watched silently as Kate and Chester left quietly through the emergency exit at the end of the hallway.

The drive back to Kate's Bakes took mere minutes. Once inside, Kate busied herself by gathering all the supplies she thought they'd need: an extra coffee maker, three thermal carafes, two cartons of half-and-half cream, a box of sugar cubes, and the remaining leftover day-old baking. There'd be a few disappointed, bargain-hunting patrons at the bakery tomorrow morning so she hastily scribbled a note for Deb, telling her to put something on sale to keep them happy.

Chester followed close behind, pushing one of the bakery's delivery carts and carefully stacking it with all the things Kate handed him. As they walked into the kitchen to grab some serving trays, Kate flipped on the lights. They flickered and then popped on with an audible click.

"You should really get those fixed." Chester was staring up at the series of pot lights that Gord had supposedly repaired that evening.

Kate rolled her eyes. "I just did. Maybe it's those new energy-saving bulbs. I don't know." Not wanting to consider having to get gabby Gord to come back, she relegated this thought to somewhere in the middle of her to-do list. Grabbing a couple of round serving trays and a handful of paper doilies, Kate placed them on the top of the cart and announced, "All done! Let's get this stuff back to Ethel before she thinks we've eloped."

Chester chuckled. Following Kate out of the kitchen, he turned off the lights. They flickered slightly and made an almost imperceptible crackling sound. Then, like a bar of Swiss chocolate, the bakery became sweet and dark.

Chapter Thirty-two

Oma's Baking Tip

Chocolate is easy to melt if you use the proper technique. It is also very easy to scorch, turning it crumbly and grainy. Use gentle heat, constant vigilance, and stir, stir, stir.

"Thank goodness you're back. I was beginning to get worried." Ethel held open the emergency door exit as Kate and Chester began to unload the supplies from the back of Kate's car. "They're pretty close to breaking for coffee and I thought you two wouldn't get back in time."

"No worries, Ethel. Chester is a great assistant. Once we get all this stuff unloaded, we can get started." Handing Ethel the serving trays and doilies, Kate dashed back to her VW Bug and grabbed the coffee urn. Chester, in the meantime, was setting one of the three boxes of Kate's Bakes goodies onto the counter.

"Oh my, that's all a lot of pastries. You're really too generous, Kate."

Ethel peered longingly through the cellophane oval on the top of one of the boxes. It revealed a mouth-watering array of tarts, croissants, cookies, and bars. The heavenly smell of chocolate, lemon, cherry, and hazelnut escaped through the seams of the sealed boxes. Ethel had to stop herself from sneaking one of the brownies tucked into the corner next to a particularly alluring coconut meringue cookie.

Kate set the last of the boxed supplies onto the kitchen counter. Hanging her coat and tam on one of the hooks near the kitchen door, she grabbed a purple apron from one of the cardboard boxes and pulled it over her head.

"Here." She tossed one to Ethel and one to Chester. "If we have to play the part, we may as well look it too, right?"

"Oh, I've always wanted to wear one of these." Ethel tied the straps of her freshly pressed Kate's Bakes apron around her waist and grinned.

"Well then, it's yours."

Ethel giggled like a schoolgirl who'd just discovered a kitten in her lunchbox. Kate admired Ethel in her new bakery uniform, then turned to help Chester, who was struggling a bit with his straps.

"Now," she said, planting her hands on her hips and surveying the piles of boxes yet to be unpacked, "let's get to work."

Out in the hall, things had gotten animated. Ursula had called upon the garden club's secretary, Mimi, to give a formal account of any new members. Since the list of names was now substantially longer than usual, Mimi was doing her best to read it quickly. Sophia had taken this opportunity to scan the crowd, once again, for Kate.

She'd done her best to find her earlier in the evening as people had begun to enter the hall. But, as the crowd had swelled, it quickly became impossible to keep track of her. Sophia had also been inundated with friendly fans, all of whom wanted to get within a snapshot's click of their favourite local TV star. Now that everyone was seated and focused intently on the stage area where Mimi and Ursula stood, Sophia had the opportunity to visually scan, row by row, the metal chairs that lined the hall.

Please let her be somewhere, she thought. Marcie had told her that she and Kate had had a good, long heart-to-heart. Marcie was convinced, even more than before, that Kate would be willing to have a dialogue with Sophia the next time they met, which should have been this evening.

Sophia's heart sank as she carefully scanned the last row of chairs. There was no Kate to be found, not even a whisper of a tam or a toss of auburn hair. Nothing. Sophia knew then that it was over. Plopping herself back down in a chair next to Brian, she let out a sigh and stared at her notepad.

"You okay?" Brian was surprised by Sophia's mood. By the look on her face, he thought she might even be under the weather. "Do you want a glass of water or something? I can get you one from the kitchen."

"No, that's okay. I'm fine. Just a little tired, I guess."

Secretly relieved he didn't have to leave his post behind the tripod, Brian looked down at her with a winning smile. "Must be those long nights out with all those boyfriends you have, huh?"

"Yeah, something like that." Not interested in a lengthy discussion with Brian about her nonexistent social life, Sophia got up and moved to stand next to Hank.

"Are we going to be able to get any decent sound in here?" Needing to distract herself from the revelation that it was truly over with Kate, Sophia plunged into her work and busied herself with the mundane technicalities of shooting the footage they needed.

"Yeah, we should be just fine," Hank said as he waved a hand in the direction of Lloyd, "as long as that guy over there with his Mickey Mouse soundboard stops fiddling with the settings."

As though on cue, a loud, ear-piercing squeak cut through the hall as people covered their ears and turned to stare at Lloyd.

"Sorry!" He shrugged and waved an apologetic hand to no one in particular.

"I think now would be an excellent time to have our break." Ursula's voice boomed across the room. She was in command again. Discreetly elbowing Mimi off to the side, Ursula took her sanctified position behind the podium.

"Thank you, Mimi, for your assistance and a hearty welcome to all our new members. As most of you will not be familiar with how our meetings are traditionally run, I suggest you take a moment during the break to familiarize yourself with a copy of our membership rules and protocol." Taking a deep breath, she continued, "Now, I understand that some of you did not receive a copy due to the overwhelming demand this evening. However, I'm sure that those who did would be willing to share. I assure you that by our next meeting, we will have enough copies on hand for everyone."

Ursula glanced towards the kitchen, getting a cursory nod from Ethel, who looked nothing less than frazzled. She pressed on. "So, please help yourself to coffee, tea, and goodies and we will reconvene in fifteen minutes."

Seeing a stream of people lunging for the back of the hall where Sophia and her crew had set up shop, Ursula hastily grabbed the microphone from its stand and loudly announced, "And if I may, I would please ask your cooperation in not bothering the film crew. They are here on official media-related business and wish to be left alone to perform their duties. I'm sure once the meeting has concluded, you will have ample opportunity to approach them."

Like scolded children, those who had made a dash for the back now turned glumly and stood obediently in the ever-lengthening line-up forming towards the kitchen.

Thank God for Ursula, thought Sophia. Having to deal with adoring, yet admittedly annoying and overeager, fans was the last thing she wished to do at this moment. All she really wanted to do was pack up her things and head home to Wendell. At least he would be willing to start a dialogue with her, even if consisted only of purrs and the occasional 'Feed me, I'm hungry' meow.

"I'm going to get something to eat. You want something?" Brian had turned his camera off for the moment and stood in front of Sophia.

"No thanks."

"Watching your weight, huh?" Without waiting for an answer, Brian strode boldly to the front of the line, knowing that his credentials as the "TV camera guy" would excuse any perceived rudeness of him butting in line.

"Just ignore that jerk." Hank stood beside Sophia, a pair of large earphones dangling around his neck. "The guy has no manners."

"That's okay." Sophia turned to smile at Hank. "I've dealt with lots of jerks in my day. He's not the worst I've come across."

"Still, he shouldn't be saying things like that." Hank sensed that Sophia wasn't in the mood to talk. Excusing himself, he headed over to Lloyd's sound set-up at the left of the hall. Thinking maybe he could give the poor guy a few tips and save them all from potential inner-ear damage, he was happy to leave Sophia to herself.

Finding herself alone, Sophia sat back down in the metal chair next to Brian's tripod. Most of the people milling about the hall with a cup in hand and serviette piled high with teetering towers of pastry seemed to respect the silent line that separated them and Sophia. Like watching a polar bear at the zoo, they were gawking at but not approaching her, as though doing so would bring the wrath of that officious club president down on them. Others stood in line, patiently waiting to be served. The noise in the hall slowly rose to a cacophony of laughter and chatter, occasionally punctuated by the sound of metal chairs scraping across the floor.

Sophia had known from the start that Marcie's plan would fail. It had been a valiant but doomed attempt to repair a broken friendship that could not be mended. The reality of it all, however, had never truly hit Sophia until now. She felt her stomach clench in that all-too- familiar way and for a moment, she thought she might be sick. Turning her head quickly in the direction of the washrooms, she realized that her last point of refuge was blocked with an overflowing line of men and women patiently waiting their turn. She felt trapped.

"Cookie?"

Sophia froze. The voice set her heart racing. She looked up in stunned silence. Standing in front of her, holding a napkin topped with a perfectly formed molten chocolate cookie, was Kate. Smiling shyly, she handed the cookie to Sophia.

"I hope you like it," Kate said, shrugging innocently. "I baked it myself."

Sophia tried to say something but the words that formed in her head stuck in her throat like a cork lodged in the neck of a bottle. She stared unbelievingly at Kate and shakily accepted the cookie.

"Well, I'd better get back to the kitchen. Ethel's a little overwhelmed and Chester," Kate said, looking down at her apron and smoothing her hands across the hem, "well, Chester needs a little guidance . . . " She paused again, looking straight at Sophia, and added, "and understanding." She let the last word linger in the air as it mixed with the tempting scent of the cookie Sophia now held gently in her hands.

Unlocking her eyes from Sophia's, Kate turned and walked back to the kitchen. She disappeared among the stragglers, some of whom had gone back for seconds.

Suddenly famished, Sophia peered at the peace offering in her hand and without hesitation, took a bite. A tear formed at the corner of her eye as she slowly chewed this little piece of chocolate reconciliation.

"Hey, there's no need to cry," Brian said with a snort as he walked past and flipped on his camera. "Nobody's gonna tell that you just devoured a thousand calories. That is, of course, unless I get you on film." Brian chuckled again and winked at Hank, who was finishing off his last bite of something crumbly.

Swallowing slowly and using the napkin to wipe the corner of her mouth, Sophia turned to Brian. "Has anyone ever told you that you're an ass?"

Not missing a beat, he said, "Why, yes, in fact, I hear it all the time."

"Good, then you'll save me having to say it again." Tossing the napkin into the wastebasket under Hank's soundboard, Sophia popped the last bite of the cookie into her mouth and chewed contentedly.

Brian thumbed in her direction and mouthed, *What's up with her?* Hank shrugged, then busied himself with his knobs and dials.

Looking back towards the kitchen, Sophia caught a glimpse of Kate busily handing out the last of the pastries and laughing about something one of the members had said. Sophia thought of Marcie and her prophesied dialogue with Kate: it had been short but, like the last morsel of cookie that she just devoured, it had certainly been sweet.

Chapter Thirty-three

Oma's Baking Tip

When baking hot cross buns, make sure your oven isn't too hot because if they burn on the bottom, the only thing that will be hot and cross will be you.

Everything had run relatively smoothly so far but now George was on a rampage. Three days of set-up for one of the nation's largest outdoor garden shows had almost pushed him to the brink of insanity. Having to deal with the logistics of moving in and prepping more than two hundred display tents, three demonstration stages, a gardener's marketplace, and an assortment of outdoor food kiosks was stressful enough. But that was a walk in the park compared to the harried preparations needed to make tonight's opening gala party a success. It was quickly turning into a fiasco and George was about to lose it.

"I don't care what Mr. Fobbs said, we need those floral arrangements in place by four p.m. Any later and I'll have his little schitzu for lunch!" George slammed the phone back into its receiver and jumped up from behind his desk.

"Stacey!"

George swung open his office door, his eyes tearing a strip across the reception room until they landed on the back of her head. Swivelling around in her chair, a half-eaten donut dangling from her mouth, Stacey cringed at the thought of another blast from her boss. His apparent warning, a couple of weeks back, that "Things would get crazy around here" neglected to include himself in that prediction.

"Yes?" she said, removing the donut from her mouth and placing it gingerly on her desk.

"Why didn't you check the schedule for the delivery of the flowers? Did I not say that the reception hall had to be completely decorated and ready to go by five today?" George leaned menacingly over her desk, "And before you answer that, my little donut-nibbling assistant, tell me why I'm the one who has to remind the violinist that she needs to begin playing at 6:30 when the doors open? Did I not tell you to contact her last week to confirm?"

Stacey blinked up at him but remained silent. She had learned this was the best thing to do when George went on the warpath.

George continued his tirade. "I just got an email from her agent saying that she'll be here around seven and ready to perform at eight p.m."

"I, uh, I don't know why they didn't—" stammered Stacey.

"Oh, it's hopeless." George huffed. "As always, I have to do everything, and I mean everything, myself." He turned to go back into his office. "The least you could do, I mean once you've finished your little snack, is to get in touch with Sophia Simpson. I want to know when she and her crew will be showing up tonight and I don't want any surprises." Slamming the door behind him, George disappeared into his enclave and Stacey let out a sigh of relief.

"Geeze," she mumbled, popping the last sugar-coated morsel into her mouth, "that guy has got to take a chill pill."

Picking up the phone receiver, she glanced quickly at her contact list and dialled Sophia Simpson's number. It rang twice.

"Sophia Simpson's office, Genevieve speaking. How may I help you?"

"Oh hi, Genevieve, it's Stacey from the Shaughnessy Gardens. How are you?" Stacey had spoken with Genevieve a couple of times and found her to be nice — efficient but nice — and Stacey envied her position. She secretly wished that she and Genevieve could switch jobs. Somehow, she thought that Genevieve would be much better equipped to deal with the likes of George Stanwell than she was.

"I'm good. Are you wanting to talk to Sophia? She's not here right now." Genevieve rarely wasted time in getting to the point.

"Actually, that's exactly why I called. Mr. Stanwell wanted to know when she would be arriving this evening for the opening night gala. Do you happen to know?" Stacey hoped she would so that she could at least show her boss that she was capable of carrying out a simple task.

"Just a sec, I'll check her calendar." After a moment's pause, she said, "She's going to get there around 5:30. Is there a problem with that?"

"No, not at all. In fact, that'll be perfect." Stacey jotted down the time on a pad and ripped that sheet from its stack. "Thanks, Genevieve. You've just helped me make some brownie points with my boss."

"Oh yeah. I've heard about him. Good luck with that." Genevieve chuckled on the other end. "Hey, you can also tell him to dress extra nice tonight because I can see that Sophia has made a couple of notes here. It says," she paused, scrolling down to the line of text on her monitor, "interviews scheduled: Ursula St. Germain, George Stanwell, and Kate Freitag. Looks like your boss'll be on camera again. That should make him happy, don't you think?"

"I should think so. In fact, you may have just made his day, and mine too. Thanks!"

"No problem. Talk to you soon." Before Stacey could say goodbye, Genevieve was gone. She had a good feeling that this juicy little tidbit of information was about to make the rest of her day a dream.

Getting up from her desk, Stacey walked up to George's closed office door and knocked lightly.

"What is it?" From the sound of the muffled-yet-annoyed tone emanating through the cracks in the door's hinges, George's mood had not improved. Taking a deep breath, Stacey slowly turned the knob and gently swung the door open. She took one step into the carpeted office and stood silently just in front of the door.

"Close it." George's voice piped from behind the computer monitor. "I'm in no mood to entertain any busybodies at this time."

Doing as she was told, Stacey closed the door. She swallowed hard and gathered her thoughts. She could hear George madly typing away on his keyboard, probably formulating a seething reply to the violinist's agent he'd mentioned earlier.

"So? Did you get an answer or are you here to hand in your resignation?" George didn't bother to peer over his monitor. Stacey was half-relieved that she was being spared a glare from his steely eyes.

"Um, yes, I uh, I um," Stacey fiddled with the sheet in her hand.

"Well, out with girl. Did you get an answer, or not?"

"Yes. Yes, I did," she blurted. "They'll be here around 5:30 tonight and. . ." Stacey paused to catch her breath.

"And what? God, you're making things so suspenseful. What is it?" George now stopped typing and peered around the potted orchid on his desk.

"Her assistant, Genevieve, said that you should be prepared and dress nicely this evening." Stacey barely got the words out of her mouth.

"Dress nicely? Who is this Genevieve? Did she think I was going to show up to our largest fundraising gala dressed in Doc Martens and a pair of soil-stained overalls?" George's voice had reached a fever pitch. Stacey took a small step backwards in preparation for a hasty retreat. Standing up, George began to move in front of his desk.

"Actually, it's because she wanted to let you know that you're going to be interviewed tonight." Glancing behind her at the closed door, Stacey quickly blurted, "Yeah, she said you and a couple of others are scheduled for interviews."

"A couple of others?" George was almost right in front of Stacey, having traversed the room in two hasty strides.

"Yes, I think she mentioned the name of that garden club president lady."

"Ursula St. Germain?" George's voice barely disguised his disdain.

"Yeah, that's it and your friend Kate too."

George stood still and stared at Stacey, as though frozen on the spot. Interpreting this as not a good sign, Stacey reached back and grabbed the doorknob. "So, that's all, I guess. I, uh, I think I hear the phone ringing. Gotta go." In one fluid movement, she disappeared behind the solid oak door, closing it quickly with an audible click.

George stood in silence. A satisfied smile crept across his face.

Another interview? he thought. Taking a glance at his reflection in the bank of windows that looked out onto the gardens, he thought how fortuitous it was that he had just bought himself a new suit for the occasion. He'd have to call Richard as soon as possible to remind him to pick it up from the tailors on the way home. Then it hit him. As he headed back behind his desk, George mumbled to himself as he quickly dialled Kate's number. Kate picked up her cell almost immediately.

"Hi, George. What's up? I'm crazy busy here." The sounds of clattering baking sheets and hectic voices filled the background. "I'm full on today and one of our ovens has decided to conk out so I'm just a wee bit stressed."

"That makes two of us, dear, but don't get me started." George leaned back in his chair. "I've got some interesting news that may not make you so happy. But being the dear friend that I am, I thought it was only right to call you right away so you'd be prepared."

"Come on, George. I can't stand the suspense." Kate covered the mouthpiece with her free hand and shouted, "Joseph! Can you please move these and put them out front? They're ready to go. We need room here for the next batch." Coming back to the conversation, she asked, "So, what is it? Please don't tell me that there's some issue with the volunteers showing up tonight. I planned on leaving work early so that I could get there well ahead of time to make sure they're all ready to go. And Marcie's supposed to meet me at home in an hour or so. She insisted on doing my hair and makeup for tonight. I still have to pick up my dress from the drycleaners on the way and then there's—"

George listened to the rising stress in Kate's voice. Not wanting to lead her on any further, he came out with it. "She's planning on interviewing you tonight."

Kate paused, then moved quickly from the kitchen and down the hallway to her office. "Just a second, George. I couldn't quite hear you. One sec."

Once behind the closed door of her office, Kate sat down. Even though she sat in total privacy, she whispered into the phone. "Did you just say that she's going to interview me tonight?"

"That's right. Looks like your peace offering has been accepted."

"That's good, isn't it?" Kate was beginning to feel nervous. Since the garden club meeting, she had not seen or heard anything from Sophia. She had no idea what her former friend was thinking.

"I guess it depends on what she asks you. I figure she'll be all business. You know, asking you about your role as the volunteer coordinator and all that. Or. . ." George paused and looked at the back of his hand, admiring his neatly manicured nails, "she could be luring you into a trap. She's been known to be a tad deceitful in the past."

"Oh, don't start that again. Let's assume she wants to play nice. What do I do now?"

"Be nice back, I guess. I mean, it's what you wanted, right? I'd suggest just playing it by ear. Be your normal sweet self and everything will be just fine. Besides, she's planning on interviewing me, too, so we'll both be in the same boat."

"Well, not exactly." Kate smiled. "You've already been interviewed by her and you're not the one she bailed on so. . ."

"You're right, but," George paused for effect, "this time, I'll be right by you. Let me tell you this: If she so much as hurts a hair on your head, I'll kick her sorry-excuse-for-a-reporter's ass off the premises so fast she won't know what hit her."

"You can't do that, George."

"Oh, yes I can. To hell with her television program. I'm not going to stand idly by and let her hurt you once again. She gets this one chance and if she screws up, she's outta here."

"But what about the exposure? It could reflect badly on the show."

"I know but," George started, then took a deep breath and exhaled, "you're more important to me than this silly show. If it means I get fired, so be it. Richard makes a good income. We could cut back on some necessities and make do. Besides, I always said I wanted to learn how to play golf so now may be just the right time."

"I love you, George."

"I love you, too, sweetie."

There was a knock at Kate's door. Deb stuck her head around the corner. "Sorry to bug you but those pot lights are flickering again. Should I call that electrician guy?"

Kate sighed. "No, don't worry about it. I'll do it. I'll be out in a sec."

Returning to her conversation with George, she said, "See what I mean? It's nuts around here."

"I so totally know what you mean. Now get back to those buns and then get yours over here as fast as you can. Tonight's the night, my dear. Quite frankly, if you don't get here soon, I may just end up killing everyone within a five-kilometre radius. Then I'd be out of a job for sure."

Chapter Thirty-four

Oma's Baking Tip

If you like the almond flavor of marzipan, add a thin layer of marzipan between a cake and its glaze. This provides a glass-smooth, crumb-free surface for decorating.

Marcie couldn't help but feel giddy as she navigated the afternoon traffic along West 41st Avenue. All of her plans were slowly coming together; her little white lies were beginning to pay off. Hopefully, by the end of this evening, Sophia and Kate would be well on their way to re-establishing their lost friendship. Once they were fast friends, Marcie could finally out herself as the secret matchmaker behind the scenes.

As she braked to a stop at Arbutus, Marcie looked out her driver's-side window at the pedestrian-filled sidewalk. She smiled broadly as she recalled her conversation with Sophia last week. Sophia had called her Tuesday evening, full of apologies for ringing so late but gushing all the same. Kate had talked to her, she said, having sought her out in the crowd at the Kerrisdale Garden Club meeting. She had even offered Sophia one of her cookies — no small gesture, Sophia had said. Buoyed by Kate's willingness to talk to her, Sophia had told Marcie she had decided to include Kate in her roster of interviews planned for the Shaughnessy

Garden Show's gala party.

"Well, I'd best get in touch with her *tout de suite* and set up an appointment to do her hair and stuff," Marcie had whispered. With Ted fast asleep beside her, Marcie had been careful not to wake him as she hopped out of bed to grab her calendar down in the kitchen.

"Yeah, but Marcie, don't tell her about the interview, though." Sophia's voice had gone up a pitch or two. "I'm hesitant to tell her about it. In fact, I'm not letting any of the people on my list know that I'm planning to do an interview with them. I want them to appear as natural as possible. I know I'm taking a risk, especially with Kate, but I believe it'll be much better this way, especially with Ursula St. Germain and George. Those two could make things difficult if they got wind of these interviews too early."

"No need to panic, Sophia." Marcie's voice had been calm and soothing. "We just need to stick to our plan. I'll give her a call and suggest that I come by next Thursday and get her ready for the big party. And you never know, maybe she'll open up and tell me all about her peace offering to you."

"Please don't blow this, Marcie. I'm really counting on you. It would kill me if Kate found out what was going on."

"Not to worry, hon," Marcie had said as she scribbled something in her calendar. "We're almost there."

As Marcie continued to reminisce about her late-night call with Sophia, she was forced to slow down just in front of Kate's bakery to let a car pull out of its parking spot. While it threaded into traffic, Marcie glanced to her left, just in time to see an elderly couple leave Kate's Bakes with a large purple box. *You won't be disappointed*, thought Marcie, as she remembered those yummy lemon scones Kate had brought with her last week when she and Marcie had had their heart-to-heart.

Marcie continued to drive her car along the final block of businesses on 41st, then took a left at Elm Park, and slowly made her way down the tree-lined street. She passed the Kerrisdale Lawn Bowling club, its neatly trimmed playing field shining bright green in the afternoon sun, then took a right onto West 45th. Seeing an empty parking spot, she came to a halt across the street from Kate's house. Glancing at her calendar to make sure she'd gotten the address correct, Marcie primped her blonde curls in the rear-view mirror, then opened the car door and went to the trunk to retrieve her roll cart.

The cart was jam packed with everything she needed to prepare Kate for her big night. Marcie carefully pulled the heavy bag across the street, avoiding the large puddle that pooled next to the sidewalk. It was just after 3 p.m. and she hoped that Kate was on time. When Marcie had called her last Wednesday, Kate had been surprised but happy to hear Marcie's voice and more than willing to have her come by to get her ready for the gala evening.

Taking a deep breath, Marcie climbed the red stairs to Kate's house, lugging the heavy bag behind her. When she finally arrived at the top step, she reached out and pressed the doorbell. Silence ensued. She was about to ring it again when the door burst open. Kate stood there looking out of sorts with her jacket unbuttoned and a dry-cleaning bag slung over her shoulder. Her curly, auburn hair stuck out in all directions from underneath a knitted orange tam. This gave the impression that she had just come through a windstorm, even though the air was still and the sun was shining.

"Hi, Marcie! Come in, come in." Kate was a bit breathless.

Marcie smiled as she stepped onto the Persian rug that lined the front entrance, then started to remove her knee-high boots. She noticed that sunshine was streaming through the living-room window to the right, filling the foyer with warmth. The house smelled delicious, like fresh bread and cinnamon. *A girl could get fat in a place like this*, she thought as she pulled off her left boot and placed it next to the other on the little rubber mat.

Looking up, Marcie asked, "Am I too early?"

"No, not at all. I'm running a bit late, as usual, and only just came in the back door when I heard the bell. Can I take your coat?" Kate had gotten hers off and was reaching for Marcie's with her free hand.

"Sure, thanks. I brought my bag of tricks," she said, gesturing to her roll cart. Marcie gave Kate a wink and added, "so we'll have you looking spiffy in no time."

"Well, thank God for that. This day has been crazy." Kate moved down the hallway. She tugged the orange tam from her head, tossed it into a bin overflowing with a rainbow assortment of other hand-knit tams, and hung their coats in the hall closet. "Please, come on in. I thought it best if we got ready upstairs."

"That sounds great. How much time do we have before you have to go?"

Glancing at her watch, Kate raised her eyebrows. "Yikes! Not much time at all. George just called me and said he needs me there by at least 5 p.m. to help with the volunteers and stuff." Kate hesitated a second, then said, "Apparently, I'm going to be interviewed tonight."

Marcie stared at her, her face frozen in a smile.

Shrugging her shoulders, Kate continued, "Not sure how well that's going to go but. . ." Her words trailed off.

"Well, that's fantastic, isn't it?" Marcie beamed at Kate. "Did Sophia contact you to let you know?" Marcie felt that sour twinge of deceit in her stomach again but did her best to keep a straight face.

"Well, no. George told me today. Apparently, he had heard from Sophia's assistant that she wanted to interview a number of people tonight, me being one of them." Kate smiled shyly. "Maybe it's because I kind of made a move towards reconciling with her last week." She turned and flicked on the light switch at the bottom of the landing.

"What? You did? My goodness Kate, that's great." Marcie's anxiety began to melt away. This was going better than she had planned.

Kate turned around. "I'm not sure but let's get upstairs so I can put on this dress. I'll tell you all about it."

Marcie grabbed her cart and followed Kate up a narrow set of wooden stairs covered with a well-worn runner that matched the Persian carpet in the front entrance. The stairs creaked a bit with each footfall and Marcie was careful not to bang the wheels of her cart too loudly on each carpeted step. As they passed a set of botanical prints that hung on the wall, Marcie couldn't help admiring the quaint décor of Kate's home. "This place is lovely," she said as they rounded the corner and ascended a second tier of stairs.

"Thanks. I inherited it from my grandparents and haven't made many changes to it since then." Kate turned to face Marcie from the top of the stairs. "I'm such a goof! Did you want a coffee or something?"

"Oh gosh, no, that's okay. Let's get you ready while you fill me in on Sophia. Then, if there's any time left, we can have a quick cup before you dash off for your big night, okay?"

"Sounds like a plan." Turning to the right, Kate disappeared into the master bedroom.

Pulling the heavy cart up the final step, Marcie thought, *Yes, plans are always good, especially when they work out.*

"Are you okay?" Kate shouted from the bedroom. "Do you need a hand with that case?"

Marcie laughed. "What, this old thing? It's a bit heavy but nothing a little girl power can't handle, right?"

Marcie managed to get the cart up the last step. She strolled into the bedroom with smile. It was small but neat. A queen-sized bed, covered with a light-pink chenille duvet, stood next to a large bay window. At the foot of the bed stood an antique vanity with a small, white, upholstered stool. The three mirrors atop the makeup table were angled to give a good all-round view. Marcie thought this vanity must be one of the things Kate had inherited from her grandmother.

"Come on," Kate said, gesturing to the bed. "Have a seat. I'll quickly get changed and then you can start on this ridiculous mop of mine." Kate disappeared with her dry-cleaning bag into the *en suite* and shut the door.

Taking a seat at the end of the bed, Marcie raised her voice slightly and inquired, "So, tell me about Sophia, already." Although Marcie cringed at her own forwardness, she just had to know what Kate was thinking.

"Well," said the muffled voice from behind the door, "I had a little talk with myself after the last time you and I met. Thanks for the styling again, by the way. After all you had told me about what Sophia went through in Toronto, you know, her trying to save her career, losing her boyfriend, and almost getting fired from her job. . ."

"Yeah?" Marcie lifted the case onto the bed and began to place its contents onto the small vanity.

"I started to really think about how hard it's been for her to try and reconnect with me. I certainly haven't made it easy on her, nor has George, for that matter. But I guess I decided that it just wouldn't be fair of me to push her away anymore."

Marcie was just about to place a bottle of hairspray on the vanity when she stopped mid-air and stared at her reflection in the mirror. Her bottom lip began to tremble.

"I'm listening," she managed to say, hoping Kate would continue.

"She made some pretty big mistakes and really let me down, but Marcie, who am I to judge her? I didn't know what was going on with her in Toronto. I blame myself, too, for not forcing her to tell me. Yes, she stole my recipe and profited from it but to be honest, if I had known she was about to lose her job, and this was her last chance at making an impression with her bosses, I would have willingly given it to her. The fact that she hardly spoke to me after Ben was killed really hurt. A lot. But now that I know the whole story, or at least what you've told me, I guess it's understandable."

Marcie sat down in front of the mirror and let out a small sigh.

"She must have felt terribly guilty. When it comes down to it, I just want us to be friends again. I'm tired of all this back and forth. It's just too stressful. Lord knows I have enough stress in my life."

Marcie brushed a tear from her cheek. Kate was on board. Now all Marcie had to do was stand back and let the magic happen. Absorbed in her own thoughts, Marcie didn't notice that Kate had come out of the bathroom.

"Are you okay?" Kate walked over and placed a hand on Marcie's shoulder.

"Oh, I'm fine, hon. I just get a little sentimental once in a while, that's all." Touching her hand, Marcie turned around on the stool and looked at Kate.

"And besides, that has to be about the cutest dress ever! It'd bring a tear to anyone's eyes."

Kate smiled and spun around. The snug cocktail dress was bright pink with yellow trim. Low-cut, it flared out just below her bust line. A lemon-yellow satin ribbon hugged her ribcage and trailed gracefully down her back in a neat bow. It was playful and sexy and Marcie was sure that Kate was bound to turn a few heads tonight.

"Do you think it's fancy enough?" Kate had stopped spinning and stood still, looking earnestly into Marcie's eyes.

"Hon, if that dress doesn't get you the attention you want tonight, I'll eat this hairbrush!" Marcie let out a girlish giggle, stood up, and patted the seat.

"Now, sit down, missy. We've got some work to do."

Chapter Thirty-five

Oma's Baking Tip

How you present your baked goods is almost as important as the treats themselves.

As soon as Marcie saw Kate's purple VW Bug pull around the corner on West 45th and out of sight, she turned around in the front seat of her car. She quickly fumbled for her cell phone, which lay at the bottom of her oversized handbag. With a shaky hand, she hit the speed dial for Sophia's number, then glanced over her shoulder once again to make sure that Kate had not returned.

"Hi, Marcie, what's up?" Sophia sounded like she was whispering into the mouthpiece.

"Did I catch you at a bad time?" Marcie's voice instinctively lowered to a hush.

"No, no, it's okay. I'm just stepping out of a meeting. Let me get into my office. One sec."

Marcie could hear a jumble of voices, then silence, then the sound of a door closing. The waiting was killing her. She fidgeted nervously behind the wheel of her car, eyes glancing upwards to the rear-view mirror, then back to street level. She registered a small woman walking her jacket-clad poodle towards the end of the block; other than that, the street was deserted.

"Okay, so tell me. How did it go?" Sophia's voice echoed Marcie's anxiousness.

"She's on board!" Marcie blurted. "Oh, my God, Sophia, this is really going to work!" Marcie grinned, finally able to share the pent-up excitement she felt.

"And you're telling me now that you thought it might not work? Oh, man, Marcie, I'm sitting on pins and needles here."

"It's all going to be okay." Marcie found herself half out of breath for excitement and took a deep inhalation before continuing. "So, I got here on time, as did Kate. We've just spent the last hour and a half getting her ready for the gala tonight. Oh my, Sophia, but she does look adorable. Anyways, while we were talking and stuff, she told me all about seeing you at the last garden club meeting and that she had made a 'peace offering of sorts.' Well, one thing led to another and she spilled the beans on her plan to forgive you and start anew. She's really going to do it, isn't that great?"

Marcie stopped to take another breath. Silence emanated from the other end of the phone.

"Hey, Sophia, are you okay?"

"Yes, yes, I'm fine." After a short pause, she added, "Thank you, Marcie."

"Oh gosh, there's no need to thank me. I'm glad to do it. You two were meant to be the best of friends and this little hiccup is just that, right?"

Marcie could hear Sophia's breath through the phone. It sounded slightly jagged like she was struggling to keep it in control. Marcie knew instinctively what was going on.

"I'm hoping those are tears of joy," Marcie said softly into the mouthpiece, "'cause if they're not, I'm going to have to come over there and give you a talkin' to." Her attempt to lighten the mood elicited a weak laugh from Sophia.

"No need to come over." Sophia cleared her throat, "I'm just relieved. Hugely relieved. You really don't know how much this means to me, Marcie."

"Oh, but honey I do, and that's why I did it. Seeing you that night in the parking lot just broke my heart. Then hearing your story while we finished off that pail of ice cream only solidified it for me. I do know how much it means. That's why I told all of those white lies to Kate." Marcie pulled her car keys from her handbag, closed the snap, and tossed it onto the passenger seat. "But now we've got one last scene to play and then the show will be over. I only hope that she can forgive me some day."

"She will, Marcie. Obviously, if she's capable of forgiving me for being such an awful, deceitful uncaring—"

"Hey!" Marcie's brow wrinkled.

"Well, it's true and even you can't deny it."

"OK, maybe, but you were under a lot of stress. That jerk of a boyfriend certainly wasn't any help either. Everyone makes mistakes, right?" offered Marcie.

"Yes, but what I did, stealing the cookie recipe and then practically ignoring her after Ben died," Sophia's voice stumbled, "that was really the icing on the cake, so to speak."

"Ah yes, but she's forgiven you all of that. At least that's what she told me today. And I believe her. You should too."

After a moment's pause, Marcie heard Sophia open her desk drawer and rustle around for something inside. The sound of Sophia sniffling revealed what she'd been searching for. Marcie pursed her lips.

"Look, if you keep crying the way you do, I'll have to pull out the big guns tonight when I do your makeup."

"You can't." Sophia sounded somewhat more upbeat.

"What do you mean I can't? I always do your hair and makeup, you silly nit."

"Not tonight. Or have you already forgotten? You and I don't work together anymore."

"Oh, shoot. You're right! I totally forgot. I guess I was so relieved after my time with Kate this afternoon that I plum forgot that part. Are you sure you'll be okay? You know you can use anything in my studio downstairs. Help yourself. If the doors are locked, just ask Carl for the key."

"I will. Don't worry."

"Okay, good. Well, mum's the word but I'm still gonna show up tonight. Kate told me about her upcoming interview and asked if I could come and do some final touch-ups." Marcie giggled with delight. "I wouldn't miss this for the world. You two are going to be best friends again by the end of the night. I'd bet my life on it!"

"Wait a second. Did you just say she knows about her interview? She wasn't supposed to find out about that." Not waiting for an answer, Sophia continued, "Whoa. Wait a second. Are you sure it's a good idea for you to show up tonight? What if one of the guys sees you?" Sophia's voice lowered to a hush.

"Oh, don't worry, honey. I'll keep well out of sight. Those two boys will never know I was there."

"Marcie, I don't know. I don't think it's a good idea." Sophia sounded worried.

"I'll keep a very low profile and be sure to know where they are every moment of the night. Besides, Hank will be too enamoured with all the free food to notice. And with all those fancy-dressed women walking around, Brian certainly won't be eyeing for me. I'll lurk in the shadows and as soon as your interviews are done, I'll disappear like a ship in the night. You won't even know I was there, okay?"

"I guess." Sophia sounded unconvinced.

Marcie put the keys in the ignition and started her car. "Hey, it's now 4:30. I told Kate I'd be there 5:30ish, which gives me just enough time to scoot home, touch bases with Ted, get changed, and get down to the gardens. What about you?" Marcie glanced into her rear-view mirror to see if there was any oncoming traffic.

"I've brought a change of clothes and will be meeting the boys downstairs in about a half-hour. Then we're heading out to the gardens. My guess is that we'll be there shortly after you so be sure to keep out of sight when we arrive."

"Don't worry, Sophia. You'll never even know I was there. Honest."

Sophia sighed. "Thanks again, Marcie. I don't know how I'm ever going to repay you."

"No need, hon. A smile on your face will be thanks enough." Revving her engine, anxious to get going, Marcie continued, "So, I guess that's it. We'll talk tomorrow, okay?"

"Sure thing." The phone went silent.

Marcie took a deep breath, grinned like a giddy schoolgirl, and tossed her cell onto her purse. They were almost there. One last scene and then this comedy of errors would magically transform itself into the heart-warming story of enduring friendship it was always meant to be. That is, if she could beat the afternoon rush-hour traffic and make it to the gardens on time. As she pulled out of her parking spot, her tires gave a little screech. Marcie giggled, thinking this was exactly the kind of thing that would happen in a movie.

Chapter Thirty-six

Oma's Baking Tip

Since overcrowding your cookie sheets will slow down the baking process, resist the urge to rush. Give your cookies some elbow room.

Mimi placed her fist against the steering wheel and pushed hard. A loud, blaring honk emitted from the bowels of her old Malibu Cutlass. Francine and Margaret cringed in the back seat, then covered their ears as the sound erupted again in three short bursts.

"Didn't I say to be ready to go at 4:45?"

Mimi glared out the passenger's-side window in the direction of Ethel's small bungalow. With curtains drawn and only a small light glowing above the front porch, Ethel's house looked quiet and deserted.

"I am not getting out of this car," Mimi announced while staring, steely-eyed, via the rear-view mirror, at her two passengers in the back seat. "It took me the best part of five minutes to get tucked in here so I'm certainly not going to venture out again until we reach the gardens." Huffing with impatience, she commanded, "Margaret, you go!"

"Why me?" Margaret moaned. "I don't want to risk getting my shoes dirty. They're not meant for outdoor walking. You go, Francine." Margaret gave Francine a swift nudge. She stared down at Francine's patent-leather loafers resting neatly atop the rubber mat on the rear floor. "You've got flat shoes on and it's only a short walk to the door."

"Well, I suppose," Francine murmured under her breath as she began to undo her seatbelt, "but I did call Ethel this morning and she said she would be ready to go on time."

The passenger door swung open and a gush of cold wind swept through the car.

"Well, hello everyone! I thought you'd never get here." Ethel clambered into the front passenger seat, placing her huge felted handbag on the floor of the car. She was extra careful not to squish her plastic rain bonnet against the Malibu's upholstered ceiling.

"For heaven's sake, Ethel. Where the hell did you suddenly come from?" Mimi tightly clutched the lapels of her black-and-white, polka-dotted raincoat to her chest. As her grip tightened around the plastic folds, it sounded strangely like a rubber balloon contorted into an animal shape by a street busker at the Granville Island market.

"I was just about to come out and get you, dear." Francine smiled timidly from the back seat as she pulled her seatbelt back into place across her faux-fur coat.

"Oh, no need, Francine. I was already waiting outside but then remembered that I left the side gate open earlier this morning when I was out in the garden. So, I popped around back to shut it. That's when I heard the horn. Oh my, but you gave me a fright, Mimi." Ethel clicked her seatbelt into its slot.

"Well, the same can be said for you, my dear. You should really learn not to sneak up on people like that. You'll give someone a heart attack some day." Mimi regretted her words as soon as they spilled out, having remembered that was exactly how Ethel's husband Sam had met his demise. The remorseful look on her face was met with a smile from Ethel.

"No need to worry, Mimi. I'm over all that." Patting Mimi's arm, she continued. "Like I always say, if my Sam was meant to have a heart attack, he was meant to have one, whether I just happened to pop out of the closet or not. I've long ago forgiven myself for doing some early spring cleaning that year. I mean," she said, turning sideways in her seat to look at Margaret and Francine, "how was I to know that he'd come looking for his old golf shoes at the moment when I needed to get some mothballs? Fluke, I guess." Turning around, she settled into her seat and reaching for the grab-handle above the passenger-door window. She bubbled, "So, on with the show, my dears! Let's go have some fun, shall we?"

"Yes, let's!" squeaked Francine like a small schoolgirl.

"All I care about is beating old St. Germain to the meeting room. I refuse to let her observe us arriving like she did the last time," Margaret said with a huff.

"Well, this time, she has no reason to complain. We look marvellous!"

Mimi revved the engine, then yanked on the steering wheel. She hastily pulled away from the curb, narrowly missing a cyclist who swerved to avoid colliding with her side door. Rolling down her window, she gave him a quick wave. "Sorry, young man, but we've got a show to do."

Luckily, she didn't see the gesture he gave her in reply. Mimi Owens was in no mood to be messed with. She was on a mission. A foul-tempered, obviously unobservant cyclist, who clearly didn't know the rules of the road, certainly wasn't going to hold her back. Besides, her gas indicator was almost on "E." She needed to get to the gardens as fast as she could before her fuel ran out.

Chapter Thirty-seven

Oma's Baking Tip

Take the time to crumb coat your cake. This first, thin layer of frosting catches all the little stray crumbs so that the second, thicker coat won't.

By the time Kate had reached the gardens, the party preparations were in full swing. Pulling her car into one of the empty slots near the entrance, she checked her cell one more time to see if there were any messages from the bakery. Deb had promised to take care of closing up so that Kate could get away early. *I have got to give that girl a raise,* Kate thought as she locked the car door and walked into the main entrance.

She quickly made her way down the hallway and past the admissions desk. Turning slightly to the left, she noticed that the doors to the reception hall stood ajar. People dressed in white shirts and black bowties were coming and going, arms laden with cardboard boxes, floral arrangements, and trays of silverware. As Kate squeezed herself past a cart of stacked chairs and hung her overcoat on a nearby rack, it didn't take her long to track down George. His booming voice could be heard above the ruckus of the evening's prep.

"Did I not say that the silent-auction tables should be set up towards the back of the room? Or was I simply speaking into thin air? And where's Boris? He was supposed to be here fifteen minutes ago to set up the speakers. Go find him. Now!" A ruffled-looking Stacey rushed past Kate, tightly clutching a clipboard under her arm.

"Hi, Kate. Cute dress. Bye, Kate." Stacey disappeared into the crowd of workers, presumably to go find Boris.

The hall looked magnificent. *George really outdid himself this time,* she thought. Neatly placed around the spacious room were dozens of round tables, each covered with a starched, white-linen tablecloth. The high-back chairs at each table were dressed in a similar material and tied with a black, satiny bow. In the centre of each table stood an extravagant, pink-lily bouquet bursting with colour. Small votive candles in glass bowls surrounded each floral arrangement. No doubt they would be lit at the last possible moment, bringing the final charm of the space into play. The catering staff was busy putting out the place settings. The overhead lighting twinkled in the stemware. It looked magical.

As Kate moved towards the small stage set up at the front of the hall, George turned, arms crossed. He looked perturbed. Despite his current disposition, Kate thought he looked amazing. In a neatly tailored grey suit that keenly matched his salt-and-pepper hair and sporting a bright purple satin tie, George looked delicious. Kate suspected that he smelled enticing too.

"Thank God, you're here!" Opening his arms wide, he took Kate into a big hug. Then holding her at arms' length, he smiled. "And you look amazing, by the way. Why, I'd be surprised if you go home alone tonight!"

Kate giggled. Even though she had no intention of finding the man of her dreams this evening, she had put a lot of effort into choosing tonight's outfit. She felt relieved to know that at least in George's mind, she looked good.

"And, pray tell, what has Marcie done with your hair?"

George spun her around and admired Kate's hairdo. Her usually unruly locks had been tamed into an elegant swirl that swept up from her neck and curved around atop her head, creating a beautiful twirl of rich auburn. She was wearing little pearl earrings and a matching pearl necklace. Her bright pink pumps went well with the colour of her playful dress. George couldn't take his eyes off of her.

"You look simply yummy. Richard won't be able to hold himself back." George batted his lashes at Kate. "And if I wasn't playing for the other team, I'd be buying you a couple of drinks tonight." George winked and gave her a small pinch.

"Now, stop that!" Kate giggled and pushed his hand away. "You'll mess my dress. Now," turning to face the room, she asked, "how can I help?"

Letting out an exaggerated sigh, George turned, picked up his clipboard, which was lying on one of the side tables, and scrolled down the list.

"Well, for starters, you can go down to Annex B and see if the doors are unlocked. If not, I'm afraid you'll have to come back here. By that time, Boris will have hopefully graced us with his presence and I'll get him to open it for you. That's the room where all the volunteers will be meeting and they can leave their coats and things in there. I need you to meet them when they arrive and get them organized." George looked at his watch. "We've got about half an hour before they get here. I'd like them to be in place before they open the doors at 6:30."

Handing her a sheet of paper that he slipped from the clipboard, George continued, "Here's that list of volunteers we've arranged for tonight and their assigned tasks. Hopefully, they all show up or we're screwed."

Kate knew that a lot was riding on this evening and George was under tremendous pressure. Even though her upcoming interview with Sophia was looming large, she set it aside for the moment and focused on George.

Taking the sheet, she grabbed George's hand and gave it a squeeze. "You're doing a fantastic job, George, and everything will work out just fine." Looking across the room, she continued, "This year, you've really outdone yourself. You should be proud."

"Well, a girl's gotta do what a girl's gotta do, right? Besides, if this is our last show, then I definitely want to go out with a bang." Smiling down at Kate, he leaned in and whispered in her ear, "Just keep that St. Germain out of my way tonight and I'll be forever grateful."

"And what about Sophia? Are you ready for your interview?" Kate knew that George was nervous about having to give an interview again. Even though she was terribly nervous herself, she wanted to make sure that he felt okay about it.

"Well, one thing's for sure: you are going to look stunning on TV. And, if I do say so myself, I will too!" George laughed loudly, then took Kate's hand and started to walk towards the entrance. "Stacey said Sophia would be showing up around 5:30 so we've got a bit of time to compose ourselves. But don't you worry: I'm going to keep an eye on her. If she tries any funny business, then—" He drew his forefinger across his throat.

"Oh, George you're so dramatic." Grabbing her coat that hung near the door, Kate smiled at him and added, "but I love you for it."

"I know you do, honey. Now, get going." He gave her hand a final squeeze, then turned to face a small group of catering staff standing idly by the entrance.

"Excuse me but what part of 'I'm here to work' don't you people understand? Now, get!" Shooing them out the door, he gave a small wave to Kate and hurried off in the opposite direction.

Thankfully, the door to Annex B was open. Kate flicked on the lights to reveal a small meeting room filled with chairs and tables. Tossing her purse and coat over the back of a nearby chair, she took a seat and began to go over the list that she and George had prepared a few weeks back. About twenty volunteers were scheduled to show up tonight; some were from the Kerrisdale club and some were unfamiliar to her.

Kate smiled to herself when she read the roster of familiar names and their assigned tasks:

Ursula St. Germain: Front desk, Admissions supervisor
Mimi Owens: Ticket-taker
Francine O'Dwyer: Coat check
Margaret Wikowski: Coat check
Ethel McCormick: Ticket-taker
Lloyd Stobbs: Silent auction
Chester Smith: Silent auction

Remembering her promise to Marcie, Kate reached in her purse and pulled out a pen. At the bottom of the list she wrote:

Marcie Mitchell: Hair and makeup

Even though Marcie hadn't been originally scheduled to come this evening, she had asked Kate this afternoon, while doing her hair, if she could arrange to let her in. Marcie had said she wanted to make sure that Kate looked her best for her interview. She had also mentioned that maybe George would like a touch-up as well. Kate smiled at the thought. Marcie seemed to know George as well as she did.

Chapter Thirty-eight

Oma's Baking Tip

If you lose power while baking, leave the oven door closed. Depending on how far along your baking was, there is usually enough heat in the oven to finish off the process, even if it takes a while longer.

Ursula was determined not to let challenges throw her tonight, even though she and four of her key volunteers were now more than fifteen minutes late.

Of all the days, of all the nights for this rag-tag ensemble of horticulturally challenged individuals to cause a ruckus, it had to be, of course, tonight.

Such were Ursula's churning thoughts as she hastily pulled into the Shaughnessy Gardens parking lot, frantically searching for an empty slot in which she could park her overstuffed Volvo station wagon. Guests had already begun to arrive and all of the parking spots near the entrance had been taken. In her haste, she drove too quickly over one of the parking lot's speed bumps, briefly jostling her passengers into mid-air. Afterwards, they settled down again, as cramped and uncomfortable as before.

Rather than hear a word of complaint, Ursula ensured that her voice boomed over the disgruntled moans coming from the back seat. "If I hear one word about this debacle at any point this evening, ladies, I will personally revoke your membership and send you packing. Is that understood?" Ursula turned her head, her eyes locking onto those of Francine, who had had the courage to take the passenger seat next to an extremely bristly Ursula.

"Yes, yes," said Francine, her voice barely a whisper. "Mum's the word, right ladies?"

"Of course," murmured Margaret. She was finding it hard to breathe, squished between Mimi and Ethel, who insisted on clutching her oversized felted bag firmly in her lap.

"We're really, very, very sorry, Ursula," pleaded Ethel. "I'm sure Mimi had no idea that we would run out of gas, right, Mimi?"

Mimi was sheepishly silent. She just shook her head and stared out the window as Ursula pulled the car to a stop at the far end of the lot.

Once in park with the car's ignition turned off, Ursula took a deep breath. "Remember: We are here as volunteers and representatives of the Kerrisdale Garden Club. We are now late, thanks to Mimi's inability to read a simple gauge and your collective helplessness to obtain the necessary supplies needed to fuel her vehicle because of improper footwear. We have thus, already, sent the wrong message to those in charge. Therefore," said Ursula, snapping her seatbelt loose and turning to face the group that stared at her in silence, "we will not waste any more time discussing the hows and whys of how we came to be late. I will simply apologize on our communal behalf and we will all commence with our duties. Do we agree?" Ursula stared coldly from one face to the next. Each nodded in silent agreement.

Opening the door, Ursula stepped out of the car, slammed the door shut, and without waiting for the others, began marching in a direct line towards the entrance.

The phone had rung just as Ursula was stepping out her front door. She had debated whether or not to simply ignore it but her innate sense of duty had pulled her back over the threshold. With house keys in hand, she had found herself rushing along the length of her hallway and grabbing the phone before it went to voicemail. She couldn't believe what she had heard: a frantic Francine was calling from a pay phone outside the 7-Eleven on the corner of Oak and 41st. Mimi had been giving them all a lift to the show and they had run out of gas. The nearest gas station was five blocks away and none of the ladies had had suitable footwear to make the trek, let alone a gas can in which to hold the necessary fluid.

"Shameful, shameful," Ursula muttered as she picked up her pace through the parking lot. Hearing the gaggle of hushed voices behind her, she squeezed the ignition key in her right hand without so much as a backwards glance. A sharp honk barked out a discordant tone as she stoically walked up to the front doors of the auditorium. A short line of smartly dressed patrons had begun to form. Brushing aside their accusatory glances, which suggested that she and her group had line-hopped to the front, Ursula was relieved to see Kate peering anxiously out of the large plate-glass doors.

"We are here to volunteer," announced Ursula in her best school-director voice, hoping this would appease some of the disgruntled looks they were receiving.

Unlocking the latch, Kate ushered Ursula and the garden club ladies indoors.

"Thank you for your patience, everyone. The doors will be opening very soon." Kate smiled apologetically to the line-up and quickly closed the doors.

"Thank God, you're here, ladies! I've been worried sick that something awful had happened."

The sound of sheer relief in Kate's voice immediately melted the stony mask plastered onto Ursula's face. Gently grabbing Kate's elbow, Ursula manoeuvred her into the foyer and away from peering eyes. She lowered her voice.

"I am so sorry, Kate." She glanced quickly over her shoulder to the guilty-looking group behind her and said, "but I had a rescue mission to undertake at the last minute. It appears Mimi ran out of gas along 41st Avenue and she had Francine, Ethel, and Margaret with her in the car. Thankfully, I was at home when they called and was able to pick up the stranded group and bring them along with me."

"Well, thank goodness you're all here now. Chester and Lloyd and the other volunteers are already at their stations and there's no time to waste." Raising her voice, Kate turned and smiled at Mimi and the gang. "I'm sorry to hear about your mishap but we've got to hurry now, ladies. Follow me and I'll show you where you can hang your coats and bags. Then," Kate said, turning on a heel and walking quickly in the direction of Annex B, "I'll quickly show you all the ballroom. It looks amazing!"

"Well, you look amazing, my dear." Ethel was already out of breath from scurrying across the parking lot but could hardly control her enthusiasm at seeing Kate in her pink-and-yellow dress.

"Simply stunning," said Francine, bringing up the rear behind Margaret and Mimi. "Don't you think so, Margaret?"

Turning her head, Margaret beamed at Francine. "You bet I do, Francine." Raising her voice so Kate could hear, she added, "I just love your hair and those shoes!"

"They're just the bee's knees," chimed Mimi as she watched Kate from behind. "You're just as cute as a frickin' bug in a rug, Kate!"

Ursula could bear it no more. She stopped and turned to face the group.

"Ladies. Ladies. We are not here for idle chit-chat. Kate has clearly indicated that we are now extremely late. As much as I'm sure she appreciates your comments, we have work to do. Am I right, Kate?"

Kate smiled, gave Ethel a quick wink, and said, "Yes, yes, of course. Come on."

As they continued on their way, the hustle and bustle of last-minute preparations was evident in the comings and goings of the catering staff. They were dressed smartly, scurrying about like an organized troupe of penguins in their black ties and crisp white shirts. A feeling of excitement filled the air. Ursula and her group quickly passed the open auditorium doors. She caught a glimpse of the television crew. Sophia, dressed impeccably in a beautiful, dark purple evening gown, appeared to be smiling at something George Stanwell had just said. Both were standing in a pool of bright light.

Ursula could feel her jaw tighten. The molars at the back of her mouth began to grind. What was it about that man that set her off? His haughtiness? His self-absorption? His domineering attitude? Yes, those things definitely set her teeth on edge. Long ago, she had got the impression that he simply didn't like her. *What was there not to like?* she wondered. She was hard working, horticulturally knowledgeable, loyal, and pragmatic. Admirable qualities, all.

Well, she thought as she caught up with Kate, *I am certainly not going to let the likes of George Stanwell get the best of me, especially tonight.* Instinctively smoothing a hand over her hair, Ursula cleared her throat and turned to Kate.

"I see our film crew has already arrived," Ursula said through slightly clenched teeth. "Not surprising, I suppose, that Sophia has chosen to interview Mr. Stanwell yet once again." Notes of jealousy caused her tone to rise towards the end of the sentence.

Kate was walking quickly and talked over her shoulder as she rounded another corner, heading for an open doorway at the end of the hall. "No, not surprising at all. In fact, I've been told that both you and I are on the list for scheduled interviews this evening as well."

Ursula felt her knees buckle slightly and blood rush to her face. Doing her best to keep apace, she stammered, "But I didn't come prepared." She glanced down at the grey tweed skirt that poked out from the hem of her snugly fitting overcoat. "If I had known, I would have picked a new outfit or at the very least, had my hair done professionally."

"Oh, no need to worry about that, Ursula," said Kate. "You're dressed very nicely and my friend Marcie is here. She's a professional makeup artist. I'm sure she'd love to give you a little going over, if you'd like. But we'd have to do it quickly because the doors will be opening in a few minutes. I still have to get you all to your posts and give you the low-down."

Considering her options and naturally wanting to look her best for a nationally syndicated television show, Ursula quickly agreed, saying, "Well, if it doesn't take too much time, I'm sure this Marcie friend of yours will do a lovely job."

They reached the open door. Following Kate like a gaggle of geese, the ladies trundled into Annex B.

Kate gestured to a middle-aged, blonde-haired woman sitting in the corner, chewing gum and filing her nails.

"Marcie? I've got another victim for you!"

Marcie looked up and smiled cheerily at the crowd that had just entered the room.

"Sounds good to me, Kate. Which one of these darling ladies is it to be?"

Ursula now had second doubts. She had never trusted gum-chewers and being referred to as a "victim" sounded too avant-garde for her taste.

Chapter Thirty-nine

Oma's Baking Tip

Unlike stirring, mixing, or beating, creaming isn't about combining ingredients — it's about aerating them. Creaming adds air. Air is fluffy and fluffy is good. Before you even start scooping the dough, something's already happened. Something miraculous. Something no one ever tells you: Creaming has just added at least five extra cookies to the batch.

The sounds of soft jazz music floated through the air, punctuated by staccato tones of laughter and tinkling glasses. After the initial rush of the evening's prep and getting all of the volunteers settled into position, Kate was relieved to see that the hectic pace had relaxed and everything was running smoothly.

She was seated for dinner at one of the tables close to the stage, along with George, Richard, and a few dignitaries from city council and the parks board. Although George was sometimes preoccupied with the comings and goings of various speakers, Kate was thankful to see that he was obviously tickled pink at how well everything had progressed. He engaged in lively conversation about the upcoming show with some of the other dinner party guests. He didn't miss a beat.

The meal had been exquisite. The violinist hired to provide dinner music had arrived on schedule, much to George's relief, and performed beautifully. Now that dinner was over and the plates had been cleared, a jazz ensemble took to the stage and began to play. On a promise to return and do a turn on the dance floor with both George and Richard, Kate excused herself and headed to the ladies' room to freshen up.

As she stepped into the ladies' room, Kate marvelled at how nicely it, too, had been transformed into something special. A fresh bouquet of flowers was set off to one side of the sinks. A wicker basket containing a varied selection of hand creams and soft paper towelettes stood in the centre of the countertop. The lighting was subdued, thanks most likely to Boris, who could work magic with any light switch. The decor reminded Kate more of a spa than a washroom in a public facility.

The swinging door closed quietly behind Kate. It was obvious from the silence that emanated from the row of stalls that she was alone. She walked up to the bank of mirrors and stood, leaning slightly forwards. Staring thoughtfully at her reflection, Kate smiled. Marcie really had done a wonderful job with her hair. Oma would have been pleased.

"Hi, Kate."

Startled, Kate darted her eyes upwards and searched the darkness reflected in the mirror for a face to match the voice. She could barely recognize the outline but immediately knew that it was Sophia, who was standing just out of the reach of lights, slightly off in the shadows towards the door.

"Hi."

"Sorry if I startled you. It's just that I saw you leaving the auditorium and I thought it might be a good time to do your interview. Do you have a moment?"

"Sure. George said he didn't need me again until they make the first announcement for the silent auction so I guess it's okay."

Coming closer into the light, Sophia stood simply. She had a small leather clutch purse tucked under one arm and her hands were clasped together, resting easily against the front of her dress. Her dark hair fell loosely around her shoulders in soft curls. She wore an elegantly cut gown made of dark purple chiffon that shimmered in the light. Kate had admired her throughout the evening but this was the first moment she had spoken directly to her all night. George had said his interview had gone splendidly and he had thought Sophia looked ethereal.

"Like a modern day Helen of Troy," he'd said. "Let's just hope she left her wooden horse at home." George was obviously still smitten and Kate could see why.

"By the way, you look wonderful, Kate. I love your hair and that dress. It's just delightful."

"Thanks. So do you. But really, all the credit for how I look goes to Marcie."

Sophia cleared her throat and stepped a bit closer. Placing her handbag on the countertop, she looked straight ahead, not meeting Kate's eyes.

"Marcie?"

"Yes. It's like she dropped out of heaven. At our first volunteer meeting, she kind of showed up out of nowhere and offered her services to do my hair and makeup. You know, I think you might even know her."

Sophia continued to stare straight ahead, then reached down and pulled a lipstick from her purse.

"I do?"

"Yes, she told me she had worked at the same TV station as you but she left just when you arrived. Don't you remember her?" Kate thought it was funny that Sophia wouldn't recall her, especially since she'd obviously had a few heart-to-hearts with Marcie. On the other hand, maybe Sophia was uncomfortable. Marcie did say that Sophia had told her things about what had happened in Toronto and that she had badly let down a friend. Kate instantly regretted mentioning Marcie's name.

"Oh right, of course, *that* Marcie. I actually saw her a couple of weeks ago at the volunteer meeting. Blonde hair. Kind of bubbly? She was nice." Pausing to check her lipstick, Sophia said, "I was sorry to see her go." She put her lipstick away and smiled at Kate.

"Maybe I'll bump into her again at some point," Sophia said. "But first things first. We've got our interview to do. Are you ready?"

"I guess so." Kate turned and looked at Sophia. Her heart was in her throat but she needed to ask, "You're not going to say anything about the shop, though, Soph, are you? Or Ben, right?"

Sophia's heart skipped a beat. Kate hadn't called her "Soph" in years. She felt her pulse race.

"No, no, of course not. We'll just talk about the show and what you've been doing to prepare for tonight. That's it. I'm sorry I even brought that up last time. It was stupid." She paused. "No. It was desperate and I'm really sorry."

"I'm sorry too." Kate looked down and sighed.

"My God, Kate. What do you have to be sorry about? It was me, not you, who screwed this whole thing up. I still can't believe you don't hate me."

Kate continued to stare at her hands.

"Or maybe you do. You certainly would have every right."

"I don't hate you, Soph. You hurt me, that's true, and I may never really understand why you did the things you did. But I can never hate you."

Placing both hands against the counter, Sophia stared at the sink, unable to lift her eyes to meet Kate's.

"The truth is, I was scared. I'm still scared. I've lived most of my life being scared. All this," said Sophia, gesturing to her dress and her face, "this is just a big cover-up. It's just my way of getting by. You know, I've never really felt very successful. I know, I've got this show and everything and people know who I am, but really, no one really knows me."

Turning to look at Kate, she continued. "You used to know me, better than anyone. After everything that's happened, despite all the letdowns, all the disappointments and the. . ."

She continued, struggling for words, "all the hurt I've caused, I just want us to be friends like we were before. I want to be able to laugh about stupid things and cry watching a chick flick on TV while munching bowls of popcorn and eating cold pizza. Right now, I don't laugh much. And crying, well, let's just say that there's a bit too much of that in my life right now."

Kate was silent. She had waited years to hear this confession. Yet, hearing it only made her feel worse than before. All she wanted to do was to reach out and hold Sophia tight.

"Oh, Kate, I feel terrible about what I did to you. I was selfish, desperate, and an awful, so-called friend. Can you ever really forgive me? Because until you—" She choked on her words and swallowed hard. Clearing her throat and struggling to find the right words, she continued, "Until you do, I'll never be a whole person again."

Kate couldn't bear it a moment longer. She stepped towards Sophia and without hesitation, wrapped her arms around her, holding her close. Sophia crumbled at her touch and began to quietly sob. Kate held her tightly as she squeezed her eyes closed. She knew that if she let Sophia go, it would be like recklessly letting her fall into the chasm of her grief. Kate was resolved to hold on.

There would be no falling tonight. No careening off the edge. There was nothing left to do. Nothing left to resolve. Kate realized there never really was. It had always been a question of understanding more than forgiveness. Feeling her friend so close, hearing her quiet sobs, sensing the relief in her touch, she knew that everything was resolved. In that instant, her touch had healed. Words were now useless.

Sophia's quiet sobs subsided and her breathing slowly returned to normal. She took a deep breath, then held Kate at arms' length, still unable to look her in the eyes. Kate spoke first.

"It's okay, Soph. I don't want to fight this anymore. Let's just let it go, okay? For both our sakes. 'Cause I honestly feel that if we don't let this go, it'll gnaw away at us both and make us bitter old women some day. Not exactly how I pictured myself. How about you?"

For the first time in many months, Sophia genuinely laughed. It started off as a soft chuckle and rounded into a smooth smile full of happiness and relief.

"So, let's get you cleaned up and let's get this damned interview over with before I lose my courage and go slinking back to the bakery."

"No way! I've got you scheduled for this interview and come hell or high water, we're going to get it done." Sophia dabbed the corners of her eyes with one of the towelettes from the basket on the counter, then pulled a compact from her purse and freshened up her foundation.

"I can go and get Marcie, if you like. I'm sure she'd love to see you." Kate smiled. "She'd have you fixed up in a jiff."

"No, no. That's not necessary. Besides, the guys are waiting in the atrium. I told them I'd be back in ten minutes and look." Sophia glanced at her wristwatch. "Oh my God, we're late. We'd better get going."

"Are you sure you want to do this?" Kate searched Sophia's eyes, looking for the sincerity she hoped she'd find.

"Hey, aren't I the one who should be asking the questions?"

"Yes, I guess you are, Ms. Simpson. Show me the way." Both laughing, they left the washroom.

After a few moments of silence, the sound of a flushing toilet broke the stillness. Ursula gingerly emerged from the stall at the end of the row. She walked up to the bank of sinks and turned the knob on the faucet. Warm water rushed from the tap. After dispensing some soap into her palms, she placed her hands under the flow and slowly washed her hands. Looking up at the mirror, she closed her eyes. A silent tear rolled gently down her cheek. She brushed it aside. Reaching out, she dried her hands on the roll of towels hanging next to the sink.

A younger woman walked into the washroom. Recognizing Ursula as the woman who had ushered her into the auditorium earlier that night, she exclaimed cheerfully, "It's going well this evening, don't you think?"

Taking one last glance at herself in the mirror, then straightening her back, Ursula smiled warmly and replied, "Yes, very well indeed."

She left the washroom, gently humming a tune, and returned to her post at the entrance.

Chapter Forty

Oma's Baking Tip

Be careful. To the naked eye, salt looks a lot like sugar.

The music had stopped and the four-piece jazz ensemble took a much-needed break. Gleeful patrons, loose from their drinks and giddy from dancing, gathered in small groups, laughter bubbling above their heads like champagne froth. George was smiling broadly. He had just gotten up to the podium to announce a few more of the silent-auction winners. Kate decided it was a good time to check on the volunteer ladies in the atrium. She wanted to make sure that they were having a good time despite being separated from the ballroom.

"I'm just going to pop out front to see Ethel and the gang." Kate leaned over and spoke into Richard's ear. "Can you tell George I'll be back right away?"

"Sure thing. But don't forget the next dance is mine, right?"

"I wouldn't miss it for anything." Kate looked into Richard's chocolate-brown eyes. Giving his arm a warm squeeze, she grabbed her pink purse and disappeared into the milling crowd. She'd made it all the way to the doors when suddenly, they swung open and Brian lunged forward, head down, obviously on a mission. He almost slammed into Kate but was able to catch himself at the last second.

"Whoa! Sorry there, Katey." He chuckled and rubbed his hands together. "I was just checking to see if there were any of those crab cakes left over. The kitchen said they were out and I haven't had a bite all night."

"No problem. There might be some left on the banquet tables near the far wall." Kate gestured over her shoulder. She had already assessed Brian as completely harmless, perhaps a little too forward sometimes, and always on the prowl, it seemed, but nothing to worry about. She turned and smiled.

"I was just heading out to check on a few of the volunteers. You know, make sure they're not too lonely out there near the entrance." Smiling again, she walked past Brian, who was holding the door open. To her chagrin, he chose to follow.

"If you're meaning that giggly group of old ladies, I wouldn't be too worried. They seem to be having a good ol' time. I could hear their laughter all the way down the hall when I came in." Kate turned to look at him and he winked, then jammed his hands into his pockets. "You know," he started, looking up and smiling a bit too widely, "in my professional opinion, if that means anything to you, I have to say that you did a great job in your interview tonight."

Not wanting to be impolite, Kate hovered for a moment. "Well, thanks, Brian, I appreciate that. I was a bit nervous but Sophia is really good at putting people at ease."

"That she is. That she is." Scuffing the floor with the tip of his shoe, Brian slowly raised his eyes up the length of her body, finally letting his gaze rest somewhere near her cleavage. Kate locked her jaw.

"And of course, you look great. Really put together. I managed to get some really good shots of you, you know, by yourself without Sophia in the way."

Looking for an easy way to exit an increasingly sticky conversation, Kate glanced over her shoulder in the direction of the coat check.

"Well, I really should get checking on that giggly group of ladies. Wouldn't want them to get into any kind of trouble now, would we?" Kate started to move in the opposite direction but Brian followed close on her heels.

"Hey, I didn't mean to scare you off. I just wanted to let you know how nice a job you did. And you really did look awesome. Marcie probably gave you a hand, right?"

Kate stopped suddenly and slowly turned to face Brian.

"Marcie?" Her eyes narrowed slightly.

"Yeah, Marcie. She did your hair and makeup, right? On these shoots, she always does a bang-up job, excuse the pun." Brian chuckled but Kate stood frozen on the spot. *Did he just say what I think he said?*

Flashes of thoughts, snippets of conversations, like a disjointed dream, raced through her head. Kate madly tried to piece the puzzle together. Brian's words resounded in her brain like when someone gets to the final number in a combination lock. The notches line up, there's a subtle click, and with a turn of the handle, the door swings wide open to reveal the cache inside.

"How did you know Marcie did my hair?" She took in a sharp breath. Kate spoke in a whisper.

"Well, she does everybody. I mean, usually." Brian stammered a bit. "When we have a big gig like this, she always comes along. Actually, Sophia insists on it because you never know what people are going to look like, if you know what I mean. Not that you look bad or anything, but. . ." His words trailed off. Brian stared at Kate, who had lost most of the colour from her face. Pointing his thumb over his shoulder, he bumbled on. "I can go and get the two of them, if you like. I think I saw them talking near the kitchen just now."

Brain's face blurred. Kate faltered. Her knees felt soft. It was as if someone had slammed the breath out of her lungs. She was barely able to speak.

"You mean, they, they. . ." Kate could only just form the words, "work together?"

"Hell, yeah. They're practically best friends. I mean, they see each other almost every day at the station. I'm just surprised to see Marcie here tonight. I thought she was on vacation but I guess duty calls, right?" Brian laughed nervously, then wiped his mouth with the back of his hand.

Kate reluctantly searched his eyes for the truth she knew was there. "But I thought Marcie was retired."

"Retired?" He let out a grunt. "She'll never retire. Hell, she loves her job too much. Besides, it gives her the perfect opportunity to gossip." Lowering his voice and leaning in close, he whispered. "I sure hope you didn't tell her any of your deep, dark secrets. Hey, are you okay?" Brian reached out to steady Kate, grabbing the crook of her arm.

Wrenching her arm away, Kate turned and ran towards the entrance. The anger that welled up from the depths of her gut raged forth with such heated fury she could scarcely see. But she knew she had to get out. The walls began to close in on her as the last of her breath squeezed out her mouth in a silent cry. She rushed past Ethel, Mimi, Margaret, and Francine, who were gathered near the coat check. She cupped one of her hands over her lips and roughly pushed on the entrance doors, releasing her into a gust of cold night air.

"Kate! Kate!" Mimi's voice echoed into the evening fog behind her. "You should put your coat on, dear. It's frightfully cold out there."

Kate didn't hear her. She didn't hear anything except her own ragged gasps as she gulped the frigid air that seared her like blasts of winter Arctic wind. As she ran towards her car, Kate shook her head from side to side, as though trying to shake off the thoughts that ran through her head. By the time she had reached her VW Bug, she felt dizzy with nausea.

Grabbing the cold metal of the car's roof rack, Kate held herself steady. Then turning and leaning her back against the driver's door, she fumbled furiously in her purse. The car keys jabbed at her fingertips.

Dragging them out of the confines of her handbag, she pushed the unlock button and flung herself into the driver's seat. Slamming the door with a strength she didn't know she possessed, she tightly gripped the steering wheel as though holding onto it would rescue her from her drowning thoughts.

Engine revving, she raced out of the parking lot, scraping the undercarriage on one of the speed bumps. She brought the car to a screeching stop at 37th Avenue, then made a quick right turn onto Oak Street and raced south towards 41st. Her sobs filled the privacy of her car, echoing off the dashboard and dripping down the windows in tears of condensation. Streetlights flashed past. The road seemed a slick black trail that loomed in and out of focus.

Kate's cell phone rang but she ignored it. She couldn't bear to speak to anyone. After three rings, it stopped.

Kate didn't know why she ended up at the bakery but she didn't care. It was closer than home and she needed to be somewhere safe. Clumsily parking her car at the back of the shop, she didn't notice Mr. Ho unloading boxes of cauliflower and broccoli from his delivery van next door. He waved and shouted, "Good evening!" but Kate gave no response as she unlocked the employee door and stumbled across the threshold. The hallway was dark but familiar. It smelled of chocolate and baked pastry dough. Kate thought for a moment she might be ill but instead of heading for the washroom at the end of hallway, she felt along the wall until her hand touched the light switch. She flicked it on. The overhead pot lights came to life.

Turning the knob on her office door, Kate entered but left the lights off, choosing instead, to inch her way along by the luminosity of her computer monitor. Her screen-saver was set to play a cascading fall of big shiny bubbles, their pastel colours glowing softly in the darkened room.

Once inside the confines of her small office, she tumbled onto the small couch that stood opposite her desk. Kicking her shoes to the floor, she pulled her knees in close to her chest and covered herself with the familiar-feeling crocheted afghan her Oma had given her many years ago. She pulled the blanket tight under her chin. Its edges slowly soaked up the stream of tears that flooded her face.

The full impact of Sophia's deception blazed behind her closed eyelids in vivid colour. The realization that Sophia had manipulated her once again was almost too much to bear. Between the ragged sobs that threatened to tear her heart in two, Kate cried out, knowing full well that the one who needed to hear her most was back at the gardens chatting idly with the film crew and planning her next move with Marcie.

Kate wrenched open her eyes and stared blankly at the computer monitor, watching the bubbles bounce in their rhythmic dance. After a few minutes, her breathing began to settle but her throat felt tight and raw. Her head ached with exploding thoughts of humiliation and anguish. A deep exhaustion pressed down upon her as she felt her body sink into the folds of the couch. She pinched her eyes closed and felt the sticky wetness of her eyelashes as they clumped together and shut out the world. Her thoughts became fuzzy, like the frazzled fringe of the afghan wrapped like a warm cocoon around her slight frame. Soon all was silent except for the sound of her breath catching slightly in her throat.

Outside in her car, Kate's cell phone rang. No one answered. It went to voicemail. "Where are you, my dear? Richard says you promised him a dance. You and I have some celebrating to do so stop flirting with whomever you're with and get that pretty little butt of yours into the ballroom right now. Or I'll send Boris out looking for you. Kisses."

Chapter Forty-one

Oma's Baking Tip

If you accidently overheat your custard, it will "break," resulting in unsightly lumps. You can rescue your custard with a good old whiz in the blender.

Sophia knew it was probably a bad idea to talk to Marcie but thankfully, the hallway that led to the kitchen was filled with the comings and goings of the catering staff who were emptying the dining hall of the dinnerware and buffet leftovers. They would be well hidden, standing next to the kitchen entrance. Sophia felt confident that no one would see them. She was glad to hear that Marcie had managed to stay out of sight all evening, hidden away in the volunteers' meeting room. When Marcie had mentioned that she had done some touch-ups for Ursula, it reminded Sophia that she had one last interview to conduct and then the night would be done, at least on a professional level.

"Did you talk to Kate yet?" Marcie looked at Sophia in anticipation.

A waiter carrying a heavy load of used plates squeezed past them. "If you don't mind, ladies," slipped from his lips as he headed into the noisy kitchen behind.

Sophia grabbed Marcie's arm and pulled her closer behind the open door.

"Yes!" she beamed brightly. "In the ladies' room, of all places. It was wonderful, Marcie. I'm not sure what's going to happen next and we still have a lot to talk about but we've definitely come to an understanding. She's so forgiving," Sophia glanced over her shoulder to make sure no one was looking or listening in, "and I really don't deserve it but I'm so relieved."

"Oh, stop it. You're gonna make me start crying." Marcie sighed, then rubbed her hands together. "All in a good night's work."

"Well, I'd best track down Ursula and get that interview done. No need to ask you if you've seen Brian and Hank, I guess?"

"Nope. Haven't seen hide nor tail of either one of them, thank God. Just like we planned." Poking her head around the door and glancing down the hallway, she said. "Guess I'll go and pack up my things." Grabbing Sophia's hand, Marcie giggled. "I'm so happy for you, Sophia. You can tell me all the rest on Monday when I'm back at work."

"Okay, will do. Thanks again, Marcie." Sophia reached out and gave her a big hug. "I don't know how I'm ever going to repay you."

Marcie looked up at her and smiled warmly. "No need. Really, no need at all." She slipped away and disappeared around the corner, heading for Annex B.

Sophia walked to the far end of the hallway, then turned left. She thought it best to track down Ursula first and then find out where Brian and Hank were. She needed them to get their equipment set up in the atrium for Ursula's interview. As she got closer to the entrance, she could hear the excited voices of some of the garden club ladies chattering away. It wasn't until she got closer that she recognized the tone of alarm in their voices.

"But she hasn't come back in yet. Poor thing will freeze to death out there without her coat." Mimi was speaking to a huddled group standing in front of the entrance doors. Her hands were cupped on the windowpane, her forehead pressed against the cold glass as she searched the fog-filled darkness.

"I think we should go looking for her. At the very least, bring the poor thing her coat." Ethel sounded worried and looked to the group for some consensus. That's when Sophia noticed Ursula coming up behind her. She was wearing her overcoat and carried Kate's pink coat draped over her arm.

"I will go and find her, ladies. I'm sure there's no need for concern. Perhaps she just forgot something in her car."

Sophia looked to Ursula with concern and gestured to the pink coat slung over her arm. "What's going on? Is Kate alright?"

Ursula stopped next to Sophia and smiled warmly. "I'm sure it's nothing but apparently, the ladies saw Kate rush out through the doors a few minutes ago. She wasn't wearing her coat and she has not returned."

"It's been over ten minutes and she looked like she was crying!" Francine couldn't contain her anguish any longer. "I'm afraid something's happened to her. Oh my, this is not good."

"Crying?" Sophia turned and stared at Francine. "Are you sure?"

"It definitely seemed like it, didn't it, Mimi? You saw her up close." Francine nodded to Mimi, who turned from her lookout position in front of the plate-glass windows.

"I think I'm old enough to know when a girl's crying and Kate definitely was."

Without hesitation, Sophia reached for Kate's coat. "I'll go. I'm sure she's out there somewhere. Who knows? Maybe she went back in through another door."

"Absolutely not." Ursula held the coat tightly. "First of all," she began, glancing at Sophia's flowing chiffon gown, "you are not dressed for the weather outside and second, there is no other way to get in. All other doors are emergency exits only and are locked to the outside. At least, that's what Kate told us when she gave us our little orientation tour earlier this evening."

"But what if something's really happened to her?" Sophia stared out into the darkness of the parking lot. "And what was she so upset about? I just interviewed her a while back and she seemed just fine—" Sophia's words trailed off as her eyes darted back and forth across the foggy darkness that clung to the light posts just outside the doors.

Pulling Sophia a little closer, Ursula said kindly, "Not to worry, Sophia. I'm sure Kate is just fine." Lowering her voice to a whisper, she added, "Remember: The eyesight of these ladies might not be what it used to be."

"I heard that!" Mimi broke in between the two of them. "Our eyes were certainly not playing tricks on us and we saw what we saw, right, ladies?" A unified chorus of enthusiastic, yet concerned, agreement welled up behind her.

"Be that as it may, I will go and find Kate," said Ursula determinedly. "Please wait here for my return. I'm sure she's fine — perhaps a bit chilled but fine just the same."

Sophia stared as the ladies parted and allowed Ursula to exit through the doors. Walking briskly, she made her way along the paved sidewalk until it sloped downwards to the parking lot. Making a sharp right, she disappeared behind the bulk of a minivan standing silently at the edge of the parking lot.

"I hope she finds her, and soon." Margaret looked to Francine for reassurance.

"Oh, she will. I have no doubt of that." Francine's words echoed off the plate glass windows of the atrium.

Sophia stepped forward and stood next to the group. Staring out into the darkness, they held a silent vigil, waiting for any sign of the returning pair.

"I don't like this one bit!" Mimi turned and started to walk in the direction of the volunteer room. Talking over her shoulder, she said, "I don't know about you, ladies, but I'm not going to simply stand by and wait. I have to do something."

"Then please, wait here." Sophia's voice was calm although her heart was racing. "There's no need for all of you to go traipsing around in the dark out there. I'll go and get one of my guys. They'll join Ursula and have a look around too." Sophia quickly walked past Mimi. "Please just stay here and wait for Ursula. I'm sure she'll show up with Kate in no time."

Trying to convince herself of her own reassuring words, Sophia walked swiftly in the direction of the ballroom. *Where the hell are those two?* she mumbled under her breath as she furtively glanced left and right. She passed numerous party guests, all of whom smiled at her in recognition.

Forcing a smile in return, Sophia walked quickly towards the ballroom. She was growing impatient as she rounded the last corner. There, to her great relief, stood Brian. He was leaning against the wall and chatting with a young woman who was blushing at something he had just said. They both laughed and then he looked up.

Sophia wasn't smiling. "Have you seen Kate?" Her voice sounded earnest but Brian remained leaning against the wall. Turning to his latest potential conquest, he chuckled and said, "Oops, sorry. Looks like the big guns are here." Gesturing to Sophia, he continued, "Gotta get back to work. You've got my number. Give me a call sometime. I'd love to show you around the sound truck some day."

The young woman smiled. She glanced quickly at Sophia and blushing, silently disappeared back into the ballroom.

"So, what's the answer, Brian? I haven't got all night." Sophia's tone was business-like. She was often annoyed by Brian's philandering and tonight was no different.

"Yeah, sure, I've seen her. She's a bit wiggy, though, you know?"

"What do you mean?" Sophia stepped closer. She could smell Brian's cheap aftershave. Its acrid scent set her on edge.

"Well, I was just chatting with her a while back and she got all uppity and left."

"What did you say to her?" Sophia felt like strangling Brian. *He prob-*

ably hit on her or worse, made some kind of physical advance, she thought. She could kill him right now.

"Nothing! Look, she was the one who got all upset. All I did was compliment her on how hot she looked and the next thing I know, she's going on about you and Marcie and blah, blah, blah. You know, girl stuff. Took off like a shot and I haven't seen her since."

Sophia's stomach lurched. She could feel a cold sweat break on the small of her back.

"Marcie? What does this have to do with her?"

"How the hell should I know?" he shouted. A couple of guests leaving the ballroom stared at Brian, who immediately lowered his voice. "How the hell should I know, Sophia? She seemed to think that Marcie was retired and that you two don't know each other. I mean, geeze, you two are practically attached at the hip sometimes. I just saw you two talking near the kitchen and all I did was set her straight. What's the harm in that?"

What's the harm in that? The words smashed inside Sophia's head like a wrecking ball. She grabbed the side of her dress, hiked it slightly, and broke into a run towards the entranceway. As she rounded the corner, she saw that Marcie had joined the group waiting anxiously at the entrance.

"Oh, my God, Marcie. She knows." Sophia blurted the words out before she had a chance to filter her thoughts. Mimi, Francine, Margaret, and Ethel all turned at once, staring backwards towards Sophia. Marcie went pale and stared open-mouthed at Sophia.

"We've got to find her. Oh, my God, I've got to explain." Sophia tore around the corner of the coat check, frantically brushing coats aside in search of her own.

"Here dear, here. Let me help you." Ethel rushed behind the counter and rustled among the coats, finally finding Sophia's long black overcoat. "I remembered this one when you came in. It looked so refined."

Sophia grabbed the black cashmere coat with a quick thank you.

Sophia struggled to get it on, then realized, "Damn it, my purse."

"We can get it later. Come on, Sophia, if we don't find her in the parking lot, we'll take my car. She can't have gotten far, right?" Marcie was halfway out the door. Sophia dashed past her. In seconds, they were gone.

The ladies stood in shocked silence. Mimi finally spoke. "See, I told you, girls. I was right all along. That Sophia Simpson has been up to no good!"

Chapter Forty-two

Oma's Baking Tip

Is it really that important to preheat your oven?
The simple answer is yes.

"I don't see her Bug anywhere."

Sophia stared out the passenger window of Marcie's car into the foggy darkness. Pools of orange light illuminated both sides of the parking lot that was filled to capacity with vehicles of all sizes and shapes. Her hands clutched the folds of her coat as she dug her fingernails into the soft cloth.

"Oh God, Marcie, this is bad. This is really bad." Sophia's voice cracked with dread.

"Tell me again what Brian said." Marcie abruptly U-turned her car at the end of the lot, then headed back towards the entrance.

"He said he saw us. He said we were standing near the kitchen. Oh man, Marcie, why did we take that chance? I told you it was too risky!"

"But I didn't see anything. Besides, we were standing behind the kitchen door most of the time. He couldn't have seen us."

"Well, he obviously did. Besides, it doesn't matter anymore. What matters is that he told Kate that you aren't retired. He told her that you still work at the station and that you and I are good friends." Sophia was suddenly silent. She turned and stared at Marcie. Her eyes, wide open, were filled with panic. "This is it, Marcie. I'm done. We're done. Kate is never going to forgive me for this one, ever!"

They had reached the entranceway. Marcie brought the car to a standstill and turned to face Sophia.

"Look. She'll understand. I'll talk to her. I'll tell her everything. It was my idea and I practically forced you into it. She'll understand. She will, I promise."

A knock at the passenger window startled both Sophia and Marcie. They quickly turned to see an imposing figure staring in on them. Ursula was peering in through the misty fog.

Sophia lowered the window, revealing Ursula's face, which was pinched with concern.

"I can't seem to find her anywhere. I just don't know what could have happened to her." She was slightly out of breath and leaned against the passenger door for support.

"We've driven the entire lot and can't see her anywhere either." Sophia wrapped her coat collar tightly around her neck as the cold, thick air settled around her shoulders like a wet shawl.

"It's obvious that something must have really upset her. You don't think she would just leave, do you?" Ursula's brow furrowed as she pondered the idea that Kate would recklessly abandon the night's festivities.

Marcie spoke up. "She may have because her car isn't here."

"Has anyone tried calling her? I don't own a cell phone but maybe that would be the quickest way to find out where she is." Ursula looked expectantly at Sophia.

Turning to Marcie, Sophia urged, "Why didn't we think of that before? Do you have your cell handy?"

"Sure. One sec." Marcie reached into her bag and retrieved her phone. She handed it to Sophia. "Do you know the number?"

"Yes." As Ursula and Marcie looked on, Sophia dialled Kate's number and waited. She didn't know what she'd say if Kate picked up but she didn't care. All she wanted to know was that Kate was okay. She and Marcie would deal with the fallout later.

After a couple of rings, it went to voicemail. Sophia looked to Marcie and Ursula and slowly shook her head. Kate's cheerful voice message chimed in Sophia's ear. "Hi. I'm either up to my arms in dough or you've just caught me at a bad time. Leave a message and I'll call you back."

"Hi, Kate. It's Sophia. I'm calling from Marcie's cell but please call us back at this number. As soon as you can. I can explain. Really." Sophia pressed the end-call button, then turned and stared at Marcie. With a slight shake of her head, Sophia handed the phone back and Marcie hastily stuffed it into her purse.

"Explain what, my dear?" Ursula ducked her head lower and stared at Sophia. "Did something happen?"

Sophia looked at Ursula. "I've made a big mistake and it's me who's upset Kate. I think maybe it's best if Marcie and I try to find out where she's gone. Maybe she went home. I don't know, but if we do find her, we'll be sure to call." Remembering that Ursula didn't own a cell phone, she reached up and touched Ursula's hand as it rested on the window frame. "I'll call my sound guy Hank and he can pass a message onto you."

"Right." Ursula straightened her back. "I'll go in and tell the ladies you've gone to look for her at home. No need to cause a panic but please do let us know as soon as you've found her." Turning to go, she suddenly stopped and leaned in close. "I'm sure Mr. Stanwell will be looking for her soon. What shall I say if he asks?"

Thinking it was too early to involve George, Sophia said hastily, "Just tell him I'm getting some extra shots with her. We'll be back soon."

"Do you think that's wise?" Ursula's eyebrow arched.

Without hesitation, Sophia looked directly into Ursula's eyes. "I do. There's no need to upset George. Besides, he still has the rest of the evening to get through and I'm sure everything will work out just fine.

Please, Ursula, can you do this for me?"

"Yes. Yes, I suppose I can," she said with hesitation, "but please promise me that you'll be in touch right away." Gesturing towards the entranceway, she said, "I'm not sure how long I can keep those ladies under control."

"I promise we will. And thank you, Ursula. I knew I could count on you."

"You'd best take this then." Handing Kate's pink coat to Sophia through the open window, she smiled gently. "No sense in me hanging onto it now. Good luck."

Sophia took Kate's coat and placed it on her lap. Ursula nodded, then turned. The foggy soup that hung in the air of the parking lot quickly swallowed her up. Sophia rolled up the window and turned to Marcie.

"Let's get going."

"Are you sure she'd go home?"

"I don't know but where else would she go?"

"You're probably right but what if she went to the bakery?"

"Well, that's easily enough solved." Sophia looked to Marcie, "The bakery's on the way to her house so let's drive by it first and see if she's there." Her voice cracked. Clutching Kate's coat in her lap, she continued, "I can't see why but it's worth a try."

Taking a deep breath, Marcie turned and stared ahead. She nodded and said, "Okay, first stop, Kate's Bakes."

Marcie put the car in gear and sped out of the lot. She turned left and headed towards Oak Street. Once on Oak, she drove as quickly as she could through the dense fog but eventually was forced to come to a standstill when the light changed at 41st. Marcie looked to Sophia, who was gently stroking the folds of Kate's coat.

As they sat waiting for the light to change, Sophia looked up, then slowly turned her head and looked directly at Marcie. Her eyes were pools of anguish. Marcie glanced at Sophia and swallowed hard.

"It'll be okay, Sophia. Really, it will."

"Not this time," was all Sophia could manage to say before she turned and stared in the opposite direction.

The light finally changed and Marcie steered them onto 41st Avenue. The streetlights cast a hazy glow above the wet pavement and traffic flowed easily through the fog until they got close to West Boulevard. The red shimmer of brake lights lit up the street through wafting mist. Things seemed to be slightly backed up in the block that ran directly in front of Kate's Bakes so Marcie made a quick decision to avoid the delay. She turned left on West Boulevard, drove half a block south, then hung a quick right into the alleyway that ran behind the businesses on 41st Avenue.

Sophia sat in silence. She stared intently ahead as Marcie navigated the speed bumps that slowed their progression along the narrow back street. Marcie was doing her best to avoid the dumpsters and delivery trucks that hugged the brick walls of the alleyway but stuck out like bony elbows blocking her passage. As they got closer to Kate's Bakes, Marcie broke the silence.

"Oh, my God, Sophia. That's her car, isn't it?" Marcie's voice was little more than a hushed whisper.

Ahead in the distance, Kate's bright purple VW Bug popped out of the fog like a cheerful beacon.

"Why would she come here?" Marcie pulled her car into the slot next to Kate's and shut the engine off.

"I have no idea. But I don't really care. She's here, which means I can finally explain." Sophia was unbuckling her seat belt and had a handle on the door. Marcie grabbed her arm tightly.

"What if she doesn't open up? What'll you do then?"

Sophia's jaw muscles clenched. When she finally spoke, her voice sounded raw and determined.

"Then I'll just keep knocking. If that doesn't work, I'll pound on the windows. I don't know. Trust me. I'll get through to her somehow. She has to listen to me, she just has to."

Sophia stepped out of the car. Grabbing the folds of her chiffon dress, she quickly strode over to the employees' entrance. She knocked on the door and waited. Nothing. Turning around to look at Marcie, who was hanging back at the car, Sophia took a deep breath, then banged loudly on the door with her fist.

A man's voice startled her. She turned abruptly to see Mr. Ho's balding head peeking around the corner of his shop next door.

"If you're looking for Kate, she is in there. I saw her go in about ten minutes ago."

"Thanks."

Sophia gave a cursory wave, then turned back to the still-closed door. That's when she noticed the smell. It was faint at first, and not something uncommon at this time of year. Many of the old houses in Kerrisdale still had wood-burning fireplaces; whiffs of smoke often mingled with the foggy dampness on these cool spring nights to create a unique scent of cool spring evenings on the west coast.

Thinking nothing of it, Sophia reached for the door handle. Turning the knob, she raised her voice, "Kate? Are you in there?"

The door handle turned easily in her palm. It wasn't locked. Sophia grasped the knob firmly, turning it completely as she pulled on the heavy metal door. Thick, acrid smoke engulfed her face. Her eyes were burning. The shock of it sent Sophia reeling backwards as she instinctively pulled her arm up towards her face.

Marcie screamed and ran forward just in time to stop Sophia from tumbling backwards onto the wet pavement.

A rippling cloud of black smoke billowed forth from the open doorway. It flowed over the upper edges of the door frame like dry ice as it snaked its way out into the expansive night air.

"Oh, my God. Kate? Kate!" Sophia regained her footing and rushed forward to the door. Gripping the frame and ducking her head down to avoid the exiting smoke, she screamed again, "Kate! Kate! Are you there?"

Turning wild-eyed to Marcie, Sophia shouted, "Call 911. Now, Marcie. Call!"

Marcie ran back to the car and leaning over the driver's seat, hastily grabbed her purse. She jammed her hand into its folds, seeking desperately for her cell phone. Frustrated that she couldn't find it, she unceremoniously dumped the entire contents onto the driver's seat. The cell phone tumbled out amongst a jangle of makeup, chewing gums, and scraps of paper. She snatched the phone in one quick grasp and dialled.

A metallic sounding voice answered almost immediately.

"911. What's your emergency?"

Marcie's voice was breathless with fear. The words spilled out of her mouth in a high-pitched shriek. "There's a fire. A fire at Kate's Bakes on West 41st. Hurry, it's bad."

"Do you know the exact address, Ma'am?"

As Marcie gasped for breath, her brain seemed to come to a standstill. Maybe Sophia would know. Her eyes flashed back to the spot where Sophia had been standing just seconds before. Marcie stared in dread at the open doorway that continued to belch thick black smoke. Sophia was nowhere to be seen.

Chapter Forty-three

Oma's Baking Tip

Baking + A Bad Mood = Guaranteed Disaster

It was completely dark. The only sound Sophia could hear was the pounding of her own heart. She had decided instantly to go into the bakery. Sophia had attended enough fires in her previous life as a journalist in Toronto to know that the time lapse between the start of a fire and death for remaining occupants was short. Since she had opened the back door of the bakery, the fire that clung to the ceiling of the hallway intensified, as if feeding itself on the foggy night air. She knew instinctively that she had only a small window of opportunity.

Crawling on her hands and knees to keep below the heavy smoke that hung in the air, Sophia kicked off her high-heeled shoes to get a better grip on the slippery hardwood floor. But the silkiness of her dress was still making the going difficult. Above her head was a sudden crackle. One of the pot lights that lined the hallway ceiling shattered, showering her path with small shards of glass. She quickly took off her coat and used it to sweep the floor in front of her as she inched along.

"Kate? Kate, where are you?" Sophia's shouts were clear and determined but no reply came. Shivers of fear ran down her back. Just ahead and slightly off to the right, she could see a colourful glow coming from an open doorway. Thinking it could be some kind of storage or work room, she picked up speed as she slid towards the opening.

Turning the corner into the small room, she recognized the signs of an office. The glowing light was coming from a computer monitor set atop a small desk to her right. Her eyes had now become accustomed to the darkness. With the monitor's help, she was able to see shadowy forms in the hazy light. Her eyes darted around the room.

"Kate! Kate, are you here?"

Even though her eyes were now beginning to burn, Sophia peered into the eerie darkness of the small office. As she twisted her head to the left, she noticed the piled-up folds of a crocheted blanket lying on a couch set against the wall. Crawling over to get a better look, she gasped. Kate's pale hand was peeking out from under the blanket and dangling limply over the edge of the couch.

"Oh my God. Kate. Are you okay?"

Pulling the top end of the blanket back, Sophia revealed the outline of Kate's face and upper body. She could barely see them through the dark smoke. There was no response. Crouching down, Sophia took a deep breath, then covered her mouth with the hem of her dress, and got up on her knees. The thickening layer of smoke that filled the room immediately engulfed Sophia's upper body. She did her best not to inhale, holding her breath tightly in her ever-constricting chest.

Kate's seemingly lifeless body was curled up under the blanket on the couch, high enough off the floor to be engulfed in the acrid smoke. Sophia ripped the blanket from Kate's body and laid it on the ground in front of the couch. Letting her hand fall from her mouth, she grasped Kate's shoulders and shook her. But there was still no response. She could see by the dim light that Kate was unconscious; her head rolled from side to side without restraint. Her eyes were shut.

Flattening herself on the floor, Sophia took another strained breath. Holding her breath tightly, she stood and grabbed Kate under her arms.

She gently slid her from the couch onto the blanket. Careful not to knock Kate's head, she laid her flat on the blanket and crawled around to Kate's feet, then knotted her own fingers through the holes in the crocheted blanket. With her back to the open doorway, Sophia tugged the end of the blanket. Kate's limp body began to slide along the polished floor.

Not knowing whether her friend was alive or dead, all Sophia could think of, as the smoke began to thicken even more, was that she had to get Kate out. The dim glow from the computer monitor flickered and went black as the last of the electrical supply cut out. In the encroaching darkness, Sophia had to go by feel alone. She continued to edge backwards. Pulling with all her strength, she slid Kate along the floor, out of the office and into the hallway leading towards the back door.

Please be alive. Oh, Kate, I never wanted this to happen. I'm so, so sorry. I love you, for God's sake. Please don't die.

Sophia could hear Marcie's screams coming from the employee entrance. She used them as her only guide through the thick smoke and darkness. With each laboured breath, her throat was tightening and she resisted the temptation to cough. At one point, she stopped, grabbed the edge of the blanket, covered her mouth, and took a deep inhalation, hoping that the fibres from the blanket would filter out some of the smoke. It didn't help much but gave her just enough oxygen to carry on.

The fire hissed angrily above Sophia as she slowly shimmied her way backwards along the hallway. Although it seemed like an eternity, with every tug of the blanket, she knew that Kate was getting closer to safety. When her foot touched the edge of the doorway, Sophia felt someone grab her tightly around the waist.

She felt an arm scoop behind her bent knees. In an instant, Sophia was lifted off the floor and out into the cool night air. Although her eyes burned and her sight was blurred with hot tears, she blinked upwards to see George. He held her closely to his chest, his face set in steely determination, jaw rigid and eyes blazing. Turning her head to the side, Sophia saw the shadowy figures of Richard and the storekeeper from next door carrying Kate to the safety of the loading dock. A full-body coughing fit engulfed her as her lungs began to take in the fresh night air and release the remnants of smoke that clung to the soft insides of her throat and lungs.

Holding her tight and cradling her in his arms like a small child, George rushed to the open door of his black Suburban.

"Are you crazy?" George whispered in her ear. "You could have died in there. Then both of you would have. . ." He didn't finish the sentence.

Bending forward with a grunt, George sat Sophia onto the driver's seat. Marcie, who'd jumped into the front passenger side, covered her with a thick tartan blanket she had found on the back seat. Leaning against the open door, George loosened his tie. His breathing was quick and ragged.

Richard's voice shot across the deserted alleyway.

"She's alive!"

Like a marionette released from its master's grasp, George crumpled onto the pavement next to Sophia. Waves of relief swept through his body. With a shaky hand, he rubbed away the tears that had pooled in his eyes. George stared up at Sophia, who sat slumped, exhausted and covered with soot, coughing into her sleeve.

"She's alive. Did you hear?" he stammered.

The piercing sound of sirens ricocheted off the brick walls of the alley. Within seconds, the glow of flashing lights lit up the darkened laneway. They were no longer alone. The sounds of shouting and heavy boots, pounding on the pavement, spread a feeling of relief as it became clear that the fire department and paramedics had arrived.

Sophia tried her best to swallow. Her voice was raspy and dry. "How did you know to come here?" she pleaded. George grabbed the car's door frame and pulled himself to his feet. Steadying himself with one hand as he gripped the door handle, he looked at Sophia as he wiped his face with his free hand.

"St. Germain. She told us everything. We figured Kate might have come here, so we took a chance."

His hands flew up to his face and covered his mouth as he stared at where Kate lay in the bright lights of Mr. Ho's loading dock. Richard was leaning over her, speaking intently to one of the paramedics. He then looked up and pointed over in the direction of George and Sophia. The two paramedics turned, gazed in their direction, and then moving Richard to one side, one of them placed an oxygen mask over Kate's face. He pulled the elastic strap behind her head and around her now-dishevelled, auburn locks.

Sophia looked at George and said, "I'm so sorry, George. I've caused all this."

Turning slowly and staring at her with tear-filled eyes, George did his best to force a smile. His lips quivered and his voice cracked with emotion.

"What you did is save her life. For that," he said as he kneeled down and grabbed her hand, "I will always be in your debt."

Sophia held his gaze, mesmerized by George's eyes. Even though his brow was pinched, his eyes belied the sincerity of his words. He looked fragile. His lower lip still quivered.

"Can you tell? Is she really going to be okay?" Sophia strained her neck, trying to see past George to the loading dock where Kate still lay atop the crocheted blanket. The two paramedics were now labouring to stabilize her. Sophia glimpsed Richard pacing beside them, distraught.

"I'm sure she will be. You saved her life, Sophia." Marcie's voice sounded soft and reassuring. Wrapping her arm around Sophia's shoulder, she whispered gently, "You do realize that, don't you?"

Sophia shook her head and let it fall onto Marcie's shoulder. She struggled to take a deep breath, filled her lungs with the night's cool air, and wept.

The voices from the loading dock became louder. George stood abruptly to witness the paramedics carefully lifting Kate from the crocheted blanket onto a waiting gurney. He felt frozen in place, unable to move. His eyes fixated on Kate. She looked so small and frail. Her petite body was still wrapped in the pink-and-yellow cocktail dress that she had worn to the gala dinner. It was now stained with dark smudges and George could see that it was ripped in places.

He tore his eyes away from Kate and looked to Richard for support. Their eyes locked. George could see that he, too, was crying. Richard shrugged his shoulders, then covered his face with both hands, his shoulders shaking. Letting Sophia's hand drop, George let out a pained wail and staggered over to where Richard stood, leaning against the loading dock for support. They embraced and held each other tightly as the back doors of the ambulance closed with a bang.

Within seconds, the siren sounded, loud and abrasive. The ambulance, with its precious cargo safely inside, slowly pulled away, its flashing lights casting an eerie red glow over everything in its path.

Sophia began to cough uncontrollably. She noticed a large, shadowy figure standing near her at the open car door. Placing an emergency kit on the ground, the fireman kneeled onto the cold pavement of the parking lot and looked gently at Sophia as she sat limply in the front seat of George's sedan.

"So, I hear we have a hero to attend to?"

Chapter Forty-four

Oma's Baking Tip

A light dusting of granulated sugar atop a cookie before baking adds a nice, crispy crunch to an already delicious morsel of goodness.

The emergency waiting room area was crowded with anxious individuals. Hospital personnel could be seen scurrying back and forth behind the glass partition that separated the land of the living from those who potentially lay on the brink of demise. Seats were scarce. Some people were forced to either sit huddled on the floor or propped up against scuffed walls that had absorbed countless hours of grief and anguish.

An undercurrent of hushed voices filled the empty spaces created by silent thoughts of worry. The lighting was clinically bright and offered no refuge to conceal the tear-swollen eyes and furtive looks of those waiting to hear news about a loved one on the opposite side of the glass.

Sophia, Marcie, and George had been fortunate enough to corral three seats in a far corner next to a vending machine that whirred softly while passively offering its fare of lukewarm coffee and stale chocolate bars.

"I can't stand this waiting." George glanced down and tapped the face of his watch. "It's been over two and a half hours since they admitted her. I was hoping we'd know something before Richard shows up with Sylvia."

"These things can take forever sometimes," Marcie whispered, "and there's really nothing you can do but wait." Her voice trailed off as memories of hospital visits waiting for news about her parents clouded her thoughts.

Recognizing her rising grief, Sophia reached over and held Marcie's hand. The gesture bolstered Marcie's courage. Giving her head a slight shake, she blurted, "Well, she darn well better be okay because I need to apologize — and I mean, in person."

"You and me both."

Sophia looked down, crumpling the paper cup that once held a much-needed sip of water, and stared at the tattered remains of her gown. It was torn in places and smelled strongly of stale smoke. George had kindly lent her his evening jacket to wear but she knew that her dress was a lost cause. Truthfully, she didn't care what she looked like. If one of the other expectant visitors happened to recognize her, so be it. Even the fireman who had attended her behind the bakery had been kind enough to make light of her disheveled looks. Even though Sophia sensed that she had been recognized, he was kind enough not to let on. After giving her a few inhalations of oxygen and eliciting a promise to take it easy for the rest of the evening, he had let her go.

From within the depths of Marcie's purse, the loud jangling of her cell phone drew annoyed looks from a few people seated next to her. A tap on the glass from the admissions nurse brought Marcie's attention to a small laminated sign stuck to the glass partition: No cell phones! Grabbing deep into her purse, Marcie quickly answered the call and recognizing the voice, turned to George and Sophia.

"It's Ted," she said while slinging her purse over her shoulder. "I'd better take this outside. Save my seat, will ya?" Rushing out the automatic doors, she disappeared into the darkness beyond.

"He's going to be worried about her for sure." Sophia continued to stare in the direction of the sliding glass doors. "I'm sure he followed the whole thing on his ham radio this evening."

Looking back to George, who was uncharacteristically quiet, Sophia noticed he was shaking slightly.

"We're not going to lose her, are we?" He turned and looked at Sophia with tear-filled eyes, desperately searching for an answer. "Because if she goes, I just don't know what I'll do."

The last few words tumbled over his lips, followed by a heaving sob that rocked his entire body. Sophia reached out and held him tight. He, too, smelled of smoke. Sophia's thoughts immediately returned to the moment when she had felt his strong grasp and the determined firmness with which he had pulled her to safety.

"I'm so sorry," she whispered in his ear. "I never wanted this to happen. I need you to know that I never wanted to hurt Kate. I only wanted to be her friend." Her voice trailed off into silence, punctuated by George's staggered breathing on her shoulder.

She held him in silence until the crying stopped. Gently opening the space between them, she looked into his forlorn eyes.

"You do believe me, don't you, George?"

"Yes, yes I do," he sighed. "I guess I really just wanted to have her all to myself. It's one of the many faults my dear husband relishes in pointing out: I don't play well with others because I don't like to share." Scratching his head, then wiping the tears from his cheeks, George smiled weakly at Sophia.

"I know you're a good person, Sophia. You would never intentionally hurt Kate. I know you were doing your best to try and rebuild whatever you had with her." He paused and took her hand. "I'm sorry I stood in the way of that. I should have been more gracious and understanding. I really should have just listened to Richard."

"Oh my God, George. It's me who should be apologizing. You didn't do anything wrong other than fiercely protect Kate, something which I sorely neglected to do."

Squeezing his hand, she mumbled, "I just hope I have the chance to tell her. . ."

"Oh, there you are!" Ursula's hushed whisper cut through the conversation as George and Sophia looked up to see her standing in front of them, neat as a pin. Taking Marcie's empty seat, she placed her handbag on her lap, then turned to them, inwardly steeling herself against the potential news to follow. "And? Will she be alright?" Ursula's voice cracked slightly, revealing the underlying emotion she kept so tightly wound inside her chest.

"We don't know yet. We've been here for over two hours and we've heard nothing." Sophia glanced at George, who was dabbing the last of his tears with his mauve pocket handkerchief.

"Well, that is most unsatisfactory." Ursula fiddled with the strap of her purse, doing her best not to look directly at George to spare him any embarrassment.

Silence ensued as the three sat staring forward, lost in their thoughts.

Ursula cleared her throat. "I do want you to know, Mr. Stanwell, that despite everything, the evening did actually finish well. Your quick instructions before you left were followed down to the T and I'm pleased to report that the facility is locked up tighter than a drum. The ladies from our garden club were most helpful in cleaning up the bits and bobs. Your custodian, Boris, I believe his name is, was very diligent in securing the facility before we all left. I've just come from home where," she lowered her voice to a barely audible whisper, "all of the monies raised have now been securely ensconced in my home safe. I'll make arrangements to bring them to the gardens tomorrow."

George smiled weakly. "You've done brilliantly, Mrs. St. Germain." He paused and turning to look her directly in the eyes, added, "I thank you. The gardens thank you for stepping in and taking over."

"Oh, no need to thank me. I felt it was my duty to help and a responsibility that I welcomed. But please do call me Ursula. I think we no longer need to observe formalities given recent events." She smiled briefly then, staring in the direction of the glass partition, furrowed her brow and whispered, "Now, if only we knew what was happening with our Kate."

As if on cue, an emergency nurse, dressed in a drab green outfit and carrying a clipboard, stepped up to the group. She looked down at George, who stared up at her with trepidation.

"Mr. Stanwell?"

"Yes?" He stood up anxiously, searching her face for a clue.

"Ms. Freitag is resting quietly."

"Oh, thank God!" George's hand covered his mouth as he looked over to Sophia, who now stood by his side. She put her arm around his shoulder and squeezed.

"Can she have visitors?" Sophia asked excitedly. Ursula, too, now stood and joined the huddled group.

"We have given her a sedative. She's on oxygen at the moment but she's doing better. If one of you would like to see her, and only for a moment, I can take you down the hall to her room."

George looked to Sophia, then clasped her hand. "You go. I can wait. Besides, someone should be here for when Richard arrives with Sylvia. We'll find out more information then. But go. Go now." He smiled broadly at Sophia as the news of Kate's state of health sank in.

"Okay. If you're sure. I can wait too." Sophia tugged at the edges of George's coat, which hung loosely from her shoulders. Pulling it closer around her chest, she clutched it tightly and swallowed hard.

"Oh, stop fussing and get going." George nudged her slightly forward. "Now, follow the nice nurse and report back to us as soon as you can. I'll wait here with Mrs. St. Ger—, sorry, Ursula. By the time you return, we will have solved the woes of the world."

George was almost giddy with delight. Plunking himself back down in his chair, he smiled broadly, took a deep breath, and looked again to his watch.

"Where is that husband of mine?"

"Yes, go dear. I'm sure she would love to see you." Ursula's words clung to Sophia as she dutifully followed the nurse down the fluorescent-lit corridor.

Sophia was convinced that Kate would not like to see her at all but she recognized that this was potentially her last chance to set things straight. As the nurse snaked her way down various corridors, Sophia did her best to keep up with her brisk pace.

Perhaps in a sedated state, Kate would not be too upset to see me by her bedside. This was her last thought as the nurse abruptly stopped and gestured to an open door to Sophia's left.

"She's in here, the last bed on the right, next to the window. Please remember, just a few moments and try to keep it quiet as the other patients are resting." Turning on her Birkenstock heels, the nurse silently walked back in the direction they had come and disappeared around the corner.

Sophia's eyes took a moment to adjust to the dim lighting in the room. There were six beds in total, all occupied. The room was eerily still. Kate's bed was enclosed by beige curtains, which offered some privacy but kept Sophia's suspense in check. She did not know what she would find behind the drapes but when she slowly pulled a corner back, she was overcome with relief at seeing Kate's bright auburn hair flared across the pillow. She appeared to be sleeping and was breathing softly. They had cleaned most of the black soot from her face but small traces could still be seen at the corners of her eyes. A clear plastic oxygen mask covered her mouth. She lay in complete stillness under a clean white sheet.

A growing, deeper wave of relief swelled in Sophia's chest. She licked her still-parched lips, her eyes filling with tears.

"Kate?"

Sophia's whisper broke the spell of silence as she stepped into the curtained enclosure. There was no reaction. Reaching out to grab the visitor's chair that stood next to the window, Sophia tried to drag it closer to the bed but its metal feet scraped annoyingly along the linoleum floor. She quickly turned her head to see if she'd woken Kate but still no movement came.

Choosing instead to lift the small chair, she placed it next to Kate's bed so that she was close to her head and could look directly at her. Sophia stared in disbelief at Kate's motionless face. She had witnessed so many different emotions play across those freckled cheeks and soft pink lips. Now Kate's beautiful face appeared serenely oblivious to the circumstances that had brought her to this hospital bed. Sophia brushed a tear from her eyes, took a deep breath, and gently held Kate's hand. It was warm and soft and felt full of life.

Taking a deep breath, Sophia's eyes rose to remain on Kate's closed eyelids.

"Oh, Kate, you deserve so much more than I have to offer."

Her words tumbled out quickly, having been packed inside her head since discovering Kate's hasty exit from the garden show fundraiser.

"I should never have done what I did. It was a stupid plan I made with Marcie and we should never have gone through with it. I want you to know that it is completely my fault though, not Marcie's. She's not to blame here. She only wanted to help me but in doing so, I put her in a very bad position, and you too."

Tears began to stream uncontrollably down Sophia's face but she made no attempt to brush them away. Instead, she chose to continue holding Kate's hand, silently hoping for some kind of reaction.

"I should have stopped it before it went too far but I didn't, and that's something I'll have to live with. I just wanted so badly for us to be friends again but I didn't know how to fix all the wrongs I'd done. There was a glimmer of hope that we could start again but I ruined it, as usual. And now," she choked on her words, "now, look at you."

Sophia looked up to the ceiling. Her shoulders shook. She was finding it hard to get a breath but the words continued to spill out.

"You're lying here and your life's work is in ruins, thanks to me. I'm so, so sorry, Kate. I know you won't want me to be around anymore but I promise you—"

Forcing herself to look directly at Kate's motionless face, Sophia whispered, "Somehow, I'm going to make this up to you. I'm not sure how yet but that's a promise."

Kate lay perfectly still, not a flicker of an eye or movement in her hand.

"I love you, Kate."

Sophia leaned in closely as she placed a solitary kiss on Kate's brow. Her words lingered in the air, then faded into the silence that buffered the space between them. Sophia dropped her chin to her chest. Exhausted and defeated, she knew it was time to leave but she couldn't bring herself to make the move to go.

In the stillness that now engulfed them both, Sophia's staggered breaths and those of Kate's mingled into a rhythmic pattern. Minutes passed.

Sophia became aware of a slight movement and realized that Kate was gently squeezing her hand.

Kate's eyelids fluttered as her eyes adjusted to the light that now poured into her consciousness. Barely able to move a muscle and struggling to part her cracked lips under the cover of the oxygen mask, she mouthed a solitary word.

"Stay."

Chapter Forty-five

Oma's Baking Tip

*Your signature bake could be a complicated concoction or the simplest
recipe in the box. It is the one that defines you as a baker; it is not one
that you seek out. It finds you and when it does, you'll know.*

"Yes. It's true. He may seem mild-mannered sometimes but even I
know better than to push my luck with Richard, especially when he's
got a bee in his bonnet. I bet that insurance company of yours didn't
even know what hit them." George's chuckles resounded contentedly
through the speaker phone.

Kate leaned back to look around her new office. The restoration
had taken months to complete but the bakery had, literally, risen from
the ashes. Even Oma's crocheted blanket had found its way back home
again. It now lay folded neatly on the new couch in Kate's office, thanks
to Mr. Ho, who had scooped it up on the night of the fire. He had had it
cleaned and had returned it to an appreciative Kate on the day of the
bakery's official re-opening.

"Well, all I can say is: I don't know what he said or did but I just got
off the phone with my insurance agent and they've now agreed to pay

my claim — in full. They've accepted that the responsibility for the fire lay in the faulty rewiring. Thank God that's at least settled." Kate sighed.

"Hey, you know what? I've also decided what I'm going to do with the left-over amount that was raised, and I've got Sophia to thank for that." Kate leaned in close and stared at the spreadsheet that beamed at her from her computer screen.

According to her calculations, she could easily cover the rest of the expenses, thanks to the restoration fund set up by Sophia. Her feature on the Kerrisdale Garden Club had aired two weeks after the Shaughnessy Garden Show had concluded. Sophia had, with Kate's permission, included a short segment about the fire at Kate's Bakes. The sympathetic response from viewers had been so great that, on behalf of Kate and on the urging of Sophia, Urban TV had set up a donation account. The money had poured in; the people of Vancouver had, once again, shown their generous hearts. The fund had more than paid to return Kate's Bakes to its former glory.

"Let me guess. You're finally going to take that vacation to Bali that you've been dreaming about." George whispered into the receiver. "I won't tell if you don't." Boyish giggles trickled through the phone line.

"Yeah, right, as though I would." Kate pursed her lips. "George Stanwell, you're as naughty as they come."

"You said it, sister, and I'm not about to change my ways! Besides, a trip to Bali, who would know?"

"I would, for one, and probably all of those lovely citizens of this beautiful city who contributed their hard-earned cash to help rebuild my bakery. Kate's Bakes burns and then Kate goes on a tropical vacation. Not gonna fly, mister." Kate laughed, knowing that George was only kidding. She silently counted her blessings while acknowledging that she was still able to have this type of repartee with him.

"If you actually want to know, I've decided to gift the remaining portion to the Shaughnessy Gardens."

George was silent.

"Did you hear what I said?" Kate looked down at the phone and cocked her head to one side. "You're still there, right?"

George's voice cracked. He cleared his throat. "You're going to do what?" he stammered.

"Well, I figure that since the insurance company has covered most of the costs and Sophia's restoration fund will cover the rest, I have a rather significant amount left over to do with as I see fit. What better way to spend it than to gift it to the Shaughnessy Legacy Garden Fund? That way, you won't have to worry about the garden show for the next couple of years. That is, if you don't spend it all on floral arrangements and jazz bands for the fundraisers." Kate's attempt at levity hung silently in the air.

"George? Are you still there?"

"Oh, hon, I'm here." Kate heard him blow his nose. She finally clued in.

"Are you crying?"

"No. Well, yes, but so what?" George's words came through staggered breaths. "Are you really serious? You'd be willing to pass that money on to the gardens?"

"Yes, of course. I think it's the best way to use it and I'm sure all those people who tuned in to Sophia's special and contributed would agree that it's the right thing to do."

"I'm not usually one to be short for words but, honey, you've got me tongue-tied. I don't even know where to begin to thank you." George's voice resounded with happiness.

"Don't thank me. Thank Sophia."

This all happened because of Sophia, thought Kate. Since the night of the fire, she had come to visit Kate in the hospital every day and continued her visits at home after Kate had been released. During the following few weeks of recovery, they had had ample opportunity to talk about all that had happened. Sophia had even brought Marcie along a couple of times. After a few awkward moments, the three of them had been laughing hysterically — no small feat for Kate, who was on strict orders not to overextend herself due to the lingering effects of her injuries.

There was a knock at the door. Joseph poked his head around the corner.

"You've got a visitor." His face was beaming.

"Anyone I know?" Kate stood up and pushed the chair into her desk.

"Yeah, I think so." Joseph nodded and gestured to the front of the bakery.

"Okay. Let me just finish this call and I'll be right out."

Turning back to the phone, Kate leaned in and whispered, "I've got a visitor. Gotta go."

"Was that Joseph I heard?" George had lowered his voice to a soft, breathy whisper. "He sounded especially delicious this morning. Is he wearing an apron?"

"Oh, my God, George. You will never change!"

"That's right, honey, and thank God for that or else I'd be elected your most boring friend who happens to be a boy." George laughed heartily. "Besides, I think I know who's coming to visit you so I won't keep you longer. Your mystery guest awaits. And Kate?"

"Yeah?"

"Thank you. Kisses."

After hanging up, Kate shook her head with a smile. She reached over and grabbed her apron from the hook by the door, tying the thin purple cords around her waist. She walked the length of the hallway that led from her office to the front of the bakery. As she emerged through the archway that separated the store from the back portion of the shop, she saw Sophia standing in front of the glass display case. A broad smile lit up Sophia's face. She held Kate's pink umbrella in her hand. Laughing as she rounded the corner of the display case, Kate reached out and gave Sophia a warm hug. Looking down at the umbrella that dangled from Sophia's left arm, Kate shook her head.

"It doesn't take a genius to figure out why you're here."

"This thing doesn't seem to want to be with you. But if you want my opinion, I think you purposely leave it behind so that you always have people chasing after you."

Kate shrugged her shoulders, eyes twinkling.

"It was fun at sushi last night with George and Richard but after you left and we realized your umbrella was still there, we fought over who got to come by this morning to drop it off. As you can see, I won." With a triumphant look, Sophia took the umbrella from her arm and handed it to Kate, who set it down behind the counter.

"And where are you off to today?" Kate turned and smiled at Sophia, who was dressed casually in jeans and a light blue cashmere sweater.

"Oh, nothing big. I got a call from Ursula this morning. She wants to show me her garden but honestly, I think she really just wants to thank me for doing the episode on the club. I'm sure she's told you already but according to her, the Kerrisdale Garden Club now has a waiting list. Apparently, that hasn't happened since 1963."

"I know, she's ecstatic. At least, that's how she sounded the last time I talked to her on the phone." Kate leaned back against the edge of the counter. "I've missed a couple of meetings since the accident but I'm looking forward to the one coming up next week."

"Well, don't be surprised if you see a bunch of new, star-struck faces. Ursula mentioned that, much to her chagrin since the episode aired, Mimi and her gang have become quite the mini celebrities in their own right. She's had to put her foot down on spontaneous autograph- signings and selfies with the ladies."

Kate smiled warmly. "I'm glad for Ursula, though. She works hard and she really isn't a bad person."

"No, she's not." Pausing for a moment to look over the scrumptious offerings in the glass case, Sophia leaned forward and looked intently at the baked goods. "Anything new you can recommend? I'd like to take something along to Ursula. Tea, you know?"

Kate moved behind the counter and pointed out a raised, crystal-glass pedestal holding a fanned display of freshly baked gingerbread. The tops of the large round cookies sparkled with crystallized sugar and the sign above them read: Oma's Genuine Gingerbread.

"How about a few of these? Our newest addition to the menu." Kate glanced sideways into the brightly lit display case. Grabbing a pair of tongs, she gently placed a few in a small purple box with white polka dots. "I have a feeling you'll like them."

Sophia chuckled. "You should put a little 'As Seen on TV' sign next to them. Then things will have truly come full circle."

"Oh, I don't think there's any need for that, Soph." Kate closed the little box and handed it over the counter to Sophia. "Things have already come full circle, don't you think? And having Oma's gingerbread back on the menu is kind of like the icing on the cake."

The bell above the door jangled loudly. Kate looked up while Sophia glanced over her shoulder. Amid a flurry of giggles, Mimi, Ethel, and Margaret tumbled into the bakery with Francine leading the way.

"So, I said to Chester," Francine was telling them, "if you continue wearing that fake hearing aid when everyone knows you can hear perfectly fine, I'll make sure it 'accidently' lands in my worm composter. We'll see how long it takes those worms to turn it into a piece of, well, you know." A renewed chorus of laughter erupted.

Kate put her hands on her hips. "Well, well, Francine. I never thought you had it in you to tell it like it is." Kate quickly wiped her hands on her apron and walked around to join Sophia at the front of the glass vitrine.

"Sophia tells me you ladies have been enjoying your newfound fame. Hopefully, it hasn't gone too much to your heads." She nudged Sophia with her elbow and threw her a conspiratorial smile.

"No need to worry about that," Ethel piped in from behind the group. "We know how to take care of ourselves, now don't we ladies? Oh, and of course. . ." Ethel stepped forward. Fumbling in her purse, she carefully pulled out a brightly coloured business card and handed it to

Kate. "Mimi's been trying to drum up some acting gigs for us. You know, just for fun. She went ahead and ordered these business cards from the Interweb and we've been passing them around."

Kate glanced down at the sparkly glitter card in her hand.

Ethel McCormick, Honourary Kerrisdale Garden Club Member
Television credits available upon request
For acting enquiries, please directly contact my agent, Ms. Mimi Owens
(see back of card)

Flipping it over, Kate saw Mimi's contact information written in flowing pink script.

"Oh my, these *are* fancy! Have you had any luck so far?"

"Why, yes, dear," Mimi chirped brightly. "In fact, that's why we're here today. We wanted to pick up a bit of sweet sustenance before I drive the gals downtown for our audition. I've been told unequivocally that the egg-salad sandwiches I wanted to prepare just don't cut it anymore. The ladies are insisting that we also bring along a few of your treats to keep us going for the rest of the day."

"Audition? What's it for?" Kate raised a hand to her mouth.

Mimi bubbled with enthusiasm. "Well," she began, drawing in a slow, deep breath to sustain the suspense for as long as possible, "we've been asked to audition for an upcoming made-for-TV movie, a suspense drama called *The Case of the Pesticide Prowler*. I gather it's all about a disgruntled gardener in a cooperative community garden plot who takes out sinister revenge on his fellow gardeners by poisoning their veggie crops. Caustic carrots, septic squash, and the like. I just so happened to hear they were holding auditions this weekend and managed to garner an appointment for all of us this afternoon with the casting director."

"Who just so happens to be related to our hairdresser!" Ethel could hardly contain her delight as she broke through to the front of the group. "Sally, you know, she's our hairdresser down at the Kerrisdale Clip 'n' Cut, well, she just can't stop talking about our television debut on Sophia's show. Her nephew is some kind of assistant to the assistant on this TV production and one thing led to another and—"

Gasping for breath, Ethel threw open her arms and rushing up to Sophia, gave her a huge hug.

"Of course, this all would never have happened without you, Sophia!"

Sophia laughed and warmly hugged Ethel in return.

"We'd only be extras, of course, you know, perhaps fumbling around in the background during the courtroom scenes but we think it would be a blast!"

"Speak in the affirmative, Ethel, or we'll never have a chance!" said Margaret. "You never know, they might take one look at us and decide that we're just perfect for the roles of those gardeners who get knocked off. Now, wouldn't that be fun?" Margaret turned back to Kate and Sophia, who stood shaking their heads. "Isn't that right, ladies?"

"Well, I think it's brilliant and I'll keep my fingers crossed for you. All I can say is that I hope Sophia and I are still as good of friends and have as much energy as you lot when we're older, hey, Soph?"

"Oh, I don't think you need to worry about that, dear," Mimi interjected. "As I've told the gals many times, from the moment I laid eyes on you two, I never doubted for a moment that Sophia coming back into your life at just the right time was simply, well, meant to be."

Francine, Ethel, and Margaret all turned in disbelief and stared at Mimi.

"Why, I just knew from the start that you two were as close as biscuits and butter!"

Kate linked her arm through Sophia's as warm laughter filled the air. It floated sweetly through the bakery until it gently settled on Kate's Bakes like a light dusting of powdered sugar.

About the Author

Pamela Dangelmaier was born in Vancouver, BC and now lives close enough that she can still smell the fresh ocean air. She graduated with a BFA in Theatre from UBC and although she's not acting full time she's still considered a bit of a ham. Co-owner of the nationally recognized mail order plant company, Botanus, Pamela has enjoyed being a 'gardening expert' on television, radio and YouTube. When she's not wearing her many hats at Botanus she's either knitting socks, tending her beehives or spoiling her two cats. Flour Garden is her first novel.

Pamela began work on Flour Garden after many 'inspirational' visits to garden clubs as an invited guest speaker. She has a keen eye for interesting personalities and revels in the uniqueness of what makes us all tick. In Flour Garden she offers a veritable smorgasbord of literary treats.

You can find out more about Pamela on her Facebook page or by visiting her website at www.pameladangelmaier.com

Acknowledgements

Many thanks to my Oma & Opa for showing me that letting your artistic talents shine is the secret to enjoying a long and healthy life. Thanks to Grandpa who sacrificed much and without whose sacrifices this book would not exist. Grandma, you were a crafty one and I'm glad I caught your crafty bug. Thank you to my parents for passing along all those creative genes and for fostering my love of the arts. To my entire family, thank you for supporting me in all I do and loving me for the quirky person I am even though you do jigs when I lose at Scrabble - you know who you are!

Thanks to the Monday night Stitch & Bitchers for being my first listening audience and especially Bonnie who fell in love with George as much as I did. I'm grateful to the Basel group (Andrea, Christine, Petra & Elke) for the enlightened and inspiring conversations we had on the rooftop and over cheese fondue. Thanks to Simon for being my silent muse and Pinkie who keeps the muse in his place. Love to Aliyah and Aria, thank you for helping me keep my priorities straight and reminding me daily that love is eternal.

Many thanks to Rachael for being such a positive inspiration in writing and in life. Thank you Alison for getting the literary ball rolling and Dorothy for your sage advice. Heather, thank you for suddenly appearing along The Way and especially for your eagle eye in making sure I crossed all my T's and dotted my I's. Wendy, your last minute proofing was a marvellous favour - or should that be marvelous favor? Mike, your cover art makes me want to pick up this book and read it, wait a second …

And to all those adorably charming garden club members I've had the pleasure of meeting over the years – you were the inspiration for this novel. The world is a better place because of your undying love for all things green.

Most of all I thank Elke for her patience in listening to every.single.word and for laughing at the funny bits. You've always kept me on track and your encouragement, enthusiasm and trust has never led me astray. You bring out the best in me.

Thank you for reading Flour Garden.
Please add a short review on Amazon
and let me know what you thought!
www.amazon.com

For more information please visit my website at
www.pameladangelmaier.com

and be sure to like my author page on
www.facebook.com

Made in the USA
San Bernardino, CA
03 June 2020

72695245R00208